PAGing DR. FReeDMaN...

A. GRIEME

STRATTON
—PRESS—
Publishing Life

PAGING DR. FREEDMAN
Copyright © 2019 **A. Grieme**

Stratton Press Publishing
831 N Tatnall Street Suite M #188,
Wilmington, DE 19801
www.stratton-press.com
1-888-323-7009

Illustrated by Angel Soto
Cover Collage by A. Grieme and Angel Soto
Cover Photography by Audrey Sedlak-Barbati
Special Artistic Contributions by Michelle Giles,
Jean Melancon and Sean Tiernan

ISBN (Paperback): 978-1-948654-67-8
ISBN (Ebook): 978-1-64345-454-2

Printed in the United States of America

To Frank and River…

Paging Dr. Freedman is a product of
the profound healing power of writing and
music. Hold fast; things can change.

I want to…I want to be someone else or I'll explode…
Floating upon the surface for the birds…The birds…The birds.
—"Talk Show Host" by Radiohead

1973

Few of us have ever actually seen her face. Very rarely do seraphim ever reveal themselves as anything but remarkable beings of pure light, but the day that I was given the most challenging case of my career as a guardian, I saw her.

The light was soft like a NYC sunrise, and the city was alive with orbs of color, bustling among animals and people. I made haste, dressed in my best vintage Burberry wool suit, my favorite golden watch fob hung from my pocket. I came to the entrance, snuffed out my cigarette on my black Chuck Taylor, and dropped it into my shirt pocket; I cleared my throat and ran my hand through my salt-and-pepper chin-length hair. I opened the door and closed the city hum behind me. The foyer was white marble, with ancient columns, floor to ceiling; a stainless water wall lined with crisp green ivy hung from the glass ceiling, defying any architectural logic.

On the far right wall, beneath a water wall that fell into an infinity pool was a marble doorway. Above the entrance in glass lettering read AKASHIC INCORPORATED. I smoothed my suit, fluffed my wings, adjusted my bow tie, and made my way toward her office.

I sauntered down the corridor lined with stainless cubicles humming with ethereal beings clad in high-fashion corporate apparel, seamlessly completing tasks. In the last cubicle at the end of the hall, an androgynous, luminescent being looked up from their desk and smiled flirtatiously at me.

"She is expecting you," they said, peering over cat-eye glasses. "Would you care for a beverage while you wait?"

"N...no, thank you!" I smiled nervously.

They sidled toward a door to open it, motioning for me to follow.

"Please...have a seat."

I walked into a rounded white room; a sectional Moroccan red velvet couch and teak table rested on a burnt sienna shag carpet. A free-standing fireplace stood opposite the seating. Taking a seat on the velvet couch, I adjusted my pant leg, nervously checked my pocket watch, and leaned over to feel the smooth grain on the large table. I was startled by a long, spider-like woman's leg that gently reached toward the fireplace and pressed a red ignition switch with a black stiletto. The fireplace ignited and I gasped.

"Don't be alarmed." Her voice smoldered and hissed behind long, shiny black hair and a deep purple veil.

"I chose *you* to take on this case because of your bold nature, Gabriel. Where is it?" She rested four of her eight delicate legs on the table between us. I was awestruck by her rare beauty.

"I am s...s...so sorry, Mother Fate! Forgive me, I'm simply smitten with your—"

"With my eight legs." She dismissed my boyishness with a wave of her delicate hand and sighed the sound of silk falling onto warm skin.

"I have a lot of weaving to do, Gabriel. Two legs aren't enough." She smiled and pushed a large file across the table toward me.

I opened the ancient book and traced my finger across bold words on one of the first pages. "Shaman, witch, queen, film actor... prostitute. She's seasoned." I winked.

Mother Fate chuckled knowingly, smoothing her purple veil.

"Yes, Gabriel, she has been around...a highly evolved soul."

Revealing ruby-red lips, she leaned into me, resting her veiled face on silk-gloved hands. I could see her coal-black irises.

"She needs *you*, Gabriel. Many other lives depend upon her will to live."

It was difficult for me to pry my eyes away from her beautiful mouth, but I managed to take my wire spectacles from my wing, slip them on, and page through the first twenty years of Ana's life, ponderously.

"Complicated," I mused. Mother Fate flipped her velvet hair away from her cheek.

"And that's only the beginning…the really critical work will begin in her twenties. Keep reading."

While I read, she slowly leaned into me and whispered in my ear, making my wings shudder, "You are a master puppeteer. I've seen your work, Gabriel. I hand-selected you for the task."

While I nervously pulled a cigarette from my wing, she slowly leaned back, crossed her eight legs with the grace of a Rockette, traced a finger over the file, and presented me with a lit match.

"Oh…thank you. I didn't even realize I took out a—Do you mind?"

She slowly shook her head and handed me an ashtray.

I gingerly closed the file and fixed my gaze on her, trying to make out the expression in her coal-black eyes.

"What Earth year is it?

"It's 1973, Gabriel."

"And the date?"

She smiled. "June 2, Gabriel. I'm sorry for the short notice, but we had some complications with the tapestry. You know the drill I presume?"

I cleared my throat and gave her my best sideways smile, having done this before.

"Yes, madam," I said, fumbling with my pocket watch.

She smiled, knowingly. "Now…when you visit the Akashic Record library, Gabriel, ask the cherub on duty for the bottle labeled "Ana Guida, June 4, 1973." Immediately report to Jersey Central Hospital, stamped beneath her name."

I nodded. She leaned into me, alarmingly close.

"Any questions?" Her voice lingered in the air. She brushed the hair away from my cheek.

"No, madam."

She grinned and folded her hands in her lap.

"Good luck."

Her voice was a whisper that dissipated into a blue orb of light. She vanished and

I touched my face where she had been.

After retrieving the bottle labeled "Ana Guida, June 4, 1973," I made my way down the hall donned in hospital scrubs past a very young Harry Guida bathed in blue TV light; it was the early morning news rerun of Channel 11 Live at 5. His face was framed with messy black hair and unkempt chops. Mouth agape, he snored shamelessly while young Peg Guida screamed, cursed, and pushed tirelessly in an adjacent room. Her long brown hair was piled atop of her head, stuck fast to her reddened, sweat-drenched face, twisted with pain, shock, and amazement. In the midst of all of the commotion, I slipped into delivery, uncorked the bottle, and watched Ana's soul, light as springtime, nestle right into her little solar plexus as she emerged from the womb. I backed out, undetected, watching Peg's softened face stare into little Ana as a doctor and a team of nurses revealed her sweet, perfect pink bundle.

"Welcome, my friend." I exhaled and closed my eyes.

Gabriel

I t all started to unravel the night she lost her dress in Connecticut. In fact, that was the first time I felt needed. Truly needed. Mental illness is a tricky thing. It manifests itself differently depending on decades. And if the mentally ill make it through their twenties medicated improperly, alive and unscathed, it just becomes more complicated. Many end their contracts there, but those who continue life beyond that decade have a mission, just one that can't quite be grasped at such an early stage.

When Ana woke with a drug-and-alcohol-induced car crash in her brain, sipping mimosas with the girls to ease the physical unease the hilarity of her missing dress flipped a switch in her mind. That day, her amygdala went to sleep; she no longer felt rational fear. There was no caution left. Until then, despite her erratic, drug-rid-dled behavior, the prudent synapses still fired intermittently. But that day, she came undone. I didn't even need to look to see it in her eyes. I felt it; I knew it was time. This was the knot in the tapestry…the one I had waited twenty-seven years to untangle. Ana had given up. I was officially on active duty.

* * *

Saturday, August 25, 2000

When Ana left Greenwich, Connecticut and her friends that Saturday evening, she slid behind the wheel of her Volkswagen Fox and lit a cigarette. She spiked a coffee with Baileys and headed down Interstate 95 South toward New York City. Her boyfriend du jour was playing at CBGB's that night, and she didn't have to be back to the restaurant in New Jersey to work until Monday afternoon. The warm evening August air washed her confusion and headache away.

"Third Planet" by Modest Mouse poured out of the one work-ing speaker when she turned off First Avenue onto Bowery. She parked in the first available spot, ignoring the sign. Ana fixed her lipstick in the mirror, lit a smoke, chugged the last of the Baileys, and opened up her door to get out. She turned to lock it, and I accosted her senses with blinding lights and a horn blaring from my SUV. She jumped back into her car, as I grazed the left front fender, ripping off the bumper like a scab. I stopped for a moment then fled the scene.

Ana jumped out and grabbed her bumper out of the middle of the street, looking around for witnesses. Not a soul. She took a deep breath, threw the bumper in her back seat, considered driving home, but then reconsidered. Shrugging her shoulders, she locked the door, took a drag off her smoke, looked back at her bumper-less Volkswagen, and sauntered down to 315 Bowery, unaffected.

Upstairs at CBGB's was Ultraspank, loud and thrashing. Not her norm, she entered the mess anyway to drink incessantly and soak in the frenetic energy. Later that evening she would surprise her boyfriend Jack and his three-piece band, scheduled to play somewhere in the club. She was elated and basking in the drunken noise; I was on high alert.

After a few beers and a shot or two of whiskey, she wandered through the smoky club, searching aimlessly for his familiar face, lost in the gaze of strangers. She worked her way outside to the sidewalk, struck up a conversation with a blue-haired girl in a Patti Smith T-shirt holding a flamingo lighter, and stared into the downtown lights. She spotted a pay phone a block away and made her way toward it to call her best friend Briar who lived on Twenty-Eight and Lexington with his boyfriend, Cal. Without booze, she would've been afraid of his reaction, as she hadn't seen him in a while…not since she freaked out and didn't show when she was supposed to meet him for a night at the Met, his treat. She told him she missed the bus; he didn't talk to her for months.

She wanted to tell him about her missing bumper…and her missing dress, when she was turned around by a shrill laugh behind her. She looked toward the sound, only to see *him*, Jack, holding up a little, dirty-blond, dreadlocked hippie chick against the wall of CBGB's, tickling and kissing her exposed, taught, and tattooed stomach, his electric guitar resting against the wall. Ana walked toward them, studying the girl as she writhed in cutesy ecstasy. She reached against the wall, grabbed the Fender Stratocaster and smacked the girl across the face with it, knocking them both down with the blunt force. The girl ducked for cover while Ana hit Jack's knees continually until the neck of the guitar cracked.

"Didn't expect to see me…and this is what I get, huh? This is it? Well, fuck you, you miserable lying piece of shit!"

The girl held her face and cowered while Jack protected only himself, yelling, "My fucking guitar…You crazy bitch!"

A crowd gathered. Dressed as a street kid, I pulled Ana away from him and the girl. She shook me off and hit a street sign with the guitar. There was a cacophony of sound then she threw the remains into the street, storming away toward her car.

Ignoring all attempts to get her attention, she walked farther away from the yells and slurs, waving her arms, crying and talking to herself.

"Can you believe that shit? Can you? Who was that *girl?* Who was *she?*"

Dissolved in tears, she searched aimlessly for her bumperless car, only to discover that it was no longer there. She blinked away tears and struggled to focus on the sign "Two Hour Parking." It had been towed; I made sure of it.

At last, I rolled up to her in a cab, rolled down the window, and asked if she needed a ride. I knew she was pondering going to Briar's place to stay until she sobered up and could find her car, but something across the street caught her eye and she was gone; there was no stopping her.

Free will is a tricky thing, especially when trying to help someone with a "no stop" button. Add intoxicated, imbalanced, and unwanted, it then becomes a game of chance. I had a job to do, and Ana was not cooperating. She ran across the street toward a group of people laughing and walking nowhere in particular.

"Who wants to karaoke?" she said, sidling up to them. It was after midnight, it was August, she was irresistibly unstable, and they couldn't refuse.

They all piled into the cab and headed to Arlene's Grocery for a karaoke party. Two nice Italian boys from Paramus, NJ, another blue-eyed and brunette boy visiting from Rhode Island School of Design graduate school, and his equally attractive twin sister, an NYU graduate student laughed as Ana recounted her crazy events of the evening. Ana took the crumpled flyer from CBGB's that featured the acts that night from her purse. "See?"

The Rhode Island boy snatched it out of her hands, smoothed it on his lap, and proceeded to roll a joint on it; his sister sprinkled some leftover powder from a bag into the concoction. He rolled it tightly, licked it, and nestled it behind his ear.

I stopped the cab across from 95 Stanton Street, and they scraped together the fare. It would've been a very short walk, but they were too drunk to know the difference. They filed out of the cab and disappeared around a corner to indulge.

Karaoke was just getting started as Ana bought a round of shots for her new friends, slowly melting into stoned oblivion. I watched from the corner as the RISD twin took the shot off the bar with his mouth, hands behind his back, beckoning Ana to do the same. They melted into each other's laughter, making their way to the karaoke stage. Ana took the mic first.

"I lost my dress in Connecticut last night," she said, choosing a song from the karaoke roster. I watched as she belted out Joplin's version of "Bobby McGee" to the applause of fellow karaoke enthusiasts. Her Rhode Island partner in crime followed her performance with a flat Joy Division classic.

"Love…love will tear us apart, again." Ana thought that maybe it was the smoldering embers of potential love.

* * *

Perhaps that was why she woke up with him on a bus to Rhode Island the next afternoon, or so she thought—no purse, no car keys, and one shoe. Ana felt a debit card, some crumpled cash in her pocket, her license, and a half-smoked joint. She opened her eyes to a shoulder she was pressed against and another car crash in her frontal lobe. The light seeped in from outside the bus window, and Ana made out a highway sign for 95 North. Then another, "Providence, Rhode Island, 20 miles." She closed her eyes to the sunlight and saw snippets of the night, day…night before flash in her brain—girl against the wall, smashed guitar, bumper in the back seat, cab driver, her mouth on a glass shot…kissing in a stickered bathroom stall, ducking into an alley, drinking from something, searching for clothing, dancing with strangers, missing someone, Port Authority, snorting something off his arm, deciding to move, sitting on the street. Forgetting the day, forgetting her name, forgetting her pain. Ana didn't even know his name.

She knew there was no getting home in this state. She was coming down hard and wanted to go home and hug her dog. The bus driver mumbled, "Next stop, Saunderstown, Rhode Island." Ana looked over at the drooling RISD student, gingerly rifled through his pockets, and grabbed a bump of whatever powder they were snorting hours before in a cellophane bag. She scored a piece of gum, took off her shoe, and stuffed it between the bus seats. She whispered, "So long," slipped the half-smoked joint into his limp fist, and sidled off the bus barefoot.

She ignored judgmental stares from people as I served her coffee at the bus station kiosk, asking her where her shoes got to.

"Forgot them." She grinned and made her way out of the station, counting the money in her pocket. She had no idea that she was laughing and crying in unison when she asked a woman and her daughter how to get to the beach. The woman pointed at a Saunderstown Cab, sheltering her child from Ana.

She waved and cried, knocking on the cab window. She asked the driver for a ride to the beach. "What day is it?" she asked, sliding into the back seat.

He gave her a once-over. Her blond hair haphazardly pushed away from her freckled face. "It is Monday, August 25."

"What?" She smacked her forehead. "Afternoon?" she asked, blocking the sunlight from her eyes.

He nodded. "12:30 p.m."

"Fuck...I'm supposed to be at work."

The driver laughed. "Hahaha! Long night, huh? Where's work?"

Ana peeked at him in the rearview mirror, wiping the corners of her mouth. "New Jersey."

Tears rolled down her face as she laughed to herself. She saw a pay phone a block away from the beach. "Drop me off here, please."

She reached in her pocket and grabbed some cash; the cellophane bag fell onto the floor of the cab. His eyes followed the bag.

"Are you okay, miss? Do you need help?"

"I'm fine," she snapped, somewhere between a laugh and a sob. She picked up the cellophane bag and walked on the hot sidewalk to the phone booth.

She picked up the phone and dialed 0.

"Collect call, please."

"Please enter the number." Ana punched in her work number.

"Hello, the Brewery," her boss answered.

"DON'T ACCEPT...just LISTEN...It's ANA. I just woke up in Rhode Island...I don't know what happened...I—"

"Yes, I'll accept." Her boss took the call. "Ana."

"Hi! Oh my God, thank you. Yes! Hi...Chris...I just woke up on a bus to Rhode Island...I—"

"What? Ana, are you okay?"

She laughed and sobbed in one breath. "Well, no...I mean, yes! I—"

He cut her off. "Are you high?" he asked, looking at the schedule.

"No...no, I'm just—" Ana squeezed the cellophane bag.

"You're fired." He closed his eyes and sighed. "Get your shit together, Ana." Click.

Ana slammed the phone down continuously. "Fuck, fuck, fuck!" She kneeled down in the booth and rested her head on her knees, sobbing uncontrollably, last night's mascara caked into the creases of her green eyes.

Her head pounded, and she reached for the cellophane bag, turning it inside out to snort whatever was left, and then licked the bag clean before she started to relax.

I walked toward the phone booth with a bottle of water in my hand. "Are you using the phone?" I asked. She looked up at me cross-eyed, not able to make out my face, hanging onto the phone receiver like a life vest. Ana reached up toward me, sinking into some oblivion.

"Would you like some water?" I whispered. The empty bag blew away; Ana fell onto the sidewalk, unconscious.

Ana

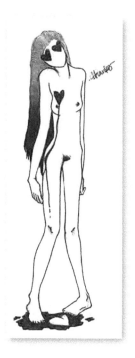

August 29, 2000 I think…

Dear Jesse,

    You've probably heard already from my parents, your mom…someone. I'm in Rhode Island. Well, on Rhode Island, at Eleanor's house. It's a big house, Jesse…284 or so beds. I'm pretty sure I came to here with a RISD graduate student with blue eyes, dark features…who I was going to marry. Handsome guy, but not the brightest.

Somehow I ended up here…not sure what happened to him. And my car was swallowed up by NYC, I think.

I don't remember much, but I know I am supposed to be at work in New Jersey. Nurse Kelsey waddles in twice a day with little blue and pink imagination slayers. I don't know if Dr. Freedman knows where I am. Not sure if he cares. But I have this typewriter at my disposal, when I can move my fingers.

You were right. I am ashamed that I am 27 years old and living above my parent's garage. It IS pathetic. Thank you for pointing that out.

But looking out the window…beyond the compound, Rhode Island is beautiful; I wish you were here…and we were at the beach. We are always happy when we are at the beach.

Love, Ana

* * *

September 6, 2000

Dear Jesse,

So I am more cognizant now, despite the Nurse Kelsey cocktail. I am no longer doing the Thorazine shuffle. I don't know why I was so overmedicated; it is not like I am any threat to anyone other than myself. By the way, it is called tardive dyskinsesia…that state. The weird tongue sometimes out-of-mouth state. Sleepwalking awake. I know you've seen it. It is apparently to "protect" the patients. Bullshit. It is yet another sick injustice…a control ploy. A way to dumb down the mentally ill so that they can be dealt with like a herd of cattle.

I have been cheek(ing) the Seroquel/ Thorazine combination at night. Fuck them. Then I crush them and hide them in my mattress. In morning, they watch me like a hawk when I take my cocktail. They also do random mouth checks where they finger sweep for pills. I have to be careful though; there are cameras everywhere. They can probably read what I'm typing to you. I wouldn't be surprised if they wiretapped this room. Maybe the RISD guy was part of this. I wonder if he lured me up here so that they could throw me away? Why Rhode Island?

Perhaps Dr. Freedman has something to do with this; he was NOT pleased that I stopped taking Lithium. I mean what the fuck did he expect? He told me that in clinical tests…Lithium mutates frogs and unborn children. Why would I take that? That is ALL I could picture! Plus…it made my hair fall out and my skin break out in cysts…or something. Horrible…and ten times worse for my self-esteem. Fuck Lithium. I'd rather swing like a pendulum.

And I have continually tried to explain to the psychiatrist that I am not an addict on top of it all, despite how I arrived here.

Me: "Honestly, I am a very smart woman, Dr. Weinstein. I was simply partying for the sake of tying one on!"

Shrink: Dr. Weinstein cleared her throat and peered over her glasses at me.

"Ana, intelligence has nothing to do with this. You were self-medicating. You are lucky that you are alive. You historically abuse drugs when you stop taking your meds. I've spoken, at length, to Dr. Freedman."

In spite of it all, I'm feeling sort of human again. I know what works. Peg, Harry, and Amber came to see me. They brought me my green backpack that you hate, and all the letters that I wrote when I left teaching. There are a ton written to you; maybe one day I will send them. My mom thought they would give me inspiration. Inspiration for what...I'm not sure. Honestly, I just feel like I am backpedaling.

I can't believe that wasn't even a year ago...

I can't believe I fell, again.

I swear things were better.

I just want to leave.

I miss Sherman.

I miss you.

Love, Ana

* * *

September 21, 2000

Dear Abby,

It is your birthday! I hope you're celebrating. Remember when I lost my dress in Connecticut a month ago? That did happen, right? Well, I haven't been home since. In fact, I ended up in in Rhode Island. Yup. I took Route 95 *North* from Connecticut...instead of *South*.

I wish it were that simple. It's not.

So...

I did, in fact, go to CBGB's after I left you and Roxy. I also had the bumper of my car ripped off by a hit-and-run. And I did, in fact, get really drunk and smashed a guitar.

I did, in fact, meet total strangers, got really high, and sang karaoke at Arlene's Grocery.

It is the rest that I am trying to piece together. By the rest I mean, how I woke in a Rhode Island State Hospital. I know I woke on a bus, 20 miles from Providence. I know I lost a shoe. I know I was with one of the strangers. And I know that I got high, again.

(sigh)

I do remember Greenwich, for the most part.

1. Roxy and I came to visit you at the palatial Connecticut paradise where you reside as a private chef.
2. The house was fantastic! They were art dealers?
3. Their grocery getter was a Mercedes wagon, and they had original Picassos hanging in their home.
4. The pool house was a fantastic building with cathedral ceilings, all naturally lit with a loft bedroom and an outdoor shower that smelled like shampoo and wet cedar.
5. The family you worked for was away, so you had free reign of the palatial wonderland.
6. We started the evening mellow, lounging back with some cocktails in the "movie theater" room designed for the kids and found a movie called *Fall?* It was so sad.
7. When the credits were rolling two or three cocktails later, you and Roxy and I were sobbing. It was worse than *An Affair to Remember*, perhaps on par with an art house version of *The Bridges of Madison County*.

8. I was in love with the poet in the film. That's all it took.

9. We all got dressed up. I wore a black cocktail dress that my mom bought me, Roxy wore a funky suit that zipped up the front, and you wore a very bohemian ensemble.

10. You took us to a French bistro in downtown Greenwich; the bits and pieces of conversations that buzzed around us were about stock portfolios, weekends on the vineyard, trips to Bali where someone had to sit in the dreaded business class, and how someone's masseuse was retiring much to their chagrin.

11. We ate and drank like queens and decided after our second bottle of wine that we needed to find some live music.

Then...

My memory is a bit fuzzy...but I do remember little film clips:

- The way you looked when you were dancing and laughing.
- The way Roxy rolled her big, brown eyes in disgust at countless advances from Greenwich men.
- The way that I spotted an older, balding man in the crowd—much older—and moved toward him to talk.

In my twisted, drunk mind he was the guy from the movie. He was sheer poetic perfection, even if he had a good twenty-five years on me. Now, this is where it gets really fuzzy, thank God. I remember sitting on the steps and talking in detail about life and art (like I know anything about either) listening to his theories about sculpture and relationships with mother earth. It turned out that he was a metal sculptor; either that or he, too, was full of shit and just really flattered that a girl who could be his daughter was doting on him.

But he had a friend, a much younger friend that you befriended and somehow, after countless more drinks, asked, "Would you all like to come over for some champagne and skinny-dipping?" Roxy rolled her eyes, the only one with sense, and the guys just about dropped their drawers right there.

I don't remember the ride much, but the rest in film clips.

Medium Shot: You took four or five bottles of champagne out of the wine cellar, and we were polishing them off, F. Scott Fitzgerald Style. Thankfully, we got to a point in the evening where both of us sobered up enough to boot them out of there and find the house.

And then...

Medium Shot: The next day over mimosas, ibuprofen, and cigarettes, we sat around and tried to recount our evening. Then you and I took a walk up to the pool house to tidy up and discard the evidence, where, alas (Close-Up) my shoes sat untouched, but my dress was missing.

Close-Up: "Those bastards took my dress." I laughed.

Close-Up: "A souvenir!" You clapped your hands together, smiling.

Medium Shot: "They must have been angry that we kicked them out, blue-balled and drunk."

So here I am...to your *North*—

Love, Ana

* * *

October 17, 2000

Dear Jesse,

So I made a friend here. Alexis. She's cool...loves music and is studying medicine but not sure if she is going to go on to med school. Her heart is conflicted. She is a pianist like Dr. Freedman; her left and right brains are both working in her favor. I told her she needs to meet Doc Freedman. He would give her sound advice about whether or not to join the ranks of the world of medicine. I think maybe music is Dr. Freedman's only escape sometimes. Imagine having to deal with the likes of me on a daily basis? Chemically imbalanced confusion? I don't blame you for not calling me.

She is currently an orderly, probably our age. We play cards sometimes. She introduced me to *Kid A*...Radiohead's latest album that was just released and loaned me an iPod to listen to it on my own. The album is transcendent. If I dare make the comparison, it is undoubtedly Radiohead's "Dark Side of the Moon." It is getting me through this, Jesse. Perhaps I can finally come out of this on the other side...wherever that may be.

Love, Ana

October 27, 2000

Dear Briar,

My parents brought me my backpack, full of letters that I wrote to work my way out of an episode. The first one I pulled out of the bag was the last letter I wrote before I ended up here. By

HERE...I mean another hospital. I wrote this right before your birthday:

August 1, 2000—Passage

Dear Briar,

Please don't take offense to the amount of time that it has taken me to write another letter to you. In fact, consider it a good thing! My time has been occupied by slinging hash and microbrews, reconciling differences between new friends (key words: new friends). I'm socializing! My self-absorption index has dwindled significantly, and I have jumped into real conversations and real laughs with real people...

I'm lying, again. GODDAMMIT! I am no longer capable of even being a good storyteller. Gone. I am simply a shadow of myself.

I will be thinking of you on your birthday, Bri. I'll be wishing that I can call you and sing "Happy Birthday, Mr. President" Norma Jean style, just to hear your sweet voice.

Wishing I can laugh with you...
in a Lower East Side Café, under
the Manhattan moon.

Wishing to see your eyes
crinkle, irises brighten
to ocean blue with
joy tears.

Wishing to see your
hand linger around
your mouth
when you speak.

Wishing I could stumble
home with you, safe inside
several aged curry cabs, washed
by city light.

Wishing to wake under
clean, white sheets, cool…
staring through bamboo
blinds at the brick
backside of 28th and Lexington.

Praying for ibuprofen to be
in stumbling reach.

But the thing is, I'm so tired of wishing, wasting, wanting, hurting. In fact, I think I am actually content with being discontent. Besides, my attempts to be discontented by lack of contentment have been, thus far, futile. I don't foresee a change in the pattern. I'm done.

I'm finished causing my otherwise content friends and family to be discontented by my whims and inconsistencies. Dis-associating yourselves from my discontentment will, in turn, leave you content in knowing that I will no longer be the bane of yours, his and her existence. I find that refreshing; you will, too. I tried. I'm exhausted.

If I squint my eyes and stare at these painted white walls, the separation between each cinder block blends together; it almost looks like I'm lying in your guest room. You will always be in my heart, Bri. I will slowly fade into your dreams. I will hold your hand there, my friend, like when we were little kids. Maybe I'll even be on time.

Possibly Maybe, Ana XO

Gabriel

October 29, 2000
Early Morning

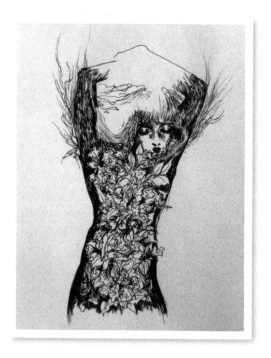

Two months in, Ana gingerly folded the last letter that she had written to Briar and slid it into her backpack. She stopped and observed the somber walls that looked almost inviting that morning. The soft light of morning twilight that fell from New England autumn leaves seemed to wrap everything around her in quiet saltwater fog. It was a new solitude for her—not forced, but gently recognizable from her childhood. She felt fresh.

The doctors and nurses deemed the environment therapeutic and, for the most part, had good intentions. Still, Ana begged to differ with their perception. In quiet thought, she paralleled the atmosphere to a painful, prolonged, emotional death. There was no quality of life inside those walls, just masked sadness, muffling and mangling memories. And if I may speak collectively for those who I encountered, I know there was a common truth regardless of sex, mental illness, addiction, socioeconomic status, race, or baggage; it was a place to recover. Some did and some didn't. They simply sought to float in peace away from their aching minds. That's all. But Ana had given up trying to find that space between sanity and madness where she knew solace lay dormant.

She left the typewriter behind with confidence, with a note in it thanking Alexis, the young orderly who had introduced her to *Kid A*, Radiohead's latest album; the Thorazine shuffle was a thing of the past.

Dear Alexis,

Thank you for sharing *Kid A* with me. It got me through this. Follow your heart, and look up Dr. Freedman for advice. He's a kindred spirit.

"Everyone
Everyone around here
Everyone is so near
It's holding on
It's holding on
Everyone
Everyone is so near
Everyone has got the fear
It's holding..."
"The National Anthem" in the album
Kid A by RADIOHEAD,

Love, Ana

She quietly whistled and sauntered off with a mission, adorned in a denim jacket that she found; I had stuffed it behind her dresser. When she put it on, she felt a bulge in the right front pocket and pulled out a stale dime bag of weed. Both were instrumental accessories to her aesthetic adjustment.

She pulled off the casual doctor facade, flawlessly. The only exception: she had no shoes, just slip-on foam booties that she acquired when admitted. Her belongings were housed in a lock-and-key abyss, and her attempt to crack the code on the lock to the room labeled "personals" was futile. In retrospect, I am confident that the slippers worked to her advantage. They were far more effective than sneakers at quelling her walk down the many corridors and echoing fluorescent stairwells.

She usually hid her head under the bleached blankets mornings when the orange and pink light of dawn snuck in through the blinds and cast dusty stripes on the far white cinder block walls. The cold, fluorescent fixtures that looked like 1950's inverted ice cube trays were off until 9:00 a.m. It was not unusual when she remained in the cocooned position far beyond her wake-up session with the shrink du jour. I suspect that when they checked on her for the morning dose of little blue and pink imagination slayers, they were not surprised to find that she still appeared to be hibernating.

Clever girl. Nurse Kelsey did waddle in, the familiar waft of bleach and mothballs at 7:30, 8:00, and 9:00 to check for life. At 9:30, she flipped on the additional reading light attached to Ana's bed, lisping orders, and pulled the covers away, exposing strategically placed pillows, sheets, and blankets stuffed into a robe and shaped in a fetal position. Ana was resourceful. She utilized her shower cap stuffed with a pillow and used a paper plate dressed with a crayon-drawn face as a disguise for her head. Perfect.

Another overlooked flaw in the facility fostered her escape: a fifteen-minute gap in time where the cameras were not scrutinized by security. She had tested it. So by the time old Kelsey sweat her way to security to begin the search, Ana would be strolling through JFK Airport holding a one-way ticket to sunny Miami.

To test this, she woke early one day, stood naked in camera view, and mimicked a Gypsy Rose Lee strip routine, using her pillow as the peacock feathers. She exposed her bare ass to the camera, lifted her typewriter, and pretended she was going to smash it through the window in preparation for a jump. During normal hours, security would have been in her room in sixty seconds flat with a psychologist and an injection of a Haldol/Ativan cocktail that would sink her into a semicomatose state for a couple of hours. I saw it happen to many others…but not during the shift change.

Ana calculated that by the time they figured out that she was the patient caught on camera leaving disguised as a doctor, and every graveyard shift sloth had been blamed for doltishness, she would be floating amidst the tropical fish. Her mission accomplished, and the second phase of my mission commenced.

She was right. The night clerks were exhausted, stuffing their faces with day-old donut holes and stale coffee before the shift change at half past six; they didn't even notice her.

Doctors strolled in methodically around 7:00 a.m. and whisked by her room toward their leisurely lounge session; they scanned the night clerk patient behavior report over coffee. With fingers clasped and furled brows, they'd sign off paperwork that directed the nurses to administer the proper antipsychotics, anticonvulsants, serotonin reuptake inhibitors, and/or sedatives to assist in dumbing us.

Ana slipped out of the main entrance with her wallet, a credit card, an ATM card, driver's license, Social Security card, and a bundle of unsent letters to long lost friends and family, here and gone, wrapped in twine. Ana never had the heart to toss the letters in the event that she wanted to drop them in the mail at the last minute; everything rested at the bottom of her tattered, green backpack.

A few days earlier, she tore up her photographs and flushed them down the toilet; she wanted no extra heartstrings weaving her into this life. I watched a tear trace the freckles on her cheek when she took a deep breath and shuddered, opening her eyes to the bowl refilling. In her war-bled reflection, she watched a remnant of a flushed photo peek out of the hole and float like a leaf in the bowl. She reached in; it was a portion of Sherman's face, her chocolate Lab who she loved with all her heart. She held it, wiped it off, and added it to the contents resting in the bottom of her backpack.

* * *

There she was; strolling across the manicured, late October lawn, frosty green with dew. She felt liberated looking at the mental health monstrosity from the outside rather than from the confines of an antiseptic robe or oversized sweat suit while pacing the fenced-in garden that doubled as a smoking deck. I watched and wondered if the same stroll Ana took was as fresh for the doctors and nurses when they left the stagnant, padded place every day to go home to their lives. Perhaps it lost its novelty. I'll bet the farm on the latter.

In all my years in this profession, I have found one universal truth. People never seem to appreciate the moment, but dwell on ten paces ahead or behind; they miss so much. I know that Ana did.

But out there that day, there were no boundaries, even to soft sound. She missed nothing, heard it all, tasted impending winter, smelled last evening's cold rain shower and felt her abdomen flutter with wild anticipation. I waited for her beyond the south gate. She felt solace in focusing on the car's distant silhouette. She was traveling away from the confines of white-washed walls and deadening psychococktails. And for the first time in a very long time, she was not afraid.

"Good morning. Thanks for being so prompt," I greeted Ana kindly, disguised as a sixty-something Boston native, with a shock of white hair contained in a chauffeur's cap.

"Seamus O'Reardan." I extended my hand to shake hers. The radio trickled a familiar song.

"Good morning, Mr. O'Reardan, sir." Ana cleared her throat. Her speech was slurred slightly by residual psychomeds slowly filtering out of her blood.

"Ana Guida. Dr. Ana Guida." She smiled. "I love this song… 'Don't Blame Me.'" She looked at me.

"Ahh…you are far too young to know Thelonius Monk." I smiled.

She smiled. "Oh, I'm older than you think."

"You are new to the staff?" I stared at her in the rearview mirror.

"Yes, I am." She flipped her hair out of her face and wiped some dried toothpaste from the corner of her mouth. Ana was well aware that she didn't look the part of the patient and never had, which had always been to her advantage. In fact, her young face, freckled skin, youthful hair, and keen ability to socialize with anyone had allowed her to escape many unsavory situations unscathed. I have watched her smile her way out of many prolonged visits to institutions and prescriptions of unnecessarily strong doses of medication that rendered her useless. I allowed her to think she had duped another man with the batting of her eyelashes.

"We are headed to JFK?" I spoke with a thick South Boston accent, turning around to peer over the seat back. I crinkled my weathered eyes curiously.

"Yes." She sighed, exasperated. Born actress. "My flight is at 11:30. I'm going to visit my aunt and uncle for a few days."

"Oh. No luggage?" I spoke to her in the rearview mirror while I started away from the gate and lit my cigarette. "Mind if I smoke?"

"No." She stared at the lit smoke in my hand.

"You want one?" I knew her passion for cigarettes.

She hesitated. "No, thank you. I don't smoke. And no, I didn't have time to pack. You know…graveyard shift." She winked at me in the mirror. "Busy, busy! In fact, I was going to ask you if you could spin by my condo so that I can change. But given the time, if you don't mind, may we stop at an outlet store or a mall so I can pick up some things?"

I laughed at her fabricated story. That's the Ana that I adore

"Sure, Doc. You don't want to travel in your scrubs, do you?"

"No!" She laughed along with me as if I were clever. "Thank you, sir." She leaned back and watched the mental hellhole disappear in the side-view mirror.

Ana thought that she had dozed off for a moment. But when I peered over the seat back to wake her at the shopping center, she stared at the clock in awe. An hour had passed.

"Dr. Guida, will this suffice?"

"Oh, yes, thank you." She had to be creative. We stopped at a super stop and shlep kind of joint. The kind that sells everything from fall fashion to dairy products, to car parts, pleather shoes, gun racks, and contraceptives.

"I'll just be a few minutes." She smiled, closed the door behind her, and checked several times to make sure that it was done properly.

I slowly lowered the tinted passenger-side window.

"Dr. Guida," I said, "we should be on the road again in about fifteen minutes to ensure that we arrive on time. We have a good two hours of driving. You know, airport traffic."

"No problem. I'll make haste." She awkwardly skipped toward the entrance, tripping over her right pant leg. When inside, she tried to stave off that familiar confused feeling that overwhelmed her in big, fluorescent places. The happy advertisements for fast=food and teen cologne flickering on TV screens disoriented her. Coupled with the slow-moving moms…children hanging on their wheeled steel baskets, begging for Twinkies and Silly Putty or something, gave her a headache. I've seen her lose it over that a couple of times. And she loathed the smell: a braid of french fries, plastic, and floor wax. But it didn't stop her from moving quickly through the fall fashion mess where she found an acceptable green cotton wrap dress, a pair of flip-flops from the summer leftover bargain bin and a pair of oversized, silver-framed aviator sunglasses. She tried them on and asked a fellow shopper, "How do I look?"

"Good," she said with a smile and endearing Spanish accent. She lifted the glasses and winked. The woman quickly shuffled away, not sure how to take her in scrubs and foam booties.

She went over to the ATM and withdrew her measly savings. It wasn't much but would suffice. It was enough to share with worthy strangers. She ran out to the car, threw her bag into the back seat, and slid in.

"Thanks." She undressed and slipped into her plastic-scented $15 ensemble; I looked away from the rearview mirror, a bit embarrassed after catching a view of her naked body when she leaned forward to adjust her dress. She noticed my supposed discomfort and turned on her charm.

"Mr. O'Reardan, in my business, a body is just a body, sir. Sometimes I forget that in your business that is not the case." I laughed at her phony confidence. "Something to tell your friends about over a couple of beers perhaps?"

I didn't comment. She leaned back and nestled into the seat, slipped on her aviators, and watched Autumn drift by. I could tell she felt good.

I watched her as she stared into the landscape at her reflection on the window; the yellow stripe on the macadam washed over her face, sprinkled with gravel, and freckled passing cars. She thought of her beautiful friend Jesse and how they used to drive Jesse's VW Bug in Autumn to her private school nestled in trees; the leaves would jump out of the way as they breezed down the long driveway.

It always reminded her of Batman's quiet ride into his cave.

Then she thought of her sweet friend Briar and how they would skip school and drive down an avenue in their quiet mountain town lined in a canopy of trees, shaded even in winter. They listened to loud Brit pop, and she felt the sprinkled sunlight in his navy blue eyes laugh on their way to nowhere in particular. Anywhere with him was perfect.

I watched her face get hot, tracing a tear with my eyes down her cheek and into her mouth. I wanted to make it easier for her, but I couldn't. Everything was as it should've been; her tapestry was already woven. But it hurt to watch her close her eyes and taste the salt, as it had always been. She had fallen so many times in her life, and I was never actually able to pick her up. I could only offer tools and whispers to help her. Whether she used them or not was debatable—or if she even noticed them for that matter. That is definitely the hardest part of this job. So I felt relieved when she dozed into a dream.

Ana dreamed that she was on a raft, drifting farther and farther from familiarity. The sky morphed into a brilliant purplish-pink. She sunk down into her raft and felt water wash beneath her back through a small hole in the bottom. She watched the indigo water, tipped white from falling sunlight slowly cover her legs and arms, and climb into her ears, muffling all sound.

Whoosh! She felt this tremendous gravitational pull beneath her, and the raft was yanked down into the water. It was that moment when she woke with a start and was lying on the floor of the car trying to regain her composure.

"Are you okay, Dr. Guida? Sorry about that. This goddamn airport traffic is ridiculous!" I wiped sweat from my brow and swore under my breath, struggling to light another smoke. I peered at Ana in the rearview mirror.

"Him! That guy...he almost caused me to send both of us through the windshield...just cut off that Atlantic City senior citizen bus!" I shook my head and inched through the traffic. She sat up, adjusted her dress and hair, and looked on to the entrance for Gate C Departure: Sun Jet, Hooters Air. We passed before she could read the last low-rent Eastern seaboard airline name.

"Gate C. That's my gate, sir."

"Gotcha, Doc."

She wondered what I would call her if I "knew" that she was actually a mental ward escapee.

"What time's your flight again, doc?"

"11:30, sir."

"That's right. Well it's 10:15," I said. "But you don't have any bags to check. Can you run in those things?" I pointed at her flip-flops while I helped her out of the back seat.

"Absolutely!" She beamed, taking in the exhaust, the honking horns, and the morning light sneaking through weird Frank Lloyd Wright reminiscent airport angles.

I had to say it. "Will you need me to pick you up and return you home, Dr. Guida?"

She slung her backpack on, dipped into her wallet, and handed me my fare plus a $100 bill. I looked at her, dumbfounded. Before I could say a thing, she stood on her tiptoes, hugged me, gave me a big smooch, and whispered, "Have a wonderful life, Mr. O'Reardan."

* * *

I felt nostalgia watching her run off like a child. I remember her little five-year-old legs carried her running to her mom, arms outstretched, when she was lost at an antique show. I found her crying beneath a table in my booth, wiped her tears, and took her tiny hand in mine to help her find her parents. That day I was Rosa, the antique quilt restoration lady.

Little Ana had wandered off after she saw a stray cat. She thought the kitty looked sad and needed her help. Ana had heard someone tell her dad that morning that the main ingredient in the egg rolls at the Asian food stand was cat. Everyone laughed; Ana panicked. When little Ana saw the kitty cat strolling around the green field surrounding the antique market, she couldn't lose the evil image of that horrible man's laughing, sweating face, red with pleasure as he caught the poor kitty and put her in a boiling pot of water.

Poor Ana started to shake, which led her on a mission to save her feline friend. Even as a little girl, she was overcome by frightening, silent confusion. Her very vivid imagination would turn frightening; she never learned how to turn it off or how to explain it to anyone. And after I led her back to her parents, she ran to her mother and told her that she got lost taking the kitty to the woods for safety from the mean man who was going to cook her. Even though her mother hugged her and assured her that the man was only joking, Ana couldn't shake it for years.

When they left that day, her parents exchanged pleasantries with everyone. That man leaned down and smiled a coffee-stained grin. He placed his hand on her cheek to caress it and little Ana smacked it away, pinching his cheek with all of her five-year-old might.

"Don't touch me," she hissed.

Despite confusion among the adults, Ana felt triumphant. That was her revenge. She included the kitty in her prayer that night.

The one that became longer and longer with every passing year and included every person, animal, bug, etc., that she encountered and needed to be safe.

* * *

Two Bloody Marys later with her face pressed against the glass staring down into the clouds, Ana had no doubt that she was in the right place at that moment. She finally thought that she understood what it meant to be an existentialist. Perhaps at one time or another, she had felt that she seized the day or lived in the moment, relishing the flavor of the now with no fear of yesterday, tomorrow, or the repercussions of what she was engaged in momentarily. But it was never to the extent that it was on that plane, in that seat surrounded by strangers sharing the same air, eating the same mass-produced sandwiches, and receiving the same smiles from androids in sassy uniform, manicured, bleached, and painted with Max Factor.

That day, she even watched attentively while they reenacted the seat belt procedure before departure and finally understood the oxygen mask drill and why you are to put it on yourself before giving it to a child or assisting a row mate. It used to seem so extraordinarily selfish to her, but that day she made sure to raise her hand when they completed the performance.

She slurred, "No questions, sir/madam, but may I say that I truly enjoyed your performance and finally have a keen understanding of the importance of your seemingly mundane explanation. Thank you for taking the time to share." She looked around. "Although judging by the blank expression on everyone's face, I feel that your zealous interpretation has fallen on deaf ears…as it usually does. And I feel compelled to apologize for that."

The android smiles faded. "You'd probably conserve your precious energy by skipping the routine, concentrating on the important things like the beverage and snack cart while just letting us bastards fend for ourselves in the event of an emergency." She laughed and held her glass up.

Their brows tensed, and I snickered. I was Dominick Pasqualo, a gemologist from Staten Island, seated in 14F, three seats away from Ana.

Disregarding scowls and groans from other passengers, she continued, "Pardon me for making an assumption, but I guarantee that a very small percentage of the passengers on this aircraft have any clue as to how to utilize their seat as a flotation device and will simply drown. But thank you for your time. I hope that people tip you. They do, right?" The attendants stared at her silently.

"Oh, and I'm not being facetious." No response.

"Okay, well, may I please have another Bloody Mary?" I leaned over to the attendant when she passed and said, "All of her drinks are on me."

The android leaned over to her with her drink, and Ana reached into her backpack for money.

"The gentleman in 14F has taken care of that for you."

Ana thanked her and leaned forward. I simply lifted my glasses and winked.

"Cheers! Thank you, sir." Ana leaned back and stared out of the window.

She used to cringe at the thought of descending in an aircraft for fear of faulty tires, crash endings, drunk pilots with ill-judgment of the landing strips who were perhaps sleeping on the job or engaged in a sordid affair with an airline attendant or two. They were all plausible possibilities, she thought. She was sure that she was not the only person who had an unfathomable fear of dying in a plane crash. In fact, she thought that it was safe to assume that it is probably one of the most common phobias. Whatever it may be, she had been forever convinced that there was a monstrosity of a shark lurking in the salty depths that has been wearing a bib with her name on it since the day she was born.

But that flight was very different. She no longer had anything to be afraid of. Not only was she drunk without fear of projectile vomiting on the stranger to her left like she did upon her descent into Ireland a few years back, but she enjoyed the nausea and pounding in her ears. The tense air, cocktail peanuts, and Miami smog had never been more inviting.

Ana was alert for the first time in twenty-seven years. She was finally going to complete a project that she had begun, successfully: Life.

Ana

February 22, 2000

Dear Briar,

   This should be the last day of February, but it's a leap year. Weird. Who the hell ever decided that every four years there should be another day tacked onto February? It boggles me. I wonder if you're outside right now, Central Park perhaps, romping around with Pup. If you are sitting up on the rocks, you know the ones that I mean, you can probably really feel impending March.

Truly, the only solace that I found today is in the wind. I sat down on my parent's balcony and listened to March. It's crazy, I can hear the seasons changing. Really. If you listen closely, you really can hear grass unearthing. Even in New York, Bri, I bet that you can hear impending spring, too. Just listen to the space between sounds; it is there. It grows like a crescendo, and tickles the senses. Spring air activates the melanin in our skin, new freckles emerge like onion grass, and hair becomes a bit more unruly.

The sun is higher now. Did you notice? It washes us in light; no more long shadows. Soon the bullfrogs will be back again, but I won't hold my breath until summer. This year I will enjoy the transition. I will dance on the Solstice, experience the green moment, taste April's rain, and hug Mayflowers. I am an existentialist...today. It is so beautiful here in June when the green is still bright, and the day is long. I swear that it is enchanted. There is this whole fairy world that lives around the pond; it is fantastic. It is so lush, green, and the fragrant wisteria climbs the spiral staircase to my apartment. I cannot believe that you haven't been here. I've had many glasses of wine out on my patio, and cheered to you and the moon, Bri. It's magical in summer. I want to share it with you someday, soon. I think that fresh air and green grass is going to help me through this.

Love, Ana

* * *

March 3, 2000

Dear Jesse,

All I could listen to today was Pink Floyd's Syd Barrett tribute, "Shine On You Crazy Diamond." Everything else made me uncomfortable. I tried listening to the Jimi Hendrix *Blues* album, but it made me so restless.

Phone Practice: "How's Marc? Really…he's such an awesome guy. You two really lucked out! God, that was a beautiful wedding on the beach! And the dolphins…remember when the school of dolphins swam behind you when you took your vows? That was really magical. What's that? Oh yes, we've got to get together soon! Perhaps we could do something this weekend? No, I promise I won't bail out. I promise. I miss and love you, too."

Love, Ana

* * *

March 6, 2000

Hiding

Dear Briar,

I am so dizzy today. I can't get my head straight. I don't know if it is the weather. It's like cold pea soup outside—that weird damp that makes you shiver all over. It's not a November damp, but a March damp. It's different. This damp smells like life, not death.

I can just make out the green mossy roof of the boathouse outside of the window, but the fog has eaten up any inkling of the pond. It's so invasive.

I wonder if it's foggy in NY today.

It probably bugs you because of the humidity; it messes your closely-shorn curls. My hair actually looks better in pea soup. It gets a little wavy, like at the beach. That's what this dizziness feels like right now.

I feel like I have just been rolled in the waves, and I am fighting the shell bottom and the tide, trying to keep my balance and composure. When I look down, and the tide is rolling out, it washes my feet and ankles, and the sand moves so quickly. Can you picture it? And then I am walking up the beach toward a nap and everything saltwater spins, like my body isn't sure if it is out of the water yet. You know that feeling? That is my brain.

Love, Ana

* * *

March 7, 2000

Truth

Dear Briar,

Pea soup again today, but I can see some skunkweed or something emerging across the pond. The contrast is inspiring. It's bright green, against the stark, wet bank of the slate green pond. I have a question that has been burning, Briar: how have you perceived my bizarre behavior all of these years? Granted, my ups and downs were always hidden behind the guise of laughter, airheadedness, drunkenness, etc. Actually, you have always brought out the fun in me…the laughter, the actress, the entertainer, the child. Very rarely have I been a miserable sod in your presence. I saved that for my poor, unfortunate family who would secretly hold up their crucifix and spread holy water when I would "grace" them with my gloom.

So what did you see me as, nuts? I miss that mania. That's what it is called. Briar, you wouldn't even recognize me, which is one of the reasons that I am so embarrassed to call you. I'm numb. I crashed. I cannot find my inner party. I don't remember how to flirt. I'm completely self-absorbed. It's gross.

I'm afraid of confrontation; I can't find that exhibitionist within anymore, Bri, you know the one who would pole dance on a subway car at 3:00 a.m. Remember?

I can tell that it makes my dad sad. I overheard him say to someone that I have lost my sparkle.

I'm trying to find the gap of silence, between sadness and light. I am going to climb in and experience it, and try to rekindle my spirit for the sake of living…for friendship. Did you think that my ability to do anything, but my inability to hold onto anything was a result of flakiness? Did you think it was because I was a Gemini? Could you tell that I was riding on a pendulum? Was I overbearing? I wish that I could stop thinking about it.

Love (your once interesting friend), Ana

* * *

March 7, 2000

Dear Mother Nature,

I love it when it rains. Amazing things happen when it rains. The dogs just went completely insane barking. So I peeked out the upstairs window, and framed by the wet pane was a car that I didn't recognize.

Usually, in a situation like this, I would hide upstairs, panicking until the car would drive away, but today was different. I ran downstairs, barefoot, sweater inside out, unbrushed teeth, totally disheveled, and I answered the door. It was beautiful, blue-eyed Nick Jones, an endearing senior student of mine, drove all the way to my parent's house to deliver a basket of flowers: roses, daisies, pansies, tulips, honeysuckle, and greens arranged in a white basket.

He stood there, a drop of rain dripping down his cheek, telling me how everyone missed me, and gently handed me a card signed from all of the students in the class. I hugged him, then breathed in the color, and like magic, I didn't care about my appearance, my ugly winter white feet in a muddy puddle, or my fear of seeing people; I was touched. I felt. It's moments like this that I surface for air, breathe deep, and remember what alive feels like.

Thank you, Ana

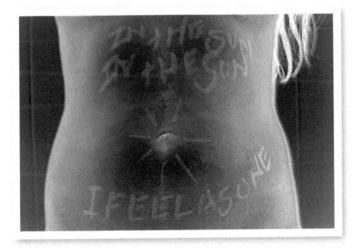

March 10, 2000

Ask

Dear Jesse,

According to the Dalai Lama's *Book of Awakening*, the Sanskrit word for ignorance or confusion is *avidya*, which means "not knowing." The Dalai Lama states, "There are several interpretations of what is meant by avidya according to the different philosophical schools and their various views of the fundamental Buddhist doctrine of anatman or no-self. However, the general meaning that is common to all the school is an understanding that there lies a fundamental ignorance at the root of our existence. The reason for this is quite simple. We all know from personal experience that what we deeply aspire to gain is happiness and what we try to avoid is suffering. Yet our actions and our behavior only lead to more suffering and not to the lasting joy and happiness that we seek. This must surely mean that we are operating within the framework of ignorance. This is how we experience the fundamental confusion at the root of our life."

So true, isn't it? Our path to happiness is inundated with the life stuff that knocks us down. It's like running up a down escalator, or climbing a slippery rope. And then when we do try to achieve that which makes us happy, something else has to give in order to get one step closer to our personal enlightenment. Perhaps this is karma—a reward system. The more we endure suffering or can learn from it, the greater the reward will be when we reach enlightenment.

I wonder if this occurs on different levels? Like, does an accomplished, wealthy actor feel fulfilled? She may have all the money that she could ever need, and all of the recognition, but does she feel that sense of gratification that we are all searching for?

Or perhaps there is someone who is married, with children, with a mortgage, a minivan, a dog, a cat, a house in suburbia, a 9–5 job, 2 weeks of vacation per year...is that her/his nirvana? Is that gratification?

Jesse, do you think that my mental illness bullshit is my suffering? My path to genuine contentment? Are you content?

Love, Ana

* * *

March 10, 2000

Wash

Dear Briar,

I sent you a letter two days ago, and I cannot stop thinking about it. I wonder what you will think? I can just picture you, fumbling into your blue, mirrored apartment building with the deco light fixtures...the smell of waxed floors and old paint. You close the city behind you, talk to Pup who you just picked up from puppy kindergarten, where all of the girls fussed over you and Pup, then you shuffle down the corridor toward the mailboxes and the neat old freight elevator that I am afraid to take, avoiding your reflection in the mirrored walls. You fumble with the keys, reach into your apt. 6C box, pull out a pile of mail...shuffle through like cards, "Bills, bill, bill, bill, check oooh, bill, bill, Ana?"

You laugh at my childlike handwriting on the envelope...silently compare it to your own handwriting, and decide to wait to read it when you get into your apartment. You and Pup move into the old elevator, you push 6 and relax into the dark, mirrored wall behind you. Struggling with the keys to open your apartment door, you go into the kitchen, greeted by Puddy the overweight, psychotic cat that I graced you with one night.

You then drop your bag on the floor in front of the window that looks out toward The Chrysler Building, walk over and check your messages. Nothing good. "Cal," you yell, noticing a half full glass of water on the counter. You notice the note: "Bri, went for a run. Be back in an hour. What are you hungry for? Love, Cal."

You fall onto the couch, followed by Pup who jumps up to gently lick your chin, then lays down, his head on your lap, and sighs. You close your eyes for a moment, then remember the letter from me in your hand, and you open it, and giggle at the crappy paper and business envelope that I folded it into. Then you fumble through my words.

The letter is my vain attempt to express how disillusioned I have been, how I have suffered, why I have been so distant, and how I am trying, desperately, to come back to Planet Goddamn Earth. And most importantly, how much I miss you. I can only hope that you are smiling now.

Love, Ana

March 10, 2000

Green

Dear Jesse,

Why is it that the most debilitating of all of the emotions is not only anger, but anger, jealousy, and shame, all wrapped up into a tightly woven bundle?

If you close your eyes and meditate on both anger and jealousy, they seemingly work as a team to knock you down...and then shame finishes you off, leaving you weaker than you were before you started.

Jealousy has a more invasive grip, whereas anger is a much more explosive. Anger I picture as a violent storm, whereas jealousy is more like a creeping poison; slow to overcome you, but when it does, it is detrimental.

Perhaps Gertrude's death in Hamlet, when she drank the poison flask of wine that was meant for Hamlet's demise, is a visual metaphor for creeping jealousy. I mean, think about it; Claudius and Laertes had premeditated Hamlet's murder by challenging him to a duel with a poisoned foil, and a flask of celebratory wine with a poisoned pearl in it. They thought that it was a no fail plan; either way, Hamlet would perish, while his mother looked on in horror.

But the fates twisted the denouement, as the audience gripped their seats in dismay, and watched Gertrude down the poisoned flask in honor of her son's elaborate sword fight move. Gertrude did not die a quick, painless death... she voiced all of the negative emotions inherent in the play on her sweating, panic stricken, dying face. The poison crept up on her while we watched, unable to change her fate.

Jealousy, if not handled properly, always leads to explosive anger. Remember when we were 7, and at one of your birthday pool parties, and I was violently jealous of your blonde school friend. Tina? Was that her name? I hated her! You were my best friend, and who the hell did she think she was? That prima donna! She had her little pink bag, and her cute little pink jellies, and she had the nerve to sit next to you when you were blowing out the candles on your birthday cake. That jealousy inched up my spine until I couldn't take it anymore. Me...tiny, goofy me.

I can't quite remember what incident finally pushed me to the next level...but all I remember is pushing my long braids and wet bangs away from my face, leaning down toward the shallow end of the pool, and punching Tina right in the face. Initially was gratifying, but then with every one of her tears, shame fell on me like rain, drenching me.

I was forced by my own guilt to say, "I'm sorry, Tina. I didn't mean to punch you." Like hell I didn't!

Love, Ana

* * *

March 11, 2000

Frightened

Jesse,

I still haven't heard from my landlord yet. I gave him a letter 11 days ago with my March rent check. I just couldn't muster up the courage to sidle downstairs to his doctor's office to tell him that I had to end my lease early because I had to leave my job; I've become a fucking charity case.

The social stigma that is attached to mental illness is pretty harsh: *One Flew Over the Cuckoo's Nest, Catcher in the Rye,* etc. Then again, who attaches the stigma to the illness? Could it be a group of inflexible pawns who belong to "moral" groups that feel that those novels shouldn't be included in the high school curriculum because they are inappropriate? Why...because of expletives? I doubt it. It's because those selections of literature are not "safe" according to the pawns, the worker bees, the ants marching.

All I know is that the only way that I could turn on my 10th grade literature students was to "be" Holden Caulfield, and read the book to them aloud. They appreciated it. They watched his mental demise. They could relate to his angst. If anything, they became more understanding, or perhaps aware of mental strife; they overcame their fear of it.

I believe this, but I still cannot push aside my own shame. I hate shame. It has a stranglehold on me. While I write this, I am panicking about the fact that I have to go over to my apartment to feed my fish and my cats. I am neglecting them because I am afraid to run into my landlord, which would probably be the best thing for me. Confrontation is key, yet I fear it. What a bizarre affliction! Here is the letter that I wrote to my landlord:

Dear Dr. Haus,

Because of the social stigma placed on mental illness, it is very embarrassing for me to address a person who I admire such as yourself initially in person about my extenuating circumstances; please accept this letter in place of a knock on your door. This year, hidden behind the guise of the flu, or a cold, etc., I have been battling Bipolar Disorder.

With the help of modern meds, I had been able to keep afloat and function as a school teacher, until recently. I had a serious episode about two weeks ago that unfortunately did not leave me unscathed; I have gone headlong into both cognitive and drug therapy as a result.

I was circumstantially granted an unpaid medical leave of absence from school for 12 weeks, to get back on my feet emotionally, although that will leave me in financial straits for a while. Sadly, I must ask you if I may end my apartment lease with you early, for I haven't a monetary choice in the matter.

Dr. Haus, I have so enjoyed living here, and I thank you for such a warm welcome into such a colorful town; I have acquired a real respect for small town economy and mentality. Milltown's self-contained success is justification for *buy local*. I welcome the opportunity to sit down and talk about the lease at your convenience. Thank you in advance for your time and consideration.

I'll tell you, Jesse, I have been praying that by the grace of some god, he would be so kind as to grant me my security deposit.

Wishful thinking, Ana

Gabriel

October 29, 2000

She was unaffected by the airline attendant whispers while stumbling toward the exit. She explained to anyone listening that she didn't have any luggage but her trusty, highly unfashionable backpack. She stopped and told everyone around her upon exiting, "Actually, I've given all of my things away to charity. It feels good! You should try it. Lighten the load, you know?" Some smiled politely, others clasped their children like possessions and pressed their pasty bodies on toward their sunny vacations. I got a real kick out of it; a sociological study on uneasy human behavior when introduced to questionable conversation from strangers.

Ana felt that it was not unlike watching people disregard the existence of the homeless, their feet wrapped in clothing and relics of shoe soles, peeking out from behind cardboard boxes, or tipped hats or used coffee cups with lipstick-stained rims. They don't exist; someone, somewhere deemed them subhuman and people listened, disregarding the fact that perhaps the haggard were born into this world with aspirations and dreams like them—only theirs were somehow shattered.

"Cheers to the homeless, to the less fortunate, to the kind souls who may have never had the opportunity to travel in an aircraft to a sunny place! May karma take care of them." She held up her imaginary glass to the flight crew and the exiting passengers and laughed at their perplexed expressions. Then she made her way through the exhaust-filled vacuum toward the airport.

You should have seen them. Everyone looked so tense; bees in a fluorescent hive, working for the queen. You could hear them buzzing about aimlessly, worrying about yesterday and tomorrow. She remembered being one of them once, wishing someone or something would ease the confusion and relax her nerves without a handful of sedatives and a quick trip to the bar for an overpriced cocktail. So she smiled. She smiled at everyone she encountered, a genuine, toothy-grin without fear that her imperfect choppers were not bleached.

Perhaps Ana had a portion of mass-produced cheese sandwich lodged between the unsightly hated space that she thought existed between her two front teeth. It didn't faze her that day. She didn't care that some looked away because many smiled back.

"Hello. Good afternoon. Great Scarf! Enjoy your trip!"

Everyone she encountered received a tailor-made message, and she felt good. I could tell. After an overpriced cocktail and an enormous tip for the angry young man behind the bar, she made her way to the car rental deck, full-knowing that her credit card only had a $100 spending limit; she did the research before she became an existential thinker. Hertz Rent-A-Car simply holds the credit card number until the car is returned then they charge you; a simple equation even for someone who is not gifted in mathematics such as herself. How will they charge her for the rental if the car is never returned? Brilliance.

"May I help you, miss?" An effeminate male with a spray-on tan and bleached smile leaned on the counter, chewing potent spearmint gum while eyeing the Polo-clad salt-and-pepper corporate serf behind her.

"It must be a real bitch to work indoors when living in Miami. I would go for a spray-on tan and Crest White Strips too. I mean, you have to hold up the image of the boys in South Beach, right?" The Ralph Lauren serf cleared his throat behind her.

"It's true, right?"

Ana turned to him and he turned away.

"Anyway, you look great."

There wasn't a response from the bronze man, just a confused stare.

"Anyhow, I would like a convertible, preferably silver and not a Chrysler."

"Okay," the attendant lisped. "Here's the paperwork. Please fill it out and take it to the excursion desk. Next?" He looked over her shoulder and whispered tenderly, "I'm so sorry about that. Can I help you?"

She entered the excursion line.

"Next, please." She was dancing to an elevator rendition of The Kinks, "You Really Got Me."

"Miss? Your paperwork please."

"Sorry. I just cannot believe that easy listening was able to cover this."

"Miss, may I have your paperwork?" Another android. I think she was a female prototype. Blonde, French twist, painted face. Ana swore that when she stared very closely, her insides were ticking mechanisms, like a clock. Perhaps she was the bionic woman, an alien…something. But whatever she was, her creator forgot to add her sense of humor. The android didn't like Ana.

She examined the paperwork, took her credit card, asked for her Social Security number, stamped her form, and without making eye contact, sent her to door number three for her prize—a yellow Suzuki Samurai.

"It's okay to smile," Ana whispered to her as she sauntered away. It was the first time the android acknowledged her; Ana considered that progress.

I watched her walk into hot, humid Miami September. A young man greeted her with a cigarette hanging from his lips and a bright blue Hertz Rent-A-Car uniform.

"Hello, sunshine." He smiled and spoke with an island tongue. "Your paperwork?"

"Gladly." She beamed. "Wow, it's so nice to be greeted by such kindness. Perhaps it's because you are outside instead of pinned behind a desk all day under fucking fluorescent light." He smiled and checked her paperwork. She leaned into him. "You are gorgeous. Have you ever considered modeling?"

He laughed wholeheartedly. "No, miss, but thank you."

"Well, you should! You'd make a hell of a lot more money than working here."

"I never thought of it." His high cheekbones and slightly blood-shot island eyes flickered a dream. Ana was enamored by the contrast against his black skin. Beautiful. He was wearing a woven cap that housed what she would only imagine to be a world of earth-scented dreadlocks; Ana always had a thing for dreadlocks, island accents, and high cheekbones.

"I'll bring your car around, miss."

"Thank you." She peered at his name tag." Peanut? That name doesn't quite suit you."

He laughed, tossed his cigarette, and a minute later, pulled around with her painfully cheerful jeep-like vehicle.

"Enjoy your trip, miss. Where's your luggage?"

"On my back," she said, smiling behind her oversized aviator sunglasses. She climbed into her rental. "You know, a couple years back, I probably would have asked you to join me for the ride." She lifted her glasses and winked.

He looked confused but still smiled a string of pearls. She reached into the pouch of her backpack and handed him a hundred-dollar bill wrapped sloppily around the stale dime bag. "Go back to the islands, Peanut. I'm sure it's kinder there." She felt good.

* * *

Ana began her journey to one of two places that she felt at peace in this life: the Florida Keys. Big Pine Key to be specific. It was late hurricane season; she was easily smitten with the thought of an ominous, crystal blue ocean, rumbled by ill-fated winds and torrential downpours. Shakespearian.

She always thought that there was something passionate about the impending deconstruction of nature by nature. It always seemed to make people communicate more. Fear brings out kindness in people, and they seem to band together to rebuild the devastation.

She swore that natural disaster happens for a purpose.

Otherwise, there would be no such thing as unity, unless politics are involved, and that is certainly questionable. She was on to something.

Ana always hated Miami. But that day she relished it, illuminated by neon on Forty-Second Avenue moving toward the Florida turnpike. It was fun making her way out of the city and South on Route 1 in a convertible; she always wanted one. The closest that she had gotten was a 1974 Volkswagen Rabbit with a hand-cranked sunroof. It was beautiful—$300 and a sixteenth birthday gift from her parents.

Later it worked as both transportation and a skate park accessory for her skateboarding cohorts; she adored it, grinded fenders and all. I watched it like a hawk.

She found a fabulous, eclectic college station. It played everything from Johnny Cash to Radiohead and tossed in some vintage punk rock in the interim.

"The Cramps?" They played their sordid, drug-induced rendition of Route 66; it was perfect. When she looked in the rearview mirror, the autumn 2:00 p.m. light that tripped through her hair and freckled cheeks sent her home for a moment.

It was a Saturday afternoon memory. Bleary-eyed and fourteen or so, she stared out of her sister Amber's window across the early September Pennsylvania corn, ready for harvest. She was probably waiting for the phone to ring or trying to muster up a faux ailment to creep up on her Sunday morning and progressively get worse.

She hoped that by evening she could convince her mother that school was not an option for Monday morning. She revisited the moment and found it weird how light, sound, or scent carried her into memory or emotion, but never the clock. Time had become irrelevant to her.

* * *

David Bowie's "Life on Mars" screamed from the Suzuki as she turned into the crackling white coral entrance to her favorite biker bar right off of the Overseas Highway in Key Largo. It was called Dick's. She found that unusually ironic having walked in on the sweaty, greasy owner Jed with his pants around his ankles inside a sundrenched nocturnal blond clad in a leather vest. There were cut-off jean shorts in a pile on the ground next to the sink that she was propped up on. Ana wasn't sure; it all happened so fast. But when she opened the door to enter the bathroom, the blonde said angrily, "C'mon, Jed, I hardly feel nothing!" Then they both looked into the shaft of light coming in from behind her—two deer in headlights.

"Sorry," she said, closing the door behind her.

She walked away, waiting to hear them lock it. Nothing. So she went back to the door, banged on it, and said, "Lock the door for Christ's sake!" I heard the bolt lock as she made her way into the men's room.

After a couple shots of Jack, she decided to sit down for a bowl of conch chowder.

"What can I get ya?" a raspy voice asked. She looked up and made eye contact with the blond doe. Led Zeppelin's "I Can't Quit You Baby" seeped from the jukebox. She turned away flustered, and Ana said, "A bowl of conch chowder, a shot of Jack, and a pint of Guinness, please." The doe blushed.

"And don't be ashamed! In fact, it sounded as if he should have been embarrassed by his ineffectual tactics."

She walked away with her tail between her tanned legs, and Ana felt bad. But then she looked up and saw Jed talking to another woman with three little children; they all danced around him.

"Daddy, I'm hungry. Is there any ice cream? What time are you coming home, Daddy?"

Bastard. She watched him kiss the tiny brunette woman coldly, barely acknowledge his children, and go back into the kitchen while the woman struggled to put everyone in the car. The doe returned with Ana's order and nervously placed it down in front of her.

"You are so much better than that," Ana whispered. "Once an asshole, always an asshole. I'm sure you're a lovely person. Don't give him the privilege of stomping on your heart, too."

The doe's eyes began to well up. "Enjoy your chowder," she said and sidled away.

Ana fantasized that the doe sat outside to have a smoke and planned her great escape. When he came outside to orchestrate their next sleazy rendezvous, she flicked her cigarette, blew her last drag into his eyes, and said, "I quit! And fuck you for treating me like vermin." Then she pushed him down in the dusty coral, stomped off to her car, took the pin out of her bleached hair, and got into her aqua-blue convertible 1974 Buick Electra.

"Go home to your wife and kids, you rotten bastard," she hissed and tore out of the gravel into the four o'clock sunshine in a cloud of crushed coral dust.

Ana was awakened from her daydream when the doe cleared her dishes and handed her the check. "Thank you." She smiled shyly.

Ana handed her a $100 bill. "Think about what I've said." The doe walked up to the register, and Jed passed behind her. He pinched her backside and leered at Ana as she crossed.

Ana bellowed, "No change, doe eyes. Treat yourself to a bus ticket out of this dump." Ana flipped Jed off then sauntered to her sunshine mobile.

"Get out of my bar, you crazy bitch!" Jed yelled.

Ana looked over her shoulder, lifted her oversized-aviators, and winked.

"Go home to your wife and children, you rotten bastard." Ana didn't look back but tore out of the parking lot, leaving a trail of dust with great hope that a piece of sharp coral gravel kicked up and landed in his eye. I steadied the wheel.

* * *

By the time she reached Bahiahonda campground on Big Pine Key, the late October sun was parallel to the Atlantic Ocean. The abandoned railroad trestle bridge that extended out over the water was sprinkled with visitors waiting to watch a magnificent sunset.

She pulled into the ranger station and registered for an overnight visit. She chose one of the cabins perched on stilts located on the far end of the island, overlooking the Gulf of Mexico. If she had chosen any other time of year to try this, she would not have been able to find a campsite.

"I love hurricane season!" she said to a family waiting to register. They smiled politely.

She observed, only to find that the majority of other campers that were registering were (a) tent campers or (b) foreign.

They were either without any inkling or fearless that they were all in the path of several hurricanes named after several unfortunate people who would probably prefer not to be associated with chaotic mass-destruction. Either way, she was impressed.

She chose the cabin located at the west tip of the island, the portion that could not be reached via bicycle and/or roller blades. Just by four-wheel drive vehicles or on foot.

She remembered snorkeling there once with a boyfriend du jour when she happened upon the funky crystal blue ravine located to the left of the site where the ocean water pooled. Adventurous kayak rowers were about the only people who ever ventured through the deep green canopy. The area was not conducive to RVs. Perfect. It was surrounded by overhanging shrubs and an occasional splash of bougainvillea—beautiful poisonous flowers.

Ana considered making bougainvillea tea for herself on her last visit…but couldn't find enough time alone. I made sure of that.

The ranger made her sign a waiver: *"Bahiahonda is not responsible for any lost or stolen goods, property damage due to natural or artificial causes, and for articles left behind."*

She peered at his name tag and signed away, handed it over, and smiled.

"Oh, don't you worry, Ranger Tom. I won't be leaving anything behind at all. It's all right here in my trusty backpack."

He smiled, blushed curiously, handed her the keys, a flashlight, a guide explaining the ecological balance that needs to be kept sacred on the island, and a parking tag for her "Suzuki Sunshine Jeep thing," as she referred to it on her registration.

"Don't forget sunscreen tomorrow, Miss Guida." He looked down at the signed agreement. "You are checking out tomorrow already?"

"Maybe even earlier." She smiled. "I just want some solace you know? Even if it is only short-lived."

"Well that's what all this natural beauty is here for." He puffed up his shoulders and cleared his throat. "You fit right in." He winked.

She reached into her denim jacket and pulled out another rolled $100 bill, closed his palm around it, and told him not to look until she was far gone. And if he could, please assure that she would have no close neighbors for the evening.

"Thanks, Tom." She winked at him then walked out into the most fabulous early evening sunshine she could remember. There was a dance of purples, braided with earthen red and yellow, soft coral, and warm pink, swirled with Crayola cornflower blue. She jumped into her ride, hung the tag from the rearview mirror. I watched her from a tree as she bounced her way toward the nest. She peered into her side view mirror and waved at Tom who wiped his balding brow and discreetly watched her slide away into the dunes and brush.

Halfway to her cabin, she pulled a pack of Camel filters from her sack that she had picked up at the Highway One liquor store along with a bottle of George Dickel whiskey. She wanted Jack Daniels, but they were sold out. It must be popular in the Keys. Judging by the statuesque storeowner's half-teeth, dipped in some sort of nicotine wash, she thought that perhaps it was used frequently as a mouth rinse or the like in lieu of toothpaste or Listerine. But his gummy smile framed by his sparse shock of white hair tied into a braid felt so genuine to her that she gave him a rolled up $100 bill, too.

"Thank you kindly for your generosity and fabulous description of George Dickel. I know that I will love it just as much as Jack Daniels. You are a good man." She looked for a clue to his name.

"Bert." He smiled and reached out his fading tattooed arm to shake her hand. "Thank you, miss."

"Now, Bert, don't unroll that bill until I am far gone. I don't want to feel silly." She winked at balding Bert with the Asian warrior braid and sunken brown eyes, and hoped that the tip made his day. She felt good.

* * *

After she nestled into the nest, I watched her struggle to start a fire outside of the cabin. She was half-in-the-bag. Her motor skills were shot by booze and residuals from the mental monstrosity.

She grabbed some musty linen they provided and curled up under the stars with her Camels and Dickel. I quietly watched her close her drunk eyes and pretend to float on the indigo sky to get a better taste of her near future. In her mind, the stars were like that of Van Gogh's—yellow, tangible, luminescent, and warm.

"'Would you like to swing on a star, carry moonbeams home in a jar?'" She climbed through a drunken memoir of her and Jack walking hand in hand during a soft, silent snowstorm. She swayed and sang that tune to him. The melody was trapped inside her scarf and wool cap. She stared up and watched flakes catch in his brown waves, peeking out from beneath a ski hat dressed with a red pom-pom. Jack stopped.

"Close your eyes. I have a special surprise for you." She remembered half-expecting a tackle into a fluffy, deep bank or a face full of snow. But then heard a vaguely familiar sound, like a dog makes when pissing hot, steamy yellow in untouched snow. Jack took her by the hand.

"Don't peek!"

He positioned her head so that she would see his creation upon opening her cold eyelids.

"Okay. You can look now."

She opened her eyes, rubbed away the blurred vision, and focused on a yellow-splattered heart in the snow.

"Talent."

She turned to him, patted him on the back. "Come on. Let's go have hot chocolate."

She thought maybe that was love; she was, again, mistaken.

* * *

Time passed. Ana's mind felt like it was dripping. She felt a strong falling sensation and was jarred awake by heat on her face coupled by that weird jerk that sometimes rouses you suddenly from dreamscape. An ember had sparked some dry hibiscus leaves that she had gathered and the fire roared, illuminating three small trees that grew parallel to the cabin stilts. It cast a wavy shadow on the quiet ocean. She sat up and coddled her bottle of Dickel, wiped hot tears from her face, and lowered onto the blanket. She dug her bare feet into the cool night sand.

I shuddered when I heard her, first shrouded in confusion, then screaming through my eyes, ears. She held her wet face to the sky pleading.

"Make it stop, please, go away! I don't exist! Go away! Go away! Go away! I don't know any yesterday. Please! Stop hurting me. Enough!"

It was then that she realized that she was yelling at herself or to the goddess or the gods or to mother fate or to the fish or to her life or to her alter ego or all of these. Why were the sad, sad memories creeping in like little fishhooks? It defeated the purpose of handing her soul over to existential thinking. God was neither alive nor dead. She knew she was then, and she was there, and she was handing in her resignation.

Ana

March 11, 2000

Righteousness

Dear Briar,

Who ever said that Lewis Carroll was a pervert? I bet it was a person of the same sick, rigid mentality that deemed homosexuals as "unfit" for society, and black Africans as worthy of only working, or women as better seen and not heard, walking ten paces behind their men. Oh, but let's not forgot the women who walk ten paces in front of their men in the event of possible land mines. What about the Lepers who are born into the caste system and destined to flounder around the bottom of the ladder only to suffer, and get trampled on by those born into a more fortunate role? Who decides?

Lewis Carroll wrote one of the most fantastic children's stories of all time, *Alice in Wonderland*, and he wrote it based on Alice Liddell…not because he had a sexual affinity for her, but because he was taken by the beauty of children; the innocence and curiosity inherent in every child.

Carroll was a mathematics professor at a university in England, and his supervisor was Professor Liddell, father to the Liddell sisters. Carroll used to take the sisters out on leisurely rowboat rides around the pond on the campus of the university, where they would make up fantastical stories, hence the dawn of *Alice in Wonderland*.

I'm sure that the unusual, unmarried Carroll was scoffed at and frowned upon by some of his colleagues for spending so much time with the Liddell girls, but their father obviously saw through the negative to the mutual joy that their story creations gave one another. Can you blame Carroll? He was the perceptive one. He was the one who saw the inflexibility and stark landscape of adulthood.

Children create their own landscape every day; they paint with their imaginations and their hands and feet. They dance when they feel like dancing. They mimic the wind. They study the earth. They love animals. They are fascinated by water. They are artists. They feel music. They laugh when it's funny. They jump up and down when they are excited. They cry when they are sad. They yell when they are mad. They nap when they are tired. They get their way because they are cute. They are not afraid to use it. They blow bubbles. They fall down, but get back up and try again. They believe in fairies. They play outside. They love colors. They are curious. They wear what's comfortable. They are colorblind. Every stifled adult should have a child mentor. We have so much to learn from children.

Love, Ana

The Evening of 3/12

Shadows

Dear Nanny,

I received the most beautiful letter today from your daughter Madeleine, my aunt, who I haven't seen since your funeral. Nanny, the letter was so endearing. It began with "I have loved you since I had my first peek at you in the hospital. I stayed with you and your mom, dad, and amber for the first week of your life. You were so pink and sweet and smelled like fresh air and flowers." I was touched, and I cannot feel much lately. Then she went on to reveal some really interesting things. Nanny, unbeknownst to family, she had bouts of depression for many years, and had been medicated for the past 25 years; like me, she had decided several times to stop taking the medication, and suffered as a result. Poor Madeleine. She has five children, and I am sure that like you, she suffered in silence for their sake. It's not fair.

Tonight over dinner, I asked my mom some questions about our lineage, and she said that you, I, and herself are not the only ones who have felt the repercussions of this debilitating genetic illness, but your sister, Aunt Viv committed suicide in her early 80s. She told me that Viv was alcoholic, and she was bedridden, and that she overdosed on pills and booze. I never knew. Again, looks can be so deceiving; I was just a little girl when Aunt Viv was still of this earth, but I distinctly remember her, polka-dot clad, a shock of white hair, huge smile, cat eye glasses, and always having mints. She was so jovial in my memory. And Nanny, how about your mom? She died when she was so young, but mom told me that she, too, suffered from mental problems. She was raised by her grandmother, so what happened to her mom? Did she suffer too? Did she take her own life? Did you ever think about ending your life, Nan? What kept you here for 86 years? Is it the same thing that has somehow kept me here so long? Hope? I miss your red lipstick that you applied with a q-tip,

Ana

Evening of March 12, 2000

Secrets

Dear Grammy,

...or should I refer to you as the beautiful Katharina from Holland? Oh no, I have not forgotten about you, except I am sure that you have reincarnated into my Niece, Jane. I can see it in her eyes. Jane loves her Bop; my dad, your little Harry.

It is you, and I am apprehensive about telling my sister this; she doesn't take kindly to anything suggested outside her realm of understanding. Who am I kidding? She already knows that I am nuts. But I like to protect her from upsetting things; I cannot stand to see her suffer.

You were one of seven siblings, so I know that you can relate. I always wished that my sister and I would've been close growing up like you and your sister Astrid. I remember you used to tell me stories about how you and Astrid used to go to the beach, meet boys, and double date. You were so beautiful, the two of you. Real 1920s and 1930s sirens! I can just picture you laughing, smoking, and deliciously flirting in the rumble seat of your flavor-of-the day's car.

Luckily, Amber hasn't been afflicted with this mental yuck. Neither were you, thank God. Heaven knows you had enough to contend with: a brain tumor, experimental surgery in the 1950s, and a husband who died in a jail cell in Mexico. That love affair is a novel unto itself—Katharina and Harry Sr.: Martinis and Mayhem. You managed to live thirty more years after Harry Sr. died in 1969. My mom told me that she asked you whether or not you would marry again, and you placed your manicured hand down on her lap and smiled, "Peg, I will never be subservient to a man, again."

I found it very interesting that mental illness did run in your husband's side of the family. I never knew that Harry's mom, a beautiful young woman from Sweden, was swept off her feet by Harry's father, who was a French/German sea captain (who knows, they were descendants of Alsace-Lorraine in France, on the border of Germany).

Because of his nomadic lifestyle, he took her away from everything she knew, including her language, and they lived from port to port. He left her for months at a time, and on his brief visits at home they had two children: my grandfather Harry Sr., and my great Aunt, Hazel. Sadly, I never met either of them.

I understand that she raised them alone; she felt abandoned, and terribly depressed. When she became pregnant for a third time, out of desperation, she attempted to abort the fetus herself, and hemorrhaged to death; a successful suicide, it seems.

Some might say, "How could a woman take her life when she has children to love and raise?" That is where mental illness sadly prevails. Someone who is suffering is consumed with thoughts of nothing but her or himself. It is the most selfish disease: dear me, woe is me, are they looking at me, why me, and why not me? You really can suffocate beneath Sylvia Plath's "Bell Jar." It exists, and it is all-encompassing. I know.

Love, Ana

* * *

March 14, 2000

Impatience

Dear Briar,

I'm beginning to really loathe the thick Lithium fog that I am living in; my 5-second delay is growing very stale, very quick. I feel dumbed-down, like I've been made into the junior edition of a board game called "me."

Briar, what if I was diagnosed all wrong? It happens more often than we probably think. Maybe my problem is physiological, not mental.

Perhaps it stems from something even bigger…something other than a chemical imbalance in the brain, a pineal malfunction, or genetics.

For instance, in all of the metaphysical literature that I sink into, illness is much more cerebral, and controlled by the mind and the environment. Psychiatrist Jung saw a direct correlation between balance, the unconscious mind, and physical wellness.

Hmmm…curious.

Robert A. Johnson (not the 1920s guitar legend), Jungian analyst and author, speaks about his theory, based on Jungian Psychology in an excerpt from *Inner Work: Using Dreams and Active Imagination for Personal Growth*:

"Jung discovered that the unconscious is not merely an appendage of the conscious mind, a place where forgotten memories or unpleasant feelings are repressed. He posited a model of the unconscious so momentous that the Western world has still not fully caught up with its implications. He showed that the unconscious is the creative source of all that evolves into the conscious mind and into the total personality of each individual. It is out of the raw material of the unconscious that our conscious minds develop, mature, and expand to include all the qualities that we carry potentially within us."

Johnson expounds further: "Jung showed us that the conscious and the unconscious minds both have critical roles to play in the equilibrium of the total self. When they are out of correct balance with one another, neurosis and other disturbances result."

I don't know, Bri, but I think that I buy it. There is no light without dark; yin without yang, love without hate; safety without fear. Balance is the key to mental stability. So what's the cure? I certainly don't think that it is to drug a person until they are deemed useless; where is the progress there? Isn't quality of life what ultimately a person suffering from any illness is striving to achieve? A renewed sense of living in the moment, not hovering above it in a highly-medicated haze.

Fuck it...I know that I want to join the party again, not just watch from a clouded distance.

Yours truly, Ana

* * *

3/13

Crush

Dear Jim,

I always felt so strange calling you by your first name. I respected you so much as a poet, and as my professor. Jim, I cannot believe that it was 5 years ago that you skipped town and I never had the chance to bid you a proper farewell.

I just want to thank you for trusting me as a writer. Your influence and recognition of my work meant so much; I hadn't an ounce of confidence before your acknowledgment.

The shape of your face is fleeting, washed in medicine, like this memory I have of you and beautiful Sarah, the girl you were dating. I remember walking briskly at twilight on Main Street next to the Coffee Shop, looking down at my sandals, and looking up only to make eye contact with you and Sarah in perpetual motion; Fu Lay Chinese neon light hung in her blonde curls. "Hi Ana," you said breezily, and rushed by with an aromatic pizza in your hands. Startled, I looked back, and you were wearing battered Vans sneakers. I loved that! You brought the essence of your California with you to Northeast academia. Your eccentricity was welcome, in addition to your Irish blue eyes and messy brown locks. Jim, thanks for holding my attention, and paying me respect.

Fondly, on fragile knees, Ana

* * *

Evening of March 14, 2000

Anger

Dear Jesse,

It's late. I'm tired, and I've been trying to force myself to smile all day. I'm just down.

I attempted to pretend for my parent's sake that I was floating comfortably above sea level, but man, I'm swimming with the fishes today. I can't figure it out! Perhaps I should just stop trying, and feel. I wish that I could just pick up the fucking phone and give you a call, or that I could answer my phone when it rings. When does it stop? How can I make this stop?

The other night I laughed. My dad took me out to a diner, and he had really bad gas; it reverberated off of the wooden seat, drawing attention from many neighboring booths. We both crumbled with laughter!

The next day when I couldn't decide whether or not I should wake up, I thought, "Good god, please don't tell me that was my high." If that was mania, what have I been reduced to by Lithium?

Perhaps this is what it feels like to be "normal." If that is the case, Jesse, I now understand people's passion for spice: fantasy novels, hallucinogenic drugs, skydiving, habanero peppers. Jesus Christ, I will take anything to add flavor.

Growl, Ana

* * *

March 15, 2000

True Grit

Dear Dr. Ari Freedman,

You probably don't remember this...but I do, and I will never forget it. It was my second stint in the hospital, not long after we met during my first hospital visit where you took me on as a patient. I bet you didn't foresee that train wreck. I apologize, in hindsight.

Do most of your patients listen to you...take their meds on time, get their blood work done, make their appointments, and not question every decision you make? I hope so...for your sake. I see your blood pressure elevate slightly with every swipe of your hand across your balding scalp when I deviate from your plan. No worries... it is nothing new; I'm well-versed in frustrating people. Historically, my name was prefaced with "Goddamnit."

"Goddamnit, Ana! What were you thinking?"

"Goddamnit, Ana! Why would you do that?"

"Goddamnit, Ana! Where is your mind?"

"Goddamnit, Ana! Who are they, and what are you doing with them?"

"Goddamnit, Ana! Use your head!"

"Goddamnit, Ana! Stop asking questions and do what you're told!"

I know I can be difficult. It's just…I sometimes do things just for the sake of doing something. I am curious. And frankly, I think I know best, in the moment.

So, I overdosed…I don't think purposely, but I did.

I may have been drinking. So, in my state of mind, I just wanted to sleep; I swallowed multiple Seroquel.

Sometimes I get restless leg syndrome from the meds I have been prescribed so badly that it is unbearable. I just kick and kick and kick; it is so vastly uncomfortable. Many nights, I have gotten out of bed in the late, late evening and taken Sherman for a long walk around my sleepy little town, trying anything to get rid of the anxious feeling in my legs. But that night, I opted for Seroquel. Usually Seroquel is a win-win, but that night, coupled with booze, it landed me on my front stoop at 3:00 a.m. in some weird sleep-state. Who knows what I was thinking. I don't have any recollection.

My boss, who was closing the brewpub, found me collapsed with a lit cigarette on the front steps. He probably wouldn't have seen me, but Sherman saw him and ran over to greet him outside of the restaurant.

He called an ambulance, Sherman stayed with him, and I was rushed to the hospital, my blood pressure dangerously low. When they revived me, I tried to leave. They sedated me.

So in and out of consciousness, this is what I remember. I could see you, I could see the nurses, I could see the lights…but I couldn't say anything. My mouth didn't work.

You didn't say much to me, but turned to the nurse in the room.

"Why is she so sedated? Who gave you orders to sedate her like this?" You searched my chart.

The nurse replied, "Dr. Freedman, when we revived her, she was physical…a danger to herself. She was trying to leave…pulled out her IV."

"I don't care what she did! She is under MY CARE! I MAKE THE CALL!"

I wanted to tell you that I was sorry, and that I just wanted to go home. My eyes were open.

"I want her off of the sedation drugs, STAT!"

"I understand Dr. Freedman…but I was ordered—"

"I don't care WHO ordered you! She is MY PATIENT!"

Your mustache twitched…a bead of sweat dripped down from under your Yarmulke.

The nurse smiled. "I understand that, Doctor, but—"

"But NOTHING! She's CATATONIC! You will do what I SAY! I'm a YALE FUCKING GRADUATE…25 YEARS IN PSYCHIATRY! UNDERSTOOD?"

You were like the Rooster Cogburn of Psychiatry! The nurse listened…and you officially became MY hero.

Thank you Dr. Freedman. And you didn't even know I was listening.

Ana

Gabriel

Evening, October 29, 2000

The fire died, and she found her way up the long staircase to the lofty cabin, made it through the door, climbed through confused intoxication meshed with a missed evening dose of antipsychotics, and collapsed onto the cedar planks. The oil lantern cast a weird light that looked like dancing cats onto the floor. She watched them dip in and out of each crack, stuffed with sand and tiny pieces of other people's lives. It didn't bother her that her face was pressed against the unkempt wood; there was no need to worry about harming her sensitive complexion. The saltwater would take care of that.

Ana lay back on her bunk, lit a smoke, and watched the ghosts dance on the wall just like she did when she was a teenager. She used to towel the crack below her door and turn the fan toward the window, nervously smoking stale Camel Lights that she kept under her bed in an old crayon box that doubled as a stash and paraphernalia holder.

"Don't think anymore, Ana." Her voice melted into the ocean air. She slugged down a gulp of whiskey and laughed. "Nan, I'll see you soon! Gram, I hope that you look like that photo of you in your bathing suit in 1930. I know that would make you content. Perhaps we'll be able to speak in person."

Her drunken eyes captured the reservation sign-in book that teetered on the edge of a rustic, driftwood table. There was a pen attached. It was an opportune time to write a letter. Not a goodbye letter full of sweet sap and garbage but a thank you note, scribbled in her painfully-disheveled handwriting, to her mom and dad. A letter to leave in the nest rather than add to the collection in her knapsack. She started to scratch down words. "Dear Mom, Dad…Dr. Freedman." No." She didn't want them to feel saddened exclusively. She hoped that they'd be relieved.

"To my lovely family, friends, animals…Dear Prudence,"

No, that was far too trite and impersonal. She stared at the screen door and listened to a ship blow its horn in the distance.

Rolling onto her back, she lit another smoke and watched the apparitions dance over the reservation book. And then she came up with what I thought was a brilliant approach to her resignation—a retrospective letter to her nanny, her mother's mother, a Wild Irish Rose who saw right through her in this life and who she was most anxious to speak to in the next. It was a no-tears approach to explaining "why" to all of her loved ones without addressing them directly. She feared leaving someone out and felt obligated to explain.

It was all so puzzling for her to live in the now. A true existentialist would not need to explain: no repercussions, no worries, and no surprises. We are everything and nothing, floating in a void or something. But that is where her perspective differed. She thought that she owed those who put up with her a "why" and those who had given up on her a "best bet." Ana felt that it was only appropriate. So she composed a letter to the after world with the hope that it would welcome her.

Dear Nanny,

I am writing this to you because you would have understood. I will kiss it, and blow it into the beautiful wind and ask the universe to carry it to you. I have been planning on telling you the details of my mental demise over a game of bridge and a cocktail smothered in laughter; like reunited friends giggling about the old dead days beyond recall. But this is simply the book jacket version for your perusal, to prepare you for the shock of seeing me at your card table, wherever you may be.

It feels like forever since you've passed. I remember you saw it; my darkness hidden behind laughter. You told me that I should write, that you had always wanted to be a writer; it's a great way to vent frustrations. You told me that you used to keep a diary and sketch ideas, but then you had a family. I remember.

And once when I was particularly down, I slumped in the chair next to your sick bed and without saying a word, or even eluding to your intuition, you chimed in with a story I will never forget. It was your gentle way of telling me that you empathized with me; you too had spent 80 years hiding a deep sadness for the sake of your family, and your marriage. You had been tortured by an overwhelming feeling of self-doubt and had been hiding a tumultuous war, forced to cry around corners and hurt yourself in private. You had struggled with depression your entire life.

Do you remember the story? You told me that you were very drawn to the moon, and that you would pray to it, and talk to it like an entity. When your mother was sick with cancer and you were just a teenager, you

spent evenings on the porch rocking chair, staring into the sky. The moon was your only solace. You felt that you were connected to it because when you would squint your eyes the moon's rays would reach out towards you, and you could touch them with your fingers. And when your mother died, you damned the moon for not hearing your cries. I have held that story so close. You and I had something sacred in common; we were both bound by souls that scream, silently.

I have this memory of you, vivid, wrapped in silence and intoxicants. Remember when you lived with my parents? I would make a point to drive to you late and find you sleeping. I used to stare so intently at your tiny, red-stained mouth, watching for signs of breath. Sometimes I was so loaded that I couldn't decipher between real movement and that created by the television, or the floating light from the occasional passing car; you would eventually sigh a muffled snore. Until I was sure there was life, I wouldn't leave you. I recall it distinctly. All of my senses were there with you. Not one hour until my 20th birthday and I had already drowned myself in several intoxicants; and feigned an illness so that I could return home from an overcrowded party. I feared that you weren't breathing. I always feared something. It would overcome me like a fog; I would try to mask it with drugs. Anything.

I leaned into the creaky wicker chair and stared out the second-story window, cradled by the slight tickle of freshly-cut grass and crickets. The 11:00pm quarter moon dripped blurred, and lingered above the old red barn. She seemed to teeter between a slowly fading weather vane

...and a vacant robin's nest atop of the old crab apple tree. Such balance. Listening to your slow, deliberate breathing was soothing. Your pursed lips, and slightly gaping mouth purred with every exhale; it was a soft rhythm, 3/4 time, a Tchaikovsky waltz. Your weathered, freckled face was washed in moving blue light from a silent television screen, ... NY Yankees after hours on Fox five. You never missed it. A Shanty Irish Brooklyn lady, you never lost your passion for a night with the Bronx Bombers, ~~and~~ I always loved that.

You are content now; this I know in my heart. I was with you when you died. Did you know that? I was there holding your hand, and so was my best friend, Jess. We saw it Nan...all of the pain, anguish, doubt and sadness left your body with your last breath. You were writhing, then suddenly your green eyes opened wide, your mouth twisted wildly into an awestruck grin, ...and you sighed. And I knew that your years of sadness were gone. The fantastic universe welcomed you into her arms, and you were warm. It must have been so liberating. I wanted so badly to touch that place, not just let you go.

The summer after you passed, when I was 21, I was diagnosed by a Dr. Latondo as Bipolar. I didn't take my diagnosis seriously. Instead I saw the drugs I was prescribed as "added bonuses;" they were most excellent additions to my crazy nights filled with drinking, cigarettes, weed, cocaine, boys, pills...later a smattering of heroin. I was completely dishonest with him and everyone I knew; I wasn't ready to tell anyonehow I was really feeling or that I really wanted something or that I was seriously bulimic; and that I had no control when it came to the male species, or that I had no self esteem, or that my moods would fluctuate severalafoy the hour. I couldn't open my mouth when the doctor asked me about the emotional mayhem that I had suffered, or the hell I put my loved-ones through because I was so unstable. Not a soul knew how to take me, what to do with my weird co-dependencies and obsessiveness, or what to expect from minute to minute. Somehow they continued to love me for that one distinct personality that I have, ... the one that smiles incessantly, compulsively lies, and is fantastically fun, too jaded and concerned with popular opinion to say a word of truth.

I think your daughter and son-in-law really began to tune into my behavior when I got wind of a birthday party they'd planned for me. I panicked because I was going to see old friends that I hadn't seen in a while, and broke down and cried "please cancel the party;" I couldn't bear to see anyone. They were simply attempting to reconnect me with the living, I know, ... but I couldn't face anyone for fear of simple conversation, or feeling their disappointment. I was convinced my old friends would think I had gained weight, or that my complexion wasn't good, or that I hadn't progressed enough in the working world, or ... that my apartment wasn't interesting enough, or clean enough or colorful enough, or welcoming enough, or nice enough. Perhaps I wouldn't dress appropriately or drink properly, or that when a photo would be taken of me I would be sick because someone, somewhere may have had an

> ill-opinion of me... or something. Anything. Nothing
> good, everything bad. Scary. And I am sorry.
> for everything. So... I'm coming to you, Nanny. I'm
> Swimming away from...
>
> jealousy, anger, frustrations, yelling, misery,
> sweetness and-light followed by complete darkness
> in a matter of minutes. I will no longer contradict
> myself and allow my right and left brain to box. It
> makes my head hurt, a lot. I'm swimming home to
> a place where I belong. I will see you soon.
>
> Love, Ana

"Perfect."

She placed the letter on the table, blew out the lantern, lounged back into her musty bedding, and stared at the egg-shaped yellow orb rising over the calm ocean.

"Good night, moon."

* * *

Morning, October 30, 2000

When Ana woke to the sun in her eyes, she stretched and had that familiar feeling in her stomach that she used to get as a child at 5:00 a.m. on Christmas morning. It was painfully-exciting. She adjusted her wrap dress, grabbed her smokes and whiskey, and walked onto the balcony to watch the water.

"Splendid."

Sitting Indian style against the cabin wall, orange sun on her face, she took a hit off of her morning elixir, lit a smoke, and watched the swirls dissipate. She considered taking a ride to the Ranger's Station to drop her bundle of letters into the mailbox then reconsidered when she remembered what she had written the night before. The letters would rest with her, tucked neatly into the green backpack.

The best part of her morning came with driving the Samurai to the edge of the ravine, releasing the hand brake and knocking her into neutral. I watched from above as she pushed the neon yellow wonder jeep thing into the ravine and beamed while it sunk slowly, effervescent until totally immersed in about six feet of water.

Mission accomplished. She sat down beneath a shady tree, watched the bubbles surface from the settling vehicle, and basked in her success.

She skipped up to the cabin, strapped her backpack to her green wrap dress, neatly folded the musty linens, cleaned up the cigarette butts, and positioned the letter neatly on the edge of the driftwood table.

She contemplated leaving her highly unfashionable knapsack for the authorities, but decided that she was naked without it. The sentiments housed in the bag were better left unsaid and untouched. They, too, would join Ana on her journey.

She placed the key and camper pass on the table next to the letter and neatly placed hospital scrubs, booties, and denim jacket. She took one last look around and shut the breeze in behind her. She kicked off her flip-flops, snuck through the bramble, and stumbled down the beach toward a driftwood log about three hundred yards away.

She sat and stared out at the perfect blue, closed her eyes, and listened to a flock of melodic island birds whistling a repetition. I was one of them. There were three notes in total; the first five were the same, followed by a sharp half step, a note drop, then back to the initial. Do do do dodo da de do. "Ring of Fire" by Johnny Cash. She couldn't believe it; it was so precise! Do do do dodo da de do. Do do do dodo da de do.

"Where are the next lines, birdies?"

She sang the tune into the breeze to no avail. It was silent for a moment then I continued with the initial do do do do do da de do. Two full days without a dose of morning meds and she felt real. She was swinging! The sun was high, the water was blue, and she was finally almost finished. I watched her guzzle down some Dickel, dig her feet into the sand, and pull the skirt of her dress up to expose her white thighs to sister sunshine. She slid down and rested her spinning head on the white-washed driftwood.

Ana felt content and dreamed of her prospective funeral. They always puzzled her; she has forever found it difficult to decipher the mood between weddings and funerals. Her only true observation was that at weddings, there were less dark colors and more hats. But the expression on everyone's face was usually very similar at both affairs. Even as a little girl, she found salty amusement in scanning the mourners at a service conjecturing what they were actually thinking about behind glazed eyes and sniffling noses. Everybody seemed to stave off any negative thought of the person.

As a child, Ana used to reenact the service she attended, wedding or funeral, with her Barbies. Her mom always wondered why she had a collection of egg cartons under her bed. She later found out that they made great caskets or beds for the eleven-and-a-half-inch honeymooners with sheaths of lumped plastic where the genitals were supposed to be.

"We are such a selfish breed, crying because we are supposed to or because we will miss the mortal comrade who has gone on to the next plateau. But really, we should celebrate because they are finally weightless and on a fresh voyage away from the scarring shackles of this life." Ana slurred to the sky pondering what everyone would talk about when she ended it all. To tickle her dark side, she would ask the fates, angels, gods, whomever she may meet upon her passage if she could kindly have the opportunity to breeze through everyone's mind to hear what they were really thinking while they stood upon a somber, grassy knoll. Her predictions were as follows:

The priest: "What do I need at the store today?"

A neighbor's boyfriend: "I'm hungry. When the fuck is this ceremony going to be over?"

A co-worker: "She was so bizarre…but nice."

A friend of a friend of her sister: "So bubbly but she had such a funny way of talking, like she had a throat-full."

A college roommate: "I didn't trust her."

Her sister: "What time is it? Forgive me God for I need to eat."

The husband of an old friend: "Catered event. Good. I wonder if there is an open bar?"

Childhood friend: "I wonder if there is going to be booze?" He reaches into breast pocket. "Shit! No cash." He notices an open bag exposing a wallet on the seat beside him, slips out the wallet, gingerly sneaks a $20 out, slides it into his pants' pocket, and drops the wallet into the bag, mustering a faux tear."

An ex-boyfriend's super-Catholic, super-confused mother: "She was such a lush. Forgive me Jesus. I hope that you cannot hear my thoughts. Hail Mary. If you can hear me God, know that I thought she was kind but nuts. I wonder if she is still loony in heaven? Or perhaps, she is in purgatory. Father told me that purgatory isn't pleasant. Honestly God. Good. She could use a little repenting from what I've gathered from conversation."

Her best friend: "I don't have to worry about her anymore. Thank you, God! Forgive me, but I have enough stress. She never returned my phone calls anyway. Freak. Jesus Christ! Where is my compassion?"

A bourgeois cousin: "She was a screwball. Good Christ, I haven't procreated yet. Please don't jinx my children's sanity! I'm sorry. She's dead. No longer. My stomach is growling."

A closet homosexual ex-fling: "I can't cry. Should I fake it? That guy is hot. Who is he, one of her one-nighters? No. They wouldn't have showed. We would have needed a few more acres to accommodate all of them. Forgive me God for I have sinned again. I shall not take her name in vain. Was that taking her name in vain? What does that actually mean? Doesn't vain mean foolish? I wonder who will inherit her clothing? Great clothes!"

A friend's father: "Her poor family. Although I bet they are a bit relieved. I'm dying for a cigarette. Can I light up here?"

A "reformed" mean girl from high school who felt obligated to show: "I wonder if you can hear me, Ana? If you can hear me, don't haunt me. I didn't mean to be such a bitch. I mean, I really wasn't cruel. You just interpreted it that way. I was young. Sorry. What did I used to call her? Oh yeah, froggie! Well, she did look like a frog, sort of. You know, when she was young. We all thought so. She used to giggle and blush. She thought it was funny, too. I'm pretty sure. No, I know it."

A random guy pal from college: "Great sense of humor. Yeah. Really funny girl. I had sex with her, I think."

A guy from hometown: "Wow, first person to kick it that I've had sex with. Hah! Weird. Sorry, God, just that it's strange."

Yet another guy from college: "What did she look like? I cannot really picture her face. Her body, yes, but not her face. Wait, green eyes? Blue, maybe? Something light. I remember now, freckles. A shitload of freckles."

A work acquaintance: "I wonder if they'll have those little wiener wraps at the after-party. Is it okay to call it that? Reception? What do you call the after-funeral thing?"

A second cousin who she hardly knew: "Thank God there was no viewing. Yuck."

A best friend: "I probably should have called her more. She wouldn't have picked up the phone."

An uncle: "I need a drink."

A friend of a friend's friend: "Oh shit, my cell phone is vibrating! I want to get it. Forgive me, God. I'll pretend I'm crying and have to step away to check my message. It could be him. I'll be discreet. Turn on tears, turn on tears."

Ana relished the laughter; it felt so good.

She dozed off for an hour or so and woke to the sun beating down on her aviators. The Dickel was hot and the cellophane on the box of Camel's was beginning to warp.

It was time. The sun was at about 1:00 from where she was lounging, and the blue sky was immaculate. She pictured Virginia Woolf, wondering if she waited for the sun to be just right for her last stroll into the water.

"Weight. I need weight or I will float to the surface."

She lit a smoke and scoured the beach for rocks, shells, and crushed coral to stuff her backpack with, skipping, laughing, and talking to herself.

"Where are you, birdies? Come sing me some more Johnny Cash."

She slurred and laughed at her ill-pronunciation.

"I think I misplaced the *j* and *c*. 'Man in Black' by Cohnny Jash."

I gave her a final do do do dodo da de do and she giggled, clapped, filled her pack, and blew kisses into the air.

"So long, birdies, I'm free! Meet you in the sky!" She blew a kiss to the sun, adjusted her aviators, lit a smoke, and danced toward the water.

"Tea time!"

She laughed maniacally, fell into the shallow water, poured some Dickel into her palm, sipped it, and poured some into Jimi Hendrix's teacup. She saw him sitting across from her, Indian style and smiling.

"'Look, a golden wing ship is heading my way!'"

He faded as she laughed and belted out "Castles Made of Sand." Big smile.

"Thanks for joining me, Jimi."

She yelled at a blue vacancy and found her way up onto two feet, regained some composure, and swore that the horizon was building up into a watery city then crumbling to nothingness in the same instance, like a film clip. And for one sweet moment, she thought she understood everything and nothing as one. Ana was Mother Ocean returning to continue the cycle. After at least a thousand times of listening to, "Turn off your mind, relax, and float downstream; it is not dying; it is not dying," she finally thought she understood what John Lennon was insinuating; in order to understand everything, we must understand nothingness. The yin-yang can only exist if opposites complement one another, creating the infinite—a circle.

She raised her head and the bottle to the heavens.

"I understand beginnings, and I understand existence. Therefore, I must give myself back to understand endings, to complete the circle. Cheers!"

It was quite a scene. Ana rested back in the water, sunk her face and hair into the salty bath and opened her eyes. She blinked away the droplets and squinted at the sun. She watched the rays dance toward her in yellowy-white strands, reached her hand up, and strummed them like a guitar. She touched them, like her nanny did with the moonbeams, stood up, smoke in one hand, Dickel in the other, strapped on her knapsack full of rocks and shells and fallen sentiments, adjusted her aviators, and walked toward a fantastic glare about a hundred feet from shore.

"Christmas morning!" she yelled.

"It feels just like Christmas morning!"

She doubled-over in laughter.

"I can't stand it!"

Her stomach felt like she was plunging off a cliff into a cool quarry. "Morning bell...morning bell...light another candle... release me...release me..." She sang Radiohead lyrics to the heavens.

"Here I come."

She padded slowly toward the dancing sunlight that called, trying not to stir the water; she wanted it to look a certain way from her tea party on the bottom. Sandy waves would only disturb the silent scene. The water crept up around her waist then shoulders, neck, and nose. She looked down and watched her green dress dance like seaweed around her legs, immersed beneath the surface, held fast to the ocean floor by a weighted pack. Ana laughed, flip-flops still intact, watching the air explode from her mouth and nose.

She sat down Indian style on the bottom and watched the bubbles rise from the bottle of Dickel. They mixed brown and green with the crystal blue seascape and rose up toward the surface. She placed the bottle to her lips, drank a last gulp of Bahiahonda, and asked a school of curious little blue fish to join her tea party. She raised her head, gazed at the sunny surface, and saw a remarkably familiar beauty. The sun danced, a plane flew over, and Ana smiled with the soft invitation of darkness.

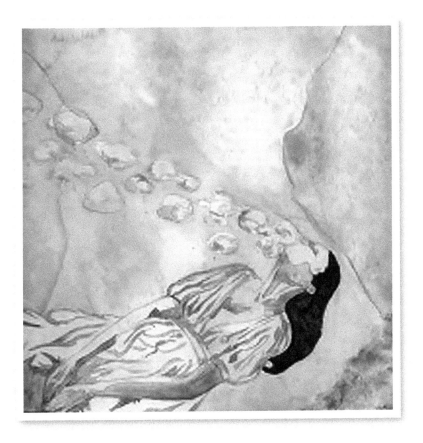

Nathaniel

October 30, 2000

"Hey! Hey! Over here! Help!" Nathaniel, a resident psychiatric patient in recovery on Bahiahonda, ran barefoot toward a ranger's truck on the edge of the beach with Ana draped over his shoulder. His drawstring T-length trousers were stuck fast to one leg from her wet hair.

"Flowers! Who in God's name is th—"

"Don't ask questions! Call the EMT, the hospital, or somebody! She almost drowned but she is breathing." He fell to his knees and gingerly lay Ana down on the sand like a sleeping infant.

"Who in the hell is she?" Ranger Dale, a young red-faced park ranger turned and spoke into his emergency response phone, dropped it, and ran over to where she was. "Nathaniel, you have no idea who this young woman is?"

"No. I saw her go for a swim and then she didn't come back up, so I—"

Nathaniel was interrupted by a distant siren followed by an ambulance. A swarm of EMTs filed out of the van followed by two police cars and another ranger vehicle. The ambulance driver looked down at her body.

"I know her. She came into my store yesterday." He shook his head, staring down at her through his sad brown eyes. "C'mon, let's get her in there."

Bert, the Highway One Liquors storeowner, led the EMT in the methodical preparation of her ashen, limp body. They ripped off her clothing, immediately strapped oxygen to her face, and injected her arm with intravenous solution, all while she was being rolled into the back of the emergency vehicle. The doors slammed and the ambulance sped off in a cloud of sandy dust washed by the blue and red light, followed by Ranger Dale. The police immediately circled Nathaniel Flowers while he held his chest and watched her disappear.

"What happened, Flowers?"

"Where are they taking her?" Nathaniel stared into the distance, speaking indirectly.

"Flowers! Who is the girl?" The policeman smacked his face to get his attention.

Nathaniel finally looked at him.

"What? I mean, I don't know! I don't know, man! I just found her!" He fell to the ground and started to cry. "Is she going to be okay?"

"Alright Flowers, get a hold of yourself."

"I did what I could. She was breathing you know?"

"We know, buddy." He smirked. "Now how did you know the girl?" One policeman motioned for the other to turn on a recording device while he took notes.

"I didn't know her. I mean, I never saw her before today! I was led to her by a crazy bird dropping cigarettes—I think." He cringed.

The policemen looked at each other and snickered.

"Flowers, have you relapsed or maybe you've been drinking salt water again?" They laughed childishly.

Nathaniel got up, wiped his face, and brushed the sand from his brown skin.

"That's what really happened!"

"Okay, okay. For the record, what happened next?"

The policeman held out the recording device

"I followed the trail of smokes to a driftwood log where I found a pack of Camels. So I kneeled down to get them. Then I looked up and saw her."

"Saw who, Flowers?"

"I saw her." He pointed in the direction of the road out of Bahiahonda. "The girl in the green dress!"

"Where did you see her?" The policeman became impatient.

"She was on the beach, heading toward the water...singing, swaying...talking to herself."

"What do you mean by 'talking to herself'?" The policemen looked at one another suspiciously.

"You know, talking. Carrying on a conversation with herself." The policeman with the recorder choked back a laugh like an uncomfortable school kid.

"What else, Flowers? Anything else unusual about the girl? Was she alone?"

"Yes, except for a bottle of whiskey and a cigarette. I thought she was just having some fun. You know getting drunk and going for a dip."

The policeman clicked off the recorder and started to laugh again.

Nathaniel got up and pointed in their faces. "That's a life...and you're laughing?"

Another ranger who had just pulled up adjusted his hat and stepped into the ring. "Okay, okay, what seems to be the problem, gentlemen?"

"They are so obnoxious." Flowers paced and spit on the ground.

"You want to go to jail you waste of life?" The policeman flexed his chest muscles and wiped a bead of sweat that slid down a swollen blue forehead vein.

The other policeman chimed in, "It would be a waste of our time. Either his uncle would pay his bail, or he would plead insanity...get sent to a loony bin for a week."

Nathaniel shook his head and stared at the ground. "Grandfather, not uncle."

"Alright, alright. Guys, could I please have a moment with Mr. Flowers—alone?" Ranger Tom was a kind, portly gentleman who checked in the young lady the prior evening.

"Gladly." One tipped his hat to Ranger Tom and turned toward the car. But that wasn't enough for the other policeman. He turned to Nathaniel, pointed a finger in his face like a drill sergeant, and spewed, "You haven't seen the last of me, Flowers. This is a national park. By law, you are not permitted to reside here. I don't care how much money your uncle hands over."

"It's grandfather, you degenerate, not uncle!"

He turned toward the car, looked back at the ranger and Nathaniel to make sure they weren't looking, adjusted himself, and yanked his industrial-strength polyester pants away from an elastic testicle pinch in his swampy cotton briefs.

Ranger Tom waddled over to Nathaniel who was sitting in the dusty sand on the edge of the beach, rubbing his eyes. He knelt down on one knee like he was proposing and let his belly rest on his leg, middle button on his brown ranger's uniform about to pop. He lay his hand on Nathaniel's shoulder.

"Look, Flowers, I know you had nothing to do with the woman drowning. Just wipe that worry from your mind. I checked her in yesterday and was curious when she said she would be checking out the next day."

Flowers rested his tan face on his folded arm and his scowl slowly faded.

Ranger Tom groaned and sat down next to Nathaniel. "I'm gettin' too old for this shit." He chuckled. "Not as limber as I used to be, Flowers." Flower's mouth broke into a grin.

"What are you, like forty now?"

Tom corrected him, "Forty-six, pal. And I ain't getting any younger. I'll tell you that!" He let out a sigh and passed gas. Flowers buried his face into his arm.

Tom shook his head, his kind eyes closed. "I thought it strange that a young, pretty woman would be all alone with just a backpack. And to stay for just one night in a great big cabin all by her lonesome? Now that's just plain weird, you know?" He turned to Flowers.

His blue eyes popped open in awe. "Weird, right? She reeked of booze to boot. I mean stunk!"

Nathaniel raised his head from his arm and stared out at the sandy road surrounded by green Bahiahonda brush and splashes of fuchsia bougainvillea.

"And, Flowers, you know what the craziest thing was?" No response. "Do you want to know what the craziest?"

"What was it, Tom?" Nathaniel asked abruptly, trying to shake away the image of her blue face.

He looked around and whispered, "She handed me a rolled up $100 bill as a tip for being so helpful! I mean what in hell was that all about, right?"

"Where are you going with this, Tom?" Nathaniel seemed to expect some half-wit story about how he thinks she's an alien, an escaped convict, or both. But he listened. After all, Tom was one of the few people who acknowledged Nathaniel's existence didn't judge his past or question his present. He had a soft spot in his jaded heart for Tom; the guy was sweet.

"Are you ready for this one?" He perked up.

"This morning around 11:00 a.m. when the campers were doing their checkout, 11:30 rolled by, then noon, then 12:30, and no Ana Guida!"

"That's her name?" Nathaniel's face softened. He pictured her seaweed-like body dancing toward the water.

Tom's round face flushed with excitement. "Yeah! But this happens, you know? Some folks just forget sometimes or sleep in past checkout or just don't feel like leavin'!" Tom chuckled. "But I started to get anxious 'cause there was an impatient French-Canadian couple waiting for their cabin, and they were not happy. I drove up to her cabin. No car. I figured she'd gone and simply forgot to check out, you know? But I found it real strange-like that I didn't see that bright yellow Suzuki Samurai pass by my gate, the one she drove in yesterday." Ranger Tom adjusted himself.

"Anyhow, I went up to the cabin. It was locked, so I used the master key and went in. It looked like there hadn't been a soul there, and then I found it."

"Found what?"

"Next to doctor scrubs and a denim jacket there was this creepy note written to a nanny character—a suicide note or something. About the same time, I heard the call over the CB from Ranger Dale."

"And there she was." Nathaniel replayed the scene in his mind. It flickered behind green-blue eyes.

Tom pulled the crinkled letter from his sweaty shirt pocket, looked left and right, and held the letter out to Nate. "See?"

Nate took the letter gently and opened it.

Gabriel

October 30, 2000

uiet. Cool. Ana pulled herself off a stainless steel table and stared at her muddled reflection; a shock of blond hair without a face, captured on a stainless steel wall, cornered by another stainless steel wall and another and another. She was in a six-foot-by-six-foot box, sitting at a sterile table, in a stainless chair in green scrubs. There were no windows, doors, or dust. She looked down at her body and touched her skin. Dry. No scent. There was no feeling. She just existed. She scratched but there wasn't an itch or even a burn. She pinched as hard as she could but felt no pain. She yanked on her hair, smacked her cheeks, and poked her finger into her eye. Nothing. She leaned back, propped her foam booties up and slammed her ankles into the edge. Nothing. No pain. Just distant sound, like she was still under water, listening.

Ana got up and jumped on the floor, searching for seams. Nothing. She walked around the room, running her hands against the wall. No smudge. No prints. "I have no fingerprints." Her palms were smooth. The fortune-telling lines were gone. No scars. She dug her nails into her face and screamed, "What the hell!" It floated somewhere outside of her, and sounded like it was stuck at the bottom of a well or in a vacuum.

She lay on her side, her face pressed against the brushed silver floor, and stared for her breath for what felt like a month then peered up toward the desk where she noticed a hidden drawer—a jar. Ana opened it and found a large white tablet with the word **open** typed in the center of the cover in bold black font. She gingerly placed the table on to the desktop and slid her finger between the cover and the first page only to find a pocket full of black-and-white photographs.

First photo: Jimi Hendrix sitting at a tea table among shrubbery, holding a fine china teacup gently in his right hand and a burning cigarette in his left. His eyes were smiling at the camera, but his expression was stoic.

Second photo: Janis Joplin spinning in a macramé poncho, eyes closed to the sky, mouth caught between a painful sigh and elation, illuminated by what felt like blue light. "Woodstock, perhaps?"

Third photo: All of Ana's deceased pets.

She could feel herself laughing but heard no sound. They were all posed in a Wild West Cantina scene.

Hannibal, her childhood St. Bernard, was propped behind a mahogany bar, lined with unmarked liquor bottles, wearing a pressed white button-down, black bow tie, and leather suspenders.

Poco, her effeminate male golden retriever, was dressed in elaborate makeup and curls in a corseted blouson, flirtatiously entertaining Rags, the neighborhood Benji, paw-in-paw with JoJo, the illegitimate, brain-damaged white poodle mix who showed up on her doorstep one windy, fifth grade afternoon.

And sitting at a card table opposite her feisty ginger cat Tangerine, donned in bar wench attire and dealing cards, was her beloved Bernadette...a temperamental Australian Shepherd mix, with a shark-like overbite and shifty black eyes. Bernie was what she thought appropriate; dressed in an androgynous black suit and western fedora...cigar dangling from her teeth.

Her eyes then followed the gaze of her sweet tabby Gepetto dressed as a sheriff, striped paw close to his pistol. He stared into the mirror at a lovely buxom gray madam behind the bar with her back turned toward him.

"Lily!" It was Lily, the fluffiest, heartiest, greatest cat in the history of yellow-eyed, fluffy gray felines. She was gazing into the mirror in a Mae West manner, unscrupulously admiring the backside of Hannibal. It was the perfect personification of Lily, who always stared flirtatiously at the opposite sex, and curled in with him in the dark of night.

Lily communicated through stare and body language because her vocal chords were damaged when she was a kitten. She couldn't meow but made only an occasional squeak coupled by a wave of her pussy-willow tail.

Ana blinked then socked her ears. She started to hear things then see things, she thought. She heard the wagon wheels roll by, kicking dust into the saloon doors, ladies laughing, and Hannibal speaking with a voice like Clint Eastwood in *High Plains Drifter.*

"What'll it be, Jack?" It was difficult to distinguish but, it was in her head and ears like she was part of the photo. She closed her eyes and just listened to the banter.

There was hushed conversation at the card table, giggling ladies, and then a distinctly gritty, distant female voice.

She said, "What does a girl have to do for some attention in a place like this? I know that I'm not invisible to you, Hanni-baby. I see you watching me in the mirror, sweetheart."

Ana heard her eyelashes wink and her whiskers twitch. She knew she did. Then she heard Hannibal's slow, deliberate footsteps. He cleared his throat, lit a match, smacked his droopy gums that made a sour pucker sound, and exhaled.

"What a lovely voice you have, Miss Lily," Hannibal gurgled in her direction.

"You should hear me sing, Ana." Ana's eyes refocused on the photograph.

"Look over here, Ana, in the mirror. Right here." She stared into the mirror, and Lily smiled and winked at her.

"So you may be coming to join us, huh?" Then Ana heard a sharp whisper lisp into her left ear. "It's not time."

The voice was followed by laughs, meows, and barks coupled with chuckles and a loud thump.

* * *

When she came to, Ana was stretched on the floor, chair on top of her, and the book entitled *Open* scattered next to her. She quickly gathered up the mess and rose to place it back in the drawer when she heard faint music. It became louder and louder braided with clinking ice, percussion, hushed talking, and the distant scent of cigarettes and fresh cut onion grass.

She peered to her left and saw a photo on the ground that must have escaped her hasty cleanup. The closer she moved toward it, the clearer the crescendo became. It was Billie Holiday's "I Got It Bad (and That Ain't Good)."

She picked up the photo and stared into a black-and-white animated film clip of her grandparents. Both couples were sitting poolside, drinking martinis and scotch. They were dressed in midfifties attire, seemingly having a magnificent time.

She had never met Harry Sr., her father's father. It was interesting to see him in action as a young socialite in a pressed Brooks Brother's ensemble. Her young grandmothers were both summer lovely, soft-spoken, cross-legged, and tanned while her grandfathers both laughed and boasted about business and Wall Street Journal headlines.

A beautiful young man with slicked-back blond hair and black-rimmed glasses sauntered out of a cabana dressed in a black-and-white tuxedo, arm stretched gracefully holding a tray of cocktails, and hors d'oeuvres. He handed both ladies a fresh martini and lit their cigarettes for them.

"Thank you." They both smiled flirtatiously at him. He began to walk away when Ana's young Nan said, "Young man, aren't you going to offer Ana a cocktail?"

"Oh, pardon me madam. How could I be so rude?" He looked up at her and slid his glasses down his nose, exposing seamless blue eyes.

"Ana, would you care for a cocktail, or perhaps some penny-royal tea?" She threw the photo into the book and slammed it shut. The young man was the late, great Kurt Cobain. *The* Kurt Cobain.

"Crazy." She smacked herself across the cheek, and this time she felt it! Ana heard herself involuntarily shower the air with expletives, like the inadvertent spritz that sprinkles the dentist's face while she or he picks and prods teeth.

There was no longer a vacuum-like void of sound. She stomped around the stainless room, relishing the teeny thump of her feet resonating from the floor.

"Where am I? Oz? Wonderland? Hell? Is this heaven?" She laughed maniacally, singing, "Heaven. I'm in heaven." She danced over to the desk with an invisible partner, fell down into the chair, and started to cry real tears.

"Where are the pearly gates?" She sobbed and sniffed, at first not noticing the stream of colors that rained from her eyes. They meandered down her cheeks and onto the floor.

"Why am I alone?" She opened her lashes, touched the primary braid rolling down her neck and onto her hands, like rain on a window shield. A rainbow dripped from her blank fingertips onto the brushed steel floor. It framed her faceless reflection smeared with viscous tears. She closed her eyes and wished her way to what she wanted heaven to be.

All of the images in that album of memories would be there waiting for her in spirit. And then she felt it—a presence loomed beyond steel walls. Me.

Ana heard nothing but felt half-sympathetic eyes on the back of her neck. When she stood slowly and stared forward, frightened to peek over her shoulder, the words *"I Exist, You Exist. Believe"* dripped across her reflection. She closed her eyes and dropped her face into her hands. "What's that supposed to mean?"

She waited for a response. Nothing.

"Are you toying with my newfound, existential way of thinking?" Nothing. Not even an echo. Still, something burned through the nape of her neck. She mustered the courage to turn her face and peer behind her and felt nothing but a feathery *whoosh*. She looked up at her reflection and standing faceless in stainless steel behind her was a statuesque figure spreading his wings. Me.

"What are you doing here, Ana?" I leaned down next to her and stared into her eyes.

"Answer the question, Ana."

My deep growl of a voice with a hint of grit startled her. Ana thought that I smelled of fresh pine and cigarettes. I was not particularly angelic in appearance: crinkly brown eyes, weathered cheeks, long, unkempt salt-and-pepper hair and navy Chuck Taylor canvas 1950s basketball high-tops. But I had wings. She knew me, I think. Recognized me from the phone booth in Rhode Island. She closed her eyes and heard me speak into her left and right ears in tandem like those weird earphone audio experience booths that they had at Disney World when she was a kid. My voice was crisp and housed inside her mind like the surround barbershop audio adventure that was definitely the highlight of her first and last Disney family adventure; sharp, clean blades of scissors sheared away at her audio locks. I love that trick.

"Open your eyes, Ana."

She fell out of memory into my disguised voice, sweetly familiar to her. I sounded of Saul the Knish cart guy who used to sell his wares outside of the Manhattan Mall Path train entrance. During her short Manhattan work experience stint on her way out of the city and back to Hoboken for the evening, she used to make a point of telling me how wonderful they smelled and to have a great night no matter how she felt that day. She never actually tried one but probably told many that she did for the sake of inciting conversation with beautiful strangers—the story of her life.

"Yoo-hoo! Ana, snap out of it!" I pinched her cheek.

"Owww!" She felt it.

"You certainly felt that Ana, huh?" I yanked her earlobe.

"Hey! What in hell is your problem?" She rubbed her ear and stared at my nicotine-stained smile.

"You're my problem, Ana." I sat cross-legged on the floor, reached into my downy wings and pulled out a pack of Camels, dropped one into my mouth, and snapped my fingers, producing a flame. Lighting it, I leaned back and blew smoke into her face. Tough love.

"I'm terribly sorry." I leaned forward to whisk the cloud away from her face, but instead offered her a smoke. "Didn't mean to be rude. Would you care for one?"

"I don't smoke."

"Bullshit." I laughed and exhaled over her shoulder.

"Bullshit?" She was flabbergasted.

"Bullshit! Lies don't work here, Ana."

"Where?" she shouted and threw her arms up.

"Where what?" I snapped back.

"Where is here?" She stood up and tripped over her pant leg, motioning to the four steel walls. "I feel like I am stuck inside some microcosmic Pottery Barn coffee table world or something."

I laughed and slid my pack of smokes back into my wing. "Now there's the Ana I know and love full of Hades!"

She caught a peripheral shot of herself in the wall; she had horns. "I have horns!" She grabbed her head and turned to me.

I slapped my knee.

"Look again, Ana." She looked and they were gone.

"You think you have horns, so you see horns. Do you follow me?" I smirked.

"No." She had enough.

"Sure you do, Ana. Think outside of yourself for once." She scowled.

"What's that supposed to mean?"

"What do you think?" I leaned over and whispered in her left ear. "You are selfish."

"Piss off!" She crossed her arms like a child.

"Hey, watch your mouth! I have wings." She started to get the flavor of Dial soap on her tongue, opened her mouth to speak, and foam seeped out. She began to choke and cough. I held my stomach and laughed.

"I love that one. Your mom should have done that years ago."

She spit the remainder of the soap and foam out onto her lap and coughed. "I don't care if you have wings. It doesn't give you the divine right to insult me like this."

I inched forward on the floor and took her hands in mine, and she immediately felt calm.

"Ana, where do you think that you are?"

"A waiting room."

I laughed. "What are you waiting for?"

She stood and threw her arms up. "Jesus? I don't know! Everyone that I love and admire who has passed over to this side of yesterday."

I smiled at her knowingly, almost condescendingly. "What side?" I reached to grab her hand.

She threw my hands away from her and started to rant.

"Here! Right here! Heaven or whatever you or I or He or She or It wishes to call it! Heaven! Pearly gates! Never-never Land! Somewhere over the rainbow! Eye of the storm! Hyperspace! The moon! The bottom of the rabbit hole! The abyss! The Milky Way! Paradise! Perhaps Dante's Inferno or—"

I lit another smoke, pulling a flame out of the air. She still wasn't impressed.

"Okay, okay, okay. Understood, understood. You think that you've cashed in, called it quits, kicked the bucket, and bought the farm."

"Died! Drowned! Swam with the fishes, literally! I am probably about to be dropped from a shark's ass to feed some hungry clams or something!" She pondered the image.

"Oh my Ana, you couldn't be more wrong." I doubled over and laughed and laughed until I coughed. "Well, I may not know a great deal, but I do know one thing that may assist you in figuring out your whereabouts."

"So, there is a hell?" She stared at me with earnest eyes that reminded me of her second-grade school picture. I leaned over, filling her aching mind like suffocating smoke. She heard my voice slice through her indignant soul.

"Ana, you are not dead."

She listened to the brassy echo and held her head to keep out the grating words that felt like a childhood earache. She was too late; they had already dripped blackened oil into her watery conscience. "You are not dead, not dead, not dead, not d…" Her body felt like it rushed to the surface of something. She opened her eyes and was standing two inches away, staring into me.

"Impossible!" she challenged me.

I challenged her, "Anything is possible."

"But not that," she argued.

"Why, Ana? What distinguishes your impossibility from possibility?"

"I am dead! Not here. I no longer exist. This is obviously some weird dream—a mental puking session or something. You know, like an acid flashback or a detox-induced delusion." She was confident but so wrong. "You don't fucking exist…and neither do I."

"But you do exist, Ana." She pictured the phrase that dripped on the wall moments ago, stared at me, and traced my weathered face with her eyes looking for patterns, answers, something. I walked toward her and she felt a warm, rocking feeling surround her like her grandmother's afghan.

"You have such purpose, kid."

She squeezed her eyes shut. She wanted to curl into the fetal position and wake under the harsh reading light in the Rhode Island hospital but couldn't close her eyes. She couldn't sleep me away.

"Shhhhhhhh—shhhhhhh," I whispered, running my hands over her face and through her hair. "Don't be frightened."

She lifted her head and stared into my gently closing downy wings, cradling her face.

"Just watch, Ana." I felt so bad for the child, but the truth is always grating on the soul. "Just watch."

I gently closed my wings around her tired lids and the filmstrip commenced in her third eye. It unfolded in her mind like a dream, only clearer, complete with sensory perception.

She was flying over a beach, looking down onto a driftwood log, the same log that was three hundred feet from the cabin that she graced in Bahiahonda. She landed in a palm tree and watched herself stumble over. Her vision was quick. Sharp. She focused on her own face and bloodshot eyes, studying herself from a third-person perspective for the first time. She listened to her feet drag through the sand and honed in on another bird who whistled, "Do do do dodo da de do. Do do do dodo da de do." It was me, but she didn't know that. To her it was the bird; the Johnny Cash bird that she was so intrigued with.

Out of her peripheral vision, she saw a man with matted, unruly hair stretch, yawn, and rub his eyes. I flew to the palm where he was stretched out, whistled...then shrieked to no avail. The man walked toward the ravine to splash water on his face, and I swooped into the water beneath him in a further attempt to win his attention.

"Whoa!" He fell back onto the bank and looked up at the tree that I landed in.

"What are you squawking about, huh?" He had a gravelly voice with a subtle softness wound into it. I screeched and followed him from limb to limb. She watched the island man perform his wake-up ritual. He peed in a bush, reached into his pocket for matches, and searched his satchel for something to smoke. He tossed a coconut shell at the tree that I was perched in.

"What is your problem?" He got up and looked around on the ground around him trying to ignore my incessant noise.

"You're lucky I haven't made you into Chong stew...Now knock it off!" Defeated, he plopped down to light a cigarette butt that he found in the recesses of his bag. I flew back to the log that Ana had sat on to pick up the remnants of her Camels. She watched in wonder from her perch while I (Johnny Cash bird) struggled to collect one cigarette at a time in my beak and gingerly place them on the ground that led toward the island man. Hearing the bird rustling on the ground, the young man looked up, mouth agape.

"I'll be damned," he muttered, rising to see what I had done.

"Would you look at that!" He looked like a skittering child, blindfolded and chasing after piñata candy.

"You are one crazy bird!" He was hunched over picking up each Camel and inspecting it. He made it to the log and found the remainder of the pack nestled in the sand, bent down to grab it, and clocked his head on the driftwood.

He slowly raised his scowling face, pushed his bleached, matted hair aside, and squinted to focus on a lovely and peculiar sight. It was Ana staggering in ankle-deep water; she was singing, swaying, kneeling, laughing, drinking, and crying. He just stared deeply with silent admiration. The Ana in the shallow water saw nothing, but he saw everything. He shrunk behind the log like a voyeur, concealed...

watching her through ghosts of cigarette smoke. Every time her face turned in his direction, he ducked.

My work was complete; he was mesmerized and afraid to speak regardless of his curiosity. The Ana in shallow water stood and stared out over the humbling blue calm. She was acting polite like a child taking communion at an altar; the sublime does that to a person. He watched helplessly while she sort of fell through the water, buoyancy aiding her hindered ability to stay upright. Ana's fading memory of her last steps into the ocean felt much more graceful than it appeared from a third-person perspective.

The man started to mumble, "She's going to take it off, take it off!" He was humming classic Sugarloaf and tapping his dirty fingers on the log. "Green-eyed lady, ocean lady." His smiling face rested on his folded arms while he waited for the naked crescendo. The skirt of her green dress floated and swayed on the surface, slowly submerging, and her weighted backpack followed. After her shoulders, her hair fanned out on the surface like a pillow when she swigged from the bottle, choking back maniacal laughter. The ocean swallowed her like sunset into an ethereal glare that held fast to the rippling surface. He watched bleary-eyed, waiting for her to rise to the surface laughing, floating on her back, kicking and squinting at the sun.

He fantasized about the green dress that would sculpt her wet body. She would be giggling like a Playboy bunny on camera. He dreamed. But the image slowly melted, leaving an uneasy look on his face.

"Oh my god!" He stumbled to his feet, dropped his smoke, and ran clumsily toward the water, kicking crushed coral sand behind him. He tripped in, stopped, turned back toward shore, then stared out at the glare that Ana had walked toward.

"Where did she walk in?" He waded toward the glimmer: a half-leap, half-swim. His overtanned back looked seal-like against blue.

He choked, "I'm on my way! Don't swim!" And then he stopped dead and disappeared into the water. His feet flipped behind him like a merman fin. His head resurfaced once, then again.

"Fuck!" He dove. He disappeared for what seemed like two minutes then broke the surface coughing, choking, and dragging her lifeless body toward shore. There was no glamour; nothing Hugh Hefneresque about her. He neared the sand, yanked her backpack from her shoulders, heaved it onto shore, and dragged her body to warmth. Ana was blue.

"You're okay…okay." He dropped to his knees and pressed his ear against her chest to listen for life. Nothing.

"C'mon, blondie!" He rolled Ana onto the side and smacked her back until her mouth dripped a little bit of yellow water, bile, blood, something. He shook, cried, and sort of smiled.

"Okay, okay." He felt her wrist then straddled her hips in desperation. "How do you do this? I forgot!" He stretched his neck toward the sky.

"Please! I haven't asked for anything in years!" He panicked holding her limp hand in his. "Please! Please, let me help her. Please?" He pushed on her chest, fell down, and listened to her heart again, hugging her and crying. He thought he heard something soft. Weak. He pressed his face into her, listening. His eyes widened then closed.

"Holy Christ!" He scrambled to the side of Ana's body mumbling, "Thank you, thank you!"

He ripped open her dress, found her sternum, leaned up onto his knees, and pressed down repeatedly, crying and cracking her ribs.

"I'm sorry, blondie. I'm so sorry!" He lifted her chin, wrapped his mouth around hers, and breathed in his life. He bent down to listen, bothered by the sound of the rolling ocean. He whipped his head around.

"Shhhhhhhhh!" He scowled at the water to quiet it as it rolled away.

"Come on, blondie!" He continually thrust his hands into Ana's chest followed by breath. Nothing. He curled his face into her sandy hair and sobbed.

"I'm sorry. I'm so sorry, so, so sorry!"

Then there was a cough, gurgle, and his crying face was splashed with booze, salt water, and countless other bodily fluids from the recesses of her abdomen.

"Oh my god! Oh my g—" He wiped his face.

"I knew it, blondie!" He stood and screamed at the sky and ocean laughing maniacally.

"Thank you!" He lifted her limp, waterlogged body over his shoulder and fumbled toward civilization.

* * *

Ana opened her eyes and wiped defeated tears from her face.

"Who are you?"

"I'm the bird. Do do do dodo da de do." I smiled, produced a soft piece of white cloth from feathered nothingness, and handed it to her to wipe her nose. I leaned back on the stainless floor and relaxed my wings behind me, brushing a cigarette ash from my shoulder like dandruff. She blew her nose and moved the fabric between her fingers nervously like she was on a first date.

"You're my guardian angel."

She said it as if she was introducing me to myself for the first time.

I leaned back to look on her knowingly.

"It certainly took you long enough to hypothesize, Ana. Is that your final answer?" She let down her guard and decided to join in my attempt at wit.

"Well, I think that it is a safe assumption." She pointed to my wings and motioned for me to toss her a smoke.

"I'm Gabriel." I pulled a lighter from my downy wing.

"Not THE Gabriel, but Gabriel, nonetheless. Please call me Gabe." She caught a peripheral glimpse of a ring of smoke encircling my head.

"Okay, Gabe, so what is that?" She pointed to the space in my wing, not visible to the human eye, from where I kept pulling random items.

"What?" I looked myself over as if I was unsure of my outfit.

"That!" She pointed emphatically toward the invisible abyss. "Is it the black hole? If I put my hand in there, will aliens in another galaxy be able to see me waving and reaching for something?"

I laughed and whispered that creepy Disney inside-both-ears thing that freaked her out before, "It's a secret."

"Oh c'mon, Gabe? I bet that is where all of the socks and under-wear go when they cannot be found."

I chuckled, dismissed her, fieldstripped my smoke, and tossed it into the air. She watched it defy gravity, float toward the ceiling, unravel like a cocoon sped up on film and change into a magnificent purple-and-orange butterfly. It fluttered a figure eight then disappeared. She pretended not to be amazed.

"Or perhaps it's like Narnia!" She studied me, anticipating a response.

"Who?" I admit. I was genuinely stumped.

"Not 'who.' Narnia is a place!"

"Where? I've never heard of it."

"Really? You've never heard of C. S. Lewis's *The Lion, The Witch and The Wardrobe*?"

"Never met the guy."

She smirked, fieldstripped her smoke, flicked it into the air, and watched it fall to the stainless floor. I giggled, reached over to pick it up, curled it into my palm, and opened it to reveal a red dragonfly. It landed on her freckled nose then took off into nothingness.

"It's not nice to play on someone's ignorance, Ana."

"Speak for yourself, Mr. Magic Trick."

Whenever she was caught, she resorted to defensive, excessive immaturity coupled with a childlike tone. She was frustrated and hated that I called her on all of the bullshit.

"Do you know what I am thinking?" She looked at me in anticipation of another magic trick.

I leaned forward, and looked into her. "I listen to what you are feeling, Ana. Emotions are honest. Words are not."

She stared at me, choking back the familiar crying knot in the back of her throat.

I gently closed her tearing eyes with my hand and whispered inside of her mind, "You are so angry, so confused. You feel like you are nothing but you are everything. Without you, the tapestry falls unfinished." She fixed her stare on me; I leaned back on my elbows, legs crossed.

"Understand?"

"Where am I, Gabe? Why am I not there if I am not supposed to be here? Where is here? What is this place?"

I laughed. "You are nowhere but everywhere all at once."

"Cut the shit, Gabe. Is this purgatory?"

I giggled again and shrugged my shoulders.

"Maybe. If you're a Catholic."

"Enough with the riddles, sphinx!" She kicked the desk and heard her toe crack when it hit. She stopped and grabbed it, hopped on one foot, and felt the pain creep like a wasp's sting.

"Oh, Ana." I reached over and helped her to the floor, handed her a tissue, and wrapped my hands around her foot, alleviating the misery.

"Enough with the passive aggressive behavior. That doesn't fly here either." The ache slowly dissipated, and she caught herself smile at me a little.

"That's better." I pulled a multicolored afghan from the recesses of my wings and wrapped it around her legs.

"Nanny's afghan!" She picked it up in amazement, held it to her face, and inhaled her memory.

"How did you?"

"It's your favorite blanket, right?"

I smiled.

"But I lost it in col—Thank you, Gabe."

"I kept it for you. The man gave it to me...to give to you. He said that it kept him warm."

Ana stared at Gabe in shock.

"He didn't live?"

"It was his time to move on to his next plateau. Don't be sad."

"How did he know that it was my afghan? I mean, I was a total stranger who pulled over to see if I could help, and he was completely unconscious, thrown from the car onto the icy highway!"

"Precisely, Ana. He saw you take the afghan from your car and drape it over him. He heard you tell him that he was going to be okay...like you saw a bird's-eye view of what happened to you. His soul was moving on. It was supposed to be, and you were meant to happen upon his accident in some capacity. That is how Mother Fate works. We are all connected in the large scheme of things. There is no denying her existence."

Ana studied my face, confessing, "Mother Fate. I say, 'Mother Fate!'"

She listened to me, smoothed the afghan, and felt reticent for the first time that she could remember. It felt different than a vacuum-like indoor silence or the inevitable void of noise and color that sneaks into us in adulthood after years of being desensitized to remain on an acceptable wavelength. Ana felt a subtle hush that could be understood by life, which she began to understand, may matter.

She lay back and stared at the ceiling's reflection of her image on the floor. She bent her knee and turned it slightly so that it looked like she was infinite then kicked her leg out to recreate a Rockette lineup.

"So, who is he?"

"Who's he? Do you mean Nathaniel Flowers?" She inhaled, picturing his beautiful face and sad light eyes hidden by sun-bleached, long, dreadlocked hair.

"Yes, why is he there? What's his story?"

I produced a piece of string and began to create a cat's cradle; the childhood game that Ana used to play on the school bus.

"He's just like you, Ana. Mother Fate knows how to match souls."

"Are you incapable of being more direct, Gabriel?" Ana was impatient.

"Well, Miss Ana, if I were more direct, then you would know all of the answers, correct?"

"Right!"

"Wrong. You're being lazy."

"I'm not lazy! I'm frustrated." She knew that she was impatient...and lazy.

"Patience is a virtue—that YOU don't possess!" I coughed and fluffed my wings.

"In order to understand the root of things, you have to take the time to investigate. If you listen to someone's answer straight away,

Ana, you'll believe it and file it under easy listening up there in your noggin'. Know what I'm saying?" I knocked on her head.

"And who said that their answer is the correct one?" She scowled at me because I stated the obvious, which she always chose to bypass for the sake of being stubborn.

"If we would've listened to the bloody churchgoers who tried to convince Magellan, Planet Earth would be a giant Frisbee floating through the universe. But no, he begged to differ, refuting that concept. Therefore, he set out to discover the 'truth' for himself. Capisce?"

I waited for her response. Nothing. She simply toyed with the cat's cradle string that I gave her lost in the image of Nathaniel Flower's blue-green eyes. "Okay, young lady. You want to know about him?"

I knew what she was feeling.

"Nathaniel Flowers is a brilliant young man, but not by the Flower family standards." She lay back.

"Thank you," she whispered, staring at her reflection in the ceiling. She saw horns peeking out of her hair again. She blinked her eyes and they were gone.

"Go on, Gabe. What's his story?"

I spread my wings enough to rest on them, crossed my arms behind my head, and lounged.

"Well, Nathaniel came from a long line of Ivy Leaguers: lawyers, doctors, Wall Street gurus, scientists, corporate cats, and the like. Anyway, Nathaniel's father was an airline pilot, a Korean War veteran. Nathaniel's mother was an international blond, blue-eyed beauty, model and airline stewardess. She was Dutch, actually. They met on a layover in Paris and that is where Nathaniel was conceived! In a bistro bathroom, I think. Anyway..." I had her attention.

She chimed in, "Well, what were their names?"

I exhaled my smoke.

"Oh yes, I'm sorry. Captain Edward Flowers and Miss Helena Staadegard. Needless to say, her modeling days were over when little Nathaniel started to brew." I gazed off as if reminiscing.

"So it was love at first sight. Cute, huh?"

Ana smiled picturing the first time she fell in love.

"So off they went. Back to the US of A, and she soon became Mrs. Helena Staadegard-Flowers in an Episcopal Cathedral in Boston, Massachusetts, on a sunny day in September 1971. She was gorgeous in a custom gown, five months pregnant. And all of the Flowers were there at the Martha's Vineyard Yacht reception, discussing politics, drinking highballs, gin martinis, and flirting with the lovely Dutch babes who came to see their Helena off into the arms of a handsome American.

Four months later, healthy, beautiful Nathaniel was born on New Year's Day, 1972, at a hospital in Rome. Edward couldn't bear the thought of traveling without his beautiful Helena, so away they flew home to Boston with their new nine-pound, eight-ounce bundle of boy."

I stopped, took a deep breath, got up, and stretched. I pulled a pocket watch from my wing and took a look.

"Oh, look at the time. I have to be going. Thanks, Ana, it's been lovely chatting with you. Good luck with everything."

I started to walk, and she grabbed my wrist and looked at the watch. The face was blank.

"Hey!" She looked at me and suddenly felt like a little kid, duped by a Jacob's Ladder, card trick, or something of that caliber.

"So you ARE paying attention. I thought I lost you somewhere in Rome with the birth of Nathaniel."

"No, I'm captivated. What happened next? Was it happily ever after? I'm confused."

I sat down and pulled a box of tissues from my wing and handed it to her.

"Are you sure you're ready, Ana?" She nodded.

"Okay. On their flight home, somewhere over the Long Island Sound on January 3, 1972, flight 316 out of Rome to Boston, Edward, his co-pilot Captain Reynolds of Houston, his beautiful Helena, and their baby boy crashed into the icy Atlantic."

Ana gasped, stared at me, and felt a stabbing pain in her heart. She felt the tragedy and I felt her pain.

"Oh god, how sad! Wait, they all—"

"All died on impact except baby Nathaniel who, by the grace of the gods, floated on debris in an air pocket at the ceiling of the plane. The plane had split in half, and he survived in the half that was not completely submerged thanks to an enormous block of January ice. The Coast Guard found him wrapped tightly in wet blankets with only his tiny face exposed, untouched physically from the crash. Not a bruise. No hypothermia. They attributed it to being held tightly by Helena upon impact, his infant buoyancy and the invention of late '60s polyester/acrylic blend blankets. They may not have been fireproof, but they were hypothermia proof. If his blankets were a natural fiber, he certainly would have frozen to death."

Ana couldn't fathom the braid of terror, sadness, confusion, and how fast it must have come undone for all of them, except for baby Nathaniel. She cried, wondering if baby Nathaniel had sensed the surge of fear or if he was just long lost in soft, sound baby sleep, cocooned in his mother's scent. She sat speechless trying to comprehend the scene.

Her mind replayed, maybe reinvented, an interpretation of beautiful Helena holding her baby boy fast to her breast. She was probably still sore from suckling when her eardrums popped and she heard the vacuum-like void of noise inside the cabin. She saw Helena struggling to brace Nathaniel in her arms, regardless of the turbulence, instinctively curling over his body to protect him.

Deaf to her own ill-fated screams, Ana thought that she must have half-believed the moment and cried out Edward's name within seconds of plummeting into the unforgiving icy depths. The image felt so real to her that she found it hard to think it a figment of her imagination.

"Oh god!" She was speechless between gasps.

"How sad. I feel it, you know?"

"What do you mean by 'feel it,' Ana?" I stared into her.

"I mean, I feel how Helena's love for the child's life overcame her own fear! She placed all of her trust and strength into saving her child, regardless!" Ana was sobbing.

"Regardless of what?"

"Of what happened to her and Edward." Ana's stomach dropped like she was on a roller coaster.

I looked at her. "Now, that's unconditional love."

She wiped her face and brushed her hands through her hair trying to gather her wits.

"So, Nathaniel…"

"Nathaniel was taken in by his eccentric grandfather, Mortimer Flowers, a world-renowned physicist with a penchant for geology and environmental science and his wife, Bess, who is an avid gardener. Neither of them were much accepted by the Martha's Vineyard socialites who they lived amongst. They were scrutinized for taking on Nathaniel, having had four boys of their own. Their youngest was a freshman Harvard law student. But Mortimer and Bess raised him with love and compassion in an affluent New England world."

I raised my right wing, unfolding an archaic film projector.

"I'm tired of talking. Hold this, please." I handed her a burning smoke, fiddled with the projector, placed it on the desk, and leveled it with the white tablet full of photos and an empty Camel soft pack. All the while I cursed to myself about how I didn't have the time for technology.

"Okay!" I laughed and plopped down in the chair next to the projector and unraveled the eight-millimeter filmstrip. "Alright, Ana, get comfortable and watch."

She snuggled on the floor, the lights dimmed, and a grainy-colored image of a man with tanned legs in Bermuda shorts, a tweed jacket, button-down oxford shirt, bow tie, and green fisherman's cap stood squinting at the camera. His hands rested on the shoulders of an adorable little fair haired boy in a prep school uniform. There wasn't any sound, but judging by the light, you could imagine late August birds chirping and crickets chanting a summer goodbye.

It was Nathaniel's first day of school, and he looked only mildly happy to be going. He waved at whom he thought was Mommy holding the camera and squinted up at Daddy who adjusted his shirt and tie and gave him what looked to be endearing words of encouragement. Nathaniel was stunning; he had the same blue-green eyes, now hidden behind matted, bleached dreadlocks. Ana couldn't see any defeat yet.

"Cute, huh?" I punched Ana in the shoulder to make sure she was paying attention. She looked up at me. I slouched knobby-kneed, cross-legged, swinging my Chuck Taylor, and staring admiringly like a mom watching her child's first recital.

She nodded. "Does Nathaniel know that they are his grandparents?"

"Not yet. They felt that his traumatic beginning should be kept from him until he was old enough to deal with the emotions, if ever. They initially complied with this request." I rolled my eyes, sighed, and cut to a later shot of Nathaniel as an awkward twelve-year-old boy, skinny legs and all, sitting on an ocean dock overlooking crystal-blue water. It was the Florida Keys. The extended family was standing around celebrating a wedding, drinking martinis in linen suits, and laughing.

"One of Mort and Bess's sons had just married an heiress from Miami, and they were married on a dock in Key Largo." I exhaled and readjusted.

"Lovely wedding."

Close-up: Nathaniel did his own thing.

Medium shot: Bess, reminiscent of Grace Kelly, was decked out in a white, polished cotton IZOD dress, espadrilles, and a woven red hat cut across the camera vue, holding a platter of fruit and a glass of something cold.

Close-up: He looked up at her, brushed his 1980s Tony Hawk blond hair from his face, and smiled, shaking his head.

"No, thank you, Mom." You could read his lips.

Close-up: Bess dripped her martini on his bare arm, kneeled down to wipe it off, teetered, smiled, and kissed his forehead.

Medium shot: Nathaniel stared down into the water at his reflection; a fish swam across his eyes. He had seemingly blocked out the chatter behind him: law school jargon, parties, clinking glasses, who knows who gossip.

"Nathaniel doesn't look impressed, right?" I chuckled in Ana's direction.

"I've never seen so many spring silk and cashmere scarves on men in one place!" I shook my head and stroked my chin as if I had a beard of sorts.

"Trends are ludicrous!"

Ana stared at the screen and watched one of the twenty-something Flowers' brothers laughing in semi-intimate conversation with another gentleman.

"Watch closely, Ana."

She looked at the screen and the camera panned in.

Close-up: Nathaniel sat swinging his legs and staring at his feet in the water.

Medium shot: Group of Brooks Brothers–clad men standing in a circle. One of them, obviously distracted by sound, squinted at the sky.

Medium shot: A plane was passing over, leaving a cloudy white trail behind it.

Pan down on Nathaniel (medium shot): Adult's perspective. He gazed into the water and kicked the surface to rumple the image of the plane. Then he looked up and watched it go over. Ana heard the dialogue in her mind.

An effeminate man's voice, standing right behind Nathaniel spoke to his martini-sipping law school comrade and second cousin.

"I wonder if that scares him, you know, Josh? I know that it would freak me out completely!"

Then Josh Flowers pressed his navy blue linen jacket with his hand and moved toward Blake. "What do you mean? Freak who out?"

Blake sipped his martini and pointed down at Nathaniel, attempting to be nonchalant. He hushed his tipsy voice but not enough to conceal it. Switching hips, he tsk'd tsk'd.

Close-up: "Him. N-A-T-H-A-N-I-E-L!"

Medium shot: Nathaniel heard his name spelled out and tuned into the conversation without being obvious.

"The plane, Josh!" He attempted to hush his tone.

"Don't you know about that?"

"I have no idea what you are talking about."

"Oh!"

Medium shot: He motioned for Josh to move five feet away to the martini bar, but it was an ill-fated attempt at concealing his voice. Ana cringed as she heard him tell Josh the story of Nathaniel's sad beginning and covered her eyes so that she wouldn't see poor Nathaniel's reaction.

Close-up: Nathaniel was tuned in, his blue-green eyes fixed on his warbled reflection.

Ana peeked out of one eye and watched Nathaniel close down staring into the water, piecing together his strange loneliness. Regardless of the love he felt from Mort and Bess, they had always felt more like grandparents to him. He was so confused.

"That jackass!" Ana threw her pillow across the room toward the image of Blake.

I stopped the projector.

"And that's all she wrote, kid. After that, he refused to tell anyone what he had heard and sought the truth himself. It all came crashing down when he found his birth certificate concealed in an envelope at the back of Bess's antique secretary one year later. While Mort and Bess attributed his reclusive, moody behavior to the onset of puberty, they were oblivious to the unraveling…until that Thanksgiving.

Nathaniel

Later...October 30, 2000

anger Tom promised Nathaniel that he would update him about Ana. Nathaniel asked that he not tell him if she died and was left to be by himself on the lonely stretch of quiet beach that he considered his home.

He smacked himself continually in the forehead trying to erase her memory; her blue face and wet blond hair wouldn't fade.

He spoke to the sky. "There was still an ounce of life, right? Just an ounce, please?"

He fell back onto the sand, burrowed his tanned feet, and buried his head into his knees. Then he cried like he had never cried before. It was a sadness that was primal, like an animal who had lost her mother in a forest.

He cried for Ana, he cried for his past, he cried to unfetter his mind for things he had done, for those he had hurt, and for those he had lost. Most of all, he cried because he was out of anger and tired of himself. He rolled onto his side in the late afternoon sunshine and focused on a sailboat out in the distant water. He envisioned himself sailing on it, felt the gentle rocking motion, felt the salt breeze on his dewy skin, and drifted into dream.

When he awoke, chilled by the orange-and-purple setting sun, he jumped up, gathered some driftwood and twigs, and headed back to his humble island home amidst a clearing in the tall brush. He started a fire but had to find more kindling, brush, dried seagrass, anything to burn when he happened on Ana's backpack that he had thrown to lighten her load. He stood and stared at it for a moment, almost afraid to touch it, for his unfounded fear of harming her somehow.

The outside looked sun-bleached from salt water. It was almost dry. So he slung it over his shoulder and took it home. It was a connection to her and made him feel like he'd done something right. It felt good.

* * *

He stared at the firelight dance on the misshapen form, changing it from backpack to frog to dragon. It reminded him of the coatrack in his childhood room; it took the form of anything remotely frightening when momentarily illuminated by passing headlights outside. He sidled over, unzipped it, and peeked inside. Lying at the bottom of a soup of salt water and shells was a water-logged pile of envelopes wrapped in twine. He turned it upside down, gingerly untied the twine, and revealed slightly smeared, addressed letters lumped together. He slowly peeled the first letter from the top of the stack and the photo remnant of Ana's dog Sherman fell onto his lap. He picked it up, looked at it in the firelight, and put it in his pocket.

Then he read the first two envelopes: "Briar Bailey 124 Apartment 4C, 28th Street, New York, NY." In spite of the water, the address was completely legible. "Jesse Giovani, 11 Dean Avenue, Zionsville, PA."

There were loads of them, many repeats of the same address. Nathaniel spread them out around the fire in an attempt to dry them out. Most were typed, some handwritten.

He stared at the first letter addressed to Briar and carefully peeled open the envelope, attempting not to tear the wet letter inside. He lay the pages out in front of him and started to sift through the erratic, water-smudged letters.

> February 18, 2000
>
> Dear Briar,
>
> Where should I begin? Having suffered the worst episode/reaction to medication ever in my history two evenings ago, I have done nothing but sleep for days. My doctor tried out a drug called Xyprexa on me. It hurts just to say the name (it should be named Xyprexa really wrecks ya and I loathe using ya as opposed to you, anyway). It was seemingly the root of all evil. Brian, I couldn't walk or move my mouth (severe cottonmouth), like three bong hits multiplied by 1000. My legs convulsed for hours as if they were their own entities. It was truly a nightmare! I finally fell asleep in the early AM, and slept all of Thursday away.
>
> I went to see Dr. Freedman today (he's my sympathetic shrink) and he's trying me on yet something else, lithium. Despite all of the neg-

ative connotations associated with the L-word, I decided to give it a shot. I mean, what could it possibly hurt? I've been a crash test dummy for the psychotropic pharmaceutical companies lately. I have taken two doses thus far (knock on wood) and somehow I am optimistic.

Bri, ever since my hospitalization in late November, I have had horrific experiences with medication. First, I was taking a cocktail of this evil substance called Geodon, cradled by Trileptal, Buspar, and Prozac. Geodon had horribly debilitating affects; I fell asleep in school while trying to teach, only to be discovered by my supervisor—the ultimate in humiliation. When the dosage was cut down later, I started to have bizarre and uncomfortable reactions in the evenings, around 8:00. It was like clockwork; my eyes would begin to shut, while my legs and body would start to twitch. Weird. Then I was incapacitated until approximately 11:00 p.m.

So my doc tried me on another, Abilify. Talk about weird; I had horrible sight impairment! My vision actually blurred to the point where I couldn't read to my tenth-grade English class. Thank God we were reading Salinger's *Catcher in the Rye*; cursing is key! If you want to get a kid motivated to read, Salinger is your writer. *Goddamn* is the most used adjective in the story. I'll write later. I wish that I could hear you. I miss you so much it hurts. Please believe this.

Love, Ana

Nathaniel lay the letter down and stoked the fire. "Sounds like my stint with Lithium. Teacher." He laughed to himself. He leaned onto his elbow and stretched his legs out in the firelight.

February 22, 2000

Light

Dear Briar,

The remedy? The beach. The ebb and flow of the tide is true solace. It was absolutely beautiful, sunny, clear, and February cold. And I thought of you and me, remember? Remember that time we went to the beach after our senior prom? Point Pleasant, NEW JERSEY?

We probably wanted to be drunk or stoned or both like so many others but didn't have the right connections that weekend. But we found true intoxication; we were invincible!

I can still feel it. The water was midday clear, six foot beautiful June waves, and you and I just kept body surfing into the rock and shell-lined shore. The more mangled we became, the funnier it was!

Remember our face plants into the sandbar and every time I emerged, my bikini was on sideways or not at all? Remember that?

You looked so beautiful, sun-drenched, and waterlogged, my playmate. We both fried in the sun, facial sunburns, and caught hell from our mothers hours later. Your beautiful mom, how I miss her, stood hip cocked, pointing her finger in desperation, pleading, "Haven't you ever heard of sunscreen? You will ruin your beautiful young skin!" Ruin? We thought we looked magnificent. Now I know what she meant, I think. I'm looking pretty rough these days.

Love, Ana

Nathaniel shook his head. He felt a little guilty, like a teenage boy who had snuck into his sister's room to read her journal. He leaned back on his elbows to stare at the stars, trying to make sense of it all.

February 23, 2000

Understanding

Dear Briar,

I am reading the ultimate book. It's called *Mama Gena's Guide to the Womanly Arts*. It cracks me up which is a rarity these days. The author refers to women as Sister Goddesses—all of us Goddesses. It's so funny—The Author's take is that whether you're thin, fat, wheelchair bound, beaten, unemployed, corporate, creative, whatever you are a Goddess, with a fantastic, underestimated Vulva. So Excellent! She talks about how women who are more in tune with their Vulva (which she refers to as the dreaded pussy, that we've come to accept as a derogatory word for the female anatomy), are more successful, happier, more in tune; I Love it! You have to read it. Yet another knock at the towering phallic inferno that we have come to love and worship: the penis. Now, I'm not knocking your genitals, Bri, I just feel that mine should hold equal significance.

I'm pretending that you are laughing now. I can hear you and see the crinkles around your eyes, your hand across your freshly bleached teeth in fear that there is a lettuce leaf lodged in between somewhere.

We are dining at an outdoor cafe, you and me. Right now. The same one that I sat at with you and Cal three years ago, the sound of downtown Manhattan behind us when I told the two of you about my recent bout with hard drugs. I was trying to justify my decision to quit graduate school two weeks before the end of the Spring semester, hop on a bus and go to NYC to act, or something. Never mind the fact that I had no acting experience except everyday life.

I hoped for acceptance…prayed that if anyone would be accepting of my decision, you and Cal would. And I was right.

But I can't help but think that in quiet conversation later…you tore me to shreds.

Right now, I sit quietly in February and write to you for fear of picking up the phone to call you. I live in memories. I'm tired.

Love, Ana

2/19

Dear Jesse-

I wish that I could call you and tell you about this. I know that you've heard it all, third person perspective, but I wish that my stupid hand could pick up the fucking phone and my crazy head wouldn't get in the way. So, I'll write. The crash test dummy crusades continue. I stopped taking Abilify about two weeks ago.

I lost my "Abilify" to see as a result of that phenomenal medicine. And the crash test dummy has been tossed into a pit of despair. It's dark. It sucks. I am more and more reclusive, desperate for sleep. I ignore all phone calls. Even Jack. I have been hiding out at my parent's house, completely paranoid that someone, somewhere may attempt to strike up a conversation with me.

I just sleep on their couch, afraid to be alone, afraid to be with people. I even lost my passion for the outdoors. Maybe because of win-

ter; I pray that it is because of winter. I wish that
I could hear your sweet voice.

Love, Ana

The evening of February 16, 2000

Drifting

Dear Briar,

Do you ever dream that you are flying? I
mean "really" flying, like a bird or a spirit. I hope
that you have, because it is an incredible experience. I used to dream that I was flying quite
frequently. Usually in the dream I was faced with
some sort of imminent danger, and I was trying
to escape it, usually trying to assist someone, and
then just in the nick of time, I would remember
that I could fly, and I would grab the other person's hand, and we would fly above the danger,
and I could feel it.

I dream of you all of the time, probably
because I miss you so much. Although, I cannot remember whether or not I have had flying
dreams with you in it. But, between you and me,
I can actually fly. I can. The dream experience is
too real; I know if I had to, I could. I feel it sometimes when I'm taking a walk outside. I haven't
done it yet, though. Only in dreams. But I will.

There are so many theories that surround
flying dreams. My favorite is astral projection;
the soul leaves the body while it sleeps and proj-
ects. That is why when we wake suddenly, we
sometimes jump. Supposedly the soul is reenter-
ing the body as the physical body wakes causing
a jumping sensation or a thumping or whoosh
sound in your ears

I haven't had any flying dreams lately. I miss the sensation. I think that my subconscious has been dulled by the medication I am taking for all of this mental mayhem. So I'm considering trying Transcendental Meditation. Have you ever tried it? Apparently through Transcendental Meditation a person can reach an extension called yogic flying. During the process, the mind and body settle down and experience a state of restful alertness, or as Deepak Chopra referred to it "the unified field" of natural law. Interesting, right?

Talk about defying physics; I am sold. I mean the mind and body work in tandem, and the mind is the puppeteer, so who says that we cannot tap into the recesses of the unused portion of our minds to make the body defy gravity. Anything is possible.

This is how the Maharishi Mahesh Yogi describes it:

"'Yogic Flying' demonstrates the ability of the individual to act from the unified field and enliven the total potential of Natural Law in all its expressions—mind, body, behavior, and environment. 'Yogic Flying' presents in miniature the flight of galaxies in space, all unified in perfect order by Natural Law. The mind-body coordination displayed by 'Yogic Flying' shows that consciousness and its expression—the physiology—are in perfect balance. Scientific research has found maximum coherence in brain functioning gives rise to 'Yogic Flying.' As the coherently functioning human brain is the unit of world peace, 'Yogic Flying' is the mechanics to make world peace a reality, and thereby bring world health, world happiness, world prosperity, a world free from suffering—Heaven on Earth in this generation."

We should take a class together. I cannot
think of someone who I would rather levitate
with. Someday.

Sweet dreams. Ana

"Wow." Nathaniel unearthed another waterlogged letter and
called to his island cat, hoping he was in the brush somewhere.
"Chong?"

February 16, 2000

Hurt

Dear Jesse,

Could you please tell me why I was so
smitten by the boys that I was when I was teenager? I mean, they dictated my life. I had a conditioned response to the sound of their skateboard wheels; I would start to salivate like one
of Pavlov's dogs or flip my hair out of my eye,
or something.

And Alex, I adored him; all surly skateboarding 5'8" of him. He was lovely, Italian and
Spanish, silky black hair, beautiful dark skin,
great style, a skilled skateboarder and surfer,
with a penchant for sniffing glue, drinking Wild
Turkey through beer bongs, smoking huge quantities of pot, dropping full sheets of acid at a
time…countless whippets.

That was all before the age of 18. Everyone
else thought he was a jackass (meaning you and
Briar) but I thought he was quietly amusing,
dead sexy, quirky and fun; I guess he was seemingly all of those things, sometimes.

And then he would change. He could
become very cruel to me. For instance, when I was

going through that really zitty stage the summer before my senior year of high school, remember?

I recall sitting across from him and doting among a whole group of "friends" in a fast-food joint, and he blurted out, "Why are you so ugly?" at me.

Everyone laughed because it was Alex, and he was so cool. I froze; I couldn't defend myself. My heart broke into a million shards.

Then later that evening after crying alone, damning my stupid reflection, Alex called, acting like nothing happened.

"Hey, can you come over tomorrow?" he asked sweetly.

"Sure. Yeah. What time?" The cycle would continue.

But the worst of the worst, Jesse, the most demeaning Alex experience that I ever had happened one night when I was about seventeen. I was driving and saw a group of my friends, including Alex, skateboarding at a park. I stopped to say hello when I happened upon their "screwing girls" dialogue:

Friend A: "Well what was it like the first time you banged Ana?"

I said, "Wow! Guys! Please. That is completely not necessary."

Alex: (complete with body language) "Oh man, it was like fucking a dead fish. She just laid there."

Friend A and Alex: (doubled over in laughter at my expense) "Hahahahahahahahahhhhhhhhh hhhhahhahahhahhahh ahahhahhahah."

I had buried that moment until just recently.

Love, Ana

Nathaniel shivered.

February 20, 2000

Dear Jesse,

Floating. It feels like Ireland today...a watery cold that doesn't require gloves and a hat but is crisp and smells like earth and impending spring. It makes my face flush ruddy and each breath tastes good.

I actually took the initiative to take a walk today. Although brief. I took the dogs. It felt good.

I am still at my parent's house and I am afraid for fear of jinxing myself to say whether or not the "L" drug is working or not. But it seems positive?

I have a gift for you—a poem:

Green river eyes,
blonde she smiles on me in dreams,
words dancing behind my eyes

like small children holding tiny hands,
spinning and spinning and laughing.

Love, Ana

Chong appeared and rubbed up against his face.

"What do you think...a girl, friend, sister, lover?" Nathaniel filed the letter in the "Jesse" pile and chuckled at his perversity. He intimately knew the chill that she spoke of, picturing a photo he had of himself and Bess. He was maybe five...six. They were sitting on a rocky ocean cliff in Maine around Easter. The image captured his innocence and froze it in time; With flushed cheeks, a hat, mittens, he was content...untouched by any harsh truth.

He read the poem again, this time aloud to Chong.

"I like that, 'green river eyes.'" He hummed "Julia" by the Beatles. "So I sing the song of Love...Juuuullllllliiiiiaaaaaaa. It's like 'Julia,' buddy, you know, seashell eyes?'"

He lost Chong to a rustling leaf by the fire pit and unfolded more letters.

Eve of February 21, 2000

Guilt

Dear Jesse,

I remember being a child and idolizing you so much. Even though I am eight days your elder you were so much taller and blonder than me. I had the ugly duckling syndrome and worshiped the ground that you graced. I remember feeling so important once when we were six; your older, infamous, experienced redhead cousins gave you two terry cloth summer halter dresses, one blue, one maroon. After a sun-filled afternoon swimming and playing outside, our parents sent us upstairs to prepare for a night out with them at an Irish pub with live music and Guinness to whet their appetite for popcorn. Exciting stuff!

You gave me the blue dress to wear so that we could be "twins," and although I swam in it, you fussed to make it fit and made me feel so special like I really was your twin sister like we secretly wished. Thank you.

Do you remember that night? I clearly recall curling up on my mother's lap later in the evening with my ear up to her chest, listening to her laughing between popcorn crunching, gurgles, and music. It was like being underwater. I imagined when I covered my other ear and listened to the night through her tummy that I was still in there; warm, floating. I had heard those sounds before; they were familiar to me. Sleep tight, Jesse.

Love, Ana

March 4, 2000

Reluctance

Dear Kenna,

I keep picturing you in the fantastic 1960s sarong that you wore to my apartment last July. You looked so incredible in that psychedelic print. You exuded freckled health. You know you amaze me. Teaching English in China, independent, fluent in Japanese and some Chinese dialects. I can just picture beautiful, blonde, compassionate you…loose in Shanghai! It must be fabulous! I bet the students think you are dynamite! I bet the color, the lights, the city is so exciting! I so admire how you can both appreciate the country and the city equally. Didn't you just complete a backpacking trip through Vietnam? I wonder what your next international adventure will be? Man, I would love to join you on one of your journeys; you really inspire me, Kenna. Someday.

You probably already know about the Four Noble Truths considering your background in Asian Studies. Just as a refresher, they are the foundation of the Buddhist Teaching: The Truth of Suffering, The Truth of the Origin of Suffering, The Truth of Cessation and The Truth of the Path. The Dalai Lama believes that by referring to someone as "good" or "nice" means that person has a more compassionate heart. We tend to overuse "good" and "nice" as much as we overdo expressions such as "cool" or "awesome." Although in your case Kenna, you really are both "good" and "nice," and I love you. I hope that you don't take offense that I never visit you when you are on your journeys. I have to quiet the voices in my head first. Keep me posted. I'll live vicariously through your exploits. You are radiant!

Love, Ana

* * *

March 17, 2000

Fairer Weather

Dear Sammy,

So many times I've wanted to pick up the phone and say hello, but to no avail. It's St. Patrick's Day and snowy, two of your favorite things wrapped into one day. Man, the fun we used to have; St. Patty's Day used to be an excuse to drink way too much Guinness and heaps of Jameson. I recall that you made it your mission to drink yourself into Irish oblivion, and I was always right there with you. You were always such a good buddy to me Sammy, and I hope that you're doing fine.

I bet that you are. I heard that you are a chef; what a gorgeous job for you. It's the perfect combination of creative and scientific.

Sammy, thanks for rolling with my punches; your relaxed attitude must have helped you deal with my bizarre behavior when we lived together in college. I didn't realize how strange my behavior was until just recently, when I started to sober up mentally, a bit. When I think of the things that you witnessed, I commend you even more for being my friend. For instance, how about the time that I snapped when we were out drinking, and I punched some big, tall football player across the face, because I had some delusion that he raped the girl standing in front of him.

Remember that? Then he freaked out on me and was thrown out of the bar. Do I have this right? The band stopped and announced, "Real cool, buddy. Way to threaten a chick. Get that guy out of here." But you believed my delusion, supported me, and we moved on to another watering hole.

Oh, and I am sure that you can't forget the time that I locked myself in my closet, crying late night, and I cannot remember if you called my parents, if I did, or if it was drug-induced, but my dad showed up at my door at 2:00 a.m. to help me. Remember? He was wearing a Burger King crown. Good old Harry!

I used to have so much fun with you... and Mini, Briana, Violet, Dewey and Kevin, and countless others that graced the palatial hovel that we resided in. I often think of all of you and swim through drunken memories to a time when everything seemed strangely okay. But Sammy, that was just the tip of the iceberg for me.

Since I disappeared, I can only describe the way that I feel as not unlike Lavinia, Shakespeare's Titus Andronicus' daughter, who was violently raped by two brothers Chiron and Demetrius, who cut out her tongue and cut off her hands so she couldn't give the crime away.

Extreme...yes, but that is what this bipolarity bullshit sometimes feels like. I feel raped of my ability to communicate, and some facet of it has instilled me with the fear of speaking to those I once loved to share life with. It's creepy, but I'm actively trying to find my way out of here. Maybe next St. Patty's Day I'll meet you at the bar for Guinness.

Love, Ana

2/24

Ghosts

Dear Aunt Carol and Uncle Bob,

We are sitting poolside, you and me. I am convincing you that everything is okay. You are reassuring me that everything is like it was when we were children, Jesse and I, Amber and Kenna...because I ask you to. You, beautiful and statuesque in your brightly colored sarong and me, tiny, long braids, envious of your tan, your gardens, and your beautiful blonde family. I sidle toward you and Bob between pale, laughing parents, unsure of myself and into your loving arms. You scoop me up and I giggle, confused and excited. You cover me in geranium red kisses, laugh and lop me into the pool, terry cloth shorts and all! I swim to the surface, sneak through blue, blink away water and fix my seven year old eyes on laughing family, lost in their afternoon, wrapped in summer green and blinding sunshine-I feel warm. My fondest childhood memoirs are there with you, Carol. Someday I will tell you this over tea. Someday I will.

Love, Ana

The Eve of 3/19

Medication

Dear Sweet Jane,

I'm sipping on a glass of wine and thinking of you. You know, the more I ponder it, you were just like me. You hid behind the most contagious laugh I have ever known, you would drink to get drunk, you were dreadfully moody, had a terrible self-image when everyone saw you as beautiful and full of life, you were addicted to drugs and the wrong guys, you were deeply affected by film, books, others' sadness, and you hurt for everyone, hiding that inside an angry, joking facade. Perhaps this was known between us; we had a quiet understanding. I could just look at your posture from across a room, and I knew what you were feeling. Did you feel that way, too? I remember sitting down on the ledge of the bathtub with you in your apartment. The two of us had been up for something like 22 hours, partying. We wanted to be eye level with the bathroom counter so we could see if there was any trace of cocaine left, even if it was mixed with tile cleaner, toothpaste, or cigarette ashes. Anything. We scraped up a line to share. Although we laughed, I think that we had a mutual understanding of that moment being the most pathetic that either of us had ever lived. I know that when I finally ventured home, suffering from a car crash in my brain, I vowed never to touch the stuff again, and I didn't…for a while.

I hope you're doing fine.

Love, Ana

March 21, 2000

Gift

Dear Kali,

Emerson said to young Thoreau, "Be an opener of doors for such as come after you." It's amazing to me how teaching is not strictly a teacher-student scenario, but an all-encompassing gift. It is a meeting of the minds between two souls who are sharing their intellect with each other. Although I may have entered your life as your teacher, you have taught me unmatched lessons in character, and suffering, and dealing with the perpetual salt in the wound called bipolarity. It pains me so much to see you suffer like I have for so many years, but the words of understanding that we have shared have been invaluable to me; in an otherwise bleak scholastic environment, our kinship made my struggle as an educator so much more bearable.

I can only hope that my presence and words of "wisdom" and empathy offered you some stability, as well. It helps to know that you are not alone, doesn't it? Only, I wish that our commonality could be something much less disturbing, like music, or our shared passion for writing, or the color green, or nature, or shopping. That would be too easy, I guess. I leave you with words from our shared favorite Transcendentalist, that I peek at intermittently when I feel discouraged:

"It is out of the shadow of my toil that I look into the light." (Henry David Thoreau)

Thank you, my sweet friend.

Love, Ana

* * *

March 17, 2000

Empathy

Dear Aunt Madeleine,

How did you raise five children with this affliction? I know that you kept it a secret because you were ashamed but how? Why? Actually, I think that I know why. It's the same reason that I have retreated into my little world. Fear: Fear of the unknown, fear of the stigma, fear of losing all control, fear of insanity. It must have been so difficult for you and your family. Not understanding your mood swings and flippant behavior. I wish that you didn't have to suffer like you have.

Apparently, when you and Uncle Sunny were just small children, way before my mom accidentally happened, there were weeks that Nanny refused to get dressed and wouldn't leave the house for months at a time.

Sounds all too familiar, doesn't it?

That must of been so hard for you and Uncle Sunny as children to understand and even worse for Nan because she didn't have any recourse. A 1940s Brooklyn housewife had an image to uphold and if I know Nanny, hers was adorned in beautiful shoes, seamed stockings, tailored skirts and hats. She must have been in pretty bad shape not to take great care in her appearance.

Aunt Madi, was your depression that debilitating? Well, if it's any consolation, you are a tremendous actor like myself. Perhaps it's because we are fellow Geminis…early June babies. My perception of you has always been that of a beautiful, statuesque woman who exudes confidence, style, and grace. Like my mother, you have such enormous spirit and presence. I have this great book. It's entitled *How to Be Happy, Dammit: A Cynic's Guide to Spiritual Happiness*, written by Karen Salmansohn. There is a passage I would like to leave you with that I hope you will enjoy:

"Life lesson # 26: You must show more respect for the invisible world. Because often what you don't see is what you get. And look at harmonic resonance—which you can look at, on any two guitars. When an 'E' string is plucked on one, it will resonate on the other. You believe harmonic resonance works with people too. When you speak openly from your heart, the hearts of others seem to open. This is because you are helping the people around you to vibrate at your same higher harmonic level. You've heard this called 'companion energy.' And you believe that in the same way the invisible germs of a cold can be contagious, the invisible energy of thoughts are contagious."

Thanks for thinking of me.

Love, Ana

"Chong?"

With tired eyes, Nathaniel picked up all of the letters and hung them on his clothesline in fear that they may blow away if he didn't. He curled into his bed and brushed his face against soft purring.

"What a day I had, my friend. Where have you been you little bastard?"

He curled up next to him, black with white paws, and fell into slumber, replaying the letters in his mind.

Gabriel

October 30, 2000

icture this scenario. Everyone was sitting around while the 'help' took the plates and Mort decided to propose a Thanksgiving toast." Gabe mimicked Mort's quirky New England accent: "'I'd like to toast my beautiful children and my growing accomplished family. I am so proud to be the father and friend to all of you fine ladies and gentlemen, and no matter what life may offer you and wherever it may take you, please know that we will always welcome you home. This is your home!'

"Everyone toasted, accept for Nathaniel who was concealing the birth certificate in his sleeve; it was like a flame burning his flesh to bone.

"'Okay, who would like dessert?' Bess stood up, straightened her navy blue suit and adjusted her shoulder pads. Nathaniel couldn't take it anymore and screamed at the top of his thirteen-year-old lungs, 'Fuck all of you, you phony bastards!'

"He kicked the turkey and stuffing into Mort and Bess' laps and poured gravy all over his 'brothers' and their guests all the while screaming, 'I hate you ALL! You're all liars! Pretentious fucking liars with no balls!'"

"Wow!" Ana laughed picturing the scene.

"Yeah! You should have seen their faces! It was mayhem! Then he pulled the birth certificate from his sleeve and held it in Mort and Bess's face and screamed, 'Tell me the truth, you liars. Tell me the truth!'

"You see, he was too young to realize that they were trying to protect him by concealing the truth until they felt that he was older and emotionally able to handle it. Unbeknownst to him, while he folded his birth certificate into a paper airplane and poured Single Malt Scotch over it one of his older 'brothers' snuck into the kitchen to call an emergency number. And while the emergency vehicle neared the Flower's residence, Nathaniel dipped the plane into the lit candelabra and tossed it at the dining room curtains setting them aflame, all the while screaming, 'So this is how I should have died, huh? Why am I still here? Why?'

"The family cowered in the corner of the room while the sous chef poured pots of water on the flaming curtains. And get this! The best part! Nathaniel grabbed the pot out of the sous chef's hands and yelled, 'Give me that fucking pot!'

"He waved it around and pretended he was going to hurl it at everyone. They all flinched and moved toward the corner in unison. He laughed uncontrollably at their subservience, gently handed it back to the chef, and demanded that everyone take the money from their pockets and throw it in the middle of the table, 'Come on, plastic too! Give it up you Scrooge bastards!'

"They did! And all the while he waved a butter knife at them. You'd swear by their expressions that it was a revolver. Nathaniel gathered it all up, shoved it into his wallet, and handed it to the sous chef. 'Here. Take this and share it with whomever you'd like…but get out of here, and fast! Go where you are appreciated. To hell with bourgeois snob motherfuckers! Go! Go!'

"Nathaniel had been studying about aristocracy and the like and found an uncanny parallel to his family structure; I guess that he wasn't impressed."

"I like that kid. He's got balls!"

Ana was hanging on the image of blue-green eyed, skateboard-skinny Nathaniel, controlling the herd with a dull object.

"A real Holden Caulfield, you know?"

"Indeed. Well, the aftermath was not particularly entertaining." I spoke solemnly and placed my wings around her face. She saw flash images of beautiful, young Nathaniel being hauled off in a straitjacket, screaming, crying, and spewing obscenities, "Let me go, you fucks! Let me go! Momma! Momma! I want to go down in the plane with you! I want to go down in the plane with you! I want to go down in the plane with them, please!"

Mort and Bess watched in guilty awe, holding one another. The ambulance doors shut them out and trapped young Nathaniel in, muffling his plea. One of the white coats tapped the end of the needle and pierced Nathaniel's fair skin. His pubescent cry slowly tapered off into whimpers, sighs, then nothing. He drifted away.

Ana knew that pinprick so well; the heat creeps into the veins and the inevitable fall into drug-induced idiocy follows. Gabriel slid his wings away from her face and wiped the tears.

"And that was just the beginning of serial boarding schools, psychiatric evaluations, psychotropic drugs, street drugs, low grades, all hiding a very high IQ. He was off the charts in creativity and toyed with the system, swimming in and out of each institution. He outwitted many, but if any teacher or doctor saw through his facade, he gave up. And eventually, he crashed." I shook my head.

"So, time passed. When he was twenty-one and 'straight' for one year, he enrolled in art school in Philadelphia. He was successful for the most part."

Ana took a deep breath. "Do I want to know the other part of 'most'?"

I cringed.

"Well, he had a bad day and decided that a trip to an old friend of his in North Phili for just one run with Mother Superior would fix it. He needed inspiration, you know?"

"And?"

"And when he arrived, he was taken into a room to wait. His acquaintance never showed…just three big guys who said that they were friends of his mate and would take care of things. So pretty New England Nathaniel placed his order, gave the city boys the money, and waited. He waited. And waited some more. Then one of the three showed up with the smack and gave it to Nathaniel who was very eager. In fact, he was too eager to fix right there. He immediately cut it out on the table and snorted it.

"'What is the matter with this shit?' Nathaniel looked up at the guy who was minding the door. Nathaniel tasted it. 'It's chalk! This shit is chalk! What the fuck?' He looked at the expressionless guy staring at him and noticed that he was armed with something. He grabbed his backpack and rushed toward the door, stopping to leave a message for the other two bastards who took his money, 'Tell those motherfuckers to rot.'

"He rushed past him toward the door, down the dimly lit stairs and through the piss-stenched hallway into the street below. He took off on his skateboard, his cheeks flushed with the night, and was stopped at the crosswalk with a fist in his jaw. Two men dragged him into an alley, covering his face. He tried to scream and fight back, but they were too strong.

"'Who's the motherfucker now, bitch? Huh?' The two guys laughed…then beat the life out of Nathaniel with his skateboard. He didn't have a chance. 'Who's the motherfucker now, pretty boy, huh?'

"Nathaniel tried to speak but only coughed up blood. He felt a boot in his face then struggled to move when he heard them chuckling behind him. 'You want chalk, bitch?' The guy screamed and spit in his ear while the other one ripped his pants off.

"'You want chalk, pretty boy? We'll give you chalk.' They spat between grunts. Nathaniel was brutally raped. They left him to die in a pool of blood."

Ana covered her ears. "Oh god!"

"He was discovered about three hours later by a newspaper deliveryman who had gone into the alley to relieve himself and was taken to the hospital. He was in critical condition for three weeks."

Ana covered her face.

"Needless to say, his stint with art school came to an untimely halt, and Nathaniel went back North. And so began his plummet into temporary insanity."

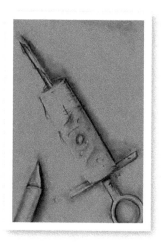

"Poor Nathaniel that poor, poor baby!" Ana turned toward me, and I handed her a hanky and a cup of chamomile tea. She didn't bother asking me where it came from.

"Thank you, Gabe." She took a sip and started to cry again.

"It's just that I know the feeling so well—THAT feeling. You know, Gabe?"

I stared into her. "WHAT feeling, Ana?"

"TH-TH-THAT!" she stuttered. "That c-c-complete loss of control, the feeling that everyone has betrayed you, and you don't know w-w-why! The feeling that nothing will ever be the same and there is no use. The feeling that the only way to exist is to numb the pain with something, anything…and to give up because of anger like Nathaniel's feeling."

I blew smoke into the air and seemed to contemplate what she had said for her sake.

"Is it giving up, Ana, or is it giving in?"

She scowled. "Giving in to what, Gabe, the dark side? What is this, Star Wars or something? Enough with the puzzles. I'm trying to express how it feels."

"That's great Ana! I am so pleased that you are opening up. It's about time. What I mean by giving in instead of giving up is giving into the negative to avoid the work that it requires to sift through it to find the positive, you know? It can be hard work to find the good stuff in life when you've hidden it from yourself for so long."

I smiled like I had just finished a happy ending to a story on Reading Rainbow; Ana dissolved in anger. She thought my rational approach to coping with mental illness was complete bullshit.

"Are you completely daft, Gabe? I bet that it is pretty fucking difficult to overcome being ass raped!" She turned her head and shook it.

"What the hell is this, Gabe, an ABC after-school special? Who are you, Captain fucking Kangaroo or something? Perhaps you're… like…the heroic school guidance counselor or something that fixes everything," she mocked him.

"That's great, Ana…I am so pleased that you are opening up."

She felt the red fade from her angry eyes when she saw me looking forlorn. And I was. I was simply someone who was trying to help her. I was an angel in uniform, and I was beginning to question my wings.

Almost immediately, Ana felt sorry. I felt her feel sorry. She was sorry for being so crass, so callous, and sorry that in the weird, delusional state of stainless purgatory that we were in, I was stuck with her.

"I'm no box of chocolates," she mumbled ashamedly.

"I chose you, Ana. You were my choice." I peered over my shoulder and flashed a half-hearted grin. Nothing was sacred, not even her thoughts.

"I'm sorry, Gabriel." She felt like she was a teenager and had just lashed out at her parents.

"It's alright, young lady. I'm paid to take your abuse!" I laughed in spite of myself, and Ana's face grew hot with anger.

"What do you mean you're 'paid'? What the hell is that supposed to mean, Gabe? Huh? I don't get it! I'm sick of it!"

She buried her face in her arms. Before I could say anything or could pull a magic remedy from my wing, she stood up and paced around the room, flailing her arms in protest.

"I'm tired, Gabe. I'm fucking exhausted! Do you hear me? I can't stand this! Please let me go…Let me go! I don't care if I wink out or if I go up into flames or if I float in space forever or reincarnate into a slug. I DON'T CARE just as long as I have no recollection of my miserable life! That's the whole point. I want out! And no, this is not just a pity party!"

She stood and looked at herself in the corner, examining her profile from both angles.

"Oh I beg to differ, Ophelia! This IS your pity party!"

She stomped over to me and pointed in my face. "Oh yeah, well I certainly feel no pity! It must be YOU that feels it for me!"

I was visibly agitated to the point of almost growling at her. "Well aren't you the most cliché basket case that I have ever had the displeasure of knowing! I was under the impression that you pride yourself on your individuality Ana…or should I say Ms. Woolf?"

"Fuck you, Gabe."

"Believe me, you little self-absorbed narcissist, it's not you I feel sorry for. You are nothing but the coward in this scenario. It is THEM."

"Who?" She looked at me, not anticipating my response.

I motioned for her to sit down and look at the far wall.

"Who? Just tell me!"

"Shhhhh."

Gabriel

October 31, 2000

The light dimmed, and I clicked what looked like a remote control, projecting an image of a coiffed brunette newscaster onto the screen, arms folded in front of her:

"Good Morning, Key West. Our top story today is a curious turn of events in our Florida Keys last evening when Bahiahonda National Park authorities discovered a woman who almost swam with the fishes. According to Sergeant Witherspoon of the Big Pine Key Police Department, she was saved from the ocean's deathly vice by an unnamed man. Officials say that the mystery twenty-seven-year-old later discovered to be Ana Guida thanks to records kept by Ranger Tom of the Bahiahonda Ranger's Association, was camping at the park when she disappeared into the Atlantic. She was later discovered alive and fully dressed with no visible signs of foul play.

She was rushed to a nearby hospital where she is still unconscious and in critical condition. Hospital officials are attempting to contact her family members. We will cross our fingers for Miss Guida. Back to you, Willy." (Static.)

"Weird." She stared at the blank wall trying to absorb a third-person perspective of her own attempt to not exist.

"Why wasn't Nathaniel named?"

I flashed her a "you're so daft" look.

"Because he's considered some sort of misfit. He's the low man on the Bahiahonda totem pole. You know how things work. There's rarely any recognition given to the good guy."

A phone rang and Ana jumped, clutching her chest. "Jesus Christ!"

"Perhaps that is who it is!" I flashed her a grin and pulled a phone from my wing. "Excuse me, Ana, I am obligated to take this."

I walked over to the corner for privacy and she tried to nonchalantly piece together my hushed tone. I spotted her eavesdropping in the reflection.

"Pardon me." I covered the phone. "Ana, I said excuse me, politely! Mind your own business, please."

"What business? I'm not listening."

I turned back toward the receiver.

"I'm so sorry. Pardon me again. Ana, please!"

I flashed her a look, and she began to hear a conversation in her mind, drowning out my low chatter.

It was the opportune time for her to see what she was about to see.

She listened to a doctor mumbling something to a female nurse.

"I have the number. I'm calling right now."

She heard the crinkling of paper, a dial tone, and eleven familiar notes

"Hello?" her mother, Peg, answered with an uneasy voice.

The nurse cleared her throat.

"Hello, is this Mrs. Guida?"

"Yes, yes, it is! Who is calling?"

"Hello, Mrs. Guida. This is Rebecca Sevigny. I am a nurse at—"

"Did you find her? Are you calling from Rhode Island? Where is she?" Ana's mother was frantic.

"No, I'm calling from Key West Medical."

"What in hell…Key West Medical?" Ana's mother's voice trailed off.

"Harry, pick up the other line—hurry up—yes, Key West—I don't know, just pick up the goddamn phone!"

"Okay, I'm here." Her dad tried being subtle in an attempt to compensate for her poor mother's rattled nerves, but she could hear the underlying panic in his tone.

"Hi, Harry Guida. Okay so you are calling—"

"Where the hell is my daughter? Is she okay?" Peg took control of the call.

"Well, yes and no, Mr. and Mrs. Guida. She is in the best of care here at Key West Medical, but in critical condition."

"Oh god!" Harry cried out.

"What do you mean?" Peg pleaded. "Please explain to us what the hell is going on!"

"All we know, Mr. And Mrs. Guida, is that your daughter almost drowned in the Atlantic at Bahiahonda State Park yesterday afternoon. Luckily, she was discovered by a man on the island before it was too late. She is alive but in a comatose state. We don't suspect foul play, although her blood was riddled with psychotropic prescription medication and a very high percentage of alcohol. Was she vacationing alone, Mr. and Mrs. Guida?"

"Vacationing? What the hell is going on? She wasn't vacationing at all! When I spoke to her three days ago, she had just finished a cognitive group therapy session!" Peg was panicked.

"I'm sorry. I don't quite understand." Nurse Sevigney sounded frazzled.

"Neither do we!" her parents almost yelled in unison. After almost forty years of marriage, they were prone to cloned phrases.

Peg chimed in, "She was an inpatient at the Rhode Island State Hospital undergoing intensive treatment for bipolar depression and schizoaffective disorder!" She could hear Nurse Sevigney scribbling into a notebook.

"Oh! I see. That would explain the blood test results. Is she suicidal?"

Peg yelled, "What the fuck do you think?"

"Okay, Peg, let me handle this." Harry attempted to be soft in his approach, aggravating Peg even more.

"No, no, Harry. I want answers! Why the hell is she in the Florida Keys?"

"I cannot answer that, Mr. And Mrs. Guida. Please, just know that she is under the best care possible and—"

"And nothing! Has Dr. Freedman been informed of this? This is pathetic! We will be there as soon as possible. Please call the state institution to alert those inept doctors and nurses that Ana is in your care, and they will be visited by the authorities and contacted by our lawyer immediately!"

Ana heard one of the lines click. Peg sighed, an older version of Ana, dissolved in tears.

"Please, please take care of our girl." Click.

It was challenging enough for Ana to see her parents shed a tear at her graduation, her sister's wedding, and their parents' funeral; but having heard that conversation, the struggle in their voices, their panic, felt different. She heard their hearts trip, fall, and weep. It was the most doleful song she had ever listened to. They were devastated, and it was all her fault. And for that, Ana was sorry. Really sorry.

Ana had never been able to deal with sadness very well. She had always been proud of her ability to shroud it beneath sarcasm, laughter, and anger, sometimes in unison. She felt that it protected her loved ones from feeling pity for her. She had never been able to accept sympathy. When she would fall and break a bone, lose a boyfriend, or learn a lousy life lesson, she was afraid that allowing sympathy would enable her family to touch her vulnerability. Being perceived as weak made her feel inadequate. For Ana, inadequacy is synonymous with disappointment.

* * *

"Enough!" She held her ears and screamed, "Enough, enough, enough! Turn it off, Gabriel, please!"

The sound faded, and I handed her a tissue.

"The truth always hurts, Ana. But that is why it is called truth, see?"

"As opposed to what, Gabriel, fucking fiction?"

"Not necessarily fiction, Ana, but denial of truth. Trying to convince your loved ones that you are a callous, unfeeling bitch is a waste. They see right through you."

She flashed me a look of disdain. "I am not a bitch!" She lit a smoke.

"Exactly! That's my point! You are allowed to feel, Ana. It's not going to hurt anyone if you are real. The burden is not on them, it is on you! You know what I'm saying?"

"No."

She stared blankly at the rings of smoke.

"Oh, don't give me that dumb routine, Ana. You know exactly what I'm talking about."

Her vain attempt to ignore me was interrupted by my wing extinguishing her smoke. I leaned into her and whispered, "The actor is you. And being phony expends a shitload of energy, now doesn't it?"

She nodded and looked down at my legs folded like a yogi.

"Good! I'm glad you're following me. Now give me a few moments. I'll be back. Just sit tight. I have a meeting with the higher-ups!"

I pointed toward the ceiling and Ana panicked.

"Where are you going? What are you doing? Don't leave me here! Please!"

I faded. "Calm down. I'll be back. Look to your left."

She needed to be alone for the next one.

"Dammit!"

She threw herself back onto the floor and stared at her reflection in the ceiling, noticing a blue orb of light in the far left corner of the room.

She rolled her head around and focused on a glowing, changing ball, suspended about one and a half feet from the ground. She half-expected it to grow horns or morph into some kind of psychedelic lesson or something. But it just hung there, waiting. She inched toward it and felt tremendous warmth dripping from its aura. She reached out to touch it and felt a soft static. Her hands cut right through the light like fingers through a flame. She played with the orb for a while then sat down and stared into it.

She saw a black-and-white tomcat and smelled morning on the beach. The image drifted over henna-scented sheets to a beautiful sleeping man hugging a pillow. His seashell eyes opened to the sound of a bird outside of his window. It was Nathaniel. She watched him.

Nathaniel

October 31, 2000
Early Morning

Nathaniel took a bottle of Dr. Bronner's Peppermint soap and stumbled toward the Atlantic for a saltwater bath. He didn't care that there was a pair of morning kayakers about a hundred feet away from him attaching gear and safety jackets to their pasty, sunscreen-slicked backs. He caught a glimpse of them in his peripheral vision awkwardly launch into the water. He waited until they were about fifty feet out, stretched, yawned, and lit a smoke all the while standing buck naked on the shore. After deliberately groaning and touching his toes, hindquarters in full view, he dove in, swam out toward them, floated on his back, and shouted over to the kayakers, "Beautiful morning, isn't it?"

They nodded politely and turned their faces away from him, trying to avoid an extended stare at what looked like a sea urchin sneaking out from between his thighs breaking the surface.

"It's nice to have extremities that double as a flotation device in the event of an aquatic emergency!"

Nathaniel threw his head back in laughter, simulating a lifeguard blowing a whistle.

"Grab on, ladies, and don't let go! My personal flotation package will keep you safe and above water."

The kayakers wobbled uneasily, a look of disdain on their faces as they tried to paddle quickly away from him. He chuckled and closed his eyes to the sun that hung in the morning. The east light washed his pretty chiseled features into the water. He took a deep breath, exhaled, allowing himself to sink to the ocean floor and opened his eyes to the burning saltwater, staring in silence. He felt peace. He wondered if it was the same peace that Ana sought to touch. He floated toward the surface and fixed his eyes on the morning sun glare that rippled on the surface. He began to feel the uncomfortable moment between consciousness and unconsciousness where the innate fight or flight reflex kicks in: sink or swim. He closed his eyes and let his lungs speak for him; they wanted to breathe again. He surfaced and gasped, water dripped from his face and ears as he pushed toward shore.

His towel got caught in the screen door, muffling the usual slam. He yanked it, dried off, lay on his bed, and dozed off.

About an hour later, he was awakened abruptly by the screen door creaking then slamming. A wet towel landed on him.

Tom yelled, "Awww, yuck, Nate! Put some damned pants on, would you? I'm tired of walking in on you buck-ass naked...damn hippy!"

He sat on the edge of the bed with two steaming Styrofoam cups of coffee.

"And enough with the skinny-dips! You're scaring the campers. Had another complaint this morning."

"They're just jealous."

Nathaniel sat up, wiped his eyes, grabbed the coffee, and took a sip. "Thanks for the coffee."

He put the coffee on the windowsill next to Chong, lounging in the morning light, one golden eye fixed on Tom.

"How is she?"

"Who?" Tom looked genuinely perplexed, passing his eyes over Chong.

Nathaniel looked at Tom and patiently waited for his synapses to fire properly.

"Who do you think, Tom?"

Tom chuckled.

"Sorry...sorry. Ana, yeah! Oh, get a load of this Nate. She's a mental ward escapee from up North. Rhode Island, Connecticut, or something."

Nathaniel was intrigued. He gulped from his cup and allowed the steam to permeate his nostrils.

"So that's her story."

Nathaniel thought of the letters, hoping Tom didn't notice them hanging on the line and spread out around the fire pit.

Tom gulped from his cup pressing his lips together to catch a drip. "Yeah!" He reached over to punch Nathaniel's arm.

"Sounds like the two of you would have had a shitload to talk about."

Nathaniel smirked at Tom's attempt at humor remembering his last stint in a state hospital setting. He pictured Doc Benny who had an uncanny resemblance to a caricature of Albert Einstein. He could even smell the antiseptic sheet tucked up under his chin and down over his feet.

Tom's voice faded into background chatter in the group therapy room memory. He tasted his dose of morning methadone that swirled with the butterflies in his stomach when he looked at Sadie Blue Eyes.

She curled into her chair and stared out over the New York winter landscape. He had never wanted to hold a person so close as Sadie, watching the steam from her morning tea wash over her pale face and through her messy black hair. The angry winter clouds rolled over her pale blue eyes, and he knew that she was trying to see something beyond our sky; it was her something that he wanted to touch.

Tom's voice trickled back into his ears.

"Hey! Where in hell do you go when I'm talking to you? You're just like my old lady, always tuning me out. Am I that boring?"

He looked out onto the porch and noticed the papers hanging on the clothesline.

"And what the hell do you have hangin' from your line?"

"Oh, just paper from my journal that I dropped in the water by accident. I'm trying to salvage it."

Tom eased his way up off the bed, groaned, adjusted his pants, and wiped his brow with the back of his hand. He turned toward the door and secured his hat.

"You're a weird one, Nate, you know that?"

The door slammed behind him. He yelled through the screen, "I'll see you later, buddy. Keep your clothes on, would you?"

Tom chuckled and walked off mumbling something and shaking his head.

Nathaniel liked Tom and never minded the required twice-a-day visit that Mort had arranged. It was Mort's endearing attempt to be proactive in his grandson's "therapeutic seclusion," as he, his wife, and their New Age psychiatrist referred to it. Nathaniel knew it more as banishment but appreciated the effort anyway. It was the first time in a very long time that he had been drug free; it was bittersweet. Drugs had been his lover for so long that he forgot what it felt like to miss someone. But then there was Sadie. He could hardly think of her for fear of impending heartache.

Chong interrupted his sad thoughts.

"Thanks, Chong."

Nathaniel scratched his back.

"You're amazing like that."

He picked up his cat, sat on the porch canopied by tropical foliage, and stared at the letters hanging from the line, crinkling in the light wind.

"Wanna read some more, Chong? Huh?"

No response. He collected the papers from the line and those scattered by the fire pit, shuffled through them, and fell comfortably into his hammock. He lit a smoke and read aloud.

Chong was his captive audience. There was never an impolite response or argument. He pulled Jesse from the pile and smoothed her out on his bare leg and exhaled.

March 26, 2000

Disappear

Dear Jesse,

It's one of those days today. One of those days that I would like to fold up neatly and tuck into a tightly sealed drawer somewhere. You know the kind of day I mean? Yesterday, I went to see Dr. Freedman and he asked me about lithium side effects. I told him that I feel like I have an impending urinary tract infection all the time.

"What do you mean?" he said. I told him that I have to pee constantly. He immediately spun around to his desk and scribbled down a lab prescription, spun back around toward me, and said, "That isn't good. We've got to have your kidney function tested today."

"Kidneys." I scowled.

"What next?" I left with my lab report, an incessant urge to pee in my pulsating urethra and headed down the highway in search of a lab. All the while I was thinking of a conversation I had with Frieda, my cognitive therapist, earlier in the week.

"Frieda," I asked, "since you are the holistic side to psychotherapy and you teach the tools to overcome behaviors, what is your take on herbal remedies as opposed to all of the chemicals that

I am swallowing daily? Do you think that they work?"

Frieda leaned back in her chair, brushed her blond curls away from her forehead, and cautiously said, "Why, are you taking them?"

"No," I said.

"But my question is, why am I NOT taking them?"

The other day I went into the health food store to pick up some vitamins and an older German man with smiling brown eyes and a thick accent greeted me at the door and sort of followed me around. So I asked him a question about the whereabouts of a specific supplement. He smiled, took both of my hands, and said, "Let me take a look at you."

Strangely I wasn't taken back. He was very kind. He stared into my eyes and told me that I needed to drink water with lemon to clean out my kidneys. Then he said, "And your liver is working very hard. Are you taking medications?"

"Yes," I confessed.

"I'm taking lithium and Prozac among other things that I am weaning off of."

"Ah," he said knowingly.

"For bipolar disorder," I said.

"Ah, you cannot tell from your smile." He winked. He then led me over to a book and opened it to a page entitled "Bipolar Disorder." There were several herbal remedy cocktails listed. One was a natural, unprocessed form of the salt lithium called Cudweed. He pointed to that and said, "It has the stabilizing effect of processed lithium but it is in its raw state so it doesn't cause the adverse side effects. Take this with you and read it." He smiled.

So I did, happily.

Frieda smiled seriously and said, "There is no doubt in my mind that natural remedies work. Nature is where all of our modern meds were extracted from but the problem that I have with them is that they are not strictly regulated. If you are taking 20 milligrams of Prozac here in the US you know that what you are swallowing is really 20 milligrams of the drug. Whereas you can't be sure when it comes to natural medicinal remedies because there is no government regulation. Is 20 milligrams of St. John's Wort actually 20 milligrams? It could be 5 milligrams mixed with 15 milligrams of filler."

Then Frieda chimed in, noticing a wave of disappointment wash across my eyes, "Although the only country other than ours that does regulate natural remedies is Germany. Their measurements are international units." All I could think of was the German man who read my irises (iridology). Maybe he was on to something.

I pulled into a small town lab and found my way in.

I was greeted by a five nothing, slim-hipped technician named Rosie who should have been home enjoying her later years. She had brilliant dyed red hair, a grandmother's charm, and a set of knockers on her that defied gravity. She was straight out of a pulp fiction magazine. She spoke to me in a raspy voice, "Hi, hon." She smiled, red lipstick on her front tooth.

"You need lab work done, dolly?"

"Yes." I smiled, silently wanting to grab an afghan and curl up on her lap to be rocked to sleep.

"Follow me, sweetie. You ever been here before?"

"No, I haven't."

"Well…" She smiled. "I'm going to put you to work then. Okay?"

She handed me a pile of legal documents to sign. She was eating a chocolate candy, turned to me, and said, "You're fasting, right?"

"Not intentionally, but yes. Unfortunately, all that I have had today is a cup of coffee."

"Good." She grinned. Then she leaned over like it was our little secret and whispered, "I'll give you some chocolate on your way out!"

I laughed. She smelled like baby powder, mothballs, and Jean Nate. Remember that after shower splash that you could get at K-Mart or Ames or any variety store like that? It came in a plastic bottle labeled cologne and was advertised as a "splash" of sexy fragrance for women? Man, I didn't think that they still manufactured it. Who knows? Maybe she stock-piled it in the 70s. Or maybe her grandchildren had wrapped it up for her for Christmas every year between 1978 and 1988, and she had filled her linen closet with it. Maybe that was her "scent," like Shalimar is my mom's scent, and my Aunt Suz's Scent and Samsara is your scent. Who knows.

She tied the rubber band above my elbow and slid the needle into my vein seemingly as easily as she poured coffee in my Pulp Fiction fantasy.

"Needles don't bother you." She smiled.

"No. I find them fascinating." She looked at me strangely.

"Not in a weird way or anything," I reassured her. I didn't want Rosie to think I was masochistic or something. After all, my lab report did say check lithium levels. She inserted another tube into the needle, and I watched it fill with my dark red blood. She pulled the needle out and pressed a piece of gauze to the tiny wound and taped it to my arm. I imagined a red blood cell holding up a stop sign and whistling beneath the surface dressed in a crossing guard's uniform to stop traffic from moving outside of my arm.

"Okay, dolly," she said, reading my lab request, "You've gotta pee in a cup for me. He's got to check your kidney levels."

"Do you know anything about that?" I asked Rosie.

"Well," she said, "I'm not a doctor, but I've been doing this a long time and medicine sometimes messes with your kidneys, so you've got to be sure." She looked at me handed me the cup and instructed me to wipe front to back with a castile soap towelette and to catch the pee midstream in the cup. Then she smiled reassuringly. I slipped into a memory of my college nurse instructing me to do that but not as kindly when I was placed on disciplinary probation for drugs.

I walked out of the bathroom and handed Rosie the cup. "Good," she remarked, like I had done a good job.

I loved Rosie like I loved my second grade teacher, Mrs. Coppola. When I was leaving, she handed me a baggy of chocolates.

"Bye, sweetie," she said knowingly.

"Don't worry, it will get easier," she said then tapped me on the back. I refrained from hugging her but I wanted to.

So why is today tough? Well, I woke up hung over. It was my own damn fault. I drank a four pack of Guinness last night, just because. I forgot how detrimental alcohol is to your body when you're taking meds. Secretly, I enjoyed the dizzying effect because I felt more human. I almost felt like I was flying high again. It was intoxicating (no pun intended). Wow Jesse...

I woke up today with a ten-car pileup in the frontal lobe of my brain and I'm not supposed to take anything to relieve it. I slept until 10:00 a.m., when I should have made progress toward my move; I have to be out of that apartment in three days. I was a bit discombobulated.

I had asked my landlord for some paint to touch up the spackle marks that I had made while filling nail holes. I decided to make up for lost time and quickly run around the living room and touch everything up. So I did. Before I left to escape the place for a while, I looked at the large white blotches on the wall, praying that they would dry to the right shade of white. When I left, the walls were still multi-tonal. I fear my return to pack more up this evening. I go in the evenings because I don't want to be seen. I'm afraid that someone might attempt to strike up a conversation with me. I feel safe in the dark.

Love, Ana

Dr. Freedman

October 31, 2000

Ari Freedman sat behind his mahogany desk, copy of the Torah, and a picture of two hearty cats draped over a piano stool in the corner. His broad shoulders filled his wrinkle-free blue button-down shirt. He leaned forward, clasped his hands together, and grinned warmly through round spectacles, nonchalantly wiping his brow. "How is everything here, Gladys?"

"Where?"

"Here."

"Where?"

"At home, Gladys."

Gladys smiled and nodded politely. Dr. Freedman motioned for her to check her hearing aids. He had a special place in his heart for the elderly, and the majority of his patients were over 75…with a few exceptions, including Ana Guida.

"Oh…yes!" Gladys lifted her fragile hand to her ear to adjust the hearing aid. It buzzed and hummed until she found the right frequency.

"Can you hear me now?" Gladys shouted to Dr. Freedman.

He smiled politely.

"Yes…I can hear you just fine. The question is, can you hear me, Gladys?"

Gladys covered her ears.

"Yes, for God's sake. You're TOO loud, Dr. Freedman. Pipe down."

Dr. Freedman smiled, stood up, and reached over to help her adjust her hearing aids.

"Better?"

"Fine…thank you," she said. "Your beanie is crooked."

"Thank you." He smiled and adjusted his yarmulke, sat back down and scribbled some notes on the chart.

"How is Zoloft working, Gladys?"

She shrugged her tiny shoulders, her freshly set white curls bounced. "It's time for me to die…Why are we trying new medication?"

Dr. Freedman smiled and leaned toward her on his desk.

"Gladys, it is all about quality of life. You are in perfectly good health."

"It must be all the bridge games." She rolled her eighty-six-year-old eyes. "I should pick up smoking again. By the way, there is a shine on your shirt. Cheap fabric. What happened to *Oxford Cloth*? Too lazy to iron it?"

Dr. Freedman smiled. "Enjoy yourself, Gladys…Life is good. This is a beautiful facility." He looked around his office at the stark landscape, sprinkled with sad Halloween decorations that the secretary hung a couple of weeks ago.Gladys dismissed him with her fragile hand, shaking her head.

"You just wait, Freedman, until someone has to change your diaper and wipe your ass three times a day. Then let's see what you think about quality of life!"

Dr. Freedman paused, then wrote a note on her file to the nurses at the geriatric psychiatric facility: "Increase Zoloft dosage to twice a day."

The door opened.

"Excuse me, Dr. Freedman, you have a call on line 2."

"Connie…I'm with a patient!"

She looked at him.

"It is important, Ari," she whispered.

He sighed and finished writing in the file.

"Two minutes, Connie."

Dr. Freedman ushered Gladys out of the office and sighed. He sat down behind his desk and looked at line 2 blinking on his phone.

He picked up the receiver. "Dr. Freedman."

"You must think you are the only one who works, Dr. Freedman. I waited two minutes."

He rolled his eyes. "Hello, Kelsey. How is everything in Rhode Island today?"

"Things could be better. Your favorite patient took a walk."

Dr. Freedman sat up straight. "What? What do you mean...She signed herself out?"

"No...She snuck out."

He started to sweat.

"What? What in the hell do you mean she snuck out? How in the hell does someone sneak out of a high-security mental facility?"

She sighed. "She is smart...timed it right."

"Oh, this is bullshit, Kelsey! I need to talk to the director RIGHT NOW!"

Nurse Kelsey waited for him to stop ranting.

"Doc, there's more. She didn't only walk, she went to Florida Keys and went for a swim."

"What the HELL ARE YOU TALKING ABOUT, KELSEY?"

"Well, Miss Guida planned it all. Had a car waiting, hopped on a plane at JFK, rented a car in Miami, and drove to Big Pine Key."

Flashes of conversation passed behind his eyes...Ana talking about her love for Bahiahonda.

"Dr. Freedman, did you hear me?"

"YES...Yes, I heard you."

"No...Did you hear me when I said that she went for a swim?"

He sat and stared. The reality settled in.

"Is she gone?"

"She is at Key West Medical...critical condition, Doctor. Coma, I think. She tried to drown herself, literally and figuratively. She was absolutely smashed."

Silence.

"Dr. Freedman?"

The blood pressure rose in his face, a crescendo of red.

"Fucking inept. DO YOU HEAR ME? YOU ARE FUCKING INEPT! EXPECT A CALL FROM MY LAWYER! I WILL CLOSE YOUR DOORS!"

He slammed the phone down, several times.

Connie stood outside of his door and waited thirty seconds before opening it.

"Dr. Freedman?"

"Connie…Get me on the phone with Key West Medical—"

"You have a patient in five."

"NOW, Connie!"

* * *

"This is Rebecca Sevigney, Intensive Care, may I help you?"

He took a deep breath. "This is Dr. Ari Freedman calling from United Psychiatric, NJ."

Nurse Sevigney sat up in her chair, paging through morning paperwork.

"Yes, Dr. Freedman." She paused, twirling her pencil. How can I help you?"

He sighed.

"You have a patient of mine under your care…a psychiatric patient…Ana Guida."

"Yes, yes Dr."—pause—"Freedman. We have been trying to locate records, as her toxicology report has many substances. We JUST received her records from a Rhode Island State Hospital where she was apparently an inpatient."

He shook his head. "How long has she been under your care?"

"Since yesterday afternoon, Doctor. She is in a coma. Alcohol poisoning…We are waiting for results of CT, MRI, and EEG. She was submerged for over three minutes, we think. Spinal tap was negative. No infection."

"Have her parents been contacted?" He held his head in his hands.

"Yes, yes they were. They were shocked, as they hadn't been contacted by Rhode Island." She paused. "Why was she in Rhode Island if you are in NJ?"

He shook his head. "Oh…long, long story, Ms."—he paused—"Sevigney?" Ari was silent.

"Okay, well I am your contact, Dr. Freedman. She is under my care, and my team will work around the clock to make sure she is comfortable." She closed her eyes. "Twenty-seven…just a child."

"I will have my secretary send you her records from my office ASAP."

"Thank you, Dr. Freedman." She smiled.

"I will call you with any changes."

"Th-thank you, Ms. Sevigney," he stuttered, blushing.

"You're welcome…and please call me Rebecca." She grinned, girlishly.

Dr. Freedman sighed…paused and sort of smiled a sign of recognition. "Rebecca, thank you. Off the record, what is your prognosis?"

She looked around and spoke quietly into the receiver, "It does not look good, Dr. Freedman. She is on a ventilator…full support."

He closed his eyes. "Please…Call me Ari."

Gabriel

October 31, 2000

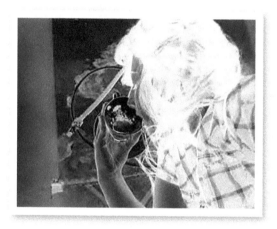

ne inch above Nate's reality, Ana sat back from the orb and rubbed her eyes feeling defeated.

"The letters…I hate that he's reading my letters." She looked around—there was no sign that I had been there and no sign that she was dreaming. She heard two female voices arguing over directions or something. It was coming from the blue light.

"You didn't ask? Well how the hell are we supposed to know what turn to make?"

It was her sister's panicky voice. Amber. Beautiful auburn Amber took control, as usual.

"There, there's the sign!"

Her father interrupted. Ana saw her mom, dad, and sister riding in a rental car, pulling into a hospital parking lot lined with tropical brush.

"Oh god."

She had no way to prepare herself for what was going to happen next. She watched them pour out of the rental car into the Key West heat and make their way toward the entrance.

They all looked so small, so silent. The antiseptic hospital smell always seems to demand some sort of calm respect for the patients or instills the fear of being a part of the sick populace. Whatever the case may be, she watched her own parents and her sister hold each other's hands in a vain attempt to comfort one another. It was most unusual for a family that loves, but almost never express affectionately.

As they rounded the bend toward the main desk in the intensive care unit, they were bombarded by television cameras and journalists who washed them in the strobe light of their gear.

"Has she ever done anything like this before, Mr. And Mrs. Guida?"

"Did you know of her plans?"

"How do you feel?"

"Was Ana a difficult child?"

"Why was she in the Keys?"

"Does she suffer from drug addiction?"

"Is she schizophrenic?"

"Sources say she's clinically insane. Is this true?"

"Was this a suicide attempt?"

"Do you believe in divine intervention?"

"Sources say she also suffers with multiple personalities. Any comments?"

"Has Ana any affiliation with a religious cult that you know of?"

Two nurses quickly escorted them to a private office, away from the media swarm.

"I'm so sorry about that. News travels really fast, and nothing is sacred around here."

"Jesus Christ, I guess not!" Peg sat down and a young nurse handed her a glass of water.

"Have a seat everyone. We've ordered security to remove the media at once. But I'm warning you, they are like Georgia Kudzu.

They'll creep up on you when you least expect it. Your Ana is hot news!"

Nurse Sevigney was a Yale nursing school graduate, but a Southern belle. She had a soft mahogany complexion, shorn salt-and-pepper curls, ruby lips, Alabama accent, and a no-bullshit attitude.

"How is she?" Amber piped in, life drained from her green eyes.

Nurse Sevigney motioned for everyone to have a seat, cleared her throat, and puffed up her shoulders.

"Well, the good news is that your little girl is alive. I usually don't get religious, but I believe that it was by the grace of God!"

Her mother interrupted. "But—"

"But as you already know, she is in a coma and has not shown any signs of consciousness. Her breathing is being assisted by a ventilator, but her vitals are unusually strong. So we have her on oxygen and an intravenous diet to sustain her. She does not respond to external stimulus, but our tests have found fluctuating but positive brain-wave activity. So when you go in there, don't you dare tiptoe around her! You need to tell her how you feel and show her that you are here. She'll know it, even though she cannot express it."

She sighed and put her mahogany hand on Peg's knee.

"I've been a nurse for thirty-five years, and I have seen many come and go. But the ones who stick around in this life are always the ones who feel that they have a reason to."

Nurse Sevigney put her hands on their shoulders.

"Make sure that she knows that she has a purpose…You hear me?"

Ana's family nodded in unison like dutiful children.

"Now, I'm not going to ask or answer any more questions. Just go on in there." She pointed toward a private entrance from the office that they were in. "I'll join you in about ten minutes or so. If you need me, there's a call button next to her bed."

Nurse Sevigney smiled at everyone and shut the door behind her.

Ana wanted so badly to look away from the blue light, but she couldn't out of fear of never being able to see their faces again.

When the door closed, it sounded like a tomb. The lights were low with the exception of the blinking vital monitors. A shaft of sunlight snuck in from the blinds, washing over Peg's weathered hands that reached to touch Ana's blanket, rising and falling with artificial breath. With the exception of Amber, quietly sobbing, the weird insulated silence was deafening. Everyone stood motionless and stared at Ana's spiritless face while her mother gently brushed a flyaway hair away from the breathing tube.

Ana's mouth was only slightly agape but enough to show the space between her two front teeth, obvious only to her. She thought that she looked like one of many baby groundhogs that she attempted to save from the clutches of her childhood dog, Bernie. She used to pry their little buck-toothed mouths open and give them rescue breaths to try to start their hearts. Ana dug many a grave for the poor little babies and rested her head on the edge to watch their chests for movement. She waited, sometimes hours, until the absolute last moment to cover them in fear that they may take one more breath and choke on the earth or cry for their mother.

Peg put her hand on Ana's forehead to check for fever like she was a child.

"Harry, is there another blanket around? She's so cold, so cold."

She stroked her forehead while Harry checked around the room aimlessly searching for anything to make her feel warm to the touch. It is amazing how a mother places her pain on the back burner and immediately functions on autopilot to protect her loved ones. Ana always admired her mother's strength but hated to think that her impending suffering was hiding in the shadows where no one saw it.

She looked up, her watery blue-green eyes spoke to Amber, lost. "It's okay. She's okay."

Amber gathered herself and walked slowly toward Ana's lifeless body while Harry stood cross-legged and cross-armed, staring out of the window, scratching his white beard helplessly. His soft brown eyes were glazed over in quiet terror.

She kneeled down.

"Hello, Ana."

Her voice was almost inaudible. She lay her head on her chest and cried.

"Her heart is beating, Mom, right? That is what I hear, right, Mom?" Peg caressed her hair.

"Yes, Amber. Shhhhhhhhhhhh. It's going to be okay. Shhhhhhhhhh."

Sadness beats a soul into childlike helplessness; beautiful, confident Amber had crumbled. She was at her mother's mercy, and it was all Ana's fault. It was then that Ana's visual perspective changed.

* * *

"What's going on? Damn you, Gabe! Please don't do this to me!"

She tried to look away, but couldn't. She saw everything from the bed instead of from above; her soul had fallen into her body for a moment. She felt her sister's tears on her chest. She saw her mother's anguish and heard her father's crying.

Her soul wept for what she had done; she couldn't hold them.

"No! Don't be sad! Please stop crying, everyone! I'm right here! Right here! I'm so sorry! So sorry! Make it stop, Gabe, please!"

She held her ears, looked away from the light, and fell into Gabe's downy wings.

"I didn't think that it would hurt them like this." Guilt echoed sickly in the hollow of her chest; she was at a total loss. The surprise of pain was just too much. She tried to block it out and cried herself to sleep.

* * *

Ana slowly woke from my nestled wings, opened her eyes, and stared into long blades of fantastic green grass and swaying dandelions. She looked down at herself, blew a downy feather from her hair, and didn't recognize her body. Her legs were longer, her skin was more fair, her stomach was fuller, but her arms were more delicate, and her hands soft and manicured. She sat up and spun her head around, searching for Gabriel.

"Gabriel?"

It wasn't her voice. She grabbed her throat and touched her lips. "Gabriel?"

She ran her hand through her hair, and it was different. It was soft, fine, shorter.

"Ik begrijp het u niet! (I don't understand!)"

Ana was speaking, but words were unfolding in another language.

"Ik spreekgeen Nederlands! Nederlands? Wat? (I don't speak Dutch! Dutch? What?)"

She looked down at her dress. It looked like a double-breasted airline attendant uniform or something. But short. Late 1960s.

She brushed her hand across her chest and pulled a rectangular pin from the breast of the uniform. It said "Helena Staadegard Serving TWA" in gold calligraphy.

"Mijnnaam is Helena? (My name is Helena?)"

She reached her hands up and felt her face; she had different skin, different features. Ana dropped her face and started to cry,

"Ik begrijp het u niet, Ik begrijp het u niet (I do not understand)." She was Ana, but it wasn't her on the outside. Her soul was there but not as Ana. She lay her head down and nestled her face into something soft, warm. It was a baby blanket, fresh with the scent of powder. She picked it up, held it to her chest, and rocked it like a child. She looked up, and I was sitting across from her, shucking wheat from a straw and smiling.

"This is a great look for you Ana, very Twiggy."

"Gabriel, war ben ik?"

She wiped away tears with the baby blanket and tried to focus on me.

"You're in a beautiful meadow. I thought that you would like it here!"

The baby blanket began to take the form of an infant and she quickly lifted the baby to her chest and rocked it.

"Shhhhhhhhh. Shhhhhhhh."

"Awwww, you are such a good mama! He's so sweet!"

Ana hugged the child peeking into his little pink face.

"Een mama? Een mama, Gabriel? Dit is mijn zoon? Gabriel, alstublieft! Ik begrijp u niet (A mother? A mother, Gabriel? This is my son? Gabriel, please! I don't understand)."

The little baby started to cry.

"De baby, moeder is hier, weinig jongen (Baby, mother's here, little boy)." The little boy opened his eyes wide and stared into the sky.

"Mooie jongen, houd ik van u mijn kleine engel (Beautiful boy, I love you my little angel)." She knew him. She knew his eyes.

"Gabriel, tevreden! Who is hij? (Gabriel, please! Who is he?)"

"Don't look at him, Ana. Look into him. What do you feel?"

Without hesitation, she said "Zuivere liefde."

Pure love. She looked into his eyes and started to weep.

"Nathaniel." She held him so close and kissed his downy hair. "Nathaniel, zonder twijfel (no doubt)."

I smiled and watched her coddle the baby boy who she thought that she had lost forever.

"Ik ben Helena, ben ikuwmoeder, and I am Ana (I am Helena. I am your mother)."

I pulled a mirror from my wing and handed it to her.

"Take a peek." I leaned back to study Ana, head cocked. She held baby Nathaniel close with her left arm and pinched the pocket mirror with her right hand, staring at a hologram reflection. It morphed between Ana and Helena, occasionally slipping from her grip.

"There is no such thing as coincidence. He found you because he was supposed to. You were brought together out of love to save one another."

She stared in disbelief at the beautiful child remembering how hard it was to let him go.

"You need each other, Ana, like your family needs you. Isn't that purpose enough to stick around for a while?"

Ana held baby Nathaniel crying into his powder-scented blanket and swayed with the windy grass.

"Ik ben hier, Nathaniel (I am here)." She was lost in his warmth when she felt him begin to slip away from her. She opened her eyes and was curled into Gabriel's wings, holding Nathaniel's blanket—

empty. She was Ana again, wrap dress and flip-flops, lying in the meadow. But that time she felt ironically different; she wanted something else.

Nathaniel

October 31, 2000

You lazy sod, get up!" Tom grabbed the hammock and flipped Nate over.

Nate held on to it, writhing like a snake. "Ouch, Tom! What the hell?"

Tom chuckled. "Just teasing you, Nate, relax! It's just you've been sleeping here for somethin' like three hours, you bum."

"Yeah, comfortably."

Tom groaned and sat on the ground against the tree opening a crinkled bag.

"You shoulda seen ya...mouth open, drooling."

He pulled a Tupperware container out and handed it to Nate followed by a steaming cup of coffee.

Nate peeked inside the container portioned like a TV dinner: chicken potpie, apple pie, and succotash.

"Thanks, man! Did you make this?"

Nate knew his wife sent it, but Tom liked to brag about her cooking, so that opened the floodgate. It made Tom feel good.

Tom cracked his knuckles and stared off.

"No, no!" He chuckled. "My girl is so good at cooking." He grabbed his belly. "The best, you know?"

Nate stuffed the chicken potpie into his mouth.

"Oh yeah. This is delicious. Please thank her for me."

He knew exactly what Tom was going to say next, so he introduced the topic. "Where would you be without her?"

Tom sipped his coffee, raised his eyebrow, and looked over at Nate stuffing his face.

"Oh, buddy, I'd be a whole lot of nothin', know what I mean?" Nate nodded and winked at him. He thought that Tom's predictability was endearing. It sort of made him sad.

"What the hell did you do all day? You sick or something?" Nate gulped down some coffee and rubbed his eyes.

"I was just really tired today."

Tom wiped his hands, stood up, and brushed the sand from his uniform.

"What in the hell could you possibly be tired from, Nate?" He laughed.

"Thinking."

Nate picked up the letters scattered all over the place and piled them neatly.

"Are you all right, buddy?" Tom punched Nate's arm.

"Yeah, yeah, Tom. There's no problem, really."

He stood up. "Thank you, Tom. Please thank Sadie for me."

Tom wiped his brow and looked confused. "Who in hell is Sadie?"

"Is that what I said? Sorry. I mean Sarah."

Tom walked off. There was an ounce of concern in his expression.

"You're wacky, buddy. See you tomorrow, you hear me?"

"Night, Tom."

Nathaniel yawned and washed out the Tupperware.

"Chong?" He sat down on the porch and stared west. The sunset was bloodred.

"Beautiful."

He grabbed his smokes and head off toward the beach.

"Chong?" Nate picked up the next letter in Ana's bundle and started to read.

"John Lennon." He smiled.

March 3, 2000

Imagine.

Dear Mr. John Lennon,

I hope that you aren't opposed to my formality, but I honestly don't know how to refer to you. I remember sitting at my dining room table, eating a peanut butter, honey and raisin sandwich on the day you died. I heard the news announced over the crackle of New York AM Radio…you had been shot.

My mother gasped…I dropped my sandwich and turned to look at her, framed by the gray December light falling through the kitchen window.

My mom rushed to the alarm clock radio and turned up the crackling and buzzing. She stared in complete dismay as the news unfolded.

"That bastard," my mom hissed at the radio.

I watched the horror creep onto her young face.

"Did he die mommy?"

I asked, singing "Lucy in the Sky…" in my head…trying to decipher what "tangerine trees" and "marmalade skies" felt like.

I wanted to taste them, so I put my six-year-old braids in my mouth, instead.

"He did," she whispered.

"Maybe he's with Lucy now," I lisped softly.

"Maybe."

My mom smiled at me, sadly.

So I'm writing to you with the hope that you can help me clarify something.

If "All You Need Is Love," as you so beautifully coined, and love is the answer to all problems, then how can I use it to cure this mental affliction that plagues me?

For instance, *How To Be Happy Dammit: A Cynics Guide to Spiritual Happiness* by Karen Salmasohn states that "life lesson #41 is Prozac Schmozac. Love is the Drug." I bet you agree, as do I, but I am conflicted. Salmasohn says:

> Love is what you're always looking for in all the things you're looking for. Even your yearning for sex is really a dyslexic search for love.
>
> You know it. And agencies know it.
>
> Love is the #1 marketing strategy, used as a promise in ad campaigns for products from cars to toothpaste to floorwax.
>
> And all this love mania reminds you of a zen saying:
>
> "Basically the archer aims at himself. If you are not a happy person inside you, then nothing outside you will ever make you happy and able to feel love."
>
> This makes sense because you already know from lesson #27 how the world is your mirror. It thereby makes sense that if you can increase how happy and loving

you feel about yourself on the inside, the more happiness and love you will see and attract from the world around you, to you.

Love radiates. It is an energy that you cannot only feel but you can see. I think that a person who truly loves herself/himself exudes light that attracts others. Do you think to knock down the self-loathing that is the scaffolding in mental illness that it isn't necessary to alter the chemistry of the brain with psychiatric medicine? Do you think there is a universal love energy that can be tapped into that is much stronger than any medicine? Is it the same mind-over-matter collective energy that you and Yoko were talking about when had your bed-in?

"War Is Over! If you want it." I mean, if you want something bad enough and direct your energy into it, it happens…right?

I would've loved to have talked to you…

Love and peace, Ana

"Huh." Nathaniel stretched to take another letter from the pile and nuzzled his face into Chong's neck.

"Hey buddy…Where you been?"

He held the letter out to Chong.

"Kindred spirit for sure."

He lay back on the driftwood log, facing west, and closed his eyes to the six o'clock sunset. He watched the patterns behind his eyes swirl a kaleidoscope of red cells, pulsating and spinning with each rush of blood. Caught off guard by a gust of autumn wind washing sand against his quiet face, Chong brushed against his leg.

He picked him up and nuzzled his whiskers.

"Yuck, Chong, what did you eat…week-old fish?"

Chong lay down on the letter, crinkling the weathered paper, bathed himself, and then chattered at some island birds. Nathaniel listened to a plane fly off into the distance, remembering a peculiar dream he had that afternoon.

* * *

He was wrapped in a blanket and listening to muffled noise: shifting, gurgling, and whispering. He opened his eyes and was suckling a breast, breathing in the dark space between. It was his mother; he could feel it. He knew the scent...like incense and rain. And although he couldn't gauge his own size, he felt helpless and infant-like.

"Shhhhh...Mooie jongen, houd ik van u mijn kleine engel." He looked up from his mother's bosom and staring down at him was Ana.

"Beautiful boy, I love you my little angel."

She was wet and unconscious like he had found her and didn't open her eyes or move her mouth when she spoke. He couldn't remember any specifics after that instance, with the exception of the timely sensation of falling fast; he never hit the ground but woke to Tom flipping him off the hammock.

He wished that he could fall asleep and continue the dream where it ended so abruptly. He missed Ana...didn't know why. He wanted to talk to her, like he wanted to talk to his dead mother and to know her and remind her that like him, she still had life.

He contemplated Ana's words, watched the sun fall into the ocean. He lit a fire and curled into the blaze in an afghan. Chong lay by his feet, switching his tail, and followed a growing shadow that skipped across the sand. It was time to listen to Ana and find out what it was that made her trip...then fall. He knew that he was one step closer to finding himself cradled inside of her mind. He smoothed all of the letters into a chronological semblance of order and held them like an ancient relic.

"The Dead Sea Scrolls," he whispered, brushed a mosquito from his hand, rested his head on a balled towel, and plunged into Ana's brain.

* * *

And one inch above his reality, I held Ana as my own, like I did so many times before, unbeknownst to her. Only that time she mourned a life left behind.

"What do I feel, Gabe? What?"

She cried and cried and sank deeper into the world beneath his wing, reading her own thoughts through Nathaniel.

As she watched and listened, I stroked her hair like a child.

"Shhhhhh...Little girl, if you didn't feel, you'd be nothing. You are everything. It's the letting go of the feeling of nothingness that hurts the most. The well must empty before it can fill again. Everything must die so that it can be reborn, a snake sheds her skin so that..."

She raised her head and looked at me.

"Okay, Confucius, I understand."

I chuckled and lit a smoke.

"Then continue to read with him, Ana. Feel what he feels." There was no argument. She read what Nate read and felt what Nate felt. And I know that somehow he felt her, too.

Ana and Nathaniel

The Dead Sea Scrolls
October 31, 2000

March 23, 2000

Voices

Paging Dr. Freedman,

Granted, I know that you are a psychiatrist and that your job is to medicate the mentally ill with good intentions of regulating their mood to a stable state of functionality and, in some cases, rationality. But I am curious about something. Does the old cliché "It takes one to know one" also apply to your profession? As a seasoned musician, you must feel that this is the case. I know it is sometimes difficult for a person who doesn't understand music to fully appreciate it as multi-faceted, rather than just a sensory stimulus that is either pleasing or not. I also know that although I love fine art, I can never entirely feel a piece of work because I haven't been trained in the technical aspects of how to create a great work of art. I can find it aesthetically pleasing, but I cannot fully understand the time and muscle that went into it.

Do you know where I am going with this? Can you empathize with those of us who have mental and/or chemical afflictions? Or do you feel that your medical expertise will suffice? I'm just curious. Personally, I feel that regardless of whether or not you are certifiable, you are a tremendous doctor and are current and well-versed in your profession. I also think that your passion for music is what makes you that way. When a person knows music in his/her soul, the senses are no longer separate entities; they meld, and the result is color that drips from a person's presence, like that of children before they become adulterated by life stuff. It is a clean intellectual energy and you have it. There is nothing clinical about you except your keen understanding of your profession. You are lucky.

Yesterday, I experienced what it feels like to not take any meds again, and it felt new or maybe just different. I ran out of lithium. I didn't take it for a day and ½. Dr. Freedman, the fog lifted for a while and I felt again. My senses were alive and I could breathe again. Even a headache felt good because I was aware of its pounding. Do you know what I mean? It was really hard for me to swallow that pill today. It was like saying good-bye to my old self even if she was unstable. I'm writing from beneath that lonely fog.

I leave you with an interesting excerpt that I read in an issue of *Prevention* magazine, entitled "Get Inside Van Gogh's Brain" by Susan Hayes:

"Creativity's personal cost: If you paint like Van Gogh or write poetry like Sylvia Plath, you're also at higher risk for madness. Could faulty brain wiring be the link between insanity and artistry? The evidence: Both schizophrenics and highly creative people possess leaky "sensory filters"—low latent inhibition, say researchers from Harvard and the University of Toronto. Their brains let in more sights, sounds, and sensations than normal. With a high IQ and a good memory, the input may be thrilling. Yet it can also be overwhelming—even deadly. To momentarily glimpse life as Plath, Van Gogh, or Mozart did (without the risk), pay close attention to a work they created. 'I think that great artists decrease the levels of latent inhibition in those who see or hear their works,' says researcher Jordan Peterson, PhD."

Regards, Ana

* * *

The Eve of March 27, 2000

Hurt

Dear Janis,

Sadly, I think that you were one of us, and nobody recognized it because of your "raw iron soul" as Jim Morrison so eloquently put it. You are a legend; you set the standard for a hard-living, hard-loving and hard-drinking blues-singing mama, but from what I gather, your perception of yourself was not good. It was the catalyst for your heroin overdose in 1970.

Apparently, you had a seemingly happy childhood, but your transition into womanhood was difficult; I can relate. As a teenager, you tended to gain weight, your hair became unruly, and you developed scarring acne that not only marred your face but your self-esteem. Then you became rebellious, drinking and drugging. You avoided mirrors and became an outcast among your peers. But luckily for you, your voice cradled you but not long enough.

Man, you were so remarkable. When I listen to your music, it exudes so much passion that I can taste it; I can also see something. I see darkness in your eyes, an unfounded shame that feeling like you weren't worthy of the attention that you received. Self-loathing. Fear of rejection. It all ate at you, and it is evident in your photos. In studio shots, you look completely lost; "Who am I?" You are embarrassed of the camera, afraid that the photographer doesn't think you are worthy of being a subject.

It seems that only models and actors learn the art of faking contrived photography…and we don't think we are worthy if we cannot emulate their grace. When truly, like in wildlife photography, I think that the best photos are candid photos. You know, like the pictures that capture the spirit in the eyes—the truth. The most remarkable photos of you, the ones that capture your exquisite beauty and spirit are the ones of you in mid-performance. You are seductive, alive and beautiful. I wish you could've seen that; maybe you'd still be around. I know what it's like to hate mirrors.

I wonder if you used to starve yourself, too? Perhaps your diet consisted strictly of whiskey, cigarettes, couple lines, and an occasional dropper full of liquid acid. You probably thought it was a sure way to stay thin, right? I did that for a while too, although my meal of choice was gin, and a whole lot of it. I did throw in olives on occasion; they are vegetables, right? Oh, and if I became hungry I would simply smoke a cigarette, or ten. Did you do that?

But my favorite remedy was to simply poison myself. I would eat two bowls of cereal, would look in the mirror, hate what I saw, and run to my "drawer" to grab the little brown bottle. I was well aware that it would make me violently ill for the next four hours, or so. I had better come up with an excuse for my flu-like behavior quick (I can barely type this without getting sick). It was called Syrup of Ipecac, and I forget how I discovered it but I did. I cannot encounter anything that even remotely reminds me of the stuff without gagging or worse (talk about a conditioned response).

Although I have grown away from the physically debilitating part of the eating disorder, it still manifests itself in different ways. Frieda, my cognitive therapist, says that it is a control issue, not a weight issue. I agree. I used to purge my negative feelings, not necessarily food. I could control what would enter and exit my body when I had no control over any other aspect of my pendulum-like emotions. I had a completely warped perception of who I was, and what I saw hidden behind my smile for the rest of the world, I hated. I wish I could have shared this with you earlier.

Ana

* * *

March 26, 2000

Introspection

Dear Alice,

    I am sure that you are THE most profound character in literary history because you represent the one commonality that every human shares. You are forced to question who you are at the ripe young age of five when most people seem to spend their entire lives searching for their true identity or at least trying to crack the surface.

    Usually the "search" begins with what seems to be a life-altering moment or with a bright philosophical or religious epiphany. You were lucky. Your search was instigated by curiosity then a long plunge down a rabbit hole into an altered reality. We certainly would be ill-developed, one-dimensional characters without curiosity:

    "Alice was beginning to get tired of sitting by her sister on the bank and having nothing to do. Once or twice she peeked into the book her sister was reading. But it had no pictures or conversations in it,

    'And what is the use of a book,' thought Alice, 'without pictures or conversations?'

    So she was considering, in her own mind (as well as she could, for the hot day made her feel very sleepy and stupid), whether the pleasure of making a daisy chain would be worth the trouble of getting up and picking the daisies. Suddenly a white rabbit with pink eyes ran close by her. There was nothing so very remarkable in that nor did Alice think it so very much out of the way to hear the rabbit say to itself,

'Oh dear! Oh dear! I shall be too late!' (When she thought it over afterwards it occurred to her that she ought to have wondered at this. But at the time it all seemed quite natural.) But when the rabbit took a watch out of its waistcoat pocket and looked at it and hurried on, Alice started to her feet. It flashed across her mind that she had never seen a rabbit before with either a waistcoat pocket or a watch to take out of it. Burning with curiosity she ran across the field after it. She was just in time to see it pop down a large rabbit hole under the hedge. In another moment down went Alice after it never once considering how in the world she would get out again. The rabbit hole went straight on like a tunnel for some way then dipped suddenly down. It was so sudden that Alice had not a moment to think about stopping herself before she found herself falling down what seemed to be a very deep well. Either the well was very deep or she fell very slowly, for she had plenty of time as she went down to look about her and to wonder what was going to happen next. First, she tried to look down and make out what she was coming to but it was too dark to see anything. Then she looked at the sides of the well and noticed that they were filled with cupboards and bookshelves. Here and there she saw maps and pictures hung upon pegs. She took a jar down from one of the shelves as she passed. It was labeled 'ORANGE MARMALADE' but to her great disappointment it was empty. She did not want to drop the jar for fear of killing somebody underneath so she managed to put it into one of the cupboards as she fell past it."

You kept falling Alice, questioning where you were falling to, what the longitude and latitude of your location was (not that you had a clue what those words meant) and how impressed everyone at home would be with your ability to endure such a fall. Then your curiosity made you lonely and you began to ponder comforts:

"Down, down, down." There was nothing else to do so Alice began talking again. 'Dinah'll miss me very much tonight, I should think!' (Dinah was the cat.) "I hope they'll remember her saucer of milk at teatime. Dinah, my dear! I wish you were down here with me! There are no mice in the air, I'm afraid, but you might catch a bat and that's very like a mouse, you know. But do cats eat bats, I wonder?" Then Alice began to get rather sleepy and went on asking herself, in a dreamy sort of way, 'Do cats eat bats? Do cats eat bats?' And sometimes, 'Do bats eat cats?' You see, she couldn't answer either question so it didn't much matter which way she put it. She felt that she was dozing off and had just begun to dream that she was walking hand in hand with Dinah and was saying to her very earnestly, "Now, Dinah, tell me the truth: did you ever eat a bat?"

When suddenly, Thump! Thump! Down she came upon a heap of sticks and dry leaves and the fall was over."

You questioned the natural order of things: do cats eat bats or do bats eat cats? It is one of the great questions: Why are things the way they are? Who created the food chain? Why is it a "given" to so many that people are the superior beings and have the divine right to smite the life of a forest creature for sport?

I remember being your age and witnessing a bloody deer carcass roped to a trailer being towed behind a pick-up truck stuffed with men with orange hats and camouflage jackets. They were laughing and enjoying the ride.

"How?"

I thought in disgust. I was horrified! It was the first time that I had encountered such sheer brutality. I asked my mother who was driving why they killed that beautiful deer? And she said, "Oh honey, don't look. Some people hunt deer."

I couldn't fathom that concept. I remember the horror that I felt. I couldn't wipe that image out of my head. Then I asked my mom, "But why, mommy? Why would those men hurt that deer? Who said that they could do that?"

I was infuriated.

"Isn't that murder?"

She couldn't answer me but she felt for me. It was the first time that I was faced with the image of cruelty and I wanted to know *why*.

So I understand why you followed the rabbit; how would we get to the bottom of anything if we didn't take the crazy route? It's humbling and you can usually find out some pretty interesting things about yourself and about human nature in general.

As Jim Morrison once said, "People are strange, when you're a stranger...faces look ugly when you're alone."

But that's just our initial response to fear of the unknown. If we take your path, Alice, the things that once seemed foreign to us become "real," and we begin to question our perception asking, "Who am I?" and "What is reality?" I think that leads to clarity.

The Caterpillar changed your entire perception of yourself with one question; "Who are you?" It was the first time that you had to step outside of yourself and question your existence. Were you simply Alice in patent leather shoes with a bow in her hair or was there more to you? The caterpillar wasn't happy with simple answers. He was a thinker and a philosopher and wasn't concerned with Alice in the physical sense. But wanted to know who the all-encompassing Alice was, which is pretty tough for a little girl to articulate but you attempted it:

"Alice looked all round her at the flowers and the blades of grass but she could not see anything that looked like the right thing to eat or drink under the circumstances. There was a large mushroom growing near her about the same height as herself. When she looked under it and on both sides of it and behind it, it occurred to her that she might as well look and see what was on top of it. She stretched herself up on tiptoe, peeped over the edge of the mushroom, and her eyes met those of a large blue Caterpillar. It was sitting on the top with its arms folded quietly smoking a long hookah and not taking the smallest notice of her or of anything else. The Caterpillar and Alice looked at each other for some time in silence. At last the Caterpillar took the hookah out of its mouth and addressed her in a languid, sleepy voice.

"'Who are You?' asked the caterpillar. This was not an encouraging opening for a conversation. Alice replied, rather shyly, 'I...I hardly know, Sir, just at present—at least I know who I was when I got up this morning but I think I must have been changed several times since then.'

"'What do you mean by that?' asked the Caterpillar sternly. 'Explain yourself!'

"'I can't explain myself, I'm afraid, Sir,' said Alice, 'because I'm not myself, you see.'

"'Don't see,' said the Caterpillar.

"'I'm afraid I can't put it more clearly,' Alice replied very politely, 'for I can't understand it myself, to begin with and being so many different sizes in a day is very confusing.'

"'It isn't,' said the Caterpillar.

"'Well, perhaps you haven't found it so yet," said Alice; 'but when you have to turn into a chrysalis—you will someday, you know—and then after that into a butterfly, I should think you'll feel it a little queer, won't you?'

"'Not a bit,' said the Caterpillar.

"'Well, perhaps your feelings may be different,' said Alice: 'all I know is, it would feel very queer to me.'

"'You!' said the Caterpillar contemptuously. 'Who are you?'"

This frustrated you but the Caterpillar went on to teach you that there is more to life than your preconceived notion of *Alice* and that if you want anything, you have to get it yourself. Between frustrating pauses filled with rips from the hookah, the Caterpillar taught you about that often overlooked space between reality and understanding: patience.

Your story should be required reading.

You are very real to me.

Love, Ana

* * *

The Eve of March 27, 2000

Dear Mother Nature,

Thank you for this lovely respite. The night is perfect. I now remember that something wonderful comes after Spring. Summer. I'm sitting on the floor of my new apartment, well new/old apartment, above the garage at my parent's place and remembering all the good things about this place. And you have everything to do with it. The balcony here has the most breathtaking view of the moon and the North Star and their reflections dance on the pond. The evening breeze is delightful. It has awakened my droopy Boston fern. I have it hanging outside beneath a floodlight; it's that warm out today. She is swaying. I'm staring at it through the kitchen window from my quiet place on the floor and drifting back to an evening with Kenna.

She came over for dinner on the patio. I made pasta and we lit tiny, white votives and sat beneath the indigo sky watching the moonrise and the horizon change. The fireflies were illuminating the dense, tree-lined path by the pond. I remember the silence, and I remember leaning over to brush a leaf from her honey-colored hair; and when I turned on the floodlight to see her down the spiral staircase to her car, I watched the shadow of the fern move across her smiling eyes.

Thank you, Ana

* * *

March 31, 2000

Touch

Dear Jimi,

Unless you have reincarnated, I know that you can feel me talking to you decades after you passed. You, too, believed in spirit guides and trusted that every person has at least one to help them through this life, either a brother or a sister from the spirit plane or a loved one from a past life that the person had a really strong connection with.

I have been so uninspired for the past couple of days.

I had begun to doubt myself, my talents, my dreams, my beliefs. I panicked when I saw the film *American Splendor* about the comic strip. I am pretty sure it came out post-1970. It was illustrated by Harry Crumb. Remember him?

There is a scene in it where the notoriously dark and skeptical wife of the main character says to herself, in reference to her husband who announces that he has been asked to appear on the highly accredited David Letterman show, "Ideas of grandeur," as a symptom of bipolarity aka Manic Depression.

My mind went into a tailspin: "Ideas of Grandeur? Is everything I am striving for in vain? What if, what if, what if, what if I lose all inspiration and can no longer write? Or what if this medication that I am taking is in the process of turning off all receptors to creativity? What if I am no longer sensitive? What if I give up? What if I am making a mistake? What if I take advice too literally? What if I can no longer feel music or see color in light? What if I lose my passion for moonlight and my limbs no longer stretch toward sunlight? What if I no longer believe in fairies?"

I began to panic. When you are in this state of mind, it is really easy to sink into a static state where you feel like you are stuck behind a television screen being pelted by viscous white/black electricity.

I think that you can probably relate judging from your musical vision. There has never been a musician like you. You made sweet love through your guitar and the result is pure color.

I had a dream today when I drifted into midday slumber out of frustration. I dreamt that I was walking through a dark, fragrant forest and the only light on the path was from an egg-shaped moon seeping through the trees. I couldn't make out what was beneath me, but it sounded like I was walking on a gravel path. I could feel it on my feet and, although the rocks were seemingly sharp, they didn't seem to hurt the soles of my feet. I felt a cool breeze rustling trees and I felt a chill. I looked down at myself and noticed that I was completely naked and illuminated by the evening. I kept walking and listening to the wind, feeling my hair flap gently against my back, tickling it. Then I heard water in the distance and was drawn to it.

I looked down and my dog Sherman was there not necessarily paying attention to me but passing by on the path. I called out to him but he didn't acknowledge me. I then reached a clearing in the woods and I looked into the distance and saw tiny flickering lights. I heard flutes playing a whimsical tune, along with earthy drums.

The air smelled of hyacinth and burning sandalwood. I noticed that the ground became more difficult to walk on. Another path forked off of the path away from the music and light that was more like the one that I had been walking on but I decided to go toward the lights.

I pushed through the trees and the briars kept scratching my naked skin. The rocks underfoot were slippery and sharp, but I was determined to reach the mesmerizing sound, cushioned by rushing water and twinkling lights. I climbed down a rocky embankment, pushed through some briars, and witnessed the most beautiful moonlit scene that I have ever encountered. There were beautiful childlike people dancing around a fire next to a waterfall that collected in a crystal pool of water. The egg-shaped moon danced on the surface. One man took my hand and led me to a soft cushion made of forest ferns and sat me down. He and I were both completely unaffected by the fact that I was naked; it was a very liberating feeling.

Everyone was illuminated by the fire and by tiny lanterns made of glass. Most everyone had some sort of instrument to play. There was one male being and even though he had long white hair his face and small stature were childlike.

He was stirring a pot of something that everyone was drinking but not a soul spoke. It is as if they communicated through music, dancing, and body language. He ladled out a cup of the pink drink and handed it to me with a wise smile and twinkling eyes.

"Thank you." I nodded, and I sniffed the drink. It smelled like hibiscus tea and dandelion wine. I drank from the clay cup and tasted a sweet, powerful flavor.

Next thing I recall I was feeling invincible and warm with the sweet drink. I stood atop a smooth rock that sat among a pile overlooking the pool of water. I looked into the waters and saw Sherman swimming around like a seal. I looked up to the top of the waterfall. At the top, next to a tree on another rock was someone standing in silence watching the water rush down. Although we were far from each other and we couldn't read each other's facial expressions, I could tell it was a male. I felt him read my thoughts and I his. It was a fantastic sensation. He wanted me to join him at the top of the waterfall. I feared there was no way for me to get to him.

Then he said, "Just fly to me." And like I had forgotten about my ability to fly, I thought, "Oh yeah," and I lifted into the air effortlessly, far above the beautiful pool of water, far above the little beings dancing in the forest and far above the waterfall. I flew straight into the man's arms.

Without words he smiled, took my hand, and we flew up to the egg-shaped moon together into the indigo sky.

It felt so real and I woke up inspired. I listened to your first album, *Are You Experienced*, and when "May This Be Love," came on I dropped to my knees and wept. Your song is so beautiful it hurts. The drums and the guitar introduction truly capture a waterfall:

Waterfall
Nothing can harm me at all
My worries seem so very small
With my waterfall

I can see my rainbow calling me
Through the misty breeze of my waterfall.

Perhaps the inspirational dream I had today was an astral experience. You believed in them, right?

The sensations were phenomenal, the feeling of the earth, the rocks underfoot, the briars cutting me, the sensation of drink, the warmth from the fire, the spray from the waterfall, the twinkle in the man's eye, the feeling of flying and the scent of the man's skin. My senses were alive.

I remember another different experience I had with astral travel. I had fallen into a deep pit of depression after a break up, existing solely on cigarettes. I remember one night; I sat on my couch to meditate in an attempt to settle my mood. I felt my spirit leave my body and I saw what it was seeing but I wasn't consciously aware of where it was going. It felt like it was attached to me by rubber bands of some sort. I watched it travel above my home like light, down one highway above another highway until it happened upon a landmark that I recognized. I remember the sensation of crying. But my soul was on a mission, and I was too curious to consciously pull away from the meditation. My soul traveled over his little town, over the lights on his street and looked down upon him sitting in his yard, playing the guitar.

It was twilight. My soul reached down toward him and his hands reached up towards my soul and we embraced. Melted.

I remember that I didn't want to let go but something made me. And when I awoke from my meditation, I cried a primal, healing cry just letting go of sadness until I fell asleep.

Thank you for your inspiration, musical color, and divine wisdom. I wish I could've known you.

Ana

* * *

Nathaniel stretched, reached over, and tickled Chong who was busy doing absolutely nothing. Nathaniel savored the surface stuff about his ocean-swept Ana. He could empathize. He knew what it felt like to be highly medicated, paranoid, and nostalgic all at once.

He reached into the pile, chose a letter randomly, gingerly opened the envelope, and pulled out a letter, perfectly childlike. "What the hell is this?"

He laughed from the gut.

"I love this girl!"

He looked closer.

DEAR ANA
WON'T YOU COME OUT TO PLAY?
...the sky is blue. It's
beautiful, and so are
you. Dear Ana...won't
you let me see smile?
OPEN UP your EYES
GREET THE BRAND NEW
DAY. THE CLOUDS WILL BE A
DAISY CHAIN SO LET ME SEE
YOU SMILE AGAIN
THE WIND IS LOW. THE BIRD

WILL SING.
YOU ARE PART OF EVERYTHING
look Around Ana,...
like a little child
LOOK AROUND
regards,   2/26
Prudence

Nathaniel slammed the letter down and yelled at the sky, "What the hell is this?"

He reread the letter again and again, looking around him thinking that somehow, somewhere, someone was playing a dirty trick on him.

"Who are you Ana? How the hell do you know me?"

He stood up, lit a smoke, and paced around trying to make sense of the sick coincidence. Lyrics from The Beatles' "Dear Prudence," which happened to be his favorite tune in the history of tunes. But that was not the sick irony. The song was synonymous with Sadie Blue Eyes, the most beautiful love that he had ever known and lost.

Nathaniel slumped down after kicking a slew of inanimate objects, inadvertently freaking out Chong, all the while spewing perverse expletives to appease himself. He slumped next to a palm tree, lay his head down in exhaustion, and watched his tears fall down toward the silty ground.

He covered his eyes in a vain attempt to quell the memory of the scent of her skin and the feel of his knees curled into her smooth body. He reluctantly reminisced about the last night he spent with Sadie in secret. He hadn't yet mastered numbing his senses without drugs. So he lit another cigarette and held his ears, unable to quiet her hushed giggles and soft breath beneath midnight blankets.

He could still see her tiny silhouette framed by the muddled light that seeped in beneath the door; he felt her mouth whisper in his ear as she put on her robe, "Thank you, Nate."

He grabbed her hand playfully.

"For what?"

She paused and stared into him. "For making me smile again." She turned to creep out of the room and glanced back. "I love you."

She smiled and snuck out into the fluorescent hallway.

The door closed and Nate held on to his chest, replaying her voice in his mind over and over. He smacked his head when he realized that he hadn't told her that he loved her, too. And he did... more than anything. She was his sole reason for wanting to exist and to kick for good. He lay back and fought off the butterflies in his stomach.

"She loves me. She loves me!"

He buried his head in his pillow, muffled a laugh of bliss, and planned their life together...when they got out of that place.

When he woke the next morning, he yawned, stretched, and looked out the barred window at a chestnut tree that slowly faded behind his breath on the glass pane. He turned to climb out of bed and focused on a letter that lay in the middle of the floor, rubbed his eyes, and walked over to pick it up. In large red letters over a pink lip print, it said "S.W.A.K." He smiled and flipped it over. *To My Dearest Nate.* He sat on his bed and opened the envelope anticipating the sweetest love letter in the history of love letters:

> "Dear Prudence ... open up your eyes...
> See the sunny skies. The wind is
> low the birds will sing, that
> you are part of everything...
> won't you open up your eyes?"
>
> I love you, I love you, I
> thank you, and I need you. That
> is why I have gone away. You
> are beautiful. Believe that. Please
> understand. We will find each
> other again. All my love
>
> Sadie xxx ooo
>
> *Just a note ...*

* * *

Time passed, and Nate cried at the inhumanity of it all. And after what felt like a very long time, he felt a strange calm. He sat up to compose himself and stared at a shadow from a coconut tree dance on the far wall of his shack and actually laughed out loud. The image looked like a wild-haired tribal dancer undulating with the rhythm of the breeze. The late afternoon sunshine captured the perfect ripe coconut placement beautifully, giving the dancer unusually large testicles. They looked authentic.

After much deliberation, consideration, and procrastination, he decided to lay on the hammock and wait for sunset instead of venturing off onto the island for "nature" therapy. His energy was spent, and in his vulnerable emotional state, a nature walk may turn into a trip to the highway, a hitchhike to Key West, and a junk binge with an old buddy on Duval Street. It has happened before.

The hammock was safe. Chong needed to be fed, and he didn't feel as lonely as usual. He had Ana and wanted to get to know her better.

April 5, 2000

It

Dear Spirit, God, Universe, Goddess, All-Knowing Entity, Prayer Collector, etc.,

Will I ever know how to refer to you? I guess it doesn't matter as long as I know you are there wherever there may be. It's definitely not one inch above my reality. I think that's where the restless souls reside, aka unresolved ghosts. I'm thinking that you are everywhere at once like Santa Claus. It's possible. He has helpers to assist him in his yearly task. Your helpers must be angels who take on human or animal form. How else could you reach your arms all around Planet Earth? That is quite a stretch.

Anyhow, here is my question. How do I prioritize my prayers? When I say a prayer, I always end up attempting to edit it as I go because I feel that it is not selfless enough. I restart the prayer a dozen times trying to hold down the prayers for myself and my thoughts of money. But I know that you can hear truth in thought or how else would you be able to determine whether or not a person is truly good or a bad seed? There are some fine actors in this world.

Perhaps it's not about language at all, but about the energy that a human radiates. Perhaps that is what you read...not their thoughts.

Wait a minute! What am I talking about? You're an all-knowing entity. See, it's really difficult for a mortal to comprehend your immeasurability. I guess that's where faith and hope come in. They are such powerful words and are two of the only words that sever skepticism, I guess.

Anyway, I have so many people that I want to pray for, but while I'm speaking to you, my mind drifts to war and repression in the Middle East. The injustice there is incomprehensible. I just cannot fathom the suffering. It certainly contorts my priorities or perhaps it clarifies them. The bothersome metallic taste in my mouth from Lithium, my negative bank account, and inability to sleep sometimes certainly isn't comparable to living in fear of suicide bomber attacks, gunshot wounds, or impending land mines.

Where are you in the face of war? I refuse to believe that you avoid it, but it is pretty difficult for me to comprehend that you are weaving in and out of all of that fear with a magic wand.

Are you there on a smaller scale like in a letter from home for a soldier or in a loaf of bread for a needy family or in the eyes of a young person training to be a terrorist who has an epiphany and realizes that something is not right with his learned mentality?

Is prayer and collective human thought what fuels you? Can it end a war?

Dhammapada (fifth-century BC) once said, "All that we are is the result of what we have thought." Is prayer really that powerful?

Love, Ana

* * *

April 5, 2000

Knots

Dear Dr. Freedman,

I found the perfect description of what a bipolar mood swing feels like. I could probably do it justice in my own words but Kafka's description in the introduction to "Metamorphoses," while it was probably not meant to represent a mood swing, is a fine parallel to severe chemical changeability. What do you think?

"When Gregor Samsa woke up one morning from unsettling dreams, he found himself changed in his bed into a monstrous vermin. He was lying on his back as hard as armor plate and when he lifted his head a little, he saw his vaulted brown belly, sectioned by arch-shaped ribs, to whose dome the cover, about to slide off compared with the size of the rest of him, were waving helplessly before his eyes.

"'What's happened to me?' he thought. It was no dream."

What do you think? Perhaps this could be a new, innovative approach for you. You could sit your patient down in the comfortable leather chair in your office and ask her to close her eyes. Then you could read that passage aloud.

Then, you ask how she relates to Kafka's description. I'm sure the results would prove fascinating. Move over Freud, Jung, and all your psychobabble cohorts. Make room for Freedman.

It may seem as if I am being facetious, but I think there is some truth to this. Why can't literature, art, and music be used as diagnostic tools (minus the ink blots)? They are used as therapeutic tools.

For instance, my gynecologist has a Monet print above her examination table. I swear that gazing at it makes placing my feet in stirrups with pot holders just that much more bearable.

When teaching Salinger's *The Catcher in the Rye*, I witnessed student reactions to many scenes in the book that were very telling about the individual's state of mind. My favorite one, that I feel would be most useful to your profession, is the scene in chapter 13 where Holden Caulfield has ordered a prostitute from the elevator man.

While he's waiting in his hotel room, he confesses out of nervousness that he is a virgin, while his mind races about his experiences with tricky bras and back seats and stopping when a girl asks you to stop. He half-heartedly figures that a prostitute will give him some practice at the art or at least some relief from his floundering mental state:

> Anyway, I kept walking around the room, waiting for this prostitute to show up. I kept hoping she'd be good-looking. I didn't care too much, though. I sort of just wanted to get it over with. Finally, somebody knocked on the door, and when I went to open it, I had my suitcase right in the way and I fell over it and damn near broke my knee. I always pick a gorgeous time to fall over a suitcase or something. When I opened the door, this prostitute was standing there. She had a polo coat on, and no hat. She was sort of blond, but you could tell she dyed her hair. She wasn't any old bag, though. "How do you do?" I said. Suave as hell, boy.

"You the guy Maurice said?" she asked me. She didn't seem too goddamn friendly.

"Is he the elevator boy?"

"Yeah," she said.

"Yes, I am. Come in, won't you?" I said. I was getting more and more nonchalant as it went along. I really was.

She came in and took her coat off right away and sort of chucked it on the bed. She had on a green dress underneath. Then she sort of sat down sideways on the chair that went with the desk in the room and started jiggling her foot up and down. She crossed her legs and started jiggling this one foot up and down. She was very nervous, for a prostitute. She really was. I think it was because she was young as hell. She was around my age. I sat down in the big chair, next to her, and offered her a cigarette.

"I don't smoke," she said.

She had a tiny little wheeny-whiny voice. You could hardly hear her. She never said thank you either when you offered her something. She just didn't know any better.

"Allow me to introduce myself. My name is Jim Steele," I said.

"Ya got a watch on ya?" she said. She didn't care what the hell my name was, naturally. "Hey, how old are you, anyways?"

"Me? Twenty-two."

"Like fun you are." It was a funny thing to say. It sounded like a real kid. You'd think a prostitute and all would say "Like hell you are" or "Cut the crap" instead of "Like fun you are."

"How old are you?" I asked her.

"Old enough to know better," she said. She was really witty.

"Ya got a watch on ya?" she asked me again, and then she stood up and pulled her dress over her head. I certainly felt peculiar when she did that. I mean she did it so sudden and all. I know you're supposed to feel pretty sexy when somebody gets up and pulls their dress over their head, but I didn't. Sexy was about the last thing I was feeling. I felt much more depressed than sexy.

"Ya got a watch on you, hey?"

"No. No, I don't," I said. Boy, was I feeling peculiar. "What's your name?" I asked her. All she had on was this pink slip. It was really quite embarrassing. It really was.

"Sunny," she said. "Let's go, hey."

"Don't you feel like talking for a while?" I asked her. It was a childish thing to say, but I was feeling so damn peculiar. "Are you in a very big hurry?"

She looked at me like I was a madman. "What the heck ya wanna talk about?" she said.

"I don't know. Nothing special. I just thought perhaps you might care to chat for a while."

She sat down in the chair next to the desk again. She didn't like it though, you could tell. She started jiggling her foot again—boy, she was a nervous girl.

"Would you care for a cigarette now?" I said. I forgot she didn't smoke.

"I don't smoke. Listen, if you're gonna talk, do it. I got things to do."

I couldn't think of anything to talk about, though. I thought of asking her how she got to be a prostitute and all, but I was scared to ask her. She probably wouldn't have told me anyway.

"You don't come from New York, do you?" I said finally. That's all I could think of.

"Hollywood," she said. The she got up and went over to where she'd put her dress down, on the bed. "Ya got a hanger? I don't want to get my dress all wrinkly. It's brand-clean."

"Sure," I said right away. I was only too glad to get up and do something. I took her dress over to the closet and hung it up for her. It was funny. It made me feel sort of sad when I hung it up. I thought of her going in a store and buying it, and nobody in the store knowing she was a prostitute and all. The salesman probably just thought she was a regular girl when she bought it. It made me feel sad as hell—I don't know why exactly.

I sat down again and tried to keep the old conversation going. She was a lousy conversationalist.

"Do you work every night?" I asked her. It sounded sort of awful after I'd said it.

"Yeah." She was walking all around the room. She picked up the menu off the desk and read it.

"What do you do during the day?"

She sort of shrugged her shoulders. She was pretty skinny. "Sleep. Go to the show." She put down the menu and looked at me. "Let's go, hey. I haven't got all—"

"Look," I said, "I don't feel very much like myself tonight. I've had a rough night. Honest to God. I'll pay you and all, but do you mind very much if we don't do it? Do you mind very much?"

The trouble was, I just didn't want to do it. I felt more depressed than sexy, if you want to know the truth. She was depressing. Her green dress hanging in the closet and all. And besides, I don't think I could ever do it with somebody that sits in a stupid movie all day long. I really don't think I could.

She came over to me, with this funny look on her face, like as if she didn't believe me. "What's the matter?" she said.

"Nothing's the matter." Boy, was I getting nervous. 'The thing is, I had an operation very recently."

"Yeah? Where?"

"On my wuddayacallit—my clavichord."

"Yeah? Where the hell's that?"

"The clavichord?" I said. "Well, actually, it's in the spinal canal. I mean it's quite a ways down in the spinal canal."

"Yeah?" she said. "That's tough." Then she sat down on my goddamn lap. "You're cute."

She made me so nervous, I just kept lying my head off. "I'm still recuperating," I told her.

"You look like a guy in the movies. You know. Whosis. You know who I mean. What the heck's his name?"

"I don't know," I said. She wouldn't get off my goddamn lap.

"Sure you know. He was in that pitcher with Mel-vine Douglas? The one that was Mel-vine Douglas's kid brother? That falls off this boat? You know who I mean."

"No, I don't. I go to the movies as seldom as I can." Then she started getting funny. Crude and all. "Do you mind cutting it out?" I said. "I'm not in the mood, I just told you. I just had an operation."

She didn't get up from my lap or anything, but she gave me this terrifically dirty look. "Listen," she said, "I was sleepin' when that crazy Maurice woke me up. If you think I'm—"

"I said I'd pay you for coming and all. I really will. I have plenty of dough. It's just that I'm practically just recovering from a very serious—"

"What the heck did you tell that crazy Maurice you wanted a girl for then? If you just had a goddamn operation on your goddamn wuddayacallit. Huh?"

"I thought I'd be feeling a lot better than I do. I was a little premature in my calculations. No kidding. I'm sorry. If you'll just get up a second, I'll get my wallet. I mean it." (J. D. Salinger)

Do you see what I mean? If a patient could empathize with that passage and could feel the sadness in the green dress hanging in the closet rather than simply seeing a missed opportunity to get laid, it could be a telltale sign that she has a heightened sensitivity and is prone to recognizing sadness in the inanimate details of life.

For example, I remember when I was living in Hoboken, NEW JERSEY and working in NYC. What someone else may have found as excitement in the fast-paced sidewalk traffic and countless expressionless faces moving quickly to a destination I found to be the loneliest that I had ever felt. I never understood how so many souls could pass each other without acknowledging one another. The people on the subway and the path rarely made eye contact with one another. That made me desperately depressed. I couldn't just ignore it.

I remember sitting and watching reflections of faces in the windows behind them change from shadow to blanched with the passing light in the train car. If I stared long enough, occasionally I would see a grin or the color of a person's eyes hidden in shadow or a book.

Each move was calculated and designed not to disturb, come in contact with or include any person in her vicinity. Granted, I was suffering from an untreated mental illness and perhaps I wouldn't have been so sensitive to these seemingly mundane things if I had been properly medicated.

But I know that when I exited the train and made my way up the tunnel, tinged with the scent of city, distant hot pretzels and urine, I understood why Toulouse Lautrec painted prostitutes pulling up their stockings instead of beautiful landscapes or still life. He, too, must have seen depth in sadness.

Regards, Ana

* * *

April 12, 2000

Spring

Dear Dr. Freedman,

Easter has come and gone. It was the first ever that I made a conscious effort not to be antisocial.

Lithium and Prozac together are helping, and the fogginess has subsided substantially.

I still have this stop, pause, and think thing that I do when I take a step. I don't quite understand it, and it's rather difficult to explain.

Oh wait, I have the perfect example.

There is a fantastic film that I recently saw called *Love, Liza*, starring Philip Seymour Hoffman and Kathy Bates. Two of the greatest.

The film is a sad, sad story about a man whose wife commits suicide and leaves him a letter, hence *Love, Liza*.

Out of desperation for self-medication for pain and to try to assuage his obsession with the unopened suicide letter from his young wife, he begins to huff massive quantities of gasoline in order to asphyxiate himself and make his time in his empty house more bearable.

Meanwhile, Kathy Bates' character, Liza's estranged yet nurturing mother, desperately attempts to convince him to open the suicide note so that they both may have a better understanding as to why she did it...to no avail.

The part of the film that I found most intriguing was the director's conveyance of deep sadness through slow human movement.

Did we already talk about this?

Every one of Philip Seymour Hoffman's physical movements was slow, deliberate, and separated by pause, by close-up shots of heavy breathing and confused thought.

The opening scene shows him pulling into his driveway in silence with a bouquet of flowers with him. The only sounds are the external sounds of trees, passing cars, birds, and his breathing as he silently stares ahead, contemplating his next move toward the house.

Nothing seemed automatic; it was too painful for him to venture toward the door gracefully; deep sadness cauterizes those nerve endings.

After painfully watching him do nothing but crinkle the cellophane wrapped around the flowers, he opens the car door into the sound of spring, closes the vault behind him, and walks. It's as if he is relearning the process of walking, which I would imagine could pose as an extended metaphor for the grieving process after losing love. Good stuff.

He eventually makes it to the door, but pauses before entering again. When he enters, the shroud of silence is overwhelming; his deliberate movement can hardly hold him up.

The camera actually reveals what "heavy" feels like. Not a heavy bag of groceries or a heavy box that is only intermittently such. But a heaviness that works with gravity in our reality in conjunction with gravity one inch above our reality where lost souls reside, shackling a burdened soul to a confused fog.

So…yeah, my weird cranial pauses feel like THAT. It used to just feel like confusion but now it has actually manifested itself as physical pauses in movement or speech, where I actually stop to reassess my thoughts and my mind is silent. And my body is silent with it. It is highly peculiar but it certainly could be worse.

Love, Ana

* * *

April 17, 2000

Kind

Dear Dr. Lee,

I wish that I would have gotten to know you better for I think that your take on spirituality was far more advanced that you allowed your medical patients to believe.

Although I was very young, I recall that you meditated with my mother when she lost her father and hypnotized her to assist her in the healing process...something that was probably unexpected from a country doctor in rural Pennsylvania who practiced out of a little house on the river.

But now she is convinced that after past life regression she knows that not only did she sink in the Titanic but she also rode alongside of Napoleon Bonaparte.

In this life she is deathly afraid of boats and has no desire to travel to France. Who knows.

You were always so kind and receptive to me as a child and a young adult and my mother told me on several occasions that you had reassured her that I would be a late bloomer, but would turn out fine. I was just torn and misdirected. I never understood how you gathered that from my countless cases of depression hidden behind the guise of a sore throat or a terminal Stomachache, but I guess I should never underestimate anyone's intuition.

I hope you received my letter of apology and accepted it when I sent it. I was so embarrassed by what happened in your office that gray day in November when I was about 22. I still don't understand what came over me, although I know that there has been one other occurrence since where my reaction was as extreme. I am afraid to open Pandora's box but I think that perhaps it is time to find out what inherently lies beneath to cause me to panic and fight like I did on both occasions.

I remember that I had chest pains that you diagnosed as pleurisy. I'm sure that my diet of Gin, Bulimia, and cigarettes didn't help the healing process. But I stayed with my parents for at least three weeks and slept the majority of the time. My mom finally convinced me to visit you. It was right before Thanksgiving and I had recently returned from a fantastic trip to Ireland with Abby.

My mom drove me to your office. We went in and we talked to you for a while. Then I hopped up onto the table so that you could examine my back and lung area and perhaps give me a shot of something to relax the muscles in my back to help with pain and pressure. Everything was fine. I have no fear of needles. I completely trusted you, my mother was there and I took my shirt off to be examined.

I lay face down on the table and as soon as your hand touched the base of my back I saw red, I panicked and yelled, "Get the fuck away from me," turned over and jumped off the table in one motion. I hit the needle out of your hand

and pushed my mother on my way to the door, hyperventilating and crying.

I ran out of the building, got into my mother's jeep, ducked down onto the floor and locked all of the doors. I shook with fear until my mother came out 15–20 minutes later. I couldn't explain what happened. I was very scared by my extreme reaction.

When my mom returned to the car, I tried to apologize and she stopped me and said, "Don't worry about it. Let's just get you home."

Dr. Lee, I was so afraid that you would think that it was something that you did when it certainly wasn't. But that was the last that I saw you because I was so embarrassed and ashamed.

My parents received a phone call from you one night and you talked to them at length about life and spirituality and how you had seen Jesus Christ at the foot of your bed when you were sick. My parents chalked the conversation up as a wonderful chat with a dear friend and doctor but you were really calling to say goodbye.

Three days later you passed on. You were so young. I'm so sorry that I wasn't brave enough to apologize to you in person. Perhaps we could have past life regressed and found a solution to that repressed angst that I violently displayed. Perhaps hypnotism would have done the trick. Maybe it is something that I experienced in this life.

Maybe not.

If you ignore it why can't it just disappear?

With all due respect, Ana

* * *

April 18, 2000

Stuck

Dear Frieda,

I may be mistaken as of late by the countless strangers that I have encountered at the restaurant. I think that I am seen as a perky, hard-working, quick-witted, server/bartender; they may pass judgment and attribute my blemished face and quirkiness to hormonal stuff. They may pass me off as ill-experienced, young, and maybe wise for my age. I never question them when they speak down to me as if I am a child. I am perceived quite often as a young adult of 18–20 who slings hash and pushes booze across a bar for drinking money.

I find it quietly amusing and sometimes use it to my advantage, however it may benefit me at the appropriate moment. It isn't often that I work during daylight hours, but I am sure that with the natural light coming through the windows, customers will be better able to read my harried face and gauge my age closer to my actual age. Although, the freckles always throw them off.

I am writing because I am at a crucial point in my mental healing progress where I usually write off any therapy or medication that I am taking as unsuccessful and leave the rest of my therapy to myself. I trust the powers that be and deem myself "healed," capable of anything and no longer in need of either cognitive therapy or drugs, at least the prescribed kind.

The sun is shining again, my spirits are high, glazed with Lithium and Prozac, and I have avoided calling you to make an appointment because I feel good, and I don't want to dig any deeper.

This is my wall.

This is where I normally quit, feel great for the summer and early fall, and start to plummet just in time for Halloween, then into complete sadness by Thanksgiving and solitary confinement by Christmastime.

It's happened so many times before, but I'm afraid that if I make the same mistake again, I won't live to see another pattern nor would I want to. It's as if when I reach this point, I simply comb the surface, bandage all the superficial wounds, and apply makeup to the scars. I am satisfied enough with the result that I portray to the outside world. I don't care to delve beneath to see what is causing the problem anymore. Masks are so much easier to put on. I really don't want to see myself in the natural light of day. I'm afraid of what lies beneath my reflection in the restaurant glass.

Frieda, I wouldn't be writing this if I didn't think that my mentality is counterproductive. My rational personality (I bet you didn't realize that I had one) tells me that I should finish digging up what I have begun to unearth. But the actor in me screams, "No! Put down the shovel, and play off of the mystery of what is unknown; feed off of the emotional mayhem."

Half of a decade ago there would have been no question as to what I would have done. But I feel that I have come this far. My pendulum is not swinging as far and as often as two months ago; it got stuck on a shard during the down swing. I'm thankful for that crash. I'm attempting to be rational and asking for your gentle assistance as my counselor and confidant. Convince me that it is okay to unearth forgotten truths and that the impending pain will only lead to healing. I want to break my cycle as a serial coward so I can join the world of the living without one of my many masks. My real reflection can't be so bad.

Regards,
Ana

* * *

April 28, 2000

Lost

Dear Joselyn,

Actress. Artist. Scholar. Real Estate Guru. Wife. Mother? God, I hope that I didn't miss that, too. I am almost at the point where I feel like I can contact you without shame, my friend. The prospect has been spinning around my frontal lobe for a good two years now. Two years! Not two months, two days—but years. It may as well be light years for fuck sake. I mean good God; of all the people in the world you would be most empathetic having gone through so much of this bullshit yourself.

I distinctly remember one instance that I felt I should never share with you out of fear that you would feel violated. It was rainy April, Junior year of College, and I heard your waxy footsteps squeak up the fluorescent hallway of our college dormitory in a drunken shuffle. You whispered and fumbled with your keys, taking care not to wake me when you slid into the room. It had been the finale of your very successful lead role in a Chekhov play and for whatever reason I skipped out on the cast party.

I almost spoke when you placed your bag and keys down but I heard your soft cry. I held my breath and watched you stare out of the window shuddering. The 3:00 a.m. streetlight illuminated a tear trickling down your beautiful face, framed by unruly brown waves that you so desperately attempted to tame earlier in the evening. I wanted to ask you what was wrong but the moment was too intimate, too alone. I was certain that you needed the solitude.

You whispered to yourself between muffled whimpers; they were real. You were not on stage. I scanned your silhouette to make sure that you were intact and hadn't been hurt. I caught the scent of your fragrance braided with cigarettes and red wine wash through the fan and across my face. Then I heard your guilt and fear; Catholic school teachings overcame you like flames and you kneeled. The window was your altar and each tear that hung from your soft eyelashes is stuck in my soft memory of you. You whispered a quick prayer, followed by silent tears and strained eyes staring through the blinds, followed by countless "Hail Mary's." I silently prayed for you to be unharmed. Do you remember?

When I rose late the next morning, I made two cups of coffee and sat down on your bunk to greet you with a sunny day beach itinerary to celebrate the finale…half expecting a response.

"Joselyn, you were pure drama genius last night, you know what that means? A beach celebration!"

You sat up smiling, demanded four Ibuprofens, and shook with maniacal laughter:

"What are you laughing about? How was the cast party?" I winked.

You pulled the cover up over your doe eyes and fell back onto your pillow laughing. "Oh my god, Ana, I was so bad, sooooo bad!"

"Jos, you little vixen!" I listened to you tell the story and laughed along with you cheering on your naughty exploits. But I knew how you felt and wanted to smack the habit-clad dictators with their oversized Crucifix. Because they molded you into a God-fearing adolescent, exacerbating your adulthood OCD and paranoia. I wanted to shake a ruler in their faces and scream, "Look what your school of thought has done to my Joselyn. It's just sex and she's allowed!"

Man, how I miss those days. I know that if I would just call you and we planned a day at the beach together like we used to, it would be as if we were never apart. I love and miss you my friend.

xo Ana

* * *

May 2, 2000

Canine Fundamentalists

Dear Nanny,

Yesterday was May 1st and the weather was fantastic but reminiscent of hot, humid July 4th rather than a May Day. With the exception of having to work a double-shift at the restaurant, the day was filled with interesting observations and the sweet scent of spring. When I woke, I tiptoed bleary-eyed down the concrete spiral staircase to the lush green grass and ancient strawberry patch below. When I reached bottom, I caught the most glorious scent; the soft, lavender wisteria that I had trained to climb the stairs and the stone building last year was beginning to bloom. I stopped, buried my face in a blossom, and breathed it in. God I love spring! Then I shuffled through the cold morning grass barefoot, wiping the dew from the blossom off of my face, to my parent's house to make a pot of coffee. I was up too late to have caught them; they were long gone by 9:30 in the morning. My schedule has been uprooted since the old dead days beyond recall when I would rose at 5:00 a.m. I can't remember what it is like but I would assume that it may give me more hours in the day to accomplish things; I'll work on it.

I wasn't even that bitter that I had to serve the public on such a day as yesterday; the effeminate Pagan dancers dulled the edge. It's true. There really was a group of effeminate Pagan dancers that came into the restaurant to share their dance on May Day.

All I know is I was waiting on a table and I heard the percussion-like loud jingling of bells; like those that would be on a horse-drawn sleigh in Central Park during the holidays. When I peered around the corner to see the source, there were three men at the bar dressed all in white with rainbow streamers and sashes. They were holding pewter and leather mugs with shin pad-like jingle bell contraptions attached to their legs right above their shoes. Several others, both male and female followed, all adorned in the same costume. They proceeded to perform pagan dances using scarves, bells, violins, accordions, and percussion sticks. Their leaps and choreography were impressive; I loved that they had no shame and were simply out to celebrate May.

The reaction from people dining was comical. There were a few men at the bar who were sitting solo, drinking beer, and eating hot wings who were visibly uncomfortable by the jingling, leaping men and women around them.

On the contrary, there were several intermingled customers who carried on, clapping out of enjoyment and appreciation. But the most comical of all were the British Dog Show judges who sidled in the door after a very serious day of not being able to decipher between the standard poodles and their owners.

Yes, Nan, in addition to the dancers, there was a dog show competition right outside town that brought in an entirely new breed of customers. Judging by the extensive traffic mounting on Bridge street outside of the restaurant consisting of predominantly RVs and vans with "Caution: Show dogs on board" bumper stickers and suction cup signs in a town that is normally graced with classic cars or imports that cost more than $65,000. The dog show was quite an event. And they all came to the restaurant.

I waited on a table of 10 and I swear to you that you could tell what type of dog they had simply by studying each person. So, I took it upon myself to guess and then I asked. Alright, so it may have been a bit bold, but would you believe out of all 10 people, I guessed correctly on eight of them?

The Mastiff was easy; the owners were a gay, male couple who were zaftig and one had an extraordinarily large neck like that of a Mastiff.

The other had sad eyes and a very low voice and sweet disposition.

Then there was an overly tanned woman, probably in her 50s, who wore a plethora of gold jewelry, had Patti LaBelle long fuchsia nails, and a remarkably curly coif atop her face, grounded by a turned up nose and coffee-stained teeth—Bichon Frise. I was dead-on once again.

The Labradors were very simple to spot. One couple had won something and the other couple hadn't. You could see the tension. Both couples were a giveaway because the women were both wearing a cap with a Labrador on them. Of course I told them about my beautiful Sherman the Tank, the 110-pound Chocolate Labrador.

"He is such a honey," I said proudly.

One of the women expressed concern. "One Hundred and Ten pounds is unusually heavy for that breed. May I ask what you feed him?"

I chose that moment as an opportune time to fiddle about for the sake of my own laughter. Without flinching, I confidently remarked, "Oh, I feed him whatever is on sale at Wal-Mart. He'll eat anything. He especially loves cat food. That I love, because it is so much cheaper! And when he's an especially good boy, I take him through the McDonald's drive-thru for a happy meal!"

Everyone at the table just stared at me, offering no advice or punishing words for my seemingly ignorant behavior.

"I'll go check on your entrees," I said grinning.

I would have loved to have heard their opinions when I disappeared especially those of the Standard poodle couple. Their posture was so erect that they made everyone around them seem strangely lazy in appearance. The Mastiff couple were content, cuddly, and washing down beer after beer in preparation for fish and chips. The "Poodle duo" sipped water through a straw, silently staring down their noses at their canine contender's post-contest commentary.

Loved it. You would have, too.

Love, Ana

* * *

May 2, 2000

Last Night

Dr. Freedman,

Later in the evening when the mayhem was dying down at the restaurant, I was assigned a table of four down by the window overlooking the ducks illuminated by fog lights on the stream.

I swallowed my iced tea, looked at the clock, and sauntered down to the table confident that my night was almost over. And when I rounded the bend to greet my four guests, I was overcome by a cold feeling that was more intense than a blast from a freezer on a hot day. It crept over me from head to toe like a web being dropped over me slowly, settling into my skin. I stopped in my tracks, turned on my heel, and walked away for a moment which I am sure looked highly unusual. Perhaps they simply thought that I forgot some pertinent item.

I shook it off, told myself that I was being ridiculous. My head was playing tricks on me. I walked back to the table, sliced through the cold feeling, and greeted the four men with Boston smiles and golf tans. They were probably in their mid to late forties; New England wealth with the dispositions of men who know better...but get away with it anyway.

I wouldn't have been surprised if any or all of them were politicians of some sort or another on a good ol' boys weekend golf outing, reliving prep school, then Ivy league glory days.

Whoever they were, my confidence completely waned in their presence and an overwhelming wave of fear and disgust overcame me. I fumbled with the ability to speak which they found highly amusing. They hissed their beer orders to me condescendingly without making eye contact, with the exception of one man. He leered at me trying to place my face, paging through the little black book in his mind. Maybe I looked like a combination of girls that had the "privilege" of screwing him in his glory days; no names, just faces.

"Do I know you?" he asked me as if I were interrupting a private meeting.

"I hardly think so," I said, feigning confidence. The guy gave me the creeps.

"Are you from this area of New Jersey originally?" he asked, a bit softer now.

"No," I replied, "I'm originally from Colorado, Fort Collins to be precise."

I turned to place their drink order and heard them speaking under their breath between dull laughs. Kelly, a girl that I work with overheard me blatantly lying to the men and asked me about it. I said, without flinching, "I don't want them to know me."

Doc...I lied. It was like some fucked-up attempt at defending myself, or something. I proceeded to tell the guy, bleached teeth, graying black hair, Polo shirt and chiseled face, my name was Andy and I was new to New Jersey. Once my identity was changed, I felt safe again.

My initial fear couldn't seep through my mask. They seemed to linger forever, and I tried to pawn them off on other servers. But they had enough of their own to contend with.

After two or three single malt Scotches, they decided to venture on to their next watering hole. I printed their check and the creepy one took it and said, "Thank you, blah, blah, blah."

I ran off and caught my breath praying never to see that man again whoever he was. He made my skin crawl, and I don't have any clue why.

When they were long gone, I went to their vacant table to clear the snifters and pint glasses and collect the check. I placed the empty glasses on the bar, nonchalantly opened the black book to retrieve the check money and receipt to add to my collection and accidentally dropped the book. I had forgotten that the bill that I had given him had my name on it and he noticed. He circled my name in a red pen and wrote a little note next to it.

"Ana. I thought that your name is Andy? Thanks for your service."

He didn't sign his name. I truly don't care to know or ever see his burnished-brown golf course/prep school face again. If I go to bed tonight as Andy from Fort Collins, Colorado, perhaps he won't be able to find his way into my nightmares.

Love,
Ana

* * *

May 6, 2000

Void

Dear Dr. Freedman,

What has happened to my libido? I am a 26-year-old female that lacks any desire to be intimate. Granted, I realize that this is very common among people who are required to take Serotonin Reuptake Inhibitors for depression. But I have been taking them for years, and it has never been like this. I am practically asexual; in order to reproduce, I'm going to have to be pollinated. I think that is how it works; I have forgotten seventh grade Biology.

With all seriousness, within the past month or so I have been scared of sex. I cower at the thought. I shy away from any physical contact. I wear clothes to hide my body. I don't enjoy kissing. And if I do force myself to engage in it, I find myself breaking into tears and trying to hide it. The idea of it pains me; my mind screams, "I hate this."

I've quit feigning illnesses, headaches, or requiring extraordinary amounts of sleep in order to forego intimacy.

I fear sex. I'm scared of it. I don't know why, and I don't want to. But I want it fixed, Dr. Freedman. Isn't there a way that I can simply fix this with a pill? Without delving into some ominous chasm of my brain that has been sealed shut, probably with good reason?

Is there any end to all of this? Finally, I am able to function beyond staring, writing poetry, then sleeping. Finally, I can work and support myself again and can laugh and smile and function comfortably. Finally, I can breathe easily, but what is hindering my affections?

Regards, Ana

* * *

May 17, 2000

Stumble

Dear Frieda,

It has been weeks since I've seen you and days since I have written in general. I saw Dr. Freedman last week. He told me that I must contact you by my next appointment with him. I think that it is 5/21. So I've thought about it. I've reenacted my prospective conversation with you. I've considered taking the cowardly way out: email. See, Dr. Freedman thinks that I really should continue with our cognitive therapy sessions. He told me that quitting now will be counterproductive and because he used the verb "quit," which has a negative connotation, braided with laziness and indecisiveness, I will contact you. Frieda, I'm afraid. I don't want to hurt anymore and I fear emotional pain; it is hard to see therapy as cathartic when I am the subject of scrutiny.

I see it as if I am an onion, and you and I have slowly been peeling away the skin, sheath by sheath, and we finally reached the soft, penetrable surface. And I ran away before we made the first cut; the one that provokes tears.

When I was hospitalized in early December and lied my way out in five days, one of the nurses who saw right through my "I feel better" facade said, "Ana, stick with it, even if it hurts."

"Thank you." I smiled, trying to appease her. Why? Why did I try to placate her? She was simply giving sound advice and once again I captured it in midair and crumbled it before it entered my ears and acted like it had penetrated my thick skull; it hadn't.

This is the first that I'd really given it much thought. It was her motherly, vain attempt at forewarning me of a prospective difficult journey. I was too busy acting. I was too drugged to know any better. But now I know different, and it is time for me to be courageous. Jesus, you'd think that I was skydiving for the first time or something. I guess that for the first time I am admitting that I need someone to hold my hand. I don't know where to begin.

Regards, Ana

* * *

May 23, 2000

Early Morning

Dear Dr. Freedman,

My hair is falling out. It is official. It is a slow process nonetheless, but it is evident. And in addition to that, my skin is breaking out in acne legions like I am 16 again. Granted, all of this therapy has made me regress back many years, but seriously, I didn't think that my skin would follow suit physiologically. Just when I thought that I was beginning to feel more like a functioning human again.

I went to see my most treasured hairdresser Audra who is also an empathetic soul and a talented artist (not that she had anything to do with the diagnosis). One of the first things she said to me was, "What medicine are you taking, Ana, because your hair is thinning?" I told her what my cocktail consisted of, which preceded an explanation as to why I hadn't been there to see her for so long in conjunction with my 2-inch roots. She explained that Lithium can cause hair loss because it is a salt and dries out the hair shaft. She recommended shampoo to counteract the side effect, and I left there feeling sorry for myself instead of being smashing, blonde, and radiant.

Dr. Freedman, I am well aware that vanity is not supposed to take precedence over my mental health, but I am a girl who, although seemingly low maintenance, requires a healthy reflection to maintain any self-esteem. In fact, one sour look in the mirror, if my face appears too wide or I have a crop of zits that hurt and shouldn't be there, overrides the effect of both Lithium and Prozac. I digress into a state of mind reminiscent of my days as a 16-year-old with horrible acne. My friend Violet called me a pizza face once, and it just about killed me. I spent the majority of my time trying to fix my skin to no avail. I've tried to make up for what I thought was lost time due to imperfections; I am perfectly aware of how shallow that is.

So the resurgence of these painful cyst-like blemishes is unearthing some pretty negative feelings, and I want them to go away. Isn't there something else that I can take? Please?

I've tried to use reverse psychology and convince myself that these reactions are not really happening, that they are a figment of my imagination and that I can simply cure any impending side effect by wishing it away. I work in public eye every day, so I desperately try to pretend that my thinning ponytail and scabbed face are not bothering me. That I'm simply satisfied that I can function and that I am working as opposed to being hospitalized or worse. My act is wearing thin. I can feel my urge for self-medication unraveling. I want to stay on a positive course. I know that I am rambling, but I am simply trying to emphasize how much this hinders my sense of self.

This is very embarrassing for me to breach during a one-on-one discussion, just like it was when I was a teenager. When I would leave the dermatologist who would prescribed heavy-duty acne medication, I always concocted an elaborate story for my parents that made it sound as if the nurturing dermatologist thought my case was minor.

"She said that it would not scar and would subside quickly and gently by utilizing the medicines," I lied.

I couldn't stand to have them look at me with vague pity; it made me nauseous. I felt downright ugly and inept. I don't think that I am being superficial but simply trying to accept this new self that isn't riding a pendulum. I accept my reflection.

Regards,
Ana

* * *

May 26, 2000 (email)

Dear Dr. Sanja,
I am writing to inquire about your services. I have seen your ad posted in health food stores

all over the county, and I would like to sit down and discuss your experiences as a hypnotherapist. I am certainly confident with your ability as a hypnotist, but I'm skeptical of one thing: my own imagination.

As curious as I am to try your technique to better my faltering situation, I fear that power of suggestion may take over my subconscious. My fantastical mind may concoct its own rendition of a memory. In my case, a not so pleasant one.

To be frank, my libido has disappeared, and I am frightened by intimacy. This has become progressively worse in the past six months or so while I have been receiving therapy/medication for my Bipolar illness. I am uncomfortable breaching the subject with either my doctor, or my therapist, simply because I am afraid of what I might find. Judging by my reactions to certain scenarios and the feeling that I get sometimes, I have reason to believe that I have fallen prey to some unsavory situations that I blocked from memory. I think that memories manifest themselves as very negative emotions and physical fears. Perhaps you can help; I want to file all of these uncomfortable feelings away. I anticipate your response and thank you in advance for your time.

Sincerely, Ana Guida

* * *

May 27, 2000 (return email)

Dear Miss Guida,

While usually I send a standard email to those who inquire about my services, which includes my mission statement, rates, credentials, etc., I found your letter intriguing so I decided to reply.

Ana, the reason that hypnotherapy is so effective is because of the power of suggestion. I do not instill ideas into the patient's mind. I only use guided, generic questions that allow the client to enter a state of consciousness that will allow her to both recall and undo certain fears, habits, obsessions, and compulsions.

My 25 years of experience as a Psychologist and Doctor of Holistic Medicine have convinced me that the mind is capable of creating physical conditions that hinder a person's ability or inability to perform certain tasks on a daily basis. And that sometimes the manifestations have nothing to do with traumatic past experience; the mind can create these scenarios to try to devise logical explanations for unfounded feelings.

Miss Guida, hypnosis is a fantastic tool for unearthing "blocks" as I refer to them. I cannot claim to cure you of anything but the results that I have witnessed in my clients have been lasting and successful. Understand that utilizing my services will not help you to simply "file away" negative feelings but will help to surface them so that you can deal with whatever it may be that is causing the block. It is a reciprocal therapeutic process. I have attached my hours, rates, and contact information for you. Call me at your convenience so we may discuss this further.

Sincerely,
Dr. Sanja

* * *

May 30, 2000 (email)

Dear Dr. Sanja,

I am looking very forward to coming in to work with you on Tuesday. Thanks for calling me back. I have a confession to make. I deliberately called you on the phone and pretended that I couldn't hear you. That was a product of something I have been working on but haven't been able to overcome as of late, phone paranoia. I sometimes freeze when the phone rings and feel panicky.

Perhaps that is something that we can work on together; it's incredibly debilitating, especially for friendships. When I called you, I simply pretended that I couldn't hear you on the other end hoping that you would ring me back and it worked:

"Good Afternoon, Dr. Sanja speaking…"

"Hello? Hello?"

"Hello, Dr. Sanja speaking."

(Talking to a fictitious person on my end of the receiver) "There must be something wrong with the phone. Hello?" Click.

Ring. (Panicking. Sweating.) Ring.

"Hello?" I asked questioningly.

"Miss Guida?"

"Yes, this is she,"

(Panic slowly dissipated)

"Hello, this is Dr. Sanja."

(I acted completely surprised) "Oh, hi! I just tried to reach you, but to no avail!"

"Yes, I heard your voice. We must have had a bad connection. Caller ID is handy sometimes."

Do you remember? So I am leveling with you, Dr. Sanja. I'm a phenomenal actress. I probably should've pursued acting as a profession.

I just hope that it doesn't hinder my ability to be hypnotized. Sometimes I just don't know which one of my personalities is going to be present at any given juncture. I fear that my subconscious is going to fabricate some elaborate scenario; I know that I have mentioned that before.

I'm looking forward to it. By the way, may I record our sessions so that I may study it later?

Regards,
Ana Guida

* * *

May 30, 2000 (return email)

Dear Miss Guida,

We have a lot of work to do, but the best mental preparation for you is none at all. Just relax. Think of me as a mental masseuse and that you have an appointment at the spa. Try it. I will see you on Tuesday, June 1. Enjoy the remainder of your Memorial Day weekend.

Sincerely,
Dr. Sanja

Ps. The sessions are always recorded.

Nathaniel

October 31, 2000
Evening

"Wake up!" Tom shook Nathaniel's arm.

"What the hell are you doing out here? Did you sleep here, you nut job?"

Nathaniel's eyes popped open, and he sat up collecting the letters that scattered while he slept.

"Tom, I need to get off of this island today!" He jumped up and ran into his shack to get Ana's backpack.

Tom rubbed his eyes. "Whoa, Nelly. What in hell are you talking about?"

Like a child running after piñata treasures, Nate henpecked from letter to letter to collect them. He stuffed them into his backpack.

"Trust me, Tom. Trust me."

Tom followed him with a steaming cup of coffee.

"C'mon, Nate…I ain't seen you with this much energy since, well, ever I guess. You alright?"

Nate nodded, mumbling the names of the letter recipients to himself and placing them in some sort of order.

"You alri—"

"Shhhhhhh." Nate continued to sort the letters. "Yes! Sorry, man, I didn't mean to snap. It's just that…"

"That what? What in hell's got into you?"

Nate looked up, stuffing the last of letters into his pack and flashed a big, toothy grin.

"Sit down over here, Nate, and have some coffee." Tom patted the ground next to him.

Nate slung his arm around Tom, causing him to spill coffee on his trousers.

"I've got shit to do, Tom, real shit!" Nate noticed the coffee on Tom's thigh and leaned over to wipe it off.

"Hey, brother, I like you, but I usually prefer 'em clean cut!" Tom chuckled.

Nathaniel laughed. "Really, Tom, I've got shit to do. REAL shit!"

"Yeah, that's what you said last time. I almost lost my job over you and your 'shit to do' stuff. Mort keeps food on my table, you know?"

Nathaniel grabbed him by the shoulders and could see a vague reflection of himself in Tom's sweaty forehead.

"Trust me, Tom, please trust me."

Tom sidled out of Nathaniel's desperate grip and cleared his throat. Raising his eyebrows, he said, "You ain't kiddin', are you, pal?"

Nate shook his head and smiled a big shit-eating grin. Tom looked around and moved closer to Nathaniel, adjusting his sweaty trousers.

"Can I just ask you what in hell this is all about, Nate?"

Nate slapped the bundle of letters down in front of him.

"It's about these." Tom looked down at the water-stained pile and picked them up to stare at them.

"What in shit's sake are these? Is this what was hanging all over your line?"

"Look closely, Tom." Nate watched Tom look closer at them without actually reading the content.

"They look like letters or something."

"Jesus Christ, Tom. Read who they are from!"

Tom scanned the page and a bead of sweat dripped onto the pile. "Let's see here. Oh! Love, Ana." He smiled at Nate.

"Okay, but who in hell is Ana?"

Nate stared at him.

"ANA! Ana! Come on, Tom. The girl who tried to kill herself." Tom wiped his head and started to chuckle knowingly.

"Oh, Ana! The girl you saved, Ana! Ha!" He stopped laughing and looked down at the letters and paged through the bundle.

"But where did these letters come from? I mean, Nate, why in hell do you have them?" He reached over abruptly, grabbed his hat pushed it onto his head, and stared at Nate accusingly.

"Did you know that girl, huh?" Nate laughed.

"No, Tom! I'd never seen her before that day, but I found her backpack on the beach filled with these letters and I read them, Tom. I read them!" Nate fumbled around for a smoke blowing sand off a half-smoked one that he found on the ground.

"They changed my life, Tom! I know her. You know what I'm saying?" Tom stared blankly and Nate exhaled, waving smoke away from his face.

"I am her. You know what I mean? I'm meant to help her or something. I know it!" Tom raised an eyebrow at Nate and wiped his brow.

"I refuse to fuck this one up, Tom! I won't do it! You hear me?"

"What in shit's name are you babbling about?"

Nate got down in front of Tom and looked up at him with childlike eyes.

"You've gotta just trust me, Tom. I need your help so I can help her."

Tom sweat beads of confusion.

"I need to go to the post office, and I need to go see her in the hospital."

Tom smacked himself in the forehead.

"Shit Nate, how the hell am I gonna pull that off, huh? You are not allowed to leave this island. If anybody finds out that I had something to do with it, I'll be ripped a new asshole...now c'mon!"

Tom placed his face in his hands.

"What are you gonna do. Mail the letters? What good is that gonna do for a girl in a coma, huh? I just don't get you Nate. I just don't."

"Just trust me." Nate put his tanned hands on Tom's knees and stared up at him; any further explanation would be in vain.

Tom raised his eyes from his hands and looked at Nate through a wrinkled brow.

"Just get your hands off my knees, Nate." Nate smiled.

He had him. Tomorrow, everything would change.

Gabriel and Nathaniel

November 1, 2000
Early Morning

Nate's Wednesday morning plan was conducive to Tom's stringent itinerary: A trip to Sunshine Supply for coffee and doughnuts for the ranger station at 7:45, drop-off at the station for punch in and delivery at 8:00, coffee and doughnuts with buddies till nine-ish, sort mail, and then leave for post office around 9:30 or so. He had to be at his front desk post by 12:30 for camper checkout, and Tom did not like his schedule to be toyed with. A day without structure left a sour feeling in his stomach, at least that is what he repeatedly told Nate. But for Nate, Tom bit his stiff upper lip, chewed an entire roll of Tums, and finagled his schedule. He added a few more steps to his Wednesday routine, including a trip to see his "aunt's sick friend" at the hospital…an extra guest concealed in the back of the Bahiahonda 4×4.

* * *

He drove up to Nate's place and slid down from the driver's seat like a crook looking both ways before crossing into unknown territory.

"Hey, Tom."

"Shhhhhhhh!" Tom looked behind, adjusting his pants and his hat, almost in unison. "Jesus Christ, Nate, keep it down!"

Nate laughed and grabbed his backpack, knocking over Chong's water bowl as he walked off the porch.

"Oops, sorry, Chong."

He leaned over and picked it up, singeing his hair with his lit smoke. He reached over and scratched his back.

"See you later, buddy."

Tom looked paranoid, violently motioning for Nate to hurry and get into the vehicle.

"For fuck sake Tom, calm down! Nobody is watching us!"

"Keep your goddamn voice down, huh?"

Nate slid into the ride.

"Sorry, sorry."

He looked at Tom who wiped his brow and checked his rear-view mirror continuously.

"Yeah, you better watch out for those backstabbing palm trees, Tom. They may slip and tell on us."

Tom slammed on the brakes.

"Enough, wise ass! I don't have to do this you know!"

Nate looked over and immediately felt like a dick; that was real fear behind Tom's inherently good eyes. Dishonesty scared him like it frightens a child or a soldier; he always did what he knew to be right. Nate had forgotten what that felt like somewhere along the way.

"I'm sorry, Tom." Tom looked forward and pressed the gas, pushed on his sunglasses, and pointed to a steaming Styrofoam cup of coffee.

"For me?"

"Well who in hell do you think it's for?" Tom motioned for Nate to drink it fast. "C'mon, buddy, bottom's up! You gotta drink that before we get to the end of this trail."

Nate took a gulp and burned his lip.

"Why?"

Tom motioned toward the back of his vehicle, and Nate's eyes followed his gesture to a pile of olive drab blankets.

"'Cause it'll be tough to drink that coffee while you are layin' 'neath them blankets." Nate nodded.

"Thank you."

Tom cut him off.

"I don't want to hear any thank you until this is done and over with, you are back on that lazy hammock of yours, and I'm back at my ranger's desk, you hear?"

Nate threw his free hand up.

"Okay, okay, no problem."

Tom gulped the last of his coffee and shoved his cup into a "Give a Hoot, Don't Pollute" cellophane bag hanging from his ashtray.

"Now, what in hell do I need to mail?"

"Oh!" Nate spoke into the coffee cup as he finished. He shoved it into the Hoot the Owl bag on his way into his satchel of letters.

"Here." He placed several bundles of letters on the dashboard in front of Tom.

"I've attached a slip of paper with the address that each bundle will be sent to. Just drop them into a padded envelope with no return address. Okay?"

Nate reached into his pocket, pulled out a credit card, and dropped it into Tom's lap.

"This should take care of all of the postage."

Tom reached down to look at it.

"MORTIMER FLOWERS? Nate, are you out of your goddamn mind?" He immediately started to sweat.

"Tom, Tom, it's okay! This card was given to me for emergencies. You just have to forge his name."

"Hell no!"

"Well, then forge mine or just write yours. No one cares, Tom, really! I used to do it all the time."

"And look where it got you!" He shook his head.

They reached the end of the trail, and Tom snatched the card from Nate.

"Get in the back and don't even whisper a sound, you hear?"

Nate paused. "You're kidding, right? Why can't I just duck down?"

Tom pointed. "Get in the goddamn back, Nate!"

"Okay, okay." Nate crawled into the back. "Under the blankets."

Nate laughed and pulled the blankets over him, watching Tom wipe his brow and inspect his blanket placement in the rearview mirror.

Tom cleared his throat.

"Now this is how it's gonna work, Nate. I'm going to pull up to emergency and drop you off. And I've got NOTHING to do with whatever in hell you plan on doing in the place, you hear?"

"Yes, Tom."

Nate hadn't a clue as to how he was going to get into her room: Alias name, mistaken identity, knock out a surgeon, steel his scrubs, perhaps feign cardiac arrest with hopes that they place him in the same vicinity as Ana.

But he had been in and out of enough hospital facilities to know that the laundry, custodial headquarters, and cafeteria were always in the basement and always run by employees that seemed more interested in the salty side of life than in six figure incomes or 401k. They actually took unabashed cigarette breaks in the loading docks, holding the security door open with a broken crutch or a bag of soiled laundry and he liked their humility; they wouldn't question his appearance. He was confident that he would be able to slide through their world unscathed. And he did. I made sure.

* * *

Nate stuffed all of the letters that were written to family and after-world recipients in his pocket wrapped in a brown paper bag with a letter from him written on it.

Dear Ant

I couldn't find the proper mailing addresses for the following letters. Perhaps you may have better luck when you wake. You will wake.

Love,
Nathaniel

That day, I was a dairy deliveryman who just happened to leave the cafeteria loading dock door ajar holding it with a case of milk that needed to be taken into the walk-in cooler. Nathaniel found it; clever guy. He looked around, picked it up, and brought it into the hospital kitchen whistling while he surveyed the scene. He tore the invoice off the box and held it like he needed a signature. He was very official.

He saw a woman loading a laundry bin with kitchen linens and saw her as his ticket upstairs. He placed the milk on the stainless counter next to the walk-in and turned to her.

"Excuse me, miss?"

She turned around startled.

"Oooh! You scared the pants off me! Who you callin' miss? I could easily be your grandmother!"

She gave him a belly laugh; her dyed red curls shook while she chuckled.

"What can I get you, doll, a signature or something?"

Nathaniel smiled, noticing the canvas laundry bags folded behind her.

"Yes. Can you sign off this shipment of milk for me?"

She wiped her hands on her apron and reached up to her hair net to look for the pen, usually poised behind her ear.

"Oh, dropped my pen. Hope it wasn't in the whites."

She looked at him and winked.

"I've done that you know." She giggled.

"I'll be right back...gotta grab a pen."

She shuffled off to the office, humming to herself. Nathaniel grabbed a canvas bag, a handful of soiled linens from her pile, and stuffed them in the bag. He put the invoice slip on the counter and snuck out the side door into the corridor.

Just as he predicted, laundry was down the stairs from the elevator. As soon as I heard the lady poke around looking for Nathaniel the dairy deliveryman, I strolled in, picked up Nathaniel's dropped in voice, and greeted her with a big smile.

"Where'd the young man go?"

I laughed. "You calling me old?"

She blushed. "No, no! I'm sorry, it's just that..."

"He's out in the truck. You can sign this for me, young lady." I winked at her from under my trucker hat, and she leaned over to sign giggling like a schoolgirl. I made her day. She stood up flustered and adjusted her red curls under the hairnet and smiled.

"What was your name?"

"I'm Gabe." She reached to shake my hand, and I bent over and kissed hers.

"Pleasure to make your acquaintance..."

"Emma." She beamed. "Emma, what a beautiful name! You have a good day now."

"And you too, Gabe."

She watched as I walked off, so I made her phone ring so she didn't notice that there wasn't a delivery truck. Mission accomplished.

* * *

In the interim, Nathaniel made his way into laundry. He found scrubs, tucked his hair into a disposable hair cap, and caught a glimpse of himself in a mirror on the way out. It was the first time that he looked like the doctor and not the patient. He smiled and whistled his way down the corridor toward the elevator. He reached down to make sure that he had the bundle of letters in his pocket and pushed sixth floor Intensive Care Unit.

His plan had originally been to simply walk through the ward confidently, snooping until he found the right room. But I foresaw major problems due to security. So, I intervened.

When he reached the Intensive Care Unit, he took a wrong turn and ended up in X-Ray. He was greeted by a young man with crooked Buddy Holly glasses, eating a microwaveable ramen noodle lunch. Between broth slurps, he gurgled, "Can I help you?"

Nathaniel thought fast. "Yes. Hi! How are you? Uh, I need to pick up the film for Ana Guidan, ICU." Nate cringed.

Buddy Holly ran his finger down a list. "Annnnna Guiiiiiida. Dr. Anjna Beri's care?"

Nate was ecstatic. "Yeah, yes, Dr. Beri."

He was sure that the guy wasn't supposed to reveal that nor did he even ask for any identification from Nate.

He walked off, grabbed the films, and slid them over the counter to Nate.

"Dude, have you seen that doctor yet? Dr. Beri, man?"

Nathaniel weighed out in his head whether he should say yes or no. "I'm not sure."

"Fucking hot, man. She's smokin'! Hot Indian chick...know what I mean?"

Nate laughed nervously, trying to walk off with the films, wondering how to nonchalantly ask for Ana's room number without seeming completely phony.

"Oh yeah? Hot?" He laughed while Buddy Holly kept on with a graphic description of Dr. Beri.

"Yeah, man, I was tempted to jump off the Seven Mile Bridge or something so that I could hurt myself real bad and request her services." He laughed and gulped the end of his soup.

"Thanks, man." Nathaniel held up the films and began to walk off when Buddy Holly chimed in.

"Oh, dude, you've got to sign those out first."

"Oh yeah, right, right."

Nathaniel walked over to the counter, and Buddy slid a clipboard over to him.

"Just initial there, dude." Nate stared at it trying to figure out what initials to write. He pointed again.

"Right there, dude."

"Oh yeah, sorry man."

Nate started to write AB, the doc's initials, but instead wrote AJ. He scribbled it out and wrote them again. AJ.

"What the hell?"

He tried again. AJ.

The guy just looked at him.

"Dude, are you a perfectionist or something? It looks fine, man." He snickered, adjusting his glasses.

Nate gave up and walked out with the films, half-expecting security to come and haul him out. But instead, while trying to gather the courage to walk into the ICU, he looked down at his feet for inspiration. Next to the water fountain was a gold tag. He reached down to pick it up. It was a doctor's ID: Aaron Joella, MD.

"Holy shit," he whispered, looked around and pinned it on himself; he was blown away.

Nate strolled into ICU virtually undetected until a portly nurse behind reception slowed his groove.

"Yes? Can I help you?"

Nate began to sweat.

"Oh yes, I'm Dr. Joella looking for Dr. Beri. She ordered these films."

The nurse placed her bifocals that rested on her shelf breast on the end of her nose and looked at Nathaniel's name tag. She studied him briefly, cleared her throat, and ran her finger down the page of a clipboard. "Berrrrriiiiiii, Beri, Beri she was just in room 115, but she signed out. Let me check the computer."

"Thank you."

Nate quickly scanned to look for room numbers while she punched the keys. And that's when I jumped in.

"Miss, miss?" I was a little old lady named Lena, complete with a walker, smudged glasses, tight white curls, and a huge, clueless grin.

The nurse looked up from the computer.

"I'll be right with you."

I chimed in very loudly.

"I'm sorry?" I tugged Nathaniel on the shoulder.

"What did she say, young man? I don't hear well."

Nate moved his face nearer to mine and spoke very slowly, "She said that she will be right with you."

"Oh, okay well that's fine but it's just that I—"

The nurse interrupted me. "I will be right with you."

She cleared her throat and sighed. So I had no choice. In order for Nathaniel to be able to go to Ana, I had to distract her 100 percent.

I farted loudly and peed through my trousers onto the tile floor, making quite a splash.

"Oh dear. It's just that I was trying to find a bathroom. I'm terribly sorry."

The nurse waddled out from behind the counter looking highly agitated.

"Excuse me doctor," she rolled her eyes.

"I'll be right with you."

"Right this way, please." She picked up the desk phone.

"Will a custodian please report to ICU, STAT?"

I chattered incessantly to the nurse while she struggled to get me into the bathroom.

"I'm sorry to bother you nurse, but could you please help me change? I keep a change of pants in my bag in the event of an emergency such as this I suppose." The nurse struggled to get my pants off.

In the meantime, Nate looked around at the silence. Just a few days had passed and already Ana's infamy had faded into recycling bin headlines; extra security was no longer necessary. It was such a quiet floor. The only sound came from hushed voices leaving loved one's bedsides and mechanical breathing coming from life sustaining machines. He peered into the office behind the desk. Not a soul. He grabbed the clipboard. "A. Guida—Room 115."

Nathaniel and Ana

November 1, 2000

The door clicked behind him, and Ana watched Nathaniel sneak in the room from above. She stared into his eyes, washed by the light from the window, and felt his heart soften as he approached her bedside. She wanted to see him through mother's eyes.

He took slow, deliberate steps as if he was afraid to wake her, whispering, "What the fuck am I doing? She's not going to wake, you ass." Ana looked beautiful to him, almost maternal regardless of tubes and the intravenous bloating. She was soft. He leaned over sheepishly.

"Well, I'm Nate. Nate, the guy who saved you."

He looked around starting to cry.

"Why am I crying?" A tear fell onto Ana's cheek. He watched it roll down her neck. He was afraid to touch her for fear of hurting her. He closed his eyes, lay his head on his folded arms, and wept.

"Why do I know you? I mean, I know you, Ana."

Ana's spirit touched his hair and his cheek.

"I just wanted to see you, to thank you. I read the letters."

His hand trembled while he pushed stray blond hair out of her eyelashes.

"I can empathize with you. But I'm still here. Won't you come back? If I can do it anyone can."

He put his face next to her ear.

"Are you listening to me?" He buried his eyes in his hands, peering at her.

"And I fucking hate this life."

Nate laughed and cried in the same breath.

"I just want to talk to you, Ana." He placed his hands on her shoulders and shook her.

"Do you hear me?" All the while, Ana's spirit caressed his hair like a child, trying to calm his nerves. He closed his eyes, kissed her hand, and touched her face.

"Please don't give up."

He cautiously leaned down to kiss her cheek and slid the bundle of letters under her blanket so that she would find them when she woke. And that's where I interfered, softly.

I had permission to lift the veil between their realities for a few, sweet moments. Then Ana's spirit closed her eyes and smiled. She wrapped her arms around Nate like a child. He shuddered at the invisible embrace and familiar scent of incense and rain. She let go of him confused by his reaction, and I whispered in her ear, "He can feel you, Ana."

Ana touched her ear, unable to see me.

Weightless, she rose above Nathaniel.

"You can touch him. Don't be afraid."

Nathaniel slowly looked over his shoulder toward the door, expecting to see security poised and ready to pounce with a straitjacket. He snapped his head back toward Ana, lying silent.

"Did you see that?" He felt a hand on his shoulder and froze. He slowly reached up and felt Ana's soft, unseen spirit hand. Speechless, he grasped it and brought it up to his cheek and let go. The hand stayed.

"Who are you?" He looked down at Ana, thinking that perhaps something was trying to protect her.

He whispered to the air, "I'm not going to hurt her."

Ana smiled at his quiet innocence; fear of the unknown evokes the hidden child in the hardest of souls. She finally understood.

She reached down, gently held both of his hands in hers, and stared into his blue-green eyes. He froze, staring at his hands awestruck.

I whispered in Ana's ear, "You can speak to him. He can't see you, Ana, but he can feel you and hear you, but just for a few moments."

Ana looked into him.

"Speak to him, Ana. He needs that."

I knew that I could only keep the veil lifted for a short amount of time.

Ana was mesmerized, slowly moving forward to rest her head on Nathaniel's shoulder. He melted, moving his face into her presence.

His eyes welled with tears.

"I can feel you. I feel you!" he whispered.

He felt soft hair on his cheek and could taste her scent. He reached his hand up to touch it and it fell through his fingers, invisible.

Ana turned her face, and he felt her breath on his ear.

"I…I'm your mother, Nathaniel."

"What?" Nathaniel's body shook. "Momma?"

Ana took him into her arms and held him as her own. He draped himself over her, sobbing into her neck and hair. He kept repeating, "Momma? I want to see you."

"Shhhhh. Uw Moeder is hier, Nathaniel. Ik houd van u, mijn kind (Your mother is here, Nathaniel. I love you, my child)." Ana held him so close.

"Please, Mama. I want to see you. Please!"

Ana closed her eyes.

"But you can feel me, mijn kind (my child)! I am here with you."

She placed her hand on his heart and wiped his tears with her other hand. He fell limp in her arms.

"Ik ben altijd hier met u (I am always here with you)."

I whispered in her ear, "Ana, you have to go soon."

She closed her eyes, took Nathaniel's head in her hands, and kissed his forehead.

"Nathaniel, you have to live. Go live! You have given me such a gift. Please, go live!"

I tapped Ana on the shoulder and pointed at the veil closing between them. She smacked my hand off her shoulder, choking back tears. Ana watched the veil close.

"Mijn Nathaniel…won't you let me see you smile?"

Nathaniel felt her slowly fall away, holding his arms out to her.

"No, Mama! Please don't go!" He collapsed onto the floor.

I pushed the panic button, and Nurse Sevigney looked up from her paperwork watching the light blink and beep.

"115?" She dropped her pencil, rushed to Ana's room, found Nathaniel on the floor, and Ana's quiet body untouched.

"What on God's green earth?"

She lifted her pants at the knee and crouched down next to Nate, reading his name tag.

"Dr. Joella?" She felt his pulse, and he jumped back into consciousness.

"Ahhhh!" He sat up and grabbed the bottom of the hospital bed. Nurse Sevigney fell back.

"Sweet Jesus!"

Nate gathered himself, realized the urgency of the situation, and helped Nurse Sevigney up. "Are you okay?"

She nodded, completely confused.

He touched her shoulder, touched Ana's face, and ran out.

"I've got to get to surgery." He rushed out, passed the front desk, and passed the nurse.

"Thank you." He dropped the pin next to the water fountain, took the freight elevator downstairs, and ran out of the loading dock unseen.

Meanwhile, Nurse Sevigney gathered herself, picked up the clipboard, and went back to her office. She sat down and slipped her pencil behind her ear.

"Directory." She entered Dr. Joella into the faculty directory and found his biography and photo. He was a bald, middle-aged biracial man. Indian, Caucasian, African American, perhaps Latino? She punched his name into another directory. No matches.

"Lord have mercy!"

She picked up the telephone. "Security, please report to ICU, STAT." She went back to room 115 and checked Ana's vitals. She was fine.

"Girl, I thought that I'd seen it all…but that was pretty weird."

She lifted Ana's head and fluffed her pillow.

"I think that I'm going to lock your door from now on."

She took a fresh blanket from the linen closet and lifted her old one, gently taking care not to disturb the life-sustaining tubes and needles. While fanning the fresh blanket, she saw a brown paper bag peeking out from beneath the sheet in her peripheral vision.

"What in Jesus's name now?" She pulled the sheet back exposing the bundle that Nate had left Ana. It was tucked neatly next to her hand.

She fingered through the letters: Mr. John Lennon, Mr. Jimi Hendrix, Ms. Janis Joplin, Nanny, Gram, Mother Fate…

"What in God's name?" She shook her head and bundled the letters together.

Nurse Sevigney wiped beads of sweat from her amber brow, hustled back to the office, and dropped the bundle of letters onto her desk.

"Where in hell is security?"

She picked up the phone to call them when I peeked in. "Excuse me?"

Nurse Sevigney put her hand in the air without looking at me, motioning to wait.

"Yes, this is Nurse Sevigney in ICU, and I called for security, STAT, at least fifteen minutes ago!"

I watched as the righteous Southern Baptist sister spirit crept up inside her veins into her shoulders and face. Her lips pursed and her posture straightened like a statuesque Nubian Queen cast in bronze. Nurse Sevigney revealed the goddess.

"I have been a nurse for a VERY LONG TIME, Mr. Whatever, and never have I witnessed such negligence in my career! Now, I suggest that you light a firecracker under their security asses and define STAT for them and spell it SLOWLY!"

She slammed the phone down, mumbling obscenities, took a deep breath, and looked at me, adjusting her glasses.

"I'm sorry, child. Can I help you?"

I was Sally, a mousy young girl with endearing blue eyes lined with far too much coal-black makeup. I spoke sheepishly, "Yeah, hi, uh, can you tell me where I can find help?"

She leered at me and raised an eyebrow. "What kind of help, dear?"

I stared blankly. "You know…help."

The nurse clasped her hands together on her desk. "Well, sweetie, I wish that you would be more specific."

Two security guards busted into her office, beeping and buzzing, muffled voices seeped from their pocket scanners.

"We're looking for a nurse"—he looked down at his clipboard— "Sev-ig-nigh?"

The nurse rolled her eyes.

"That's me. Excuse me, gentlemen, for one second. Sweetie, where are you trying to go?" I raised my frail arms exposing two bleeding, bandaged wrists. The nurse jumped up.

"Oh lord, take her to behavioral health, STAT!"

The guards looked confused.

"But we were ordered to—"

"I don't care what you were supposed to do! Behavioral Health, NOW!" She pushed a folded wheelchair toward them.

"Open this." They fumbled with it. She pushed them out of her way, opened the chair, and guided me into it.

"It's okay, honey." She barked at the men and her voice echoed in the corridor, "Now MOVE!" They fell all over each other.

"Jesus, Mary, and Joseph! To the top floor, gentlemen!"

They tripped down the hallway toward the elevator with me while the nurse called the behavioral health unit to alert them of my impending arrival.

When we arrived, I was rolled into the psychiatric nurse's emergency cubby to await admittance while they attempted to explain where I came from.

I found this the opportune time to disappear. And boy, were they surprised when the wheelchair was empty. I giggled from afar; like three blind mice, they ran amuck trying to retrace my steps.

* * *

Undoubtedly, shapeshifting, defying time, space, reason and gravity is by far my favorite job perk of work as an ethereal artist. Perfect.

And Nate? He was tucked neatly under the green blanket in Tom's Suburban still adorned in hospital scrubs. By the time the hospital staff gave up looking for the suicidal girl, Tom's blood pressure had settled below hypertension level and he was perched comfortably, donut in mouth, behind his desk.

* * *

Later, Nate lounged on his hammock with Chong. He purred and kneaded the hospital scrubs that Nate used as a pillow. Nate lay trying to absorb the surrealism of his morning, watching soft smoke rings disappear into the fuchsia bougainvillea.

"I did it, Chong!"

He stroked his back, imagining each letter a floating entity, creeping into each person's hands with eerily gentle harp-like precision, frightening them into seeking solace in the comfort of their own rooms, away from doors and telephones. The letters would unravel quietly at first, then slowly wake dormant ghosts and secrets. Ana's tale of falling down her own private rabbit hole would be revealed.

Gabriel and Ana

November 1, 2000

You have a choice, Ana."

I sat with her in the same meadow that we had been to before. Ana slumped, looking desperate like I had seen so many times before throughout her life. She smiled subtly but her vacant eyes seemed strangely content with disenchantment. It was a look that I was afraid of, but half-expected.

She toyed with a strand of wheat, the color of her hair, wrapping it around her finger like a noose.

"But I've done my job, Gabe. I've given Nate a reason."

"A reason for what, Ana?"

"I don't know, Gabe. A reason to live I guess. The void has been filled. He's going to be okay now. My job is complete."

She stared at me with the vague expression that passes over a person's eyes before believing a lie or before the onset of delusion.

I lost my patience; I couldn't help but mock her melancholy bullshit.

"'My job is complete'! How selfish, Ana…how selfish you are! What about OUR job, MY job, Ana? Is this all in vain?"

Ana sobbed. "Gabe, thank you! Thank you so much for all that you have done. You are remarkable! This is all so amazing, and now I know why I ended it! You justified it. It is clear to me now that I am more helpful in death than I was in life. This is where I am going to stay, Gabe, right here. Pull the plug. I've seen it all, and there is no more to see."

I stood, cleared my throat, and spread my wings. "Goodbye, Ana."

She lifted her green eyes to me, blinking away tears. "I'm sorry, Gabe, it's just—"

"Just nothing, Ana. You are a coward!"

I shook my head and lowered my eyes, vanishing into a cloud of cigarette smoke.

"I am hardly a coward!" Ana shouted into nothingness, sitting cross-legged on the grass, coddling Nathaniel's baby blanket.

"I'll be fine, Gabe."

She yelled into the vacant sky, half-expecting the miracle of my face to appear. She closed her eyes, counted to five slowly, and opened them. Nothing. It was the same meadow, green dress, baby blanket, but no Gabriel.

"Everything's cool." She forced a smile, lifting herself off the ground, brushing her dress. She turned in a circle and looked around at the rolling landscape. She kicked off her flip-flops and dug her feet into the soft ground.

"It's so beautiful here." She walked, feeling the strange wind on her face, pushing down the fear that crawled up her spine. In the distance, she saw a field of little red and white flowers sprinkled with purple. She ran toward them like a child, flailing Nathaniel's blanket behind her, closing her eyes and taking in the scent like springtime... her mother's perfume. She pushed down the memories that it magically evoked.

Black magic, she thought.

Tumbling into the field for a cat's eye view, she felt the flowers tickle her face and laughed into the sky. She lay trying to get a handle on the concept of freedom without the constraint of time when she heard the breathing. She rolled her face over and looked into Dr. Freedman's eyes staring up from the earth.

"Doc!" She reached her hand over toward him, and he was gone. She felt a crinkling beneath the grass where his face was, dug into the grass, and found a letter addressed to him. She looked around for me and caught a chill.

"Where are you?" She stood up, shaking the letter toward the sky. "Please, please don't do this to me, Gabe! I beg you!"

Clouds rolled in faster than Seattle fog followed by strong gusts of wind. Ana sat down and draped Nate's blanket around her shoulders.

"C'mon, Gabe, no more tricks." It started to snow.

"Ahhh, Jesus Christ, Gabe!"

She stumbled through the meadow, shivering and blinking away snowflakes, holding the letter in front of her eyes to shield them from the wind.

"What is this? Have I been condemned to this frozen hell because you're not happy with me or something? Is this hell, you bastard?"

The snow quickly accumulated around her flip-flops, making her slip and fall.

"Fuck it!" She took the flip-flops off, held them in one hand, and the letter in the other.

"Well, you blew it! I can't freeze to death, can I!"

She stubbed her toe.

"I'm already dead!"

"Not yet, remember?"

She stopped and whipped her head around toward my voice. "Gabe?"

I wasn't there, just in her mind. I was trying to orchestrate the moment, which was one of my most difficult challenges. Ana was too stubborn to pick up on the subtleties that made the moment easier for her to contend with.

"Gabe?"

She slipped, fell, got up brushing the snow off her and off the letter. The snow began to slow. She shook the letter, tried to remove the condensation, and the more she shook it, the warmer she felt.

"What the fuck?"

She continued to walk and the snow began to fall again, coating her hair with white crystals. She used the letter to brush away the snow and the snow slowed to a halt. She stopped and stood perfectly still. The snow began to fall fast again. She looked at the letter and shook it. The snow stopped.

"I'm like Mother Nature!"

She rubbed the letter and the clouds began to dissipate in the sky. The snow began to melt and she felt warmer.

There was a clearing on the ground where a patch of soft grass was revealed.

She jumped to it and sat down. She lay the letter down next to her. The clouds immediately started to roll in again and the temperature began to plummet.

"Okay, okay, I've got it, Gabe!"

She took the envelope addressed to Dr. Freedman and unfolded it. Her hands quivered when she read the introduction. Ana slapped the letter down and closed her eyes. An image unfolded in her mind's eye like the part in a silent family eight-millimeter that you almost cannot watch for fear of feeling.

"Stop it, Gabriel!" She knew what was coming next. Eyes open or closed, she couldn't avoid their reality.

Peg, Harry, Amber, and left Ana's room with Nurse Sevigney and were handed the bundle of letters that Nate had left with her. Ana saw it. It looked like the nurse was trying to explain how the letters just appeared. But the only one listening was Harry, who stood cross-legged staring off into nothingness with a perplexed brow. Amber, Jack, and Peg stood huddled, shuffling through the letters, shaking their heads in disillusion.

Ana watched as Amber and Peg both took the envelopes addressed to them and slid them into their bags. You could read Amber's lips and body language.

"I just can't read it now."

Amber motioned for a cup of coffee, wiping her eyes, as she and Peg walked arm and arm out of the office and down the corridor. Harry walked over to Ana, eyes welled, cocked his head, and touched her shoulder, rising and falling. He forced a crooked smile.

"We're going downstairs, Ana." He sighed.

Ana could read his lips.

Her dad turned to leave and stopped. He held on to the railing, closed his eyes, and shook uncontrollably. His knuckles whitened, tears escaped his closed eyes, rolling down his cheek..., disappearing into his white beard.

He leaned down so that he wouldn't be heard. "Was—" He choked. "Was it something we did?" He sobbed. "I'm so sorry, kiddo...so, so sorry if it was. Your mom and I never meant to hurt you. We tried...We didn't know you were so sad...so, so sad."

Peg came in and helped him up. "Oh, Harry...It's going to be..."

She dissolved into his shoulder. Ana felt every word.

Meanwhile, Amber sat on a bench outside of Key West Medical in the shade of a palm tree in a vain attempt to regain her composure, remembering Ana's letter in her purse. She unfolded the letter, pushed her auburn curls to the side and read reluctantly:

The Evening of April 13, 2000

Dear Amber,

A female customer referred to me as "well-adjusted for a bartender" today, and I thought of you. Because you would've countered that comment with something brave and perhaps callous yet intelligible whereas I quietly reproached and repeated her statement incessantly in my head. I tried to interpret it as many ways as possible, smiling and exchanging money for hand-pumped beer and booze all the while.

My final interpretation: her comment was meant to be demeaning. She may as well have said, "You're alright, for a girl."

She was so fucking shallow that I actually felt sympathy for her on some level. She felt that her lot in life entitled her to judge my character, aloud for the sake of somehow empowering herself and her dinner date through laughter...at the expense of me. I only wished that I would've had even an ounce of your assertiveness for just one sweet moment. Any that I have seems to evaporate into thin air when I am in the presence of obnoxious women. On the other hand, I have no problem telling men where to get off the bus.

That is something that I so admire about you, my beautiful big sister. Although you look at the world through rose-colored glasses, your jaded pink perception has made you intolerant of anything slightly off-color but not in a judgmental way. I love that about you. You are a protector and you speak your mind with true conviction and confidence in order to assure the best for those that you love and yourself. I am working toward acquiring your caliber of confidence as part of my therapy. Have you ever been shy?

I remember working at mom's store with you. You and I were behind the counter together sharing the holiday sale duties; you wrapped the order neatly, something I am incapable of, and I rang up the order. One lady tried to pull a fast one by handing me, the younger one, a faux receipt, trying to return something that she hadn't purchased for money.

I stared at the incorrect receipt, fumbled over how to broach the subject with the woman, thinking about how desperate she must have been financially to try this silly stunt, and you simply snatched the receipt out of my hand and said, "I'm sorry miss, but we cannot honor this receipt," proceeding to take the stolen goods from her hand. I stared…completely blown away by your unabashed assertiveness. She tried to argue but you simply knocked her down off her pedestal with your brilliant public relations skills. She backed down, defeated, and walked out of the store with her tail between her legs. You simply turned to me.

"The nerve of her. Did you see her diamonds? She's obviously loaded."

And then that rainy day in March when I called you, right after I had started taking Lithium, and I simply wanted to talk but broke down into tears, confessing that I just made myself throw up for a good hour.

"Why?" you pleaded.

"I don't know," I confessed, unable to make sense of anything, tired from the physical strain of purging.

"You've got to stop this," you said, as if I were making childish decisions and needed to be reprimanded. But I understood your manner of speaking, and I am thankful for it. I was at a complete loss and needed to be spoken to like a lost child. That is how I felt. You calmed me down and told me to take a nap but to keep the phone nearby. Unbeknownst to me, you called Dr. Freedman and explained my weird behavior to him. He was emphatic that if I was going to continue this behavior it could cost me my life. Lithium doesn't mix with purging. It's salt and changes the chemistry affecting the level of electrolytes.

You scared the shit out of me. Your melodrama worked, Amber—good work. Your "take the bull by the horns" approach single-handedly cured me of bulimia. I haven't succumbed since. Well, not really. Thank you. You make it seem okay for me to color inside of the lines on occasion.

I love you—Ana

Amber put the letter against her forehead and cried.

* * *

"Enough! Enough, Gabe!"
"Forget it, Ana. In order to truly see, you must feel the truth."
"This is too much, Gabe, too much."
Ana curled into the fetal position on the patch of grass, coddling Nate's baby blanket and closed her eyes...wishing away everything.

Sadie

November 1, 2000

When Ana opened her eyes again, she was in the far corner of a stark apartment in low natural light. There were half-completed paintings on easels and cotton rags on the floor. It smelled like New York downtown: oil paint, exhaust, fried food, and salt air. Ana liked it. She peeked through some sort of chink in the wall, not quite aware of her size. Her head moved in quick jerking motions from left to right, and she reached up to itch her twitching nose on the verge of a sneeze. She used a weird, brisk punching motion; it felt like onion grass had sprouted from the side of her face.

"Whiskers."

Ana looked down at her tiny, round white belly and pink feet.

"A rat, Gabe?"

"A cute one. It's a propos, I think."

I whispered into her left ear, and she looked, only to see a cockroach scurrying off into a dark corner. And then she heard it.

"Hi, um, I'm trying to reach an inpatient. Or at least I think he's still an inpatient. Maybe not…Nathaniel Flowers? My name is Sadie. Yes, Flowers. Is he still there? Well, do you know where I could find him? I understand the privacy act. And yes, I know the liability issue, but I think that you may know me, too. I was an inpatient along with Nathaniel. Sadie Bartholomew. Yes. I'm aware of that. I know that I didn't finish my term, but I'm clean and sober. Why am I telling you this? I don't owe you anything. LOOK…I simply called to find my friend. Do you know where he is? Thank you. I'll hold."

Ana watched as Sadie leaned back in her chair, folded her legs beneath her, and stared at a photo on her wall. She and Nate were cuddled together on a barred window seat, light pouring in behind them, washing out the angst on their faces. She brushed her black hair away from her pale blue eyes and leaned over to pick up her coffee from a makeshift desk.

"Yes. Wait, let me grab a pencil. What do you mean you can't find his address? Well…what about his family? Can I call them? I TRIED to get their phone number! Unlisted. Please, if this is a confidentiality issue, I PROMISE that I will not share the information with anyone. PLEASE!"

Sadie slammed her coffee onto the desk, knocking the table top off the wooden horses and shattering the mug. She jumped up to wipe the hot coffee off her lap.

"Shit! No, no, I'm not talking to you. I spilled coffee all over myself. Alright, I'm calming down, just, please I beg you! But isn't there any way to find out where he is? Thanks for your time."

Sadie smacked her head with the cordless phone and folded into a ball, screaming into her lap. She looked up at the photo and cried.

"Why not?" She threw the phone at the wall and watched it smash into pieces and fall to the floor.

"I'm so sorry I left you there, Nate…so, so sorry."

Ana twitched her whiskers and peeked around the corner to take a closer look, trying to speak.

"It's okay, Sadie. Nate is fine."

Sadie turned to look toward a small squeaking noise coming from the chink in the wall, wiping tears away from her face; her long black hair matted with sleep. I got a charge out of Ana's squeak. She turned to my voice and attempted to speak, "Shut the hell up, Gabe," but all that passed through her yellowed buck teeth was "eek ek ik sek, ak." It was amusing…to me.

Sadie turned toward Ana and smiled in amazement.

"Awww! Hello, sweetie! Don't be afraid."

She walked over to the refrigerator and opened it. It was bare except for a can of coffee and a package of processed cheese slices. She opened a slice of cheese and looked over toward Ana sitting on her hind legs, itching her nose.

"You are so cute."

She slowly walked over leaned down and gave her some cheese.

"Thank you."

Ana squeaked then nibbled.

Sadie laughed.

"You're so adorable, little mousie."

She slowly moved her hand toward Ana to touch her. Ana felt her shaking hand stroke her head while she nibbled.

"Hi, little friend."

Sadie smiled, her blue eyes glazed with tears. Her nose was painted with peppered sunlight.

"Are you my little friend?"

She smiled and cocked her head.

"Are you trying to talk to me? Huh?"

I whispered into her ear before she became too comfortable, "Ana, finish your cheese. It's time to go back to your hole."

"I kind of like being a mouse, Gabe."

"A rat, Ana."

"Whatever."

Sadie sat back and clapped her hands. "Your squeak is so sweet, little mouse."

Ana nibbled the last of the cheese.

"Do you want some more, little mouse?" She got up and went to the bare fridge to grab another cheese slice, and Ana scrambled back through the hole in the wall.

Sadie turned around unwrapping the cellophane.

"Oh, where did you go, little friend?" She tiptoed around looking under paint rags, in boxes, in piles of clothing, behind the bathroom door. She walked over to the hole in the wall and kneeled down trying to peek in. Ana watched her blue eyes' vain search. Sadie leaned back from the hole, shredded the cheese into little pieces, and gingerly reached her fingers into the chink, poking Ana in the eye.

Ana woke with a start on the patch of grass holding onto the baby blanket.

"Sadie Blue Eyes. Will Nate ever see her again?"

"Ana, I've got it all taken care of."

I sat back, lit a smoke, and watched her face begin to soften. "You know, 'chance' encounters are commonplace, Ana, but second chances are only given to those who haven't given up on hope."

Nathaniel and Gabriel

November 2, 2000
Early Morning

Nathaniel woke with a start, shivering on the hammock; the palms and bougainvillea were swaying all around him in the salt air. It was pitch-black except for a few stars peeking through salt air clouds.

"Brrr…What time is it?" Nate looked around at the sky and reached for the scrubs that he used as a pillow, putting them on and running into his shack.

"Chong?" He shook the cat food bag. He came out from under the bed, stretching.

Nate was groggy, so I had to be crafty in order to make him recall what he had just dreamed about.

"Hungry, pal?" He poured food, missing the bowl.

"Shit." He kneeled down to scoop the food back into the bowl and noticed a pack of smokes underneath the ledge of the counter.

"Oooh!" He reached under. Empty. He tossed them into the garbage noticing something on the back. He bent down to stare at the image of Sadie and himself cuddled together in front of the barred window in rehab. Nate picked it up and stared at it remembering what he had just dreamed about. Sadie sat on a ledge overlooking a quiet city street, her long, raven hair blowing against her cheek, tossing bread to pigeons below. A willowy, blond woman strolled by hailing a cab. It was Ana. She stood beneath a street sign: Mulberry and Spring. The taxi pulled away then screeched to a halt.

"Hold on! I'll be right back. I forgot to do something." Ana ran to the building that Sadie sat on top of and dropped a letter into the mail drop addressed to:

Sadie Bartholomew
52 Spring Street, Apartment 2 New York, NY 10012

"Oh my god!"

Nate ran to pick up his journal, scrambling for a pen.

"Don't forget, asshole. Don't forget! 52 Spring Street Mulberry Street something. New York. Definitely New York." He scribbled it down, closed the book, and walked onto the porch to have a smoke. He leaned back, exhaled, and stared up to the sky watching a blinking plane soar far beyond sound's reach. For the first time in a very long time, he felt butterflies in his stomach.

He ran inside and stuffed all of his worldly possessions into Ana's backpack: toothbrush, wallet, T-shirt, shorts, and flip-flops. He blew the sand off his duffle bag, cut some small holes into it, and stuffed Chong's food and water bowl into the front pocket. He lined the bag with the scrubs and slipped into a pair of sneakers and a sweatshirt that were collecting dust on the floor. After folding the blankets and placing them on his bed, he sat down to compose a letter.

Dear Tom
 Before you start
swearing and cursing
because I am not here
just know that you will
not be blamed for my
leaving. I snuck away in
the middle of the night;
no Tom I am not on a key
west binger. I am simply
starting anew. It is time
... but no worries, mate. I
will leave a phone message for
Mort and Bess explaining my
decision and emphasizing
that you had nothing to do with it.
I promise. Take a deep breath...
Breeeeeaaaaaaathe, deep
breathe now, drink my coffee
for me, and give Sarah my love
and thanks, too. You've been a
real friend to me Tom.
 Thank you. I'll be seeing you
                Nate.

Nate picked up Chong, hugged him, and gingerly placed him in the duffel bag much to Chong's chagrin.

"You'll be fine, buddy, I promise. Shhhhh…You have to be quiet. We are going on a journey. Shhhhh…It's okay, buddy."

Nate zipped the bag enough so that Chong couldn't wiggle his way out but enough that he could fit his hand in to pet him. He turned around, pushed his smokes into his pocket, switched off the light, blew a kiss, and headed down the path toward the Overseas Highway.

"Thank you, Ana."

* * *

I knew that it wouldn't be impossible but highly unlikely, even in the Florida Keys, for anyone to pick up a young male hitchhiker with dreadlocks, a backpack, and a lumpy duffle bag wandering along the Overseas Highway in the darkness of early morning. The scenario is simply too close to the premise of any episode of *Unsolved Mysteries*. So I assumed the identity of Ruthie the truck driver, a feisty redhead with a pirate smile and a Dolly Parton figure. My rig was just as hot: Yosemite Sam "Back Off" mud flaps, an airbrushed "Foxy Grandma" insignia across the hood, and a "Sexy Senior Citizen" bumper plate.

I had a CB, pictures of grandchildren pasted along the roof of my cab, bumper stickers from all over the world, and a collection of self-sticking bobbleheads lining my dashboard. And my favorite cab accessory was a proud set of pink plastic handcuffs with "What Happens in Vegas, Stays in Vegas" etched into them. They hung from the ceiling where I was sure they would garner extensive beeps from passersby.

I pulled over when I saw him and put on my hazards. Nate started to run with Chong in the duffle bag, then picked it up, and held it tight.

"Sorry, buddy."

I opened the passenger-side door. "Where you headed, kiddo?"

Nate was exasperated.

"Hi, uh, thanks so much for stopping. I need to find my way to an airport, bus station, train, or something. I'm heading to New York." Nate smiled at the new sound of hope, even confidence in his voice.

I leaned over adjusting my bra straps. "New York? Well hell, young man, you've got a lot of miles to cover." I looked at him suspiciously for legitimacy's sake. "Wait a minute, what's in the bag?"

Nate paused.

"I'm not going to lie to you. It's my cat, Chong, and he's scared shitless. He's never been off the island."

"Awwww, poor little baby. I love kitty cats. Climb on in here, young man. And let that poor cat out of the bag. Hah!"

I laughed at my own pun. I reached in the back retrieving a sack of cat litter.

"Well, I'll be damned! I've got a bag of kitty shitty back here from when I had my little pussy willow on the road with me."

I poured the litter into a cake pan on the floor next to the sleeper. "My poor pussy is no longer." Nate fought back the giggle with a cough. I reached into one of the many glove compartments and pulled out a value package of Magic Trees, bubblegum scented. Chong immediately ran into the back and started to scratch in the litter, kicking it all over the floor.

"C'mon, Chong, keep it in the box please?"

I bellowed. "He really is scared shitless, ain't he?"

Nate struggled to open one of the Magic Trees and waved it frantically around the cab. "I'm so sorry."

I laughed and adjusted my mirrors. "That's nothing, baby, don't you worry." I smiled and winked at him. "My name is Ruthie." I motioned toward the makeshift cat box. "Now I know that you're Chong, but who's your daddy?"

Nate fumbled to find a place to hang the Magic Tree noticing the pink handcuffs. "I'm sorry. I'm Nathaniel. Thank you so much for stopping for us. I had my doubts that I would be picked upon the side of the road in the middle of the night."

"Oh, honey, I could tell from a mile away that you were a good boy. I've been around a long, long time." I looked at Nate and smiled knowingly. "And I just happen to be heading through Miami on my way north. Do you want to go to the airport, honey?"

Nate settled into his seat. "Yes. I think that the airport would be the best bet."

I pulled onto the highway, pulling a smoke out of my gingham shirt pocket, stretched too tightly across my weathered bosom. When I reached for my lighter, I popped a button, and it landed on Nate's lap.

He pushed his hair off his face and reached over to hand me the button, noticed my gaping blouse and blushed.

"Oops."

I laughed. "I guess that I've outgrown this blouse. What do you think?" I lit my smoke. "Oh, mind if I smoke?"

"No, no, in fact, I'm glad that you smoke. I mean I'm not glad that you smoke, but I smoke and I've been itching for one."

He reached into his pocket. "Do you mind, Ruthie?"

I flashed him a look.

"Thanks. We smokers are a dying breed you know."

"Hah!" I leaned over and smacked his knee. "You're cute all right. So, are you going to see family, or are you running away from the law?"

Nate smiled. "This time I'm not actually running away from anything."

"Well, she must be awful pretty." I shot Nate a knowing look.

"Who?" He wasn't sure how to respond.

"Well, Jesus Christ, darlin', if a young, good-lookin' man ain't running from the law in the middle of the night then he is surely following his heart." I looked at him and snuffed my cigarette out in the ashtray. "Feels good to follow your heart, don't it?"

Nate leaned back and closed his eyes. Chong jumped into his lap, looking surprisingly calm. "Better than I could have ever imagined."

I leaned over and switched on the radio. "The only thing that comes in down here until we get closer to Miami is this station. I think its Sunny 100 Soft Rock, something like that. Ooooh I love this tune! 'Woke up it was a Chelsea morning and the first thing that I...doo...dod do do o do dadoo doo dododo da de dedadoo.' Ahhh, Joan Baez?"

"Joni Mitchell, actually," Nathaniel quickly corrected her.

"I know, I know. Just seeing if you're a hip cat like old Grandma Ruthie over here. How do you know the difference between Joni Mitchell and Joan Baez, huh? You're too young!"

"Ahhh!" Nate kept his eyes closed in exhaustion and laughed. "To this day, I still fantasize about the first time Joni and I kissed."

"You're pulling my leg!" I cackled and slapped his knee. "Get out of town on a fast train, kid!"

"Well, it was more like I kissed her cardboard image on the front of the *Blue* album. She kind of kissed back. My six-year-old imagination helped matters. She was tucked in some uncle's album collection between David Bowie's *Ziggy Stardust* and Johnny Cash's *Live at Folsom Prison*. That record player was my sanctuary...how I avoided shitty conversation with my phony super-tanned aunts and such."

I chimed in, "Now I know Johnny Cash, but I'm not real familiar with David Bowie. I just know that one catchy tune, 'Little Chinese Girl.'"

Nate cracked up, scaring Chong into the back of the cab. "For future reference, it's actually called 'Little China girl,' not Chinese girl."

"Oh, don't be so fresh! Chinese, China...What the hell's the difference!" I looked over at Nate. His eyes were heavy, and he began to slump in his seat.

"I'm sorry, Ruthie. I'm so tired all of a sudden."

"Don't be silly. Take a nap. You have a very long journey ahead of you, child. It'll be a good one. I know it."

Nate smiled. "Thanks so much, Ruthie."

I watched him fade into slumber, knowing that he could take the Sun Air red-eye to JFK at 6:15 a.m. I got him there in plenty of time. I pulled into Sun Air departure zone at 4:58 a.m. and woke him up by lighting a smoke for him. He yawned, stretched, and looked around bleary-eyed, taking the smoke from me.

"Thank you, Ruthie." He looked around. "Sun Air?"

"Yes, doll. While you slept, I did a bit of research. There's a 6:15 direct flight to JFK Airport. From there, you can take a cab, bus, whatever, to wherever you may be going. Does that work for you?"

Nate looked at me in awe. "Well, yeah! That's great, Ruthie. Thank you so much." He fumbled around the cab searching for Chong.

"Oh, honey, I forgot I had a carrier from my late great pussy." I pointed to a carrier next to the cat litter. Chong was peeking out. "My pussy used to snuggle in there for hours. You can have it, Nate.

You'll need it to fly with him. Easier than a duffle bag to lug around, you know?"

Nate fought away laughter. "Ruthie, how can I repay you for all of this?"

"Nonsense. Go find what you are looking for and take good care of her." I turned to Nate and winked. "Now get going. I've got places to go, kid."

Nate strapped on Ana's backpack, grabbed Chong, and started to climb from the cab. He got out, inhaled the exhaust-filled early morning air, and grinned, staring into the Sun Air terminal.

"Get going. I can automatically shut the door from over here... newfangled security device."

"Thank you so much, Ruthie." He started to turn toward the entrance, then turned and ran back to the truck and knocked on the door while I pulled away. I rolled down the window, and he stopped dead in his tracks. "Dear Prudence" was playing on my radio.

"What is it, dear? I've got to get this rig out of here." Nate stood, listening. "Her name is Sadie."

"Well, get the hell out of here and go get her!"

Nathaniel

November 2, 2000
Morning
Day Four

"Spring and Mulberry, 52 Spring Street, Apartment 2." Nathaniel hopped into a cab outside of Port Authority Bus Terminal oblivious to the fact that someone else was in line ahead of him for the same cab.

"Hey! What the hell is your problem?" Nate simply smiled at the woman flailing her arms at him. He leaned down and talked to

Chong in the crate. "You like New York, buddy?" Chong looked shell-shocked. "We're almost there, Chong."

The cabby kept looking in the rearview mirror suspiciously.

Nate leaned forward. "I'm talking to my cat, dude." The driver only acknowledged him with a partial nod and eye contact. Cross town traffic was intense, but Nate didn't mind. He rolled down his window and rested his head on the frame, fascinated by all of the people, wandering in packs, headsets and briefcases intact, talking to someone on the other line, but to no one in close proximity. It had been awhile since he had been in the northeast during an early November rush.

The closer Nate got to downtown, the more his stomached flip-flopped. He had quit the what-ifs hours ago and was prepared for anything except Sadie not being there. And the dream having been wishful thinking. But either way, sober New York City seemed like a great new place to hang his hat. He knew in his soul that Ana was giving him a second chance.

He had tunnel vision when he fumbled to open his wallet outside of 52 Spring Street. He didn't even hear the cabdriver tell him how much he owed and simply handed him a fifty-dollar bill.

"Thank you. No change."

The walk to the front stoop felt like eternity. It was exactly like the dream. He stared at two door buzzers: S. B. Apartment 2. He closed his eyes, gritted his teeth, and pushed the button. No answer. He pushed it again. No answer. He hit the buzzer what seemed like twenty more times and his heart sunk to his knees. He looked down the block toward a coffee shop and started toward it. His legs felt like rubber, and his eyes began to well up.

Just then, he heard the creak of the front door of 52 Spring Street.

"Hello?"

He turned and stared into Sadie's sleepy blue eyes, speechless.

Briar and Jesse

November 2, 2000
Morning
Day Four

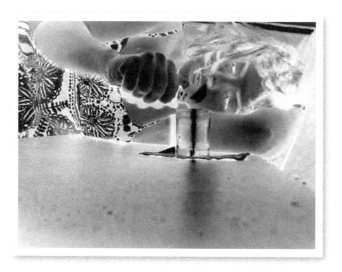

Inside 124 Apartment 4C, Twenty-Eighth Street, New York, New York, Cal closed the door, leaned down, played with Pup, and dropped his stuff on the table. "Bri?"

Briar sauntered up the stairs with a toothbrush in his hand. "Hey! How was your run? I'm sorry. I just couldn't do it again. God, I feel like such a pig. I have to start working out." He looked at his perfectly trim stomach and shrugged. "We are going to be late, not that I care. I have a car coming for us at 11:30 a.m. The wedding starts at 1:00 p.m., right?" Briar flitted about searching for a bottle of wine. "I know that I had a bottle of wine for them. Have you seen their gift?" He found a package from Tiffany's.

"Is it too early for a cocktail? Oh god, I hate going to these things. I mean, who gets married on a Friday?"

"At least it's on the beach." Cal fingered through the mail, staring at a strange bundle addressed to Briar and handed it to him.

Briar looked at the bundle and opened it, paging through the contents. "What the hell? Oh no, Ana," he said it quietly to himself while Cal fussed with a bottle of champagne for mimosas and talked about a new client. Briar slowly moved toward the sofa, Pup in tow, and fell into it. Cal's voice disappeared into his background.

March 3, 2000

Realization

Dear Briar,

I have a whole lot of time to think but I don't mind. And when I don't want to think, I read. I read a lot. I actually cradle my books like I used to covet cigarettes. It's weird but I'm learning I guess. I wonder if the psycho meds are altering my brain so much that I am actually retaining everything in some other portion of my head. Perhaps they have inadvertently made space for my newly found perception of old files. I don't know, but I do know that many of the books that I am rereading for the sake of not thinking are having a profound effect. I have a new understanding I think. For instance, Sylvia Plath so eloquently referred to it as living within the vacuum of a bell jar. I used to think that being bipolar was much more violent than that. My depression was more torrential, less predictable. I would do outlandishly generous things one minute and would spiral into tears within a day, drowning my confusion with wine or Guinness or pot or whatever was available. Definitely pills. My mother must have wondered what happened to her supply of Xanax. They were my solace…washed down with red wine. And then I would wake, function, and start the cycle all over again. The worst was if I didn't have any drugs at my disposal. Then food became my tool and my comfort followed by the same pattern of complete elation, then a vicious downward spiral within a day. I would sink to seclusion, tears, anger, food followed by guilt, then hours of puking. Psychedelic yawn. Tossing my cookies. However, you would like to refer to it. It was painful and gratifying in tandem. Sick. Depression was torture; underneath my guise of happiness, my soul screamed and choked for air.

But now I understand the bell jar. Lithium is a vacuum. I smile but I feel nothing. It's like I am in a vortex of my life and the film called my reality dances across the screen surrounding me. I can see love, hate, fear, sex, passion, longing, truth, and touch slowly move down through my film credits, illuminated by the red sunrise and the setting brilliant moon; I can appreciate it like a painting, but I can't feel it like music. I am in the jar.

XO Ana

Cal, still speaking, walked in to hand Bri a mimosa; he was engrossed. "What is it?"

Briar looked up. "They are letters from Ana."

"Ana?" Cal reached out to hand Bri the cocktail. "I'm confused."

"Me, too." Brian fluffed the pillow behind him and sipped on the cocktail. "Thank you."

"We have to get ready, Bri."

"I know, I know, it's just—go ahead down and get showered. I'll be down in a few."

Cal finished his mimosa and leaned down to kiss Briar's forehead. "Okay."

March 12, 2000

Unjust

Dear Briar,

Did you see the film *Before Night Falls* about Cuban writer and revolutionary Reinaldo Arenas? It is filmed in a sensual, watery light that capture Arenas' memoirs in Cuba. It's like a journal of images, documenting his childhood in lush, green Cuba, his young, gay experiences in adolescence, his hedonistic life in Havana as a revolutionary, writer, and lover and his jailing, which eventually led to his suicide in New York. It is so sad. He was persecuted for being homosexual and expressing himself through art. He was a lover, a poet, a dreamer, and a giver. He gave himself selflessly to others and shared his writing and his passion for the beautiful. He lived and suffered the consequences of the other half; the rigid people, unable to attempt to understand that he was only human. Homosexuality is not a conscious choice, it is an innate sexual preference and it is a goddamn shame that people are judged by what sex he/she is sleeping with. Perhaps society ought to take a look at mental exercise for some wisdom; those of us who stretch and are flexible are strong people whereas those of us who are stagnant are rigid and weak.

My question is how do the stagnant, inflexible, and weak people still have so much clout? This isn't a political issue either; this is humanitarian and universal. We need a new consciousness so the negative in history will stop repeating itself.

When I think of the emotional struggle and the lies that you have had to hide beneath just to function before you felt safe being gay, it breaks my heart. Why should you have to be ashamed of who you love? I wrote you a poem a long time ago; around the time when you were ducking into the Chelsea shadows in secret trying to conceal what you thought would break your dying mother's heart:

> The city breathes outside white walls,
> July ceiling fan whirs,
> drowning out noise in your tired mind,
> you lie with him in soft sheets,
> admiring his sleeping face,
> wishing you could take him
> home for the weekend,
> like a prom date,
> or that beautiful girl in college
> who you promised the world to,
> and your brother announced, "She's sexy,"
> after one too many cocktails;
> you felt so much shame
> every time she rolled over,
> kissed you, and whispered,
> "I love you," and fell to
> silent slumber while you watched,
> wished for something else and
> felt unsafe.

Love, Ana

While Briar closed his eyes and held the letters against his heart, 150 miles away, in Northeastern Pennsylvania, Jesse leaned into her cabinet to put away a wineglass, the last of a dishwasher load, when she was startled by her husband Marc wrapping his arms around her waist.

"Got you!" He leaned down and kissed her.

"You scared me!" Jesse spun around and rested against the kitchen counter.

"I have to get to work. Do you need me to pick anything up at the store on the way home tonight?"

"A four pack of Guinness." She wiped her hands on a towel and leaned over to give him a kiss. "Be careful."

He grabbed the keys, smacked her bottom, and headed toward the garage. "Oh, there was a big package for you in the mail. It's on the table. Have you been shopping again?" He smiled, and the door shut behind him.

Jesse listened to the car back down the driveway, then poured a coffee, and opened the refrigerator—no milk.

"Shit."

She rifled through the freezer and found a freezer-burned pint of Ben and Jerry's chocolate chip cookie dough, spooned out a dollop into the coffee, and sunk into the oversized chair, switched on NBC's *Today with Matt Laeur and Katie Couric*, and sipped her coffee. Out of her peripheral, she saw the package on the kitchen table and strolled over to "What is this—Florida Keys?" She refilled her coffee, wrapped into her nana's afghan, sunk back into the chair, and peeled into the package.

February 19, 2000

Dear Jesse,

I wish that I could call you and tell you about this. I know that you've heard it all from a third-person perspective. I wish my stupid hand could pick up the fucking phone and my crazy head wouldn't get in the way. So I'll write. The crash test dummy crusades continue. I stopped taking Abilify about two weeks ago. I lost my "Abilify" to see as a result of that phenomenal medicine. And the crash test dummy has been tossed into a pit of despair. It's dark. It sucks. I am more and more reclusive, desperate for sleep. I ignore all phone calls. Even from males. I have been hiding out at my parent's house, completely paranoid that someone, somewhere may attempt to strike up a conversation with me. I just sleep on their couch, afraid to be alone, afraid to be with people. I even lost my passion for the outdoors. Maybe because of winter. I pray that it is because of winter. I wish that I could hear your sweet voice.

Love, Ana

"Oh my god!" Jesse gulped her remaining coffee and pulled out another letter.

The Evening of March 18, 2000

Third Eye

Dear Jesse,

Although it pains me that I am not making money while I am sifting through all of this chemical garbage, there is something profoundly important about quiet observation; I am beginning to see things again. I'm noticing things that you don't notice when you're preoccupied with life stuff. I'm concentrating on the sound of Sherman's soothing Labrador snore; I trace his sleeping face when he naps. I noticed that my mother's Christmas cactus is sprouting brilliant fuchsia blooms; a sure sign of spring. I notice the child light in my father's sixty-year-old eyes and my mother's beautiful profile. I've rekindled my passion for *Handel's Messiah* and I've rediscovered Brit Pop and Mozart's *Twinkle, Twinkle Little Star*. I hear the symphony in silence again.

I noticed that my sister's face grows even more beautiful with age, and I accept that she is lucky. If I could paint her, her husband Colin, and her beautiful children, it would be an autumn scene in a sunlit pumpkin patch. Like a close-up photograph that I love of three-year-old blue-eyed Elijah sitting in a pile of autumn leaves, smiling. His hair was just wisps of white blond. He looked so proud that his dad was taking his photo. Elijah and Jane would be preserved forever as they are; beautiful young children, full of joy, life, fun, and laughter. I just don't want them to ever feel any of this pain, just happiness. Dr. Seuss said it best in *I Can Read With My Eyes Shut*: "Young cat! If you keep your eyes open enough, oh, the stuff you will learn! The most wonderful stuff!"

"There are so many things you can learn about, BUT you'll miss the best things if you keep your eyes shut."

Love, Ana

"Ana." Jesse's tears fell onto the pile of letters. She pushed her blond hair away from her eyes and continued reading the rest of Ana's words.

And tucked neatly into a leather sofa with Pup in Manhattan, Briar continued to read:

March 18, 2000

Vision

Dear Briar,

Okay. This may seem really far out to you, and no, it is not some drug-induced delusion that I had. I think you may enjoy this. Have you ever pondered why you and I have always loved each other so much but never consummated our love? We certainly have had more than enough opportunities, but it never happened regardless of how randy we were in teenage years. Well, this may be of some interest to you, Bri. Enjoy it for what it's worth even though you don't believe in reincarnation.

Last year, I met this wonderful channeler who I befriended. She specializes in reading past lives among other things. She is a remarkable woman. Anyway, after our first session, I started having lucid dreams about being beheaded. In the dream, I was looking out over the country-side through a gothic-shaped stone window, and I was wearing very ornate rings on my hands.

I couldn't see my body, but my hands were very pale and small, almost childlike. Then in my dream I felt intense fear then I was beheaded, and I heard a puppy whimper.

When I had a second session, without sharing my dreams with her, she channeled a past life that I am somehow rectifying in this life. She told me that I had been Mary Queen of Scots. I'm not sure if you know anything about her, but she lived a very dark life. She was born to Mary Guise and James V of Scotland and he died the same year. She was crowned Queen of Scots before she was one years old. She was married for the first time at the age of 15 and her teenage husband died a few years later. He was the love of her life. Then she married a man who died not long after, then married another man, her cousin, and gave birth to James VI, her only son. Because of her Catholic faith, she was imprisoned and had to leave James behind; it almost killed her emotionally. Her third husband died while she was in prison.

Carole (the clairvoyant) told me that a platonic love I have in this lifetime is my son, James, reincarnate. Mary and James had an incredible connection; she fled to keep him safe from the Catholic/Protestant struggle. After years of imprisonment, Mary was found guilty of plotting Queen Elizabeth's murder; she was sentenced to execution by public beheading. Mary was relieved; she wanted to be free of persecution and imprisonment. As a devout Catholic, she would die a martyr.

On the day of her execution, she entered the courtyard smiling and cordial. When her ladies-in-waiting wept and disrobed her, she made a joke. She said, "That she never had such grooms to make her unready and that she never put off her clothes before such a company." Story has it that she kneeled down and placed her head on the execution block without faltering, with no sign of fear. The executioner hit her neck twice and grabbed Mary's head off the ground to show the crowd; everyone gasped! Her mouth continued to say the Latin prayers that she recited before her execution and her head fell out of his hand onto the dirt ground. Although she was only approximately 44 years old, her hair had grown completely white and she had worn an auburn wig to conceal it. He was still holding the wig, while her white hair framed a young, praying face lying on the ground.

So here's the clincher, Bri. Mary had a puppy that she had trained to stay beneath her skirt to protect it from the prison guards. When she was beheaded, the puppy began to cry and the bereaved ladies in waiting went over to her clothes that they had taken off of her and the puppy was cowering underneath. When they tried to pick it up, it ran over to Mary's body and lay down between her shoulder and her head on the ground for hours, soaking her blood until it finally allowed the ladies to pick it up to bathe it.

Her son James VI became the king of Scotland. Later, when Queen Elizabeth died, he became James I of England. He was historically the first guy to become king of both Scotland and England and he never married. You may be asking, "Why the history lesson?" Well, Briar, let me ask you this: Do you ever have dreams about being a king with two crowns?

Love, Mary

* * *

March 21, 2000

Weary

Dear Briar,

Happy spring! The first real day. I welcome it with open arms and a pineal gland in need of some serious sunshine. Apparently if you stare at the sun with your eyes closed for at least 15 minutes a day, it is supposed to generate mad amounts of vitamin D, serotonin, and all of that jazz. I remember one day sitting outside of the high school that I worked at, eating lunch in the sun and a fellow English teacher, an intuitive eccentric, read my mood through the cafeteria window and came out to share her sun theory with me. She told me to kneel down with my back toward the sun, brush my hair to the side, and allow the sun the bake the back of my neck for a few minutes. She said that there was a "sensor" that if saturated with sunshine helps to remedy a sour mood.

The two of us must have looked like ancient Mayans, bent down in a worshiping position, exposing the soft underbelly of our necks to the sun. All I know is that I felt much better after my "prayer" session. All I know is I could really use some vitamin D today. I woke up almost chipper but now, four hours later, the mere thought of taking off my pajamas and joining the world of the living is overwhelming. God I hate this! What will it take to make this pendulum stop swinging? I'm getting sea sick. It's like a perpetual feeling of dropping into a steep roller-coaster incline. You know, when your stomach is in your throat? I'm there, but it won't go away. How does this happen? If this cocktail isn't working, then what will? I thought that Lithium was the cure-all? Perhaps people have mistaken "Lithium dull" with normalcy. Who am I kidding? How could a salt possibly fix this? I simply feel like a more tightly wound version of what I'm trying to fix. I'm restless but dull.

Perhaps this is what potential energy feels like. Like an appliance that is turned off or a ball sitting on a ledge, waiting to fall. My body and my mind are detached from one another today. They are not working in tandem. My mind is distracted and agitated, and my body wants to run a fucking marathon. It's frustrating. I have an appointment with Dr. Freedman tomorrow. Maybe I'll be able to explain all of this to him. I don't know. Then again, tomorrow could be a totally different experience. I may wake up on the wrong side of the bed and eventually taste some clarity throughout the day. You never know.

I could wake up with a crusher headache but feel completely stable or I could wake up feeling content, my tea may taste too weak and it may send me into a mental tailspin. I will not allow it to affect those around me; for their sake, even if I am feeling bad I will put on a "humor" show. I know it is counterproductive, but when I act like I feel around others, I watch their energy plummet. It's not fair to them; everyone has their own baggage to lug around. I'm exhausted.

Love, Ana

Briar's brow was tensed, and he ran his hand through his closely shorn hair. He heard Cal's voice sneak through the constant water. "Bri, do you want me to leave the shower on for you?"

Bri sighed and buried his head into Pup's side. "Be down in a minute."

"What?"

Briar turned his face toward the spiral staircase. "Be down in a minute!"

"Okay, it's just we don't have that much time!"

Briar snapped, "Yes, Cal, I know!"

"Sorry!"

March 23, 2000

Sink

Dear Briar,

Did you know that Jerry Garcia died the day of your 22nd birthday? I remember it well. It was the evening between August 8 and August 9 in 1995. He died at a drug rehabilitation center. I swear that my heart sunk for all of the 40 and 50-something burnouts who did nothing for 20 years but get wasted, follow the Grateful Dead and live day to day off of their cash crops and kitchen LSD. Their demigod had passed, not to mention the innovator of the jam band, talented musician, and a seemingly downright jolly guy. That was the first thing that I heard when I woke on August 8, Seth's 22nd birthday. Let me tell you, it foreshadowed one of the weirdest days of my existence.

I remember that I spoke with Seth, and we planned a birthday night of anything goes, which I thought consisted of booze, pot, perhaps a line or two of coke and a birthday cake. I remember I had dinner with Jesse, Nana, my sister, my parents, and my friend Lea, who read our palms after dinner. I then went off to Seth's only to find booze, a joint, a birthday cupcake, and two lines of heroine waiting for me on the kitchen counter. "That doesn't look like coke," I said to Seth who I knew had been dabbling all too much in this new world. "It's not. Try it," he said. "You snort it up just like coke. You'll love it."

I polished off the beer I was drinking, pulled my hair back into a ponytail, and snorted both lines, feeling it burn and drip into the back of my throat. It tasted different than coke, chalky and yellow like it looked. It didn't numb my teeth and my nostrils, and it didn't give my saliva that familiar metallic taste. But I was immediately drawn to the denim couch in the soft light of Seth's cedar den, sunk down into its blue cushioning, and fell into the most overwhelming euphoria that I had ever known. I felt like Alice in control of my speed as I drifted down the rabbit hole. I was wrapped in chemical warmth and I was frightened for a moment, not by the sensations, but by how good they felt. For a split second I understood addiction. All my crazy feelings, insecurities, and inhibitions melted and I didn't hurt. I was wrapped in a cloud.

Later, the nightmare set in. When I was coming down, I felt like a child, lost in a public place, panicking and screaming for my mother. All I wanted was to be comforted, and all Seth wanted was to be alone. I have memory clips of me crying, then laughing and shivering and walking up the picture-lined stairs to Seth's bedroom, looking at childhood pictures of him and his brother. I wondered where it all went wrong for Seth. I didn't see it in his young face. I made my way into his dark bedroom, climbed into bed with him, searching for a blanket, comfort, anything. I kept curling up closer and closer to him and he just moved away.

I lay there, and my reality started to creep back into my mind: your birthday, waiting tables, Jesse's smile, my parent's snoring, the blue light of the Yankee's game dancing on Nanny's face, Violet's advice, and I just wanted to be in my bed snuggling with my cat, Henry—safe.

Love, Ana

* * *

The evening of March 26, 2000

Twister

Dear Briar,

This is a real trip, isn't it? Life. We are like game pieces. "King me," or "I won," "Sorry," or "I'll take Entertainment, please," or "Oh Balderdash," I forgot "You sunk my battleship," and "Park Place for $5000." "Right-hand red, left-foot blue," Briar. What will it be? I wonder who's playing our pieces or if we are in complete control like the Caterpillar said. "Survey Says," I don't think so. There are just too many coincidences to be chalked up as such. Is "worthwild a word?" "Connect Four." I used to think that it was all a game and that death would be a game too. I began to compose these letters with the intention that they would be my vain attempt at saying goodbye to those that have touched my life and given me life if I had to fly. It's really hard feeling this way, and I've felt like a burden for so long.

I don't know exactly how I would have done it, but it would have been far away from everyone I loved so that they didn't have to deal with funeral preparations and the unnecessary pain of having to see my lifeless body. I would have just given my letters to everyone, then the other day happened.

I had an appointment with Frieda. I was feeling unusually low although I pretended to be OK. The entire time I drove there, I tried to plot my suicide, half-serious half-depressed. When my appointment was over, I decided to drive to my sister's house to visit in search of solace. When I walked in, my mom was working in the office. My sister was at the doctor with little Jane who was sick. I descended the stairs to the den and my mom greeted me with a great big smile from the office on the right. On the left, Elijah's six-year old eyes lit up and he yelled, "Ana, did you miss me?" he said with his little arms outstretched. "Is that why you are here?"

I melted onto the couch next to him. He curled up onto my lap, gave me a great big hug, and showed me his missing tooth. I hugged him and kissed his freckled nose and his blond hair. "How are you, El?" I said. "Good, I missed you! Would you like to go to the movies with me sometime? We could go see 'Home on the Range,' just like when we went to see the 'Cat in the Hat.'" Then he whispered so my mom, his Gaga, couldn't hear, "Maybe we could get some candy and play some video games." He giggled deviously. It was our secret. He continued to tell me all about the Bugs Bunny cartoon that he loved, wide blue-green eyes smiling, and his voice dripping with love drifted off. I knew at that moment, choking on my own selfishness that I couldn't ever possibly take my life. It would break little Eli's heart. He just wouldn't understand.

I spun and got a "free turn," Briar. I am back in the game.

Love, Ana

* * *

April 4, 2000

Sound

Dear Briar,

The clocks were turned ahead today, and I thought I was doing alright when I rose from a pile of blankets at 11:00 a.m., only to find when I ventured downstairs to my parents for a cocktail of coffee, Lithium, and Prozac that it was actually noon. That's a weird way to start the day. My intent was to wake up relatively early and write among other things, but to no avail. My mattress on the floor is just way too cozy, tucked behind a couch, nestled into an exposed stone wall and hidden from any natural light. I could've easily slept the entire Sunday away. It's rainy and windy and the sound on the roof is so soothing, especially while nestled into soft striped sheets and my favorite fluffy yellow blanket. My only incentive to venture into the outer world in addition to the necessity of medication was to appear alive and motivated to my father. He was tinkering around with an ancient Macintosh computer of his, trying to unearth some old eBay files that he had saved. My dad is up with the sunrise. He sits and listens to talk radio and drinks a pot of coffee, solving all the world's problems by the time anyone else rises. He scoffs silently at those who sleep the morning away. I cannot take the feeling of disapproval even though he never voices it. I certainly can sense it unless that too is a figment of my warped imagination. I'll probably never know.

Last night, in an attempt to organize this mess of an apartment that I have created, I decided to separate the photo albums from the silverware and find a proper home for both. In my struggle, I happened upon a photo scrapbook that my sister had created for me many moons ago. It documented my life up until about age 15. It features my evolution from a sweet, innocent, green-eyed, long braided tomboy into a most unattractive and awkward junior high student, complete with a hairdo reminiscent of the '80s band Flock of Seagulls, braces and a nose that was way too big for my confused eyes, and underdeveloped chin; I hadn't quite grown into my features yet. And featured on the same page was your seventh grade class picture. I couldn't quite make out your eyes because the lenses in your glasses had darkened from the flash and your expression was that of impending doom (as if the camera was going to attack you at any minute). Your hairstyle made up for the inability to see your eyes; it was the dreaded year when you were hit hard with puberty and your straight feathered locks became curly. The transition was tough for you.

I think that you decided to go the safe route with your newly found curls, and when you went to the stylist, you simply said, "Short on the sides, leave some length on the top and back." It wasn't quite like Lionel Ritchie in the "Hello" video nor was it like Michael Jackson in his transitional hair phase between "Off the Wall" and "Thriller." It definitely wasn't a mullet, a style synonymous with our hometown, laden with souped-up Camaros and loud hair rock.

Even at 12, you had way too much style for that nonsense. It was more like Richard Marx. You remember him, right? He was a love song-extraordinaire: "Hold on to the Night," "Endless Summer Nights," etc. He was a huge hit at '80s high school dances and roller rinks. For a while there, he was played almost as often as "Stairway to Heaven" as the slow, last minute make-out song of choice when we searched for the one lonely soul in the crowd and asked him/her to dance and awkwardly spun around in a circle trying not to chew our gum too loud. I remember shifting in order to not to feel a strange protrusion in my dance partners' young trousers, or in your case, maybe you attempted to slowly inch your nimble hands down toward her bottom.

Whatever the case may have been, we had one thing in common. When "Stairway to Heaven" sped up and when we looked around, everyone seemed to lose their "spin slowly in a circle groove" and they talked to their partner and made plans for after the dance. "So, what time's your mom picking you up?" "Do you want to go to McDonalds? I've got some gin in a jelly jar in my purse. We could mix it with soda." And while we discussed such topics, the lights would begin to come up with, "and she's buying the stairway to heaven" exposing those who were passionately smooching on the dance floor and in dark corners of the bleachers. We had a much less sophisticated group of youngsters that we grew up with in a slate mining town, than our neighboring Italian town, Roseto, where the private school swarmed with lovely Italian boys. Sometimes their dances would end with something much more hip like "Love Song" by The Cure. I remember that I thought that simple detail made them a much more exotic bunch.

But, Briar, in addition to our fantastic junior high school photos (by the way, we were both wearing paisley button-downs in our class pictures, you with suspenders and me with a faux gold and pearl broach), I found photographs from our circus in either first or second grade. They are priceless! Remember? We had a parade in school, and everyone dressed as a character from the circus. There's a picture of me in a red, satin polka dot leotard thing, white tights, and tap shoes. I had my hair down and a red satin arm garter on; I think I was going for acrobat. In fact, I'm pretty sure that's what I wanted to be when I was six and seven, in addition to a veterinarian.

But you were smiling shyly in the background with your adorable glasses that you forever loathed and feathered hair. You were dressed as the strong man. It was so cute. I remember that I had such a crush on you. That whole day I kept getting upset if any other girls would talk to you, namely a particular blonde who we went through school with who often had rug burns on her knees back in high school. She seemed a floozy even at seven.

I remember she used to lift up her shirt and show boys, girls, whomever, the content of her pasty, seven-year-old chest. She would say, "Chinese, Japanese, dirty knees, look at these," and would peel up her Garanimals polo shirt or her baby doll dress. I just couldn't compete.

Looking at the photos inspired me to make you a mixtape like we used to do for each other in high school. Perhaps you have a Sony Walkman relic stashed in a drawer somewhere to listen to it.

There is something innocent about mixed tapes. Forgive me while I reminisce. I cannot help it. I seem to associate modern audio technology with "Video Killed the Radio Star." This must have been how photographers felt when digital came out or how my parents felt when they could no longer buy 8-track tapes for their Buick Electra.

I remember once when I was really down, after Gino dumped me, you made me the most fantastic mixed tape that I still have. It has everything from Brit Pop to Edie Brickell. You introduced me to The Stone Roses..."I wanna be adored."

The cover had smiling faces and clowns all over it and the inside had inspirational quotes about laughter. It was such a thoughtful compilation. Nothing heals better than music as far as

I'm concerned. Hence, the song list that I put together for you:

"Queen Bitch" by David Bowie
"Just Like Honey" by Jesus and Mary Chain
"100%" by Sonic Youth
"Talk Show Host" by Radiohead
"She Came in through the Bathroom Window" by The Beatles
"Blue Light" by Mazzy Star
"Just Like a Dream" by The Cure
"Nervous Breakdown" by Black Flag
"Tomorrow Never Knows" by The Beatles
"Spit on a Stranger" by Pavement
"Just Like a Woman" by Bob Dylan
"Moonshadow" by Cat Stevens
"Blue" by Joni Mitchell
"Baby Blue Sedan" by Modest Mouse
"Good Morning Heartache" by Billie Holiday
"Rainy Day, Dream Away" by Jimi Hendrix
"Dig a Pony" by The Beatles
"My Funny Valentine" by Chet Baker
"Sunny Afternoon" by The Kinks
"Janine" by Soul Coughing
"Waiting Room" by Fugazi
"Oh, You Pretty Things" by David Bowie
"Dear Prudence" by The Beatles
"Feel the Pain" by Dinosaur Jr.
"Ten Years Gone" by Led Zeppelin
"Milk It" by Nirvana
"Pretty in Pink" by The Psychedelic Furs
"Hallelujah" (Jeff Buckley Version) "Black Star" by Radiohead
"Johnny Sunshine" by Liz Phair
"Shady Lane" by Pavement
"Seeing Red" by Minor Threat

"Waltz # 2" by Elliot Smith
"Crying Song" by Pink Floyd
"Bulletproof" by Radiohead
"Afterhours" by The Velvet Underground
"Half a World Away" by REM
"Leave Me Alone" by New Order
"Pictures of Matchstick Men and You," the version by Camper Van Beethoven
"Best of Jill Hives" by Guided by Voices
"Gigantic" by The Pixies
"A Good Idea" by Sugar
"Stop Breaking Down," the version by The White Stripes (No disrespect to Mr. Robert Johnson)
"She's So High" by Blur
"Save Me" by Aimee Mann
"Thirteen" by Big Star
"Exit Music" by Radiohead
"Motor Away" by Guided by Voices

I was feeling nostalgic. That is my disclaimer.

Love,
your old friend Ana

Fifteen minutes later, Cal skipped up the stairs took one look at Briar snuggled into Pup, letters scattered all around them, sat down next to him, and wiped a tear from his cheek. "Are you okay, baby?"

Briar turned and looked at Cal through tears. "The letters are so fucked up. I had no idea, Cal, I just didn't know!" He buried his face into Cal's lap.

"Is she okay?" Cal spoke gently.

"I don't know, and I'm afraid to keep reading."

Cal stood up and mixed Briar another mimosa.

"The car is going to be here in fifteen minutes." He handed Briar the drink.

"Do you want me to call the driver and tell him that we need more time?"

"No, Cal, go. Just go without me. Tell them I'm sick or something. Okay? Just make something up."

Cal adjusted his tie and leaned down to kiss Briar.

"Are you sure?"

"Yes, I'll be fine. I just need to be alone."

"Call me if you need me. I won't be late, okay?"

Briar smiled and Cal blew him a kiss, closing the door behind him. Their cat Puddy jumped onto the leather sofa next to Pup and walked over him to get to Briar.

"Hey, Pud." Puddy stretched and dropped her zaftig body onto his lap.

"Jesus, Pud, you weigh more than Pup."

He leaned over, trying not to disturb either of them, picked up the scattered letters, and dropped the already read pile back into the envelope.

He leaned back and closed his navy blue eyes.

"I don't think that you've ever met Ana, Pup, but Puddy has. Right, Pud? Ana dropped you off in the middle of the night when you were just a baby."

He scratched her chin.

"Remember, Pud? She thought that I seemed lonely in my Brooklyn apartment and needed a friend."

Puddy purred.

"And I don't get it. You hate her and all other females you little misogynist."

Briar stretched and gingerly picked up the remaining letters. He took a deep breath and settled into the sofa.

The Evening of April 4, 2000

Are you there, Briar? It's me, Ana.

Do you remember that book? Well actually Judy Blume entitled it, "Are You There God? It's Me, Margaret?" Did you read it, or did you sneak a copy from your sisters and read it with a flashlight beneath the sheets? It was considered borderline racy when we were able to read beyond

Dick, Harry, Jane, and Spot ran to the park. It was about the "P" word as Eugene described with a heavy Brooklyn accent in Neil Simon's great "Brighton Beach Memoirs," pew-buh-dee, aka puberty. It was Margaret's coming of age story. For any parent who wasn't particularly well-versed in the art of talking about anything pertaining to pubic hair, menstruation, cramps, crushes, erections, or budding breasts, it was a saving grace. A prepubescent elixir to help understand the crop of zits that were sprouting on our cheeks, especially mine. My parents had a very interesting approach to talking about adolescence with me; they simply didn't. Sex Ed. took care of that. Remember those horribly embarrassing videos that we watched in sixth grade? Boys were in one room and girls were in another, but we all came together for the childbirth video. I think that it is safe to say that was education's vain attempt to prolong abstinence. It was bloody, graphic, full of screams, and one girl had an epileptic seizure in our class when the baby crowned. Do you remember?

I don't blame my parents for tiptoeing around the subject. I was pretty difficult to talk to at that age; I didn't speak at all or I yelled. But most of the time I was being yelled at for my indignant behavior; no one knew it was the unfolding of a disease, not even me. My family thought that I was becoming a stereotypical teenage girl much to their chagrin.

Oh, I forgot, there was a sex talk. When Jesse and I were about 15 or 16, right about the time that we all drank a gallon of strawberry wine and you sucked a ring of hickeys around her neck. Remember that? We tried to pass it off to our parents as a serious case of neck poison ivy. Well, Jesse and I were sitting together in the front of my parent's van while my mom drove us somewhere. I remember that Jesse and I were speaking in code, planning our drug/boy fest for the evening, and my mom pulled the van over turned to us and said, "I've got one word for you girls: abstinence." The she pulled back onto the road and turned up the radio. Jesse and I looked at each other shaking with hidden laughter and I whispered, "What does that mean?" Jesse replied, "I have no idea!"

The sex talk that really backfired was when I was about five. I remember climbing into my parent's big, brass bed on a Saturday morning having already been up for two hours, watching cartoons. The day before we had been swimming at our neighbor's house and there was a woman there who was very pregnant and applying Bain de Soleil to her exposed skin; her belly defied gravity. Being the precocious little girl that I was, I sat down next to her, touched her tummy, and asked if a baby was growing inside. She smiled and said, "Sure is," and pinched my cheek. I remember not being satisfied with that. "But, how?" I asked. She smiled, putting the cap back on the orange tanning gel, leaned back, and shook her straight blond hair behind her tanned shoulders, winked at me, and said, "It's magic."

That did it for me. Although she wasn't aware of the depth of my young imagination. At that age, I was convinced that Barbie, who I worshiped, was secretly plotting to end my life via Barbie perfume and that when the lights went out at night, the red carpet in my bedroom was a place where all demons resided and if I stood on it longer than two seconds I would be dragged down into the fiery recesses of some hell...but my sister was immune. So if I jumped quickly into the room, then onto her bed and fell into mine without touching the ground beneath us; I was safe. When my sister would growl, "Why must you jump onto my bed every night? I'm trying to sleep," I would say, "Sorry." I couldn't have possibly explained what I thought. I was afraid of reactions even then.

So the evening before the "sex talk" I cried myself to sleep, rubbing my tummy and hiding the tears from my sister. "What if I'm pregnant? She said that it's magic." I remember that I convinced myself that there was a baby growing in my tummy just like her; I believe in magic. I crawled between my snuggling parents and my mom asked, "What is it, sweetie?" "Mommy, how did I get here? Was it magic?" My dad giggled, climbed out of bed, adjusting his boxers and V-neck T-shirt, and lumbered down the hall to fulfill his morning ritual. First stop, the can; second stop, the kitchen radio; third stop, the coffee maker. My mom watched him go. They glanced at each other knowingly but she had the look of "Thanks a lot, Harry" in her eyes, too.

So she climbed up in bed, and I snuggled into my dad's side, still warm from recent slumber. "Well," she said, rolling over toward me, pulling the cover over her shoulder and smoothing it around me, "You see," she was searching, "I have a beautiful garden inside my tummy." She placed her hand on her stomach and all I could picture was my Nanny and Poppa's strawberry patch and peach orchard. "Your dad," she said endearingly, "has a special seed, and he planted his seed in my garden." She smiled softly. Thank god she told me that before I discovered Cabbage Patch Kids or I would've wondered why my bum hadn't been signed. "And that's how Amber and I were born?" I leaned back and stared at the hairline cracks in the plaster ceiling that looked like my Fischer Price United States puzzle. "In a roundabout way, yes." My mom has always loved to speak in metaphors.

I remember that I was satisfied with her response and began to climb out of their bed, "So there's no chance that I am going to have a baby?" My mom started laughing hysterically, "No, sweetie, don't you worry." I didn't worry for a long time Briar until one day, a year later. We were doing an agriculture project and learning about farmers. Do you remember? Each of us received a Dixie cup from Mrs. Overdass, and we had to fill it with dirt and corn seeds, among other things. We were going to plant our seedlings outside after we had nurtured them in the window for a while.

I received my cup, filled it with dirt, and panicked when the student teacher, Mr. Santiago came around and gave us seeds to put in our cup. He placed them in my palm, and I kept counting them over and over again making sure that I knew how many I was putting in my cup before I placed it on the windowsill with the rest. Somehow, I was distracted. I cannot remember if I fell or if Mrs. Overdass began to give directions, but I had forgotten how many seeds I had in my hand. I panicked. "Oh no," I thought, "I ate one! I'm going to have a baby!"

I swore that I felt the seed trapped in the back of my first grade throat and started to cough terribly, in an attempt to dislodge it. When the teacher came over to me asking what was wrong, I started to cry and looked at her desperately, "I think I swallowed a seed!" She ran and got the packet of seeds to look up whether or not they were toxic, while Mr. Santiago comforted me and Chris Liebman, a classmate and neighbor of mine, came up to me and asked, "What's wrong?" "I swallowed a seed," I said as if he knew the consequences. He started to laugh and said, "Uh oh, you're going to have a big watermelon growing in your tummy and corn stalks growing out of your nose and ears!" With that I cowered even more. Mrs. Overdass had to escort me to the nurse's office where they asked me why I was so upset; the seed wouldn't hurt me. "Honey, accidents happen," said the nurse with the beehive that I always thought was detachable. How else could she have slept at night?

I proceeded to explain to them that I felt that I was too young to have a baby and I wasn't ready. They all held back their laughter and asked me to explain to them why I thought swallowing a seed would make me pregnant. So I did. I was escorted into another room and given a snack and a blanket to calm me down while the nurse called my mom from her office. I remember I could hear the nurse speaking in muffled tones between hushed giggles and 20 minutes later my mom was there to take me home and to reassure me that I wasn't going to have a baby. On the ride home, I remember feeling so much better until I began to doze off and I swore that I felt corn creeping up the back of my throat. I had a funny tickle in my nose and ears, too. Who says that physiological ailments cannot be caused by the mind or healed for that matter? If all else fails, they can definitely be helped by a mother's kind word, a snack, and a blanket. That should be one of the universal truths. Do you agree?

Love, Ana

* * *

April 16, 2000

Open

Dear Briar,

Exactly two months ago today I left school hearing voices, never to return. But today I sit naked on a sunny patio writing to you on my trusty typewriter. I couldn't find my bathing suit, so I simply blanketed the patio. I'm soaking up the sun like a new leaf. My April skin is so pale that I fear it is deflecting the sun's rays, but I don't care. The heat feels magnificent and my skin has been enshrouded for months. I feel healthy with the exception of my desire to smoke. This, too, shall pass. Two months ago I didn't think I would ever see the light of day again. At 6:00 p.m. today I will work at the restaurant selling my soul for tips. It's amazing that a salt compound and a little serotonin can make the difference between life and death. I have to admit that out of boredom I am experimenting on myself. I'm not sure if it is strictly out of curiosity or if it is my latent desire to impair myself for the sake of self-satisfaction. But I have neglected to take my Prozac for about four days simply to see what might happen. I just want to know whether or not it simply has the placebo effect or if it actually does placate my moods.

Today is the first day that I have noticed anything, and I must say it is relatively drastic. I spoke with Jack on the phone, and I wasn't pleased with his response to something that I said. So when he hung up, I continued to pretend to talk to him and proceeded to take the phone and throw it across the room at a stone wall, smashing it into several pieces. Then I lay down in the fetal position on top of the broken phone and screamed and cried for about 15 minutes. Then I was fine except I got up and felt something on the side of my face. Thinking it was strictly a blind Lithium zit (I've had several of them lately) I looked into the mirror to find a jagged piece of the phone lodged into my face. I stared in complete amazement. I had been so self-absorbed with unfounded anger that I hadn't any recollection of how it got there. It was relatively small, but the face bleeds freely and there was a small river of red blood spiraling down my freckled cheek. It meandered around scabbed blemishes like river rocks and dripped onto the vanity below. I ran my finger slowly across the vanity and smeared the viscous drips into a picture of a flower.

I gently dislodged the plastic piece from my cheek and stared at the incision that it made. It looked like a smile seeping blood. I found that quietly amusing and it reminded me of that thing that I used to like to do when I was a child in the bathtub. I would live vicariously through my dolls. I would pretend that they were super-human mermaid-like creatures that would fight to the death, and I would talk through their battle feeling the good vs. evil and would eventually cause the evil mermaid to perish, brutally. I took bath water into my mouth and let it seep out while I mumbled the bad mermaid's last words. I remember it felt warm and thick as it pulsed out of my lips and ran down my chin; I could have sworn that it was actually evil mermaid blood.

I doused the smiley face with witch hazel and started to laugh at my confused, maimed reflection realizing how ludicrous the fit of rage had been. When the bleeding stopped, I skipped downstairs, disregarding the shattered mess on the floor, and I grabbed my dogs to frolic around the pond. Delicate Dolly tiptoed around the edge while Sherman barreled into the water after countless sticks and tennis balls. I sat barefoot on an over turned boat in the afternoon sun, smiling at the early spring scene. I was calm again. I curled up in the sun and fell into a half-dream, half-wake state. I was reliving a night at the restaurant when I awoke from bullet-like drips of freezing pond water from Sherman's saturated, shaking 110-pound coat. I jumped up and freaked out completely as if it were a shower of bullets. I lost all control and screamed at Sherman as if he did something very wrong, and he cowered and ran away. Then I appropriately stepped in a hole, overturned my ankle, fell over, grabbed my foot, and cried for the next 15 minutes. Not over the pain but over my lunacy and over the fact that although I verbally assaulted poor Sherman, he still came to my aid when he heard me cry, licking my wounds.

I had thankfully forgotten about behaving this way. Prozac does not have the placebo effect. I am convinced; that is my result.

Love,

Ana

* * *

April 20, 2000

Purpose

Dear Briar,

I just remembered that it's Cal's birthday. I hope the two of you are celebrating in a warm, sunny place or over gin martinis somewhere in NYC. I've been feeling a little better, more in control. The weather has helped and so has a job. It was fantastic out today; seventy degrees and sunny with a warm breeze. I had a day off and played with Sherman and Dolly, throwing stick after stick into the pond for Sherman to swim to. He waddles when he swims and looks like a big, happy seal. I swear that he must be a direct descendent of the seal family.

I sat barefoot in the mossy grass with a collection of sticks and tennis balls next to me. So when Sherman climbed out of the pond, he didn't have time to shake all over me; I immediately tossed another into the blue-green water. The weirdest thing happened, Bri; I moved to the edge of the bank and sat down amidst some sprouting periwinkle and wildflowers and waited for Sherman to waddle back to shore with the stick du jour. When I looked down into the water at the clouded reflection of the cloud spotted sky framing my shadowed face and messy hair, my mind was hit with a memory. Whether it be this life or a past life I don't know. It spooked me to the core.

I remembered being a child, surrounded by other children and teenagers, sitting on the edge of a lake or pond, feeling alone and uncomfortable and staring down into the water, when I was scooped up by one of the older male kids (I could feel his bare chest against my back), and was taken into the pond. Everyone was laughing and playing and I was being playfully tossed between kids. But I had this feeling that something wasn't right. I kept looking toward the bank for my mom or my sister...somebody safe. The faceless male kept me afloat, but I was dreadfully frightened by him, to the point of being afraid to cry out for my mom. I feared that he would hurt me somehow and no one would know.

Sherman shook and sprayed me with an April shower, scented with mud and dog and pond, waking me from what I hoped was a deluded concoction of my sick imagination. It just felt too familiar, even though the children in the pond remained a faceless sea of voices and laughing. They were hidden beneath the confusing sun dancing on the surface...shards of light masked them from my young eyes. Fucked up.

I walked Sherman and Dolly up to the house, dried them off, and brought them in for snacks and water. I ventured back down to the pond alone to see if I could rekindle whatever it was that I experienced. Although it spooked me, I wanted to know more. But I think that my subconscious fear of revealing something that I didn't want to unearth overtook my rational mind, and I wasn't able to rehash the memory. Perhaps I was trying too hard; I don't know. But something was there, Bri. Something scary that may help me to explain a lot of unfounded fears and repulsions and insecurities that I have always attributed to yet another facet of the dreaded psychobabble term that I have come to hate so much, bipolarity.

Nothing surprises me anymore.

Love, Ana

* * *

April 30, 2000

Shame

Dear Briar,

Half of the reason that I am so afraid to speak to you is for monetary reasons, which I completely don't understand. But I think I've mentioned them before. As of today, things are getting a bit easier. At least I don't think that I am going to bounce another five checks this month. In the three weeks, I have been bartending and waitressing, excuse me, serving (politically correct), I have accumulated enough cash to pay a bill or two and that is a relief. It is very humbling, not that I have ever had large sums of money, but I had piece of mind and a salary/benefits when teaching; I guess that it is all relative because I'm simply paying off past self-medication credit card bills. I know that if I were discussing this with you over a gin martini you would say, "Ana, it may seem like Cal and I make a lot of money but we spend accordingly; the bigger the salary, the bigger the spending. It all evens out." And then you would smile and nod knowingly yet softly like a fairy godfather, reassuring.

Why is it so embarrassing for me to be slinging hash and beer? It is completely reputable. On the surface I have never been one to care what people think but for some reason since I have worked there again I feel compelled to tell everyone I encounter of my other endeavors. I would like to think that it is because I am proud of myself. I want to share my passions for writing with them, but somewhere in my heart I think that I need to be perceived by the public as special or different and capable of creative things. Briar, I am not knocking the service industry. It is one of the most difficult ways to make ends meet, but it is mindless chaos especially on a busy afternoon or evening. And if a customer lacks the gift of empathy or even sympathy for that matter for the multitasking server in the interim, he or she can single-handedly make life dreadfully difficult for the server and for all of the other customers that she or he is juggling. Negativity definitely has the ripple effect in a restaurant setting. One small incorrect beer pour, coffee without creamer, or delayed ketchup bottle delivery and the unsavory guest will turn into a wild animal and bite the server with a look of disapproval, foreshadowing a really lousy tip.

It's a form of selling yourself—culinary prostitution. I feel obligated to charm the pants off a customer, not necessarily for the tip but simply for the sake of acknowledgment and a sense of belonging. I guess that happens in every industry and that it is fair for me to assume that ass-kissing to prove one's ability to be worthy in the corporate world is justified because there is a more substantial pay check attached.

You know, Bri, I'm making such progress with this bipolar thing that I am so afraid to be underestimated and mistaken for the unstable me of yesteryear. I feel I must verbally express my artistic intentions to prove my competence. God knows I'm not gloating, just reaching for acceptance like a child.

"Mom, watch! Mom, watch!" Fucking pathetic, really. I must admit, I also may be trying to overcompensate for my fear of falling back into my old life of mental confusion that by repeatedly talking about my big goals. I will keep them at arm's length through power of suggestion. That way they cannot fly away into never-never land like so many other things that I have dreamed of or embarked upon that I never allowed to come to fruition. I refuse to allow that to happen again.

I guess I always have the impending fear that nothing is different and deciding not to go back to teaching is yet another random (bipolar) decision that I made. And that my writing goals are unrealistic and that I am just a loony tunes with a zillion great ideas who lacks the ability to reach the next plateau, sadly floating in a world of indecision and discontent. Doubt is a very powerful thing, Bri. But regardless of those moments I think hope has much more clout. I mean that. I can actually say, without fear of a jinx and without crossing my fingers, eyes or any other body parts, that I actually trust myself for the first time.

I'll talk to you soon.

Love, Ana

* * *

May 21, 2000

Blah

Dear Briar,

I spent the last two days bedridden and/or with my face in the sink and my ass on the can. What a drag! I must have picked up some kind of killer 24-hour flu at work; it was the most intense headache that I have ever encountered; worse than a gin headache, worse than a cocaine headache. During moments of solace when everything flu-like subsided for a split second, I imagined that I was being prepared by the powers that be for childbirth; the pain had to be the equivalent.

My mom came to check on me. When she walked in, she heard a fate whimpering between weird coughs. She found me in the fetal position shivering on the bathroom floor, coddling a towel like a blanket.

"Ana, what's wrong?" She knelt down and rubbed my shoulder.

"Just cut my head off."

I remember her trying to wash my face off with cool water, but there was no water pressure. I cannot remember the dialogue, but I know that I ended up lying on the living room rug, with a towel for prospective puking spells, a blanket for comfort, and my feather boa hot pink Barbie sleeping mask on to keep the morning light out.

I was physically incapable of moving. So I made my home on the floor between the can and the couch. I was cradled by my dog Sherman. Angel.

My body finally felt some peace. When I attempted to open my eyes, the light that seeped in beneath my pink satin mask, reminded me of the light that illuminated the outside of that one chi-chi SoHo bar that we've gone to a handful of times. I had great experiences there with you and Cal. But the time that I went with girlfriends was very different. Did I ever tell you about it?

Frankly, I've attempted to erase it from my memory but to no avail. In moments of complete physical vulnerability like lying in an immovable heap on the floor, it creeps back into my memory and claws its way to the surface.

I went to the bar with a girlfriend of mine who in turn invited one of her college girlfriends. My girlfriend, whom you haven't met, is very starstruck, media-savvy, and all that good stuff. She is in the know, unlike me.

She mapped out places where a male actor that she idolized had made recent appearances according to some magazine. Even though it sickened me slightly, I got a kick out of her voracious appetite for name-dropping and girlish desire for an autograph, so I played along. I'll admit that it was entertaining. She and her college friend sat huddled at the bar, laughing and gossiping over Cosmopolitans while I sipped a Bombay Sapphire Martini with five olives and watched the crowd.

There was a very attractive, very effeminate brunette male sitting at the end of the bar, intermittently checking his cell phone, obviously waiting for someone. He was wearing a fitted black-and-white horizontally striped crew neck T-shirt reminiscent of Simon Le Bon of Duran Duran, fitted Diesel Jeans, and black Italian beetle boots.

I kept catching wafts of his scent, Chanel Egoiste. You used to wear that. I love that scent. So I looked over at the girls who were still laughing and gossiping and decided to move down and strike up a conversation with the Duran Duran guy.

Bad idea. He treated me as if I were a scourge of some kind.

"Look," I said, walking away from him to the back area of the bar, "I simply felt bad for you." He hated that.

I wandered to the back lounge behind the bar for a private seat and a cigarette, and sat next to an older couple who were pawing at each other.

"Do either of you have a light?" I asked.

"Sure, honey," the woman said, reaching into her bag. I watched her very large manicured hand and followed it up her well-dressed arm, over her neck, through her brown ringlets, and onto her freshly made-up face. She was a he that made a lovely she. And he was a he, who loved that she was a she/he.

I sat and smoked and talked to them for about 15 minutes. She was from Manhattan and her name was Jade, a Cabaret singer. He was a horse-whisperer from Salt Lake City, Utah. Apparently, they had met after one of her shows at a club where he, Sexy Benny as she referred to him, was at a bachelor party for a friend in New York.

"I fell head over spurs," he said with a cow-boy twang, tickling Jade.

"When I retire, I'm going to move out to Utah with ol' sexy here," Jade said, kissing him. I laughed, picturing Jade in a cowboy hat and full makeup.

I left sexy Benny and Jade to their smooch-ing and peeked around the bar to check on the status of the girls that I was with; no change.

They were still in the same position, giggling over cosmopolitans. So I helped myself to another gin martini and had a seat in the back lounge where I sat for what seemed like eternity while the same male cocktail server kept checking on the status of my drink; he refilled it once.

I recall that my left eye starting closing involuntarily, but only my left eye and I couldn't move my feet quickly. I picked up a magazine that was on the table and tried to read it but my eyes would not focus.

"I've only had 2 ½ drinks. I feel bizarre," I said to the waiter when he passed.

I remember that I put my head back and closed my eyes for a moment, trying to regain my composure. But all I could do was listen to the spiral of noise: muffled laughter, clinking glasses, igniting matches, swinging kitchen doors, lounge music, and then blackness.

The next thing that I remember is waking up on the bathroom floor of my friend's apartment, with my slip over my head and my face in a puddle of vomit, whimpering and shivering with the chills. There was a car wreck in the frontal lobe of my brain, and I could recall nothing. I wasn't able to move or function until 12 hours later when my friends filled in the blank for me.

Apparently, they had looked all over the bar and found me slumped over in a dark corner upstairs in the other lounge. They said that I had a blank expression on my face and didn't recognize them. They walked me out of the bar and I didn't speak. I got into a cab with the help of two "hot" gentlemen as they had referred to them. They said that I was completely quiet and unresponsive to them, but I was able to move. I walked out of the cab and into the elevator in the apartment building and lay down on the floor. They covered me over with a blanket.

It was no four-day hangover, Bri; I was drugged. Ruffinol, I think; the date rape drug. What sick fuck decided that I would be the perfect victim that night and how many other helpless, unknowing candidates had fallen prey in the past? At a chi-chi lounge nonetheless!

It seriously took me four days to really recover, and I never fully recollected the events of the evening. I just pray that it was as innocent as my friend described, but I don't know.

I remember shivering on the bus ride home from the city staring at the winter gray landscape unfold outside my window. I closed my eyes and tried to solve the mystery. I pictured everyone that I spoke to repeatedly, reliving every facial movement, every word, every gesture. Whoever it was had to have access to my drink before I did, which would leave the bartender and the cocktail server.

Neither seemed devious in any way.

The Duran Duran guy wasn't crafty enough to do something so cruel; he was far too self-absorbed to expand any of his precious energy thinking of harming someone else. I wasn't important enough for that effort.

"Ana, you okay?" My dad peeked over the back of the couch that divides the living room from the bedroom.

"Uh-huh, I'm just laying here."

I lifted the pink mask and escaped that reality for a moment. I heard him fumble around and seconds later, I repositioned the mask and felt a soft blanket fall over me followed by a quick smooch on the forehead.

"Nice pink thing," he said and stumbled out of the apartment.

Bob Dylan's *Blonde on Blonde* album had been on repeat since the night before, but I didn't have the strength to get up and shut it off. I started to doze.

"Rainy Day Woman" snuck through the wind, the birds, the leaves, my headache. Then I remembered something from that night that I hadn't thought of thanks to Bob Dylan. When I was talking to sexy Benny and Jade, "All Along the Watchtower" was playing in the lounge and we had a brief discussion as to our opinions of when Dylan was better; before or after the motorcycle accident. I happened to notice four, 40-something well-dressed guys sitting around on dimly lit couches, sipping scotch and smoking cigars. I couldn't see their faces but they had wandering expressions; they watched all the girls walk by, between commentary and low laughter.

I'm not sure whether they were simply great tippers, VIPS, celebrities, or he wanted to sleep with all four but the cocktail server gave them extra special attention. I thought nothing of it because I was not impressed by their Italian shoes and jingling rocks glasses.

I have a vague recollection of having gone off to the ladies' room. On return to my solo lounge position, the cocktail server lisped, "Excuse me, but the gentleman over there would like to buy you a drink." He stood and stared at me with his hand on his hip expressionless.

"Oh, thank you. That's very kind." I waved over to the four men in smoky shadow. I think that they were expecting me to join them but the crowd was too unassuming and upscale to accept a "Hey! Come on over and join us for a drink, honey!" So they remained partially anonymous and I was relieved. Then came the martini that I finished half of before the cranial Ruffinol onslaught.

I cannot recall their faces, Bri.

Love, Ana

Briar fell asleep after he read the final letter and woke from a restless slumber about an hour later. He threw on some clothes and grabbed his sunglasses, having stopped to look at his face in the mirror.

"Jesus Christ! I look like I've been beaten up. C'mon, Pup. Let's go get some coffee." Pup slid into his leash, and they went out the door, closing it behind them.

* * *

Jesse took the bundle of letters and stepped barefoot through the soft, green grass toward the coy pond in her herb garden 150 miles away. She lay down among the lavender in the October sunshine. She sighed and caught a glimpse of herself in the water; a golden fish swam through her reflection, warbled by a fallen leaf. She rolled onto her back, exposing her soft underbelly to the sky and cautiously dove into them.

March 14, 2000

Kind Planets

Jesse,

I'm writing back because for whatever reason, the sun, my big cuddly Sherman, the pair of ducks, and the geese couple that are ruling the pond flapping at Sherman and Dolly whenever they dare to near them, my cup of tea is just right.

I slept well. I feel better today than I did yesterday. Granted, I am still spaced-out but it isn't coupled with gloom and doom and looming sadness. Thank God. I thought that those emotions were strictly saved for melodramatic teenagers. At least I hope in most cases that it is strictly synonymous with hormones, acne, too much makeup, '80s melancholia, and black crushed velvet (The Cure, The Smiths, Echo and the Bunnymen, The Church, House of Love, Peter Murphy) all of which I know very well, as do you.

Since I am on a roll, let's delve into astrology. I just finished looking up our horoscope: Gemini, the sign of the dual-natured whack job. Growing up, I always thought that it was so cool that you and I were born eight days apart and were both born under the sign of Gemini. I have been scoffed at for putting so much stock in the study of astrology but I don't care. I find it fascinating. The correlations between astrological signs and character traits are uncanny; I'm not talking about basic fortune telling that you read every day in the paper (at least I do). That's entertaining, too, but I am talking about the art of astrological study and character analysis. It is something else!

Have you ever had your chart done? It's based on the position of the sun, the earth, the moon, the planets, and the time when and where you were born geographically. It is so complicated but so interesting. My personality analysis was super accurate and that is pretty hard to imagine, considering I suffer from personality disorders and I am a bit flippant (without psycho meds). When my sister had Jane, her youngest child two years ago, I had her chart done and my nephew Elijah, but I never gave them to her for fear of freaking her out. Although I think that they could provide some insight into raising them considering it points out both positive and negative personality traits and how to efficiently deal with them.

Speaking of positive and negative traits, how about I share with you some of our own, that you may find ironic, dear Gemini Jesse? According to Dr. R. Donald Papon, a homeopathic physician, Jungian astrologer and New Thought Minister (whatever that may entail), Gemini is the sign of the artist or inventor:

"In the Hebrew Zodiac, this sign refers to the tribe of Benjamin and among early Christians it was used as the mystic emblem of Christ and his redeemed. In Greek mythology, Castor and Pollex, who on account of their dual nature are constantly at war with each other, represent the sign Gemini. To the Arabs, the heavenly twins were twin peacocks; to the Ancient Egyptians, twin planets; to the Indians, twin gods; to the Chinese, something like Siamese twins." Interesting, right? Dr. Papon expands on this, delving into the personality traits indigenous to the Gemini:

"There are no people more affectionate and generous than those born under the sign of Gemini. They are courteous, considerate, kind and gentle to all. These qualities make them very magnetic and hypnotic. They take great pride in their family and its accomplishments. Neither selfishness nor meanness is found in such natives. They are usually far too generous for their own good. Often they will neglect themselves in order to assist others to the chagrin of their family."

Very complimentary, right? Here are the traits that I find uncanny:

"There is a bit of the schizophrenic and a bit of the manic-depressive in every Gemini personality. The former is more pronounced than the latter. Certainly, astro-analytical case histories contain disproportionately high percentage of Gemini Schizophrenics. Impulsiveness, overactivity, overtalking, bizarre activity, and hypochondriasis are all too familiar figures. Faced with real or imagined hostility, Gemini will employ acid sarcasm or any other means to vindicate his imagined wounds."

Sound familiar?

Love,
Ana

* * *

Evening of April 8, 2000

Dear Jesse,

I've spent the last twenty to thirty minutes staring at a reflection of my own pupil on the inside lens of my glasses. I swear that you can see the cells move around in the ebb and flow of my eyeball. It almost looks as if I am looking at DNA dancing around beneath a microscope. It's mesmerizing, especially when I can almost shut it out like a shutter lens with my eyelashes. They slowly swallow up the image like a Venus flytrap or if you'd prefer a less gruesome description, like the body-size feather fans of a Burlesque stripper. Sneaky, feminine, vicious. I know that I've experienced these phenomena before while in bright sunlight, wearing sunglasses. I probably was out enjoying the weather, not sitting Indian-style on my couch with big, brown, stinky Sherman and two cats, wondering why I cannot sleep, again for the fourth night in a row.

Sherman is sleeping like a bear and snoring like one, too (not that I have any clue whether or not bears snore). But he is very bearlike; you haven't met him yet. He is spread out next to me, all 110 pounds of him, and he looks like a big, chocolate teddy bear but he smells like a sewer. He's so adorable and so full of love that I don't mind his stink. He's got a boxy Chocolate Labrador face and a very stout build with beautiful fur, huge paws and a roly-poly belly. He is so sweet. Before he fell asleep, he was cleaning my cat, Mimi. She acquired that name because of her uncanny ability to meow incessantly at the most inappropriate hours of the morning. Usually she'll run in circles, scratch the furniture, climb the wooden beams, and meow at the top of her lungs, for no apparent reason. But what can I expect? She had a tough beginning. She was a garbage dump cat at a bar where I worked. She and I befriended one another when I would sit on the pavement at 2:00 a.m. and feed her and pet her after work. And what do you know? One day she followed me to my car meowing the entire way. I'm a regular goddamn Snow White.

Right now she sleeps sweetly like Sherman. Her tabby ears glisten from being groomed by him. Cat's look so peaceful when they sleep all balled up. She looks so comfortable.

...Okay, I'm not alone. The fish are awake although I've never noticed any difference. Do fish sleep? They must. Don't they need to be in constant motion to ensure oxygen through their gills? All I know is that Mini and Maude are seemingly doing what I was doing for 20 to 30 minutes. They're swimming in tandem around and around the base of their tank looking at their reflections in the glass. It's sad really, I should go turn off the light on the tank so that they cannot see their reflection anymore but I'm afraid they will think that they lost their friends on the outside. I'll just let them live the illusion. Besides it's tremendously entertaining for both me and Gato, a fantastic, old long-haired tabby cat who I love, who resides here as well. She's spread out on the chest next to the fish tank with her little face just resting on her outstretched paw, watching the dizzying fish like I am. It seems to be tiring her; her big yellow eyes are slowly disappearing behind coal-black lined Egyptian-looking frames…and she's asleep. Maybe if I stare long enough it will put me to sleep, too.

Thinking of you, Ana

* * *

Early in the morning

April 9, 2000

Dear Jesse,

The fish are still talking to their friends in the reflection. I tried talking to my reflection, but I became immersed in staring at how strange my mouth looks when I speak. I have rarely seen anyone else look this strange. I have never encountered this weird mouth phenomena on television or among movie actors. I don't even know how to explain it.

When I eventually tired of looking at my weird reflection, I began to go through all of my clothing, half of which I gave to Goodwill, to see how much I have available to sell at a yard sale. Yes, I've decided that I am going to have a yard sale very soon out of complete necessity. I am out of money and have missed two credit card payments this month already. This wouldn't have bothered me a month ago when I broke down and was so highly medicated. Then everything seemed like an emotionless dream. Now that I am swimming toward the surface, I can feel it. I guess that's a good thing but it is nerve-racking. Wait, that's got to be a good thing too! I can feel it. I feel genuine discomfort again. But I also have the urge to remedy the situation creatively, not just with a quick monetary or drug-induced fix.

I have accumulated so much debt as a result of my bipolar binges that it ate all of my teaching income. I bought anything to appease the pain and it worked in the short term. Now, with a closet full of things worn once and a negative bank account, I have reevaluated the importance of things.

Okay, I'm going to try again. Sherman's snore is lulling me into relaxation. Perhaps I can record it and market it as something like "animal meditation." I'm pretty sure that National Geographic made a mint off of recordings of the humpback whales. Why not the snore of a Labrador?

Good night, I pray

Ana

* * *

Early in the Morning April 10, 2000

Dear Jesse,

Ironically Cat Steven's "Morning Has Broken" is coming out of my speakers as I write this. I'm starting to become very confused. This backward sleeping thing. Tonight I'm going to break the pattern. I received the thumbs up on sleeping pills or "a" sleeping pill as my pharmacist emphatically suggested. I can do it. A month ago I would have seriously considered washing down the entire bottle with some wine but today I want to sleep when the moon is up and wake when it is down. I don't think that is too much to ask. I'm beginning to hallucinate, at least I keep seeing Kurt Cobain in my kitchen. I question nothing.

Sleep deprivation is a weird thing. I feel like Alice in Carroll's, "Through the Looking Glass." Remember that story? Alice is the heroine in a fantasyland where everything is reversed. The world exists just behind the mirror over her mantel, and she becomes a pawn in a crazy game of chess involving all of the characters in the story. I've often wondered what it would be like to be on the outside looking in? Or would it be on the inside looking out? It would be great to soul switch for a day with someone, even for an hour. Just to see what it's like to literally wear their skin and see through their eyes. Do you ever do that? See a person and close your eyes and try to envision yourself inhabiting her/his body? If you practice, it becomes much easier. I used to find myself doing it while I waited in waiting rooms at doctor's offices. I swear that I could feel that person's ailment.

So this is how I do it. I study a person and nonchalantly pretend I'm reading a magazine or lean back to close my eyes for a moment. Then I carry my soul over to that person, and I hop inside and envision opening my eyes as her/his eyes. I study my new perspective, then turn on the five senses. I rub my hands together, up and down my arms and feel the texture of my new skin. Then I wash my hands over my face and through my hair, or lack of hair, paying attention to the scent as my hands pass my nose. Then I run my tongue across my teeth and rub my lips together. Then I look down at my attire and I move my legs and wiggle my toes. Is it easy?

Do I feel any discomfort? The weirdest thing of all is trying to perceive what sound would be like through another person's ears. I also like to turn my/her/his hands over and study the palms imagining what her fortune reads.

Strangers are easy but the most challenging for me is jumping into a family member because we already have our preconceived notions of what the person sees or feels. What I've learned by practicing this is that people are so quick to pass judgment about others, based on strictly superficial observation that we miss the beauty in individuality. We project our ideas of what is good or pretty or acceptable or moral onto other human beings based on our learned perception. When it comes to our family members, those that we think we probably know the best because of genetics and proximity, they are the people that are the most difficult to understand.

Jumping into my mother was like being on the other side of the mirror; I saw myself through her eyes, arm's length from her tired hands and I read the expression on my face and didn't like what I saw. So when I reconvened with myself,

I adjusted my attitude in her presence because I had experienced her human frailty, inherent in all of us. Sometimes we forget.

Love, Ana

* * *

April 2, 2000

Us

Dear Jesse,

We truly were compulsive liars growing up, feeding people elaborate stories about our lives and our childhood together, our eight-minutes-apart birth, when actually we are not related but were born 8 days apart. We told of our schooling, our friends, our young sexual experiences, anything for the sake of spicing up a conversation with a stranger, remember? It was so much fun and I felt so important being your imaginary fraternal twin that when our vacation or excursions were over and I had to go back to my reality I went through Jesse withdraw.

Did you?

I forget. When did we start telling the truth, or did we just continue to live imaginary lives just for the sake of excitement until we drifted into adulthood and jobs and long-term boys/ men? Sometimes I have a very difficult time deciphering whether some of my memories of our experiences are truth or fiction.

My imagination like yours is vast and ripe with color. I sometimes fear that memories that recently crept into my consciousness are fabrications of a host of memories perhaps braided with past life experience, as well. They are very dark and feel very real. I touch them, taste them, hear them, smell them, you get the picture. But that is what a poet is supposed to do best right? She is to create imagery with the senses and snapshots with words. At least that is what I think. How can I believe my memories when I know that my mind is capable of fantastic fabrication that I can feel? How can I tell the difference and trust myself? Do you trust your own mind? I don't know what I think.

Love, Ana

*　*　*

Jesse stumbled into her kitchen in disbelief. She opened her pantry cabinet for a new box of tissues and her address book. "Briar, Briar." She lounged next to the phone holding onto her tummy and contemplated calling him. "I feel like he should know this."

"Hi. You've reached Briar and Cal. Please leave a message, and we'll get back to you."

"Hey, uh, Briar. Hi, it's Jesse. Yeah weird that I should be calling you out of the blue during the week. I'm sorry, I don't have your work number. In fact, I'm not particularly sure where you work. God, what has it been, like three years since we've seen one another? No, it can't be that long. Anyway, hi. I just need to talk to you. It's about Ana. I received letters in the mail from her. A lot of letters and I, well, I'm confused. Sad and confused. Have you seen her? Have you spoken to her? I just don't know what else to say. I…please call me when you can. Soon though. Bye. Oh, my number should be on your ID."

Minutes later, Briar walked into the apartment and caught his reflection in the stainless steel refrigerator door. "Look at my eyes, Pup." Pup shook and jumped up onto the sofa to snuggle into the corner. Briar opened the freezer door to grab the spoons that he had freezing for a quick eye-puffiness fix, noticing the blinking phone. He flopped back onto the couch next to Pup, rested the spoons on his swollen eyes, and clicked the phone remote. "Hey, uh, Briar. Hi, it's Jesse." He sat up to listen to the message and the spoons fell into his lap.

"Holy shit!" He jumped up grabbed the phone and called her back. "Briar!"

"Jesse! Oh my god, how are you?"

"Did you get my message? Duh, obviously, you called me back."

"Jesse, she sent me letters, too!"

"No way. Weird."

"They are weird, and so sad. I had no idea."

"Neither did I. No idea! I just thought that she was avoiding me again. I stopped calling."

"What about her family?"

"They said nothing. I'm afraid to call them."

"Do you want me to try?" (Silence.)

"I don't know."

"What if she's—" Jesse's voice began to crack.

"I know, I know."

"I feel so bad, Bri."

"Me, too. Terrible. But how were we supposed to know? She hid from us!"

"That's how I feel. But I cannot help but feel guilty for some reason."

"I feel sick." (Silence.) "I'm going to call Peg and Harry. I'll call you right back, Jess."

"Okay. Thank you, Briar."

"It's great to hear your voice, Jess."

Briar hung up the phone, took a deep breath, and rang them. Just as he was about to hang up after several rings, someone answered, "Hello, the Guida residence."

"Wow. Hi, Peg?"

"No, actually this is their neighbor Liz. I'm feeding their pets while they are away."

"Away?"

"Yes, they are in Flor—Who is this speaking?"

"I'm sorry, Liz, my name is Briar and I'm an old friend of Ana. Is everything okay?"

"Hi, Briar. Well things are a bit strange right now, and I don't really feel comfortable talking about it because—"

"Liz, I received a bundle of water-damaged letters in the mail today from Ana, postage stamped in the Florida Keys. Please, what the hell is going on? Is she okay?"

(Silence.) "Ana tried to drown herself, but didn't succeed. Someone found her and revived her, but she was too far gone. She's in a coma, Briar. They don't know if she's going to make it."

Briar grabbed his chest and started to cry. "Where is she, Liz? Please. I have to know."

(Silence.)

"Key West Medical. But it's not quite all the way down in Key West, it's…"

Briar scribbled down the information. "Thank you, Liz. Take care." He hung up the phone and immediately called his travel agent. "Hi, this is Briar Bailey. Yes, how are you? Listen, I need two tickets to Key West, a rental car and accommodations, preferably a bed-and-breakfast. Please, no chain hotels unless there is a five-star suite available, okay? I would like to leave later today, please. Yes, I know that it is short notice, but it is an emergency. Okay…I'll hold. Thank you."

Briar slid down the wall listening to a lousy Muzak rendition of "Lucky Star" by Madonna as he awaited his itinerary. "Please, please, please!" He kept picturing himself and Ana as teenagers on the beach laughing, drunk. He watched her dancing by herself in gay clubs in Manhattan, unaffected by fear or embarrassment. He felt her shaking ten-year-old hand in his while roller-skating around the rink in strobe light and parachute pants and laughed to himself.

"Yes. You do, great! Sun Air, flight 216 to Miami 8:30 from Newark to Key West Charter from Miami, 12:00 a.m. Perfect! Thank you. Okay, Briar Bailey and Jesse—oh god, hold on, I'm not sure of her married name. You must think I'm insane. Hold on." He clicked through his phone ID. "Are you still there? Good, it's Giovanni, Jesse Giovanni. Thank you so much. You have my card number. Thank you."

"Jesse?"

"Hey, Briar!"

"I need your address so I can send a car for you."

"What? What's going on?"

"She's in a coma at Key West Medical."

"What? Oh god!"

"Listen, I'll tell you about it on the flight."

"Flight?"

"I booked us a flight from Newark to Miami, Miami to Key West at 8:30 tonight. I'll have a car there for you at 4:30. Okay?"

"Okay, okay. Thank you, Bri. I don't know what to say. What the hell do I tell Marc?"

"Just tell him the truth. He'll understand. The ticket will be waiting for you at the Sun Air desk. We'll talk over cocktails. See you at the departure gate."

"Wait, my address Bri, 11 Dean Avenue, Zionsville, PA."

"I suck with directions. Where is that near?"

"Allentown, Bri."

"Jess, I'm home!" Marc dropped his stuff opened the fridge, grabbed a Guinness, cracked it open, and poured it into a pint glass leaning down to pet his dog.

"Jess?"

He went outside to enjoy what was left of the October afternoon sun. He noticed a piece of paper taped to the screen door. Jesse knew his afternoon ritual.

"What the hell?"

> Dear Marc,
>
> First of all, please don't worry. I'm fine. I tried to call you at work to no avail, so here's a letter. Ana is in a coma in the Florida Keys... that's all I know. I'm flying out of Newark with my and Ana's old friend Briar at 7:55 p.m., Sun Air, flight 216. Briar made the arrangements last minute. We have to go. I'll be fine, and I'll call you when I get there. I'm sorry that I had to leave you a letter. DON'T WORRY!
>
> I love you,
> Jesse xo

* * *

150 miles away, Briar kissed Pup and Puddy goodbye, left a note on the table next to an unopened bottle of wine for Cal, and slid out the door with his overnight bag.

Day 4

November 2, 2000
Early Evening
Dr. Freedman

ri Freedman walked into his dark apartment and tossed his work bag onto the antique settee.

"Girls?"

He turned on the recessed lighting, dimmed the switch, and closed the blinds.

"Girls?"

He opened the refrigerator, grabbed a day-old carton of lo mein, emptied it into a bowl, and put it in the microwave.

He hit the power button on the sound system, starting the CD shuffle.

"Girls!"

The microwave beeped three times and Mozart's "Sonata in C Major" floated from the speakers.

"Girls! Want some lo mein?"

Two lazy green-eyed tabby cats sauntered into the kitchen meowing and rubbing up against his pants, stretching and yawning. Ari took some noodles from the bowl and coaxed the girls to eat it out of his hand.

"Tough day, girls?"

He put a dollop on top of their food, grabbed chopsticks and a beer from the refrigerator, and settled into the settee. He rested his head against the wall and closed his eyes, listening to Mozart.

The music paused and the CD changer shuffled disks; a solo piano trickled out of the speakers. "Bulletproof" by Radiohead... pianist Christopher O'Reilly's rendition. Ari took a sip of his beer and got lost in it. He looked to his right and saw a bundle of mail on the floor that had been dropped into the mail slot. He sighed, slurped the remainder of the noodles, and picked up the mail.

Everything looked standard: Bill, bill, bill, bill...except for a brown envelope with no return address, postage stamped from Florida.

"Florida?"

He finished the remainder of his beer and tore into the envelope, pulling out a water-damaged bundle of letters. His heart stopped.

"Ana."

* * *

Listen

Dr. Freedman,

I'm sitting here typing in the 2:00 sun on my balcony wondering how you are. I missed another appointment. The Sun Fish must be laying their eggs around the edge of the pond right beneath my balcony; I am staring down and I can see dozens of them lazily swimming in the sun drenched, light green water. It's quite remarkable.

A very large fish, perhaps a trout, keeps circling the celebration. Perhaps it is a female and she has nested in the same vicinity. I hope she is not planning to eat one of the Sunnies for lunch. Or maybe she was hired by the Sun Fish as a bouncer, and she/he has to patrol the area protecting it from any unwanted pond creatures: snapping turtles or largemouth bass. I'm sure that there are pond politics just like on dry land.

I'm relaxed now. Lulled by the sound of crickets and droning cicadas. But earlier today I was very uneasy. I went to see a hypnotherapist named Dr. Sanja yesterday. I know what you are thinking...bullshit.

I did it anyway. Story of my life.

I left her office feeling like I needed a blanket, a pacifier, and a dark corner to rock back and forth and hum to myself in. That was even before I listened to the recorded session.

Please don't misinterpret me. She is fantastic. In fact, you would have loved her.

I pictured her as a Native American medicine woman in one of her past lives. She has that air about her. She is tall, potentially Rubensque, perhaps if she hadn't led such a rich life but was too weathered to appear pale and doughy. She has intense Joni Mitchell blue eyes and long white hair framing her tanned face—not quite leathery but worn in a beautiful way. She wore multicolored reading glasses on the end of her intricate small nose. Her smile was warm and pink, framing naturally white teeth. I think that she was probably a natural blonde in her youth and a striking buxom one at that. If I could draw my interpretation of an Earth Mother or Mother Nature or a goddess, it would be her; she is wise and beautiful, maternal and soft.

I liked her manner. She welcomed me into her office, painted in fantastic southwestern greens, blues, yellows, and washed reds and covered in rich green plants and a goldfish pond in the waiting room. It smelled of sandalwood with a hint of cold water. You know that scent I mean?

"Welcome, Ana, oh, I forgot to ask you in our emails whether or not you are allergic to cats."

"I adore cats, dogs, rats, bats—you get the picture."

"Oh good, I have grown so tired of psychiatry without pets. Now that I am old and have hung up my stethoscope, I feel entitled to have pets running around my practice. They are very healing, you know." She looked at me down her pinched nose and smiled.

"Oh, they most certainly are. I love pets." I immediately told her in detail about my arsenal of pets, some saved, some purchased, all adored and spoiled.

"Oh good." She chuckled, leading me down the blue/green hallway trimmed in yellow to her meditation room.

I had such a good feeling when I walked into the warm, indigo room adorned with mirrored tapestry that she said she picked up in Bali, and an overstuffed olive green ultra-suede couch. It rested on a hand stitched Indian rug; it was blue with sage green and bright yellow and orange dragonflies on it. I loved her style.

"Have a seat and get comfortable." She smiled. "What kind of tea do you like, chamomile, ginger, lemon zest, hibiscus?"

"Hibiscus, please."

She left the room. I fell back into the couch, closed my eyes for a moment, and tried to take in everything. I heard her whistling something in the distance while preparing the tea. I reached over to grab a throw pillow from the edge of the couch. Nestled behind it was a big, fat orange tabby cat who opened one eye and sized me up. Apparently I seemed safe; he didn't move an inch.

"Well hello there, sunshine," I said, reaching over to pet his oversized tummy.

"Oh, you've met Stanley," Dr. Sanja said, sneaking into the room with two cups of steaming, fragrant hibiscus tea, gently pushing the door shut behind with her matronly hip.

"He's an angel," she said.

"He's almost eighteen years old and spends the majority of his geriatric years sleeping in this room. He's such a honey."

She smiled, reached over to hand me a cup of tea, and scratched Stanley's orange chin.

"He loves this." She giggled. She relaxed into an overstuffed red chair across from me, gently blew the steam off the top of her tea and took a sip. She placed her tea on a coaster on the mahogany coffee table between us, nonchalantly wiped a drip from her chin and asked, "Tell me why you've come to see me?"

"Why I've come to see you?"

I pondered, not sure how to answer her question cohesively. Because I wasn't really sure how to glue my scattered thoughts together. She stared through me with warm eyes.

"Well, I know that I intimated my concern to you in our email," I confessed without making eye contact.

"Yes," she said questioningly, "but the first step in my helping you to surface and relinquish some of your angst will be through your verbalizing concerns that you would like to be addressed."

I sipped my tea, scalding my bottom lip, and nervously placed my tea down on the table.

"Dr. Sanja, I am frightened by intimacy." I took a deep breath.

"Go on." She nodded and smiled approvingly.

"And I feel an overwhelming loathing sensation in my gut when I encounter most men with the exception of my father, my Uncle Bob, my best friend Briar, and a few others."

I looked at her for a reaction. Nothing.

"I can eventually trust most men if I feel as if they don't have an ulterior motive."

She sipped her tea and placed it in her left palm, gently holding it with her right hand.

"Okay. What do you think is the definitive point when you feel that you can trust a man?"

"I don't really know how to define it Dr. Sanja."

That was my attempt at being vague and playing dumb when I knew exactly how to answer her question. She saw right through my indifference.

"Okay. Then may I ask you this: Do you have a history of being promiscuous?"

Dr. Sanja stared at me intently. I was taken back by her question.

I choked on the word for a moment. "Yes."

Dr. Sanja nodded and noted something in her mirrored notebook; I watched her, unable to grasp that I confessed to my sordid past. One word: Yes. She smiled at me.

"Did you ever consider that possibly you were dabbling in sexually deviant behavior because you were seeking to trust a man?"

I sipped my tea and tried to inhale some confidence.

"Frankly, Dr. Sanja, I don't know what I was looking for. But all I know is that it certainly wasn't surface pleasure because the majority of the time I was highly intoxicated from a cocktail of illicit substances. It was never a sober affair."

She spoke to me softly, "Did you trust those men?"

I sipped my tea nervously and contemplated her question for a moment.

"Honestly, I don't recall if I felt trust or not. The day after I only had vague recollections of the evening before followed by a week-long crush that lead to nothing but the realization that I was just an object, seeking affection, and acceptance from the opposite sex."

I started to get choked up.

"I feel pathetic."

"Good!"

Dr. Sanja giggled to lighten the mood.

"Not good that you feel pathetic but good that these feelings are surfacing. You are verbalizing things that you have internalized for a very long time I imagine."

She leaned over and handed me a box of tissues.

I started to sob uncontrollably.

"I'm so fearful that if my parents understood my past mentality, they would judge me harshly and that I would lose their acceptance."

I began to calm down and Dr. Sanja smiled warmly.

"You know, Ana, hypersexuality is characteristic of bipolar sufferers. It's common. There is no need to feel shame."

I regained my composure.

"But, Dr. Sanja, hypersexual behavior is a thing of the past. That's the issue! Now I suffer from the antithesis of it. I want nothing to do with sex. I feign illness to avoid sex. I pretend I am asleep to avoid sex. My mind tells me that I hate it. It sometimes makes me cry. I don't know why!"

I started to become very upset again.

"I continually blame my loss of libido on the cocktail of drugs that I take for my chemical imbalance but…"

Dr. Sanja nodded knowingly. "What drugs are you taking, Ana?"

"Lithium, Prozac, Lamictal."

I took a deep breath and shuddered.

"Prozac has been known to destroy the libido so that may have some bearing. But you and I are going to explore other options as well."

She reached over and patted my knee in a motherly kind of way.

"Have you ever been hypnotized, Ana?"

"No. I've tried self-hypnosis but to no avail. My mind kept drifting, and I couldn't follow the prompt."

Dr. Sanja laughed. "You couldn't concentrate on one subject? I find that very hard to believe." She winked facetiously and inched out of her chair to prepare the room for a hypnosis session. She closed the bamboo blinds,

"Do you mind incense?"

"I love incense." I perked up. Her bohemian approach was so comforting.

She handed me three scents to choose from: lavender, musk, and sandalwood.

"This one." I handed her the pungent sandalwood. The scent used to lull Violet and me to sleep when we lived together in college.

"Do you mind if Stanley shares the couch with you?" Dr. Sanja tried to coerce Stanley from his nest behind the pillow.

"That would be great."

I placed my empty cup of tea on the table in front of me and leaned over to scratch Stanley's chin.

Dr. Sanja removed everything from the coffee table in front of me and placed a terra-cotta bowl full of river stones and water in front of me and lit a white floating votive candle in the middle. She placed two sticks of sandalwood incense in holders on either side of the bowl and lit them illuminating her shiny white hair with match light. She gently closed the door and opened a cabinet revealing a hidden stereo.

Turning to me, she asked, "Forest or ocean?"

"Ocean."

"Debussy or Chopin?"

"Both are perfect."

I watched her finger through her CD collection then play the sound of waves rolling onto a beach with a distant piano on the wind. Debussy...Clair de Lune. It was beautiful. I thought of you, Dr. Freedman.

"Now, it is most effective when you are in a lounging position so that you may completely relax."

She arranged the overstuffed pillows behind my head while I nestled into them. Her voice softened.

"Contrary to popular belief, I will not be using a swinging pendulum to mystically send you into a hypnotic trip."

She smiled.

"Close your eyes and concentrate on the sound of the ocean waves. You are in a comfortable, safe boat and gently rolling toward shore. You feel the warm sunshine caress your skin and hair. You feel like a leaf, gently drifting across the surface. You will hear three snaps and will fall into deep comfort. All anxiety will dissipate like ocean spray."

I remember entering into a realm that felt like I was dreaming, but I was still conscious. In the back of my mind, somewhere I thought, "So this is the space between the waking and dream state."

The rest is what she recorded verbatim:

Snap, snap, snap. "You are comfortable, relaxed, warm. What do you smell?" Dr. Sanja asked gently.

My voice was recognizable but less confident.

"I smell the ocean marshmallows roasting. I smell the sun."

"How do you feel?" she asked. I could hear her leaning back into her chair and flipping a page in her mirrored notebook.

"I feel better than I've ever felt. I am not even paranoid about the sharks in here." My voice smiled.

"In where?" she asked.

"Swimming under me in the ocean. If I don't stir the surface, they won't know that I am here. Lying down, I am safe," I explained.

Dr. Sanja paused then asked, "Do you feel like you have to hide from them?"

"Yes," I said emphatically.

"Why?" she questioned me.

"Because I am afraid of them. They look scary…sinister like planes or something. I can see them but they cannot see me. They have small eyes. Creepy."

You could hear Dr. Sanja scribbling something in her notebook.

Dr. Sanja questioned me, "Ana, do you know the sharks?" I didn't answer.

"Why are you curled up?" she asked me, apparently observing my behavior.

"Shhhhhhh!" I whispered loudly. "They will hear us."

"Okay, I'm sorry. I'll speak more softly." Dr. Sanja quieted her voice to appease me.

"They heard us. They want to hurt me. I'm alone." I sounded like I was in a quiet panic.

Dr. Sanja reacted quickly, "Ana, you will hear two clicks and you will no longer fear the sharks. They are simply swimming along with you. They are not trying to hurt you." *Click, click.*

"How do you feel?" Dr. Sanja sounded genuine.

"They are swimming away now. I am a leaf again." I sounded more reserved.

Dr. Sanja took a deep breath.

"Okay, Ana. You are now drifting softly toward shore, and as you float, you are venturing back into your memory. Allow your childhood to unfold as safely as the ocean waves. What do you feel?"

"I feel the sun on my face." My voice sounded almost childlike. It was eerie.

"How old are you, Ana?"

I paused. "I am four. I had a guitar cake for my birthday."

I sounded young.

"Where are you, Ana?"

"I am floating in a donut—a big, blue pool."

"Where are you?"

Silence, followed by, "Aunt Brenda and Uncle Frank's house."

"Are you alone?" Dr. Sanja spoke to me like I was a child.

"Yes. But my sister is over there."

"In the water?" she asked.

"No, sitting on a towel reading a book. She's almost nine," I explained. "She's smart."

I hear Dr. Sanja giggle a bit. "Is there anyone else around?"

"Uh, yes. I can hear my mom and dad laughing. There are people in the caboose. I mean the cabana. Aunt Brenda did a cartwheel. I saw it." (Pause.)

"I'm sliding. I can't say anything. I'm slipping through the middle of the donut and falling slowly in blue, watching the sun on the cement walls. I can hear my mom's voice like when I was in her belly. I feel peaceful. I'm sitting on the bottom and looking up at my floating donut and the sun. A plane crossed the sky. I'm fading.

"The surface is broken, and my sister is swimming down to me...she tugs me to the surface. My mother is standing on the edge, reaching down to the water to grab both of our arms. I'm coughing, but I won't cry. I want my sister to get this attention. I liked it better down there at the bottom of the pool. The light was softer, quiet."

Dr. Sanja paused.

"Why do you want your sister to get this attention, Ana?"

"Because she is all alone. Nobody plays with her."

My voice became quiet, almost a whisper. Dr. Sanja took a deep breath.

"Okay Ana, you are back in the safe boat drifting forward in time. You are but a few years older, perhaps school age. What are you experiencing?"

"I'm so dizzy." I giggled. My young voice smiled.

"Tell me more," she said.

"I'm rolling, rolling down a hill, so fast!"

"Where are you?" Dr. Sanja asked gently.

I paused. "It's a very green, very steep hill. All the kids are rolling. I see my sister, my older cousins. It's a race. I'm losing. We are rolling down to the pond to go swimming. I've stopped on the hill to look up and see my progress. My aunt's cottage and the sound of clinking glasses and ice are long gone. I'm holding on to my towel. My sister is looking up. I mimicked her. 'C'mon, Ana, you're almost there.' I'm so small. Maybe five. I have two long dirty blond braids covered in grass clippings hanging past my elbows on either side of me. I'm wearing a green-and-blue striped bathing suit one-piece. It is my favorite.

"Ana, what is at the bottom of the hill?"

"A pool—no, a pond that looks like a pool. A pond-pool. That's what Hunter called it."

"Hunter? Who is Hunter, Ana?"

Silence. "He is my teenage cousin. He's home from boarding school in New England."

Dr. Sanja sighed before asking more about Hunter. "Is your cousin rolling down the hill, too?"

I sounded childlike. "No. He and his friends are already down at the pond-pool. I don't know his friends. My sister seems embarrassed around them. They're bigger. Hunter told my mom that he would watch us."

Silence. Dr. Sanja was scribbling in the mirrored book. She must have observed me sniffing a scent in the air.

"Where are you now, Ana?"

"I am walking up onto the cabana porch. The four boys are laughing, passing a bottle between them and smoking a pipe. I'm walking up to them and my sister is grabbing my hand to go to sit on a bench by the water. I'm annoyed with her. I want to hang with the big kids. I asked her why we can't sit at the table and my sister said, 'They are doing teenage stuff and we're not teenagers.' I feel annoyed."

"Where are you now, Ana?"

"I am walking into the water. The bottom feels like soft sand. It's warm. I don't have to hold my nose anymore. I can swim underwater, and I want to show off for the boys. I can dive, too."

"Where is your sister, Ana?"

"She's right next to me. I'm trying to swim ahead to the dock. My sister is telling me to stay in the shallow end, 'Mom said.' I'm climbing the ladder up to the dock. 'I can swim fine,' I snapped back at Amber. Amber followed me up on to the dock and sat and watched me dive after dive after dive until she felt confident."

Silence. Dr. Sanja must have observed a change in my mood.

"What are you doing now, Ana? Are you in the water?"

"No. I'm taking a break. I'm wrapped in a towel that smells like home and dryer sheets."

"Where is Amber?"

"Lying on a towel next to me. The boys are walking onto the dock. Hunter and his three friends. They are all giggling and laughing. Hunter's eyes are as red as his hair but he is kind. He's smiling. 'Ana, you can dive now! I saw it!' he said, walking toward me. His friends are making fun of him for talking to me like that.

'Quit it,' he says. 'She's my little cousin!' Amber is completely immersed in whatever is playing on her Sony Walkman. I don't know how old the boys are, but they have scratchy deep voices. Not quite like a man but not quite like a boy either. I'm not sure if I like them. I don't know how to act. Hunter is sitting down next to me. He smells like a parent party. He's sitting Indian style and showing me a coin trick that he learned at school. I think he's neat.

"A huge tire tube just grazed the top of my head and splashed into the pond. Amber is still listening to her headphones. Maybe she wasn't splashed like me and Hunter. The dock is shaking and the three boys all ran and dove over our heads into the water. Amber is sitting up abruptly. She is angry and wet. 'Hey, my Walkman is wet.' The boys don't care. I'm reaching over and loaning her a corner of my towel to dry it off."

Dr. Sanja is scribbling.

"Are you still on the dock, Ana?"

"Yes, but Hunter is asking me and Amber if we want to play on the tire tube with him and his friends. 'No, Ana.' Amber is looking at me not wanting me to go in without her and not wanting to go in herself. 'I'll watch her, Amber. Don't worry.' Hunter just picked me up and I'm on his shoulders. I feel like I am going to slip off. He's holding on tightly to my knees and walking into the water. I'm laughing out of nervousness. 'No splashing, guys. Ana's gonna play.' Hunter is smiling. We're rocking the two of them on the tube. They are trying to knock each other off.

"Hunter is putting me up onto the tube. 'Hold on,' he's saying, while swimming me around the pond and making engine noises. I'm laughing and bouncing my feet on the opposite side of the tire, and I'm wondering how these inflatable tubes hold heavy cars. I'm embarrassed to ask. I'm sitting up on one side, and my little legs are stretched across the donut hole and barely reach the other side.

"I see something swim beneath the donut hole and up through the middle his white fingers are climbing. I'm scared to death! 'Du dah, du dah, du dah, du dah du dah du dah du dah.'

"He's singing the Jaws theme—he's laughing a screechy teenage boy laugh—climbs up onto the other side of the tube to sit down. His weight pushes me way up into the air.

"'Did I scare you?' His eyes are beet red and his hair is long and brown. I'm spooked."

Silence.

You can hear Sanja open her mouth.

"Are you comfortable, Ana?"

"No. Yes. Now I am."

"What do you mean?"

Her chair creaks, and she is scribbling something.

"The other boy is here now. He seems friendly. He is pulling us around on the tube."

"Who is on the tube?"

"Me and the boy with long, dark hair."

"Where is Hunter?"

Silence.

"He is playing a card game on the dock with my sister. We are playing a game in the water."

"What game, Ana?"

"The boys call it dizzy. We are spinning and spinning on the tube until we feel sick. 'Stop! I'm going to fall off!' My sister doesn't notice.

"'Here, hold on to this!' The brown-haired boy is grabbing my hand and shoving it down his wet denim shorts. His friend is laughing and shoving his hand in my bathing suit. He's scratching me and it hurts! I'm trying to pull my hand away, but he's holding my wrist.

"'Hold on to it!' he's demanding. His friend is laughing even harder.

"'To what?' I'm struggling. I feel a wet heat and something different. Changing. I feel sick.

"'No, you're not doing it right! Do this stupid!' He's becoming very impatient and holding my arm really tight, moving it around inside his pants.

"'That's better.' He's seems more content now. I'm crying. I don't understand and I can't scream. Amber cannot see this because it is all underwater.

"'Why are you crying? It feels good, right?' He's breathing heavy and moving his other arm under the water. His friend's eyes are closed, and he is smiling with his head back on the tube. I don't understand."

Silence.

"Are you okay, Ana?" Dr. Sanja sounds maternal.

"I feel like I am going to throw up."

You can hear her preparing me for a potential accident. The garbage can is shuffling towards me.

"The boy with the long brown hair is uttering things under his panting breath, and I'm still struggling to pull my hand away. His friend's face is turning red...I feel saliva filling my mouth like I'm going to puke. I want my mom.

"'I want my mommy!' I'm screaming. 'I want my—' *Slap.*

"The boy with the long brown hair's hand has smacked me across the mouth. 'Shut up you stupid little bitch.'

"I am gagging and I'm throwing up my lunch all over his hand. He's turning bright red with anger and is pushing me away in the water. My sister and Hunter see me struggling in the water, and they dive in after me.

"'What the fuck, guys, you're supposed to be watching her!' Hunter is grabbing my arm and carrying me over to my sister. She looks panicked.

"'What happened?' My sister is wrapping me in a warm towel. I'm embarrassed, and I don't know why.

"'Can we go home now?' I'm speaking between sobs. Amber has put me on Hunter's back and the three of us are walking up the big, green hill to the party. I'm falling asleep with my face pressed against his freckled back; my little legs are gently wrapped around his skinny waist. I can hear the clinking of glasses, music, and my father's laugh. I'm asleep."

Dr. Sanja is scribbling in her mirrored notebook.

"Ana, you are very relaxed and back in your boat again floating towards shore. When you wake, you will feel refreshed like you just had a long nap. You feel comfortable and calm. You feel as if a weight has been lifted from your soul. Your soul is light, white, content without sadness.

"With the ebb and flow of the water, your body cleanses itself. You can feel love again, Ana."

Silence.

"You are drifting gently toward the present. You will hear two claps and will return to the now."

Silence.

Clap. Clap.

"Just relax."

Dr. Sanja shuffles toward the recording and *Click.*

Dead air.

And Dr. Freedman, the most amazing thing is that I do feel lighter. Something has been lifted. I feel like my heart has opened a little; there is not as much darkness. I have forgiven something or someone, I think.

I just wanted to share it with you.

Love, Ana

Ari closed his eyes and held the letter to his chest. He went to the refrigerator, grabbed another beer, and unfolded the next letter.

June 24, 2000

Light

Dear Dr. Freedman,

It's actually July 1. I began to write to you a week ago but couldn't put my experience down into words. My fate is all so strange but liberating at the same time. I had to absorb it before I could share it. I still don't know what to do with my new tangible understanding, but I finally feel like I am swimming toward the surface. I'm closer to the blue sky. I am awake.

I had a second session with Dr. Sanja. We spent the majority of the first hour discussing the first hypnosis and my disturbing recollection of the stoned, teenage boys.

It's difficult for me to even write this word: molestation.

I guess that would explain my preoccupation with fear of intimacy or my need to separate commitment from intimacy, maybe? What do you think?

I'm guessing. That is my self-diagnosis. My first taste of "sex" was violent, not consensual, cold, shallow, hollow, foreign, and frightening and I buried it deep in a chasm of me. My Kundalini. Metaphysical stuff.

It affected every other facet of my being. Every one of my chakras had been slightly tainted as a result perhaps exacerbating my bipolar imbalance.

I am only able to hypothesize this because of my experience with being attuned to Reiki… light/love healing. I think that I told you about that.

Sorry to digress, but I'm not certain that you're familiar with what I studied on one of my manic swing, self-realization kicks; I am not being cynical about Reiki itself but about my initiation into it.

I may have been afraid to share details with you for fear of being silently scoffed at. At that point, I thought that I was going to be a Reiki practitioner. Although that fell through, Reiki has been a very useful healing tool for me. I've been able to help many or at least open their minds to alternative healing methods and options.

In addition, I freak people out completely because of the sensation they feel when I place my hands above or near any one of their chakras or a body part plagued by pain or illness. There is no scientific explanation; you'd dismiss it.

I'm digressing...but you need a brief explanation, Dr. Freedman. There are seven main chakras in the body that are essentially invisible orbs of energy that house past lives, emotions, intuition, sexuality, communication skills, etc. Above the head there is the crown chakra, violet in color that is representative of cognition, followed by the third eye or intuition chakra, indigo in hue, somewhere between the eyes.

When you move down to the throat, there is a blue chakra representative of communication and moving down the body, suspended in the upper chest is the heart chakra, represented by the color green...love and emotion.

Then when you drift down to the solar plexus region there is a brilliant yellow chakra that houses a many-faceted power followed by an orange glowing orb of energy located in or around the crotch (for lack of a better description). This chakra houses issues pertaining to sexuality. Somewhere between the thigh and the soles of our feet there is the root chakra or kundalini that is red in color and is a pillar of strength and emotional stability.

So, do you see the correlation here? If I housed my ill-experience in my Kundalini, inadvertently hindering my emotional stability it must have sent a wave of darkness through the other six chakras: imbalance.

I think that it makes perfect sense and that is exactly what Sanja and I discussed.

But Dr. Freedman, what I learned in the hypnosis session following our discussion will never cease to amaze me. It could justify Nietzsche's

"God is dead" philosophy for those who allow it or who take his carefully chosen trinity of words literally rather than diving deeper to understand the premise of his philosophy.

And if I didn't know better, I would judge his words at face value because my faith and trust in the inherent good of the majority of mankind would simply seem a shattered myth or pipe dream after what I have learned from my own subconscious.

On the surface, no god = no conscience, and no conscience = no morals, and no morals = no remorse, and no remorse = no fear, and no fear = no repercussions, and no repercussions = evil; hence the all-encompassing god is as good as dead.

But I've delved deeper Dr. Freedman; I now know that the universe offers so much more than what we see physically. We have to learn to "see" it with our senses. We have to wake up our third eye intuition to even begin to understand that there really is "good."

"God" is not dead but is very much alive in life lessons. As far as I am concerned, whoever coined the euphemism "What doesn't kill you makes you stronger" had it all figured out.

Okay, I will reiterate to you verbatim the contents of our recorded hypnosis session.

Dr. Sanja quietly spoke, cradled by the sound of the ocean wave recording.

"Ana, you are comfortable, rocked gently by the ocean and drifting in a boat toward the safe shoreline. The sun is caressing your skin and you are at peace, one with the sea, sky, and sun."

Long pause.

"As you float toward the white, sandy beach, you are moving toward your current age of 27. Feel the change in your mental state, your physical self, and your emotions. You are floating gently through time. Watch time pass. Focus on events, faces, people, pets, scents. Feel them. Experience them."

Long pause.

"Why are you crying and smiling, Ana?"

"I am so sad, but relieved. She sees more than we do here."

Dr. Sanja asked gently, "Whom are you speaking of, Ana?"

"Jesse is with me. I feel her sympathy. She is so kind. She is stroking Nanny's freckled face. I wish that I could close her mouth, but I am afraid that her spirit needs for it to remain open. Her green eyes are peaceful. They are no longer clouded, old."

Dr. Sanja scribbles in her mirrored notebook. "Who is peaceful, Ana?"

"My nanny. She wasn't supposed to die, but somehow I knew that she was going to. I slept by the phone last night. She stares at something we cannot. She looks amazed like a child on Christmas morning. I'm following her gaze and I see nothing but a sterile, white hospital ceiling. I want to be where she is but I won't tell Jesse. It would upset her. Jesse is sad, a little confused I think. Nan looks so content. There is something really beautiful that embraced her after she exhaled and didn't inhale again."

Silence.

"How do I tell my mother that her mother died?"

Silence.

Dr. Sanja is scribbling. "You are very strong, Ana. You are an old soul. There is a brilliant white light surrounding you, Jesse, and your grandmother. It is peaceful. Embrace it and know that she is weightless, free, and surrounded by warmth and kindness. Your mother knows this. Ana, you are not afraid. You are comfortable."

There is approximately three minutes of silence.

Sanja clears her throat.

"Now you are drifting in the boat, at peace, feeling the ebb and flow of life in the gentle waves. You are tapping your fingers. Do you hear something, Ana?"

"There is music in the distance. I...I'm being sucked into the music, darkness."

You can hear the turning of a page, and Dr. Sanja adjusting in her chair. "Where are you, Ana?"

"I am sitting at a bar. It's wintertime. Everyone is pale and dressed for the cold. My friend is cackling next to me talking to her friend. They are not interested in including me. I'm fine with that. I'm watching people. I feel like a fish out of water. I don't belong here in New York City. I'm smoking a cigarette, trying to pass time. I feel alone. I wish I were at home."

Dr. Sanja clears her throat again. "Why do you wish you were at home Ana?"

Silence.

"Let me ask you again. Why do you wish you were at home?"

"I don't belong here. I have nothing to talk about with these people."

My voice sounds agitated and Sanja asks me what is bothering me.

"Girls," I almost shouted. "I hate the gossip! I'm going into another room to be alone with my cigarettes and my gin martini. I feel guilty that I don't like them, but I am tired of pretending. I'm not like them."

Dr. Sanja allows time to pass.

"Where are you, Ana? You are seemingly more relaxed."

My voice has changed.

"I am sitting in a big red chair. It looks more comfortable than it is. I'm watching an obvious first date illuminated by red and blue lounge light. Body language is so telling. The woman is seemingly standoffish, and leaning back into her chair with her fishnet legs crossed and one arm crossed over her stomach. Her other is holding a cocktail. A cosmopolitan I think. I cannot make out her eyes, but her lips are bright red, framed by short black bangs; she has a page-boy haircut. Her face is pale and her hands are nondescript."

"Why are you giggling?"

Dr. Sanja is obviously getting a kick out of my changing demeanor. My speech is beginning to sound a bit slurred and stoned.

"It's just that guy!" I laugh.

"He's so awkward but making a desperate attempt to be suave. He just leaned over to light her cigarette and his dangling scarf knocked her cosmo glass into her lap! He's trying to blot her fishnets with the tablecloth and she isn't taking this well. She is sidling off the chair while brushing the drink from her faux fur cuffed sweater. It's the most animated I have seen her! She is cat-like…walking her way toward the facilities, and he is sitting back in his chair looking around to see if anyone witnessed his faux pas."

Sanja is getting a kick out of this. You can hear her giggling while scribbling in her notepad.

"Holy shit, the table is smoldering! He doesn't see it! He is leaning back brushing his shaggy dyed black locks away from his eyes, watching toward the ladies room direction. I cannot move and I'm laughing! He still hasn't noticed. Others are looking around to try and figure out what the stench is. 'What's that smell, what's that smell? Burnt hair? A joint?'

The peanut gallery is reacting in whispers.

An attractive, effeminate, angry cocktail server struts his way over to his table and stamps out the smoldering tablecloth with a bar towel. The guy is saying, 'Oh, I'm so sorry I—'

"'What, are you a complete fucking asshole?' Just as his date is walking back up to the table, grabs her coat, and snobs her way toward the door.

"'Wait!' The guy is fussing with his scarf, pulls some bills from his wallet, and gives them to the server.

"'Sorry.' He is jetting out the door after her, pushing the half-open wallet into the back pocket of his punk plaid pants.

Silence.

"Jade and Jed are pawing one another."

"Who are Jade and Jed?"

"She's a he that makes a pretty she and he's a cowboy that likes that she is a he/she.

Dr. Sanja giggles and scribbles in her notebook.

"Where are you, Ana?"

"In the lounge. They're lighting my smoke, telling me their story. They are whispering and cooing or something. I feel mildly uncomfortable. I'm watching the effeminate server cater to a group of men in the corner, hidden by the shadow of a pillar cast in red light. All I can make out is the clinking of their glasses…single malts, some on the rocks. And their shoes. Expensive. And their mumbles…You should see the waiter. He is kissing their asses with his hand on his jutting hip like a flirting schoolgirl. He's shifting uncomfortably, fixing his hair. He is trying to impress them. It's sad, really. He is looking over his shoulder at me. I quickly try to look occupied. Cigarette in my mouth, I search my bag for a light. I feel awkward, doughy, contrived. I'm being scrutinized. The waiter is turning on his heel. He's breezing by me. I'm finishing with my martini. I love olive juice. I'm being careful not to look too desperate to eat the five olives at the bottom of my drink. Fuck it. I'm eating them one by one, plucking them from the Napoleon glass with my fingers. I am nonchalant."

Silence.

"Ana, why has your face changed? What's wrong?" Sanja is gentle in her question.

"I am sipping another martini, waving at the four gentlemen in shadow that bought it for me. I asked the waiter to thank them for me. They are looking over. There are four of them. I am mouthing, 'Thank you.' I feel young. Uncomfortable."

Silence.

Ocean sounds. Sanja clears her throat.

"Ana, what is happening? Why are you leaning back your head? Are you tired? Do you want to go home?"

"My left eye is shutting. I cannot control it. My head hurts. I feel comfortable. No, uncomfortable. I'm closing my eyes. The smoke, the music, the conversation are all one feeling. They are braiding in the front of my mind. I'm opening my eyes but I cannot focus. I'm walking toward the light…the bathroom. I feel really stoned but different. It feels like heroin…but different. Not friendly."

Silence.

You can hear crying, like the quiet whimpers between vomiting episodes when you await the impending horror of the next involuntary purge.

Dr. Sanja sighs. "Where are you, Ana?"

"A redheaded girl with red lips is helping me to a blue room. 'I'll get you some water. Are you alone?' There is an echo. I am laughing and crying in tandem. There are people there. They are ignoring me. 'Why don't you like me?'

"I am yelling to them, 'Why don't you like me?' They are turning their backs toward me. The redheaded angel is here with water. I am thanking her. I'm reaching up to hug her, and I'm falling to the floor. She's trying to catch me. The glass is broken. I hear it. I don't see it. I feel it. I am lying in it. She is pulling me toward the wall and brushing the glass from my cheek. I am propped up against the wall like a rag doll. Someone is laughing.

"'C'mon, Brigette,' a guy is whispering impatiently.

"The sound cuts me. 'I can't just leave her here!'

"'Let her sober up. C'mon. We have to go.' He sounds annoyed. She's leaning down to me. Her breath smells sweet like schnapps.

"'You'll be okay,' she is saying. She is holding my face in her hands. The boy is pulling her away, and I cannot see his face in shadow."

Silence.

"Why do you scowl, Ana?"

I'm crying. "I cannot speak. I hear a male voice asking about me." Silence.

"Someone slaps my face gently. A man. I cannot focus but I see his shoes. It was one of the men who bought me the drink. I cannot speak.

"'Are you okay? Do you want to come home with me?' He whispers, 'Did I do this to you?'

"I hear other male voices coming in the corridor. He's taking my face in his hands, kissing my mouth with single malt slobber, and I'm focusing but cannot physically push him away. He's looking at me. It's the man—THAT man!"

"What man, Ana?"

"That man who I saw at work—who I waited on! It's him! Crisp polo shirt—the one who jeered at me and asked, 'Do I know you?' It's him! He's doing this to me! He's kissing me violently! I'm screaming and he's covering my mouth! I'm biting his hand as hard as I can.

"'Ouch, you stupid little bitch.'

"I'm screaming as loud as I can! He's getting up, brushing himself off. He's holding his hand and he's kicking me. He's walking away. I hear his voice in the corridor with the other male voices. I am crying but I cannot move my limbs easily. I cannot get up!

"'Please come here…Over here!'

"Who are you speaking to, Ana?"

"I hear my friend asking the men in the corridor if they have seen me. 'No, but can I buy you a drink?' She is giggling; I am screaming as loudly as I can! She doesn't hear me. I cannot get any sound out. I can hear them flirting with her. I am alone, but there is part of my broken glass next to me. I'm reaching for it. I have it! I can hold it. It's cutting me, but I can grip it. I'm flinging it toward the corridor. She's looking into the lounge. She sees me!

"'Ana, what happened?' She's running over to me, wrapping her scarf around my bleeding hand.

"'Oh my god, what's wrong?' She's running to the corridor for help, and to yell to her friend."

Silence.

The ocean music is playing and I've ceased to whimper.

"Why are you shivering, Ana?"

My voice sounds wintry and my teeth are chattering. "I am really cold. I can't stop shaking!"

"Where are you?"

Pause.

"I don't know, really. On a tile bathroom floor? My eyes are fixed on the claw-foot of the tub. I cannot tell if it's a face—a lion's head perhaps? There is quiet city light falling onto the tub—a powdery shadow. I think that it is snowing. I am calm now. I'm inching my way up to lean against the tub. My dress is in a pile on the floor. There is puke all over it and in my hair. Everything hurts. My right hand hurts. There is a big gash on my palm. I feel like I'm going to get sick again. I'm remembering what happened—sort of. My body looks so pale. I'm only wearing underwear. I see the guy's face in my mind's eye. I'm untouched. I wasn't raped. I feel the radio softly playing a classical rendition of 'Oh Tannenbaum' outside of the door, colored

Christmas tree light is peeking underneath. I'm in my friend's apartment. Safe.

"I cannot move to the toilet and I'm getting sick..."

Silence.

You can hear a softened thud, like a muffled version of falling onto the bed when you're really tired. Dr. Sanja is scribbling in her notebook.

"Okay, Ana, you're back in your boat drifting softly toward shore. The sun is slowly going down and you are cool and comfortable."

Silence.

Waves crash.

"You are floating back toward the present—here with me on a soft couch, safe. You will hear two claps and will lay silently in peace."

Clap, clap.

Silence.

"Ana, you will hear two snaps and will slowly wake up refreshed, rekindled, and relieved. A world of anger has been lifted from your heart. You will feel a soft sense of renewal and inspiration."

Snap, snap, then *click.*

The session ended.

I feel different. I am lighter and blown away by the six degrees of separation between people, places, events, and that word called *coincidence.* Another lesson I can feel.

Love, Ana

Ari wiped tears from his eyes, shaking his head. The girls were snuggled into his thighs, Clair De Lune floated from the speaker... unfettered piano keys comforting them.

He put the letter down and walked over to the bookshelf. He pulled *Textbook of Anatomy and Physiology Anthony & Kolthoff Ninth*

Edition 1975 from the shelf and sat down at the piano. He closed his eyes and opened up the front cover. There he was, a younger version of himself nestled into a couch with beautiful Rebecca, holding up a glass of champagne toward the camera…the floor littered with New Year's confetti and streamers. Her smile lit up the photo, faded from time; her gorgeous mahogany skin glowed. He turned over the photo.

> To My Ari…
>
> May this photo be a reminder of how grateful I am to you for helping me to pass Anatomy 101 ;). I will be forever grateful for your tutorials, late into the evening. What would I have done without your studious assistance?
>
> Love, Rebecca

He closed the book and smiled.

"Hi, Connie…sorry to call after hours. Listen…please cancel my appointments for tomorrow. Something has come up, and I have to leave town for a couple of days. Yes…yes, my parents are fine. No…I will explain later. I have to fly to Miami. Tonight."

Day Four

November 2, 2000
Evening
Briar and Jesse

With the exception of time passed, there wasn't a lull in the conversation. It was as if they had lunch together yesterday. That's the way Ana wanted it to be. They reminisced about their teenage sexual liaisons with strangers, with one another, the parties, their significant others while they smothered each other with much deserved compliments.

"Your skin looks amazing!"

"Thanks, Bri! Jesse blushed thousands of feet above the ground. She felt like a sexy teenager again.

"No really. What are you using?"

"Nothing. I think it's just, well, marriage... maybe?"

"You know, that's what I need to do, just leave my face alone! I put so much shit on my skin. I think it's overkill, you know? I'm going to need work done soon if I don't stop with the facials. I'm addicted."

Jesse cracked up, enjoying the camaraderie. It had been a while. "You look hot, baby! Don't change a thing." She growled. It felt good.

And one inch above their reality, I sat with Ana, sort of rosy-cheeked again, lost in Briar and Jesse's conversation.

"You wish you were there, don't you?"

Silence.

"Well, don't you?" Ana fumbled with Nate's baby blanket, smoothed her green dress and stared into the distance.

"May I have a smoke?"

I tossed her a smoke, watching her eyes well up with tears while she tried to act preoccupied with inhaling.

"Queen Thespian."

"Please, Gabriel... leave me alone."

"See how much they love you, Ana?"

She smiled, and I traced a tear down her freckled cheek with my eyes.

"I miss them, Gabe. I miss them all so much, but I—"

"But what, Ana?" I stopped and took a deep breath so I didn't lose my cool.

"You WHAT?"

She shook her head.

"I don't know. I can't explain. It's just that I can't live like I did. I existed without living, you know? All of my loved ones. They're living their existence."

"What, you can't turn that around? Huh? How about Nate?"

I flashed an image of Nate and Sadie, naked as children staring into each other's eyes beneath white sheets, in the soft light of downtown Manhattan dusk.

Ana smiled and closed her eyes.

Then I showed her mom, dad, and sister sitting around a table with Uncle Sunny and Aunt Mary drinking beer. Wild-eyed, Peg pushed the letter from Ana toward Uncle Sunny who smoothed his strawberry blond comb over into place.

He cleared his throat and read it aloud:

April 2, 2000

Spark

Dear Mom and Dad,

    I have never heard of a wedding quite like yours. I wish I could've been a fly on the wall of the women's detention center that April Fool's

Day, 1965. Your wedding should have given you keen insight into what the fates had in store for you as a couple, as business partners, as parents, and as grandparents. It certainly was a bumpy ride in the back of your 1945 Army Jeep, now parked and collecting dust in a barn, home to mating neighborhood cats. But out of all of the vehicles, don't you think Jeeps are the most fun to ride in?

Your story is most unconventional, and I wouldn't expect anything else from either one of you.

It was "The Dawning of the Age of Aquarius." You were kids in love, with no money and bad real estate blood between your two families.

For a long time, I questioned whether or not you were an inmate, mom. Hey, what the hell? The only preacher in town was there that day and he drove a cool old Jeep to boot, right, dad?

The photos are priceless. The two of you, Uncle Rat and Aunt Eve as your witnesses and your preacher with the salt-and-pepper brush cut and thick black cat eyeglasses, hiding the expression in his eyes behind the Kodak glare.

Dad, you were skinny, early 20s and looked like Dustin Hoffman in "The Graduate." And mom in a traditional white dress? Not even close.

Wasn't it satin, bright yellow, Coco Chanel with an edge, with a mink stole and a hat? Fantastic! You had your long dark brown hair draped across your forehead in a severe side part with thick black eyeliner on your upper lid… very Audrey Hepburn.

Your 20-year-old face looked so elegant and confident; a bit crazy and full of secrets. You had a new one to throw into your closet.

Uncle Rat looked like a blond, rosy-cheeked kid, full of fun. Aunt Eve was the only serious looking one in the crowd. Her beautiful porcelain face framed with dark hair smiled, but her eyes and her posture were nervous, like she thought the marriage police were going to break down the door and split the two of you up any minute. What a scene!

How did you keep it a secret for so long? What was it…six months? Then a bouquet of flowers came to Nanny and Poppa's for you, mom, addressed to Mrs. H. Guida. And Nanny hand delivered them to you accusingly. Do I have it right? You must have felt so uncomfortable.

Did the two of you have to rendezvous in secret? Were you forbidden to see each other? Was it like the Montagues and Capulets?

Now…years later, it certainly wasn't a Romeo and Juliet ending. I can just picture the two of you running off for a makeshift, one-night honeymoon. When you are young and in love, I'm sure that even a one-night honeymoon feels like a week in an exotic place. And you had the element of "secret" braided into your nuptials. That must have made it all the more exciting!

What did you do when you got home, mom? When Nanny asked, "How was your night, Peg?" What did you say?

"It was OK," then disappear upstairs to your bedroom, secretly smiling? Or did you make up some rambling, elaborate story like, "Oh, it was OK. Eve and I caught a movie and dinner. Nothing too spectacular," and then sat down at the kitchen table tapping your fingers, silently praying for forgiveness for this one, thinking about the guy you left behind for my dad.

Between bites of a sandwich you put together, you tried to figure out how you were going to tell Gunnar, the artist in Germany that you were engaged to, that you fell in love with and married someone else. Maybe Nanny broke your deep thoughts with a parental, "A letter came in the mail from Gunnar today," then she gave you the eye. You probably picked it up and dismissed it like it wasn't important and slipped it into your purse when your mom turned her back. Then sidled upstairs with it.

It was April 2, 1965, and the two of you were married one day. And you wonder where my rebellious streak comes from? I may have a genetic predisposition to bizarre decision-making. Granted, the flippancy of my personality and the inconsistent patterns that I show are directly related to my chemical imbalance. But my passionate decisions are based solely on love. Granted, some may scoff at my decisions and some may find me reprehensible. But I feel that what society dictates as "the norm," sometimes is devoid of emotion, namely love.

I digress.

When you look into someone's eyes and feel like you have finally made it home, that is love. Whoever that soul may be or whatever the scenario may be, it's good. I'm sure that the reason you married out of passionate desperation like you did was because you saw the same thing in each other's eyes. You felt something that you never encountered with anyone else; that is real.

If I were a fly on the wall on April 1, 1965, this is what I think that I would've seen:

To Mom—

Standing unsure, pressing red lips together, smoothing your yellow dress with nervous hands, you bend down to brush away a scuff from patent leather shoes, hardly recognizing your own ankle, wrapped in silk stockings…straightening up, you smooth your mink stole, and smile politely at the preacher, who is preparing for your union… brown eyes burn into your flush cheek.

You turn and look out the window staring at the freshly shorn lawn and barbed wire fence, drifting into memory.

Eleven years old and sitting with Suzy Stiles, licking ice cream cones on the popcorn scented

Coney Island Boardwalk, looking at the Steeple Chase…just closed down and surrounded by fencing and wire to keep the kids out.

Suzy pointed to a just married couple…

They laughed, carrying on with a bottle of whiskey.

"Look how flouncy her dress is. Yuck. When I get married, I'm going to wear something much more chic. Simple. More Manhattan. Aren't you?"

Your brown-eyed groom touched your shoulder.

"You're okay?"

"Yes," you said.

"I was just thinking."

He smiled warmly.

"The preacher's almost ready."

Thank you for rolling with my punches, mama y papa.

Love, Ana

"Don't even go, Mary," Peg cried.

"You won't recognize her. She's not there."

Mary's beautiful brown Irish eyes tried to comfort Peg while Harry looked at Amber knowingly and lowered his tired eyes. Uncle Sunny, never at loss for words, hung his head and folded the letter.

"No, Peg, we are going to see her in the morning."

Mary piped up, "Absolutely."

* * *

Ari Freedman took a 9:00 p.m. direct flight from Allentown Pennsylvania to Miami, with a connecting flight to Key West, arriving at the hospital with an overnight bag and a heavy heart at 2:00 a.m.

Much to the night nurses' chagrin, Dr. Ari Freedman called on his way and asked that a piano be set up in Ana's room upon his arrival.

"This is Dr. Ari Freedman calling. I will be arriving at Key West Medical to tend to my patient, Ms. Ana Guida in ICU."

"Good evening, Dr. Freedman. That is fine."

The night nurse looked at the time.

"What time will you be arriving in the morning...so I can arrange for your arrival?"

"In approximately two hours. About 2:00 a.m."

The nurse looked confused.

"Dr. Freedman, that won't be necessary. You can meet with Dr. Beri in the morning—"

"I SAID—" He took a deep breath to gain composure. "I said 2:00 a.m. That is when I will arrive. I am her primary psychiatrist, flying in from the Northeast, and I require her records...and a piano."

The nurse was perplexed.

"A piano...I'm sorry, Doctor, we don't have access to a piano."

"I require a piano...There is always a piano in maternity. Wheel it into Ana Guida's room."

"Dr. Freedman..." She looked around for advice. "Dr. Freedman, I don't think that is allowed."

"LOOK...I KNOW Nurse Sevigney. SHE would understand. My patient NEEDS music."

The nurse cleared her throat. "I will see what I can do."

"NO...you WILL do what I ask, or Nurse Sevigney will be told that you DID NOT COMPLY...understand?"

The nurse was agitated. "Okay."

Ari hung up.

The nurse dialed the phone.

"Good Evening Nurse Sevigney. I am sorry to call you...Dr. Ari Freedman called and demanded that a piano be placed in Ana Guida's room. Apparently he will be at the hospital at 2:00 a.m. He says he knows you."

Rebecca looked at the clock and sighed, remembering a much younger Ari Freedman from nursing school. She smiled and bit her bottom lip. "So what is the question?"

The nurse paused. "So you know him?"

Rebecca laughed. "I do...if the doctor wants a piano...a piano he will have. Now don't call me in the middle of the night with such ridiculous questions!"

Rebecca hung up the phone and smiled.

"Ari Freedman. Dr. Freedman."

She nodded her head in laughter and awe. She looked up toward the ceiling and smiled.

"You move in mysterious ways."

She looked in the mirror and fluffed her beautiful, salt-and-pepper raven black curls.

* * *

Early Morning
November 3, 2000

Two hours later, Ari Freedman found his way to room 115, opened the door, and closed it like a tomb. Avoiding looking at her, paging through her chart, he gingerly placed the chart down and hung his head. He had many geriatric patients over the years who winked out because of illness, loneliness, or loss of hope…but never a young person. A vibrant person with so much life; he felt like he failed her.

Ana looked on as Dr. Freedman sat on the cot listening to Ana's rhythmic breathing muffled by the oxygen mask. The piano had been rolled into her room as requested. He walked over and touched the keys.

"Twinkle, Twinkle Little Star…"

Silence. He closed his eyes.

He walked over, unable to focus on Ana's face. He kneeled quietly next to her bed, and said a prayer in Hebrew:

וכרב האל לחר ,הקבר, הרש בקעי ,קחצי םהרבא וניתובא דורב ימ יאמ
תואירב התוא רובע הלמח אלמ תויהל שודק דורב תא זכתיי .הנא טעמ תוחאלו
האלמ התוא חולשל לק שיח םיהולאש .תמצוע תא תויחהל ןתינ התוא רזחשל ןתינ
ןמא ונל ונתנ ,שפנהו ףוגה לש שודיחה

(May the one who blessed our ancestors, Abraham, Isaac and Jacob, Sarah, Rebecca, Rachel and Leah, bless and heal little Ana. May the Blessed Holy One be filled with compassion for her health to be restored and her strength to be revived. May God swiftly send her a complete renewal of body and spirit, and let us say, amen.)

Dr. Freedman stood and sat down at the piano, took a deep breath, looked at Ana's body, riddled with tubes, and felt a childlike sadness…a hopelessness that only crept into his heart in the most vulnerable of spaces. He was lost, too.

He started to play Debussy, "Claire de Lune."

It started like a soft rain. His eyes closed and his fingers weaved the sound into a tempest…wind, heartache, love, life…hope. He played like no one was listening. He played from his heart. He didn't hear the door open and close but felt the soft presence of a lost lover sit down on the bench beside him…a warmth that cannot be described. He would've known her anywhere.

"You play as beautifully as the first time I heard you." Rebecca lay her head on his shoulder. "Hello, Ari."

"Hello, Rebecca."

He smiled.

Decades disappeared, and they sat in comfortable silence. Time stood still.

Ana

Early Morning
November 3, 2000

either Briar nor Jesse could sleep when they arrived in Key West in the middle of the night, and that's the way I wanted it.

"I won't be able to get any rest until I go and see her," Briar said.

"Me neither. Should we go, Bri, right now?"

"How are we going to get in? I'm sure that they won't let two people into ICU in the middle of the night."

Jesse looked at Briar with her old familiar impish grin.

"I'm sure that we can figure it out. Worst-case scenario"—she pointed to her tummy—"we'll pretend I'm pregnant! Think of the possibilities!"

And just as I had hoped, when they arrived at the hospital at 4:00 in the morning, the graveyard shift zombies were becoming restless, leaving their posts for coffee, conversation, stale doughnuts, cigarettes, anything to alleviate the pain of waiting until sunrise relief came along. Jesse and Briar walked in, still tipsy from the flight. Jesse confident, Briar uncomfortable, they breezed past the sign-in desk to the elevator.

"See how easy that was?"

"Shhh...Don't talk. I don't want to jinx it." Briar fixed his hair in the brushed, stainless steel reflection on the elevator door.

The door opened to ICU. It was like a ghost town.

"How the fuck are we going to find out what room she is in?" Briar panicked, seeing an orderly flit between desks in an office across the hall."

"Leave it to me, Bri."

She walked up to the front desk and peeked around for a floor roster, sign-in book, anything.

"Can I help you?" The young orderly saw Jesse and Briar and approached them suspiciously.

Jesse grabbed Briar by the arm and snuggled into him. He smiled nervously.

"Yes, hi. My husband and I are wondering if you can tell us where our doctor is. I am about to be admitted into maternity."

The orderly looked confused but tried not to draw attention to the fact that she didn't appear to be pregnant "Well...uh..., this is the Intensive Care Unit. Maternity is down on the second floor."

"Yes, sir, I am aware of that but the nurse in maternity said that he may be up here."

"Okay, well I am relatively new here so I'm not familiar with all of the doctor's names. I will do my best to look him up for you." He opened the computer registry.

"Last name?"

Jesse's green eyes scanned the room and fixed themselves on a mobile oxygen unit in the corner.

"Dr. Respirar." Briar flashed Jesse a look.

The orderly punched the computer.

"Respir...how do you spell that?"

"R-e-s-p-i-r-a-r." She looked at Briar and motioned toward the oxygen unit.

"I think that it means breathe in Spanish." Briar squeezed her hand, rolling his eyes.

"Well, I can't find it in the directory. Let me go check the list in the office. Wait right here. I'll be right with you."

"Thank you."

Jesse immediately grabbed the guest sign-in list off of the desk.

"Here's Peg and Harry, 115!" Jesse grabbed Briar's hand and started to run.

"Wait!" Briar pulled her back to the counter.

"Excuse me, sir, we have to go downstairs for a moment." He motioned to Jesse. "Bathroom emergency."

The orderly nodded knowingly and went back to his search. They rushed down the hall toward 115 and stopped outside.

"Oh god, I feel sick." Jesse stopped and put her head on Briar's shoulder.

"Shhhh...Me, too." Let's just do it. They peeked in through the window and Jesse started to cry.

"Poor Ana! Oh god, Briar, look closely." Briar closed his eyes and slowly opened the door. They snuck in closing the door behind them. Everything was quiet, save for the respirator, forcing life into Ana's limp, frail body.

* * *

"I'm so scared, Gabriel."

Ana and I watched them from above as they inched toward the bed, holding each other up.

"Don't be scared. It's time you did this. Look how much they adore you, Ana. Don't believe anyone when they say that love isn't enough. Really, it's the only thing that keeps a person going."

I looked at her and winked.

"I'm so sorry, Gabe."

"What for?" I took her hand and held her shivering body inside my wing while Briar and Jesse approached her like they were going toward an altar.

* * *

Jesse held her hand, and Briar gently touched her face.

"We snuck in, Ana." He leaned over and gently kissed her forehead.

The sun just began to crest on the horizon, changing the midnight sky to a perfect navy blue.

"Are you okay?" Jesse whispered to Briar.

He nodded and whispered into Ana's ear, "We received the letters yesterday…both of us. When did you send them?" He brushed her hair off her forehead.

"Did YOU send them?" Jesse lay her head on Ana's leg and cried, quietly, noticing the piano in the room.

The deep blue sky slowly brightened with coming sunrise. They stood and held each other hopelessly, at the end of Ana's bed, like little kids left out of a game. Jesse buried her head in Briar's shoulder and cried quietly. Briar stroked her blond hair…neither of them noticing Ana's hand twitch. They walked together to the window to watch the changing sky, unaware that Ana's head had jerked. Briar leaned on the windowsill and stared into the twilight, rubbing his weary face, while Jesse sat back to adjust Ana's pillow. She neatened the sheets and stroked her hair. And when she reached to brush a piece of lint from her cheek, Ana opened her green eyes slowly. A faint smile washed over her lips.

"Welcome Home, Son" by Radical Face

Sleep don't visit, so I choke on sun
And the days blur into one
And the backs of my eyes
Hum with things I've never done

Sheets are swaying from an old clothesline
Like a row of captured ghosts
Over old dead grass
Was never much but we made the most
Welcome home

Ships are launching from my chest
Some have names but most do not
If you find one
Please let me know what piece I've lost

Peel the scars from off my back
I don't need them anymore
You can throw them out
Or keep them in your mason jars
I've come home

All my nightmares escaped my head
Bar the door, please don't let them in
You were never supposed to leave
Now my head's splitting at the seams
And I don't know if I can…

Here, beneath my lungs
I feel your thumbs press into my skin again

CPSIA information can be obtained
at www.ICGtesting.com
Printed in the USA
BVHW060105110519
548023BV00005B/46/P

9 781948 654678